Gulliver's Travels

Gulliver is, perhaps, the world's most famous traveler. His journeys begin when he is shipwrecked and lands on Lilliput, and they continue until he has seen more strange sights than almost any other man in the world.

Lilliput is inhabited by a race of people only six inches high. It takes six hundred of their beds pushed together to provide a place in which Gulliver can sleep. He rewards their hospitality, however, by helping them win a war when he tows the enemy fleet to shore.

On his other travels, Gulliver visits the land of giants, the land of horses who govern themselves, and the abode of mathematicians and musicians—all recognized by adults as brilliant satires on the actual world, but loved by children as inventions which rival their wildest fancies of what remote places must be like.

Jonathan Swift's most famous book, it has increased steadily in popularity since it originally was published in 1727.

I stepped over the great Western Gate

JONATHAN SWIFT

Gulliver's Travels

REVISED AND SLIGHTLY ABRIDGED

ILLUSTRATED BY

JO POLSENO

COMPANION LIBRARY

Grosset & Dunlap

PUBLISHERS
NEW YORK

Contents

PART I

A Voyage to Lilliput

PART II

A Voyage to Brobdingnag

PART III

Voyages to Laputa and the Country of the Houyhnhnms

PART I

A Voyage to Lilliput

CHAPTER 1

Gulliver Is Shipwrecked and Made a Prisoner

———————

M Y FATHER had a small estate in Nottinghamshire.
I was the third of five sons. He sent me to Em-
manuel College in Cambridge at fourteen years of age;
where I resided three years, and applied myself to my
studies. But the charge of maintaining me (although I
had a very scanty allowance) being too great for a
narrow fortune, I was bound apprentice to Mr. James
Bates, an eminent surgeon in London, with whom I
continued four years. My father now and then sending me small sums of money, I laid them out in learning navigation, and other parts of mathematics useful
to those who intend to travel, as I always believed it
would be sometime or other my fortune to do. When
I left Mr. Bates, I went down to my father; where, by
the assistance of him and my uncle John, and some
other relations, I got forty pounds, and a promise of
thirty pounds a year to maintain me at Leyden. There
I studied physic two years and seven months, knowing
it would be useful in long voyages.

Soon after my return from Leyden, I was recommended, by my good master Mr. Bates, to be surgeon

to the *Swallow*, Captain Abraham Pannell commander. With him I continued three years and a half, making a voyage or two into the Levant, and some other parts. When I came back, I resolved to settle in London, in which Mr. Bates, my master, encouraged me, and by him I was recommended to several patients. I took part of a small house in the Old Jewry, and married Mary Burton, second daughter to Mr. Edmund Burton, hosier, in Newgate Street, with whom I received four hundred pounds for a portion.

But, my good master Bates dying two years after, and I having few friends, my business began to fail. Having therefore consulted with my wife, and some of my acquaintance, I determined to go again to sea. I was surgeon successively in two ships, and made several voyages, for six years, to the East and West Indies, by which I got some addition to my fortune. My hours of leisure I spent in reading the best authors, ancient and modern, being always provided with a good number of books; and when I was ashore, in observing the manners and dispositions of the people, as well as learning their language, wherein I had a great facility by the strength of my memory.

The last of these voyages not proving very fortunate, I grew weary of the sea, and intended to stay at home with my wife and family. After three years' expectation that things would mend, I accepted an advantageous offer from Captain William Prichard, master of the *Antelope*, who was making a voyage to the South Sea. We set sail from Bristol May 4, 1699, and our voyage at first was very prosperous.

It would not be proper, for some reasons, to trouble the reader with the particulars of our adventures in those seas. Let it suffice to inform him that in our passage from thence to the East Indies we were driven by a violent storm to the northwest of Van Diemen's Land. Twelve of our crew were dead of immoderate labor and ill food, the rest were in a very weak condition. On the 5th of November, which was the beginning of summer in those parts, the weather being very hazy, the seamen spied a rock, within half a cable's length of the ship; but the wind was so strong that we were driven directly upon it, and immediately split.

Six of the crew, of whom I was one, having let down the boat into the sea, made a shift to get clear of the ship and the rock. We rowed by my computation about three leagues, till we were able to work no longer, being already spent with labor while we were in the ship. We therefore trusted ourselves to the mercy of the waves, and in about half an hour the boat was overset by a sudden flurry from the north. What became of my companions in the boat, as well as of those who escaped on the rock or were left in the vessel, I cannot tell; but conclude they were all lost.

For my own part, I swam as fortune directed me and was pushed forward by wind and tide. I often let my legs drop, and could feel no bottom. But when I was almost gone, and able to struggle no longer, I found myself within my depth; and by this time the storm was much abated. The declivity was so small that I walked near a mile before I got to the shore, which I conjectured was about eight o'clock in the evening. I then advanced forward near half a mile, but could not discover any sign of houses or inhabitants; at least I was in so weak a condition that I did not observe them. I was extremely tired, and with that, and the heat of the weather, and about half a pint of brandy that I drank as I left the ship, I found myself much inclined to sleep. I lay down on the grass, which was very short and soft. There I slept sounder than ever I remember to have done in my life, and, as I reckoned, above nine hours.

When I awakened, it was just daylight. I attempted to rise, but was not able to stir. For, as I happened to lie on my back, I found my arms and legs were strongly fastened on each side to the ground; and my hair, which was long and thick, tied down in the same manner. I likewise felt several slender ligatures across my body, from my armpits to my thighs. I could only look upward; the sun began to grow hot, and the light offended my eyes. I heard a confused noise about me, but in the posture I lay could see nothing except the sky.

In a little time I felt something alive moving on my left leg, which advancing gently forward over my breast, came almost up to my chin. Bending my eyes downward as much as I could, I perceived it to be a human creature not six inches high, with a bow and arrow in his hands and a quiver at his back. In the meantime, I felt at least forty more of the same kind following the first. I was in the utmost astonishment and roared so loud that they all ran back in a fright; and some of them, as I was afterward told, were hurt with the falls they got by leaping from my sides upon the ground. However, they soon returned, and one of them, who ventured so far as to get a full sight of my face, lifting up his hands and eyes by way of admiration, cried out in a shrill but distinct voice, *Hekinah degul.* The others repeated the same words several times, but I then knew not what they meant.

I lay all this while, as the reader may believe, in great uneasiness. At length, struggling to get loose, I had the fortune to break the strings, and wrench out the pegs that fastened my left arm to the ground. By lifting it up to my face, I discovered the methods they had taken to bind me, and at the same time, with a violent pull, which gave me excessive pain, I a little loosened the strings that tied down my hair on the left side, so that I was just able to turn my head about two inches. But the creatures ran off a second time, before I could seize them; whereupon there was a great shout in a very shrill accent.

After it ceased, I heard one of them cry aloud, *Tolgo phonac*, and in an instant I felt above a hundred arrows discharged on my left hand, which pricked me like so many needles; and besides they shot another flight into the air, as we do bombs in Europe, whereof many, I suppose, fell on my body (though I felt them not) and some on my face, which I immediately covered with my left hand. When this shower of arrows was over, I fell a-groaning with grief and pain. Then as I strove again to get loose, they discharged another volley larger than the first, and some of them attempted with spears to stick me in the sides; but, by good luck, I had on me a buff jerkin, which they could not pierce.

I thought it the most prudent method to lie still, and my design was to continue so till night, when, my left hand being already loose, I could easily free myself. As for the inhabitants, I had reason to believe I might be a match for the greatest armies they could bring against me, if they were all of the same size with him that I saw. But fortune disposed otherwise of me.

When the people observed I was quiet, they discharged no more arrows; but, by the noise I heard, I knew their numbers increased. About four yards

from me, over against my right ear, I heard a knocking
for above an hour, like that of people at work. When
I turned my head that way, as well as the pegs and
strings would permit me, I saw a stage erected, about
a foot and a half from the ground, capable of holding
four of the inhabitants, with two or three ladders to
mount it: from whence one of them, who seemed to
be a person of quality, made me a long speech,
whereof I understood not one syllable. But I should
have mentioned that, before the principal person began his oration, he cried out three times, *Langro
dehul san* (these words and the former were afterward repeated and explained to me).

Whereupon immediately about fifty of the inhabitants came, and cut the strings that fastened the left
side of my head, which gave me the liberty of turning
it to the right and of observing the person and gesture
of him that was to speak. He appeared to be of a middle age, and taller than any of the other three who attended him, whereof one was a page that held up his
train, and seemed to be somewhat longer than my
middle finger. The other two stood one on each side
to support him. He acted every part of an orator, and
I could observe many periods of threatenings, and
others of promises, pity, and kindness. I answered in
a few words, but in the most submissive manner, lifting up my left hand and both my eyes to the sun, as
calling him for a witness. I was almost famished with
hunger, having not eaten a morsel for some hours before I left the ship. Indeed, I found the demands of
nature so strong upon me that I could not forbear
showing my impatience by putting my finger frequently on my mouth, to signify that I wanted food.

The *hurgo* (for so they call a great lord, as I afterward learned) understood me very well. He descended from the stage, and commanded that several ladders should be applied to my sides, on which above a hundred of the inhabitants mounted. They walked toward my mouth, laden with baskets full of meat, which had been provided, and sent thither by the King's orders, upon the first intelligence he received of me. I observed there was the flesh of several animals, but could not distinguish them by the taste There were shoulders, legs, and loins, shaped like those of mutton, and very well dressed, but smaller than the wings of a lark. I ate them by two or three at a mouthful, and took three loaves at a time, about the bigness of musket bullets. They supplied me as they could, showing a thousand marks of wonder and astonishment at my bulk and appetite.

I then made another sign that I wanted drink. They found by my eating that a small quantity would not suffice me. Being a most ingenious people, they slung up with great dexterity one of their largest hogsheads, then rolled it toward my hand, and beat out the top. I drank it off at a draught, which I might well do, for it did not hold half a pint, and tasted like a small wine of Burgundy, but much more delicious. They brought me a second hogshead, which I drank in the same manner, and made signs for more, but they had none to give me. When I had performed these wonders, they shouted for joy, and danced upon my breast, repeating several times as they did at first, *Hekinah degul.* They made me a sign that I should throw down the two hogsheads, but first warning the people below to stand out of the way, crying aloud, *Borach mivola.* When they saw the vessels in the air, there was a universal shout of *Hekinah degul.*

I confess I was often tempted, while they were passing backward and forward on my body, to seize forty or fifty of the first that came in my reach, and dash them against the ground. But the remembrance of what I had felt, which probably might not be the worst they could do, and the promise of honor I made them soon drove out these imaginations. Besides, I now considered myself as bound by the laws of hospitality to a people who had treated me with so much expense and magnificence. However, in my thoughts I could not sufficiently wonder at the intrepidity of these diminutive mortals, who dared venture to mount and walk upon my body, while one of my hands was at liberty, without trembling at the very sight of so prodigious a creature as I must appear to them.

After some time, there appeared before me a person of high rank from his Imperial Majesty. His Excellency, having mounted on the small of my right leg, advanced forward up to my face, with about a dozen of his retinue. Having produced his credentials he spoke for about ten minutes, often pointing toward the capital city, whither it was agreed by his Majesty in council that I must be conveyed. I answered in few words, but to no purpose, and made a sign with my hand that was loose, putting it to the other and then to my own head and body, to signify that I desired my liberty.

It appeared that he understood me well enough, for he shook his head by way of disapprobation, and held his hand in a posture to show that I must be carried as a prisoner. However, he made other signs to let me understand that I should have meat and drink enough, and very good treatment. Whereupon I once more thought of attempting to break my bonds. But again, when I felt the smart of their arrows upon my face and hands, which were all in blisters, and many of the darts still sticking in them, and observing likewise that the number of my enemies increased, I gave tokens to let them know that they might do with me what they pleased. Upon this the *hurgo* and his train withdrew with much civility and cheerful countenances.

Before this, they had daubed my face and both my hands with a sort of ointment very pleasant to the smell, which in a few minutes removed all the smart of their arrows. These circumstances, added to the refreshment I had received by their victuals and drink, which were very nourishing, disposed me to sleep. I slept about eight hours.

It seems that upon the first moment I was discovered sleeping on the ground after my landing, the Emperor had early notice of it by an express. It was determined in council that I should be tied in the manner I have related, that plenty of meat and drink should be sent me, and a machine prepared to carry me to the capital city.

These people are most excellent mathematicians, having been encouraged by the Emperor, who is a renowned patron of learning. This prince has several machines fixed on wheels for the carriage of trees and other great weights. He often builds his largest men-of-war, whereof some are nine feet long, in the woods where the timber grows, and has them carried on these engines three or four hundred yards to the sea. Five hundred carpenters and engineers were immediately set at work to prepare the greatest engine they had. It was a frame of wood raised three inches from

the ground, about seven feet long and four wide,
moving upon twenty-two wheels.

This engine was brought parallel to me as I lay. But
the principal difficulty was to raise and place me in
this vehicle. Eighty poles, each of one foot high, were
erected for this purpose, and very strong cords of the
bigness of packthread were fastened by hooks to
many bandages, which the workmen had girt round
my neck, my hands, my body, and my legs. Nine
hundred of the strongest men were employed to draw
up these cords by many pulleys fastened on the poles,
and thus, in less than three hours, I was raised and
slung into the engine, and there tied fast. All this I
was told, for while the whole operation was perform-
ing, I lay in a profound sleep. Fifteen hundred of the
Emperor's largest horses, each about four inches and
a half high, were employed to draw me toward the
metropolis, which was half a mile distant.

About four hours after we began our journey, I
awaked by a very ridiculous accident. The carriage
being stopped awhile to adjust something that was

out of order, two or three of the young natives had the curiosity to see how I looked when I was asleep. They climbed up into the engine, and advancing very softly to my face, one of them put the sharp end of his half-pike a good way up into my left nostril, which tickled my nose like a straw, and made me sneeze violently: whereupon they stole off unperceived, and it was three weeks before I knew the cause of my awaking so suddenly.

We made a long march the remaining part of that day, and rested at night with five hundred guards on each side of me, half with torches, and half with bows and arrows, ready to shoot me if I should offer to stir. The next morning at sunrise we continued our march, and arrived within two hundred yards of the city gates about noon. The Emperor and all his court came out to meet us; but his great officers would by no means suffer his Majesty to endanger his person by mounting on my body.

At the place where the carriage stopped, there stood an ancient temple, esteemed to be the largest in the whole kingdom, and in this edifice it was determined I should lodge. The great gate fronting to the north was about four feet high, and almost two feet wide, through which I could easily creep. On each side of the gate was a small window not above six inches from the ground. Into that on the left side, the King's smiths conveyed fourscore and eleven chains, like those that hang to a lady's watch in Europe, and almost as large. These were locked to my left leg with six and thirty padlocks.

Over against this temple, on the other side of the great highway, at twenty feet distance, there was a turret at least five feet high. Here the Emperor ascended with many principal lords of his court, to have an opportunity of viewing me, as I was told, for I could not see them. It was reckoned that above a hundred thousand inhabitants came out of the town upon the same errand. And in spite of my guards, I believe there could not be fewer than ten thousand, at several times, who mounted upon my body by the help of ladders. But a proclamation was soon issued to forbid it upon pain of death.

When the workmen found it was impossible for me to break loose, they cut all the strings that bound me; whereupon I rose up with as melancholy a disposition as ever I had in my life. But the noise and astonishment of the people at seeing me rise and walk are not to be expressed. The chains that held my left leg were about two yards long, and gave me not only the liberty of walking backward and forward in a semicircle, but, being fixed within four inches of the gate, allowed me to creep in, and lie at my full length in the temple.

CHAPTER 2

The Emperor of Lilliput

WHEN I found myself on my feet, I looked about me, and must confess I never beheld a more entertaining prospect. The country round appeared like a continued garden, and the enclosed fields, which were generally forty feet square, resembled so many beds of flowers. These fields were intermingled with woods of half a stang, and the tallest trees, as I could judge, appeared to be seven feet high. I viewed the town on my left hand, which looked like the painted scene of a city in a theater.

The Emperor was already descended from the tower, and advancing on horseback toward me, which had like to have cost him dear. The beast, though very well trained, yet wholly unused to such a sight, which appeared as if a mountain moved before him, reared up on his hinder feet: but that prince, who is an excellent horseman, kept his seat, till his attendants ran in and held the bridle, while his Majesty had time to dismount. When he alighted, he surveyed me round with great admiration, but kept without the length of my chain.

He ordered his cooks and butlers, who were already
prepared, to give me victuals and drink, which they
pushed forward in a sort of vehicle upon wheels till I
could reach them. I took these vehicles, and soon
emptied them all. Twenty of them were filled with
meat, and ten with liquor. Each of the former af-
forded me two or three good mouthfuls, and I emptied the liquor of ten vessels, which was contained in
earthen vials, into one vehicle, drinking it off at a
draught; and so I did with the rest.

The Empress and young princes of the blood of
both sexes, attended by many ladies, sat at some distance in their chairs. But upon the accident that happened to the Emperor's horse, they alighted, and came
near his person, which I am now going to describe.[1]
He was taller by almost the breadth of my nail than
any of his court, which alone was enough to strike an
awe into the beholders. His features were strong and
masculine, with an Austrian lip and arched nose, his
complexion olive, his countenance erect, his body and
limbs well proportioned, all his motions graceful, and
his deportment majestic. He was then past his prime,
being twenty-eight years and three-quarters old, of
which he had reigned about seven, in great felicity,
and generally victorious.

For the better convenience of beholding him, I lay
on my side, so that my face was parallel to his, and he
stood but three yards off. However, I have had him
since many times in my hand, and therefore cannot be
deceived in the description. His dress was very plain
and simple, and the fashion of it between the Asiatic
and the European. But he had on his head a light

[1] This could be a portrait of George I.

helmet of gold, adorned with jewels, and a plume on the crest. He held his sword drawn in his hand, to defend himself, if I should happen to break loose. It was almost three inches long, the hilt and scabbard were gold enriched with diamonds. His voice was shrill, but very clear and articulate, and I could distinctly hear it when I stood up. The ladies and courtiers were all most magnificently clad, so that the spot they stood upon seemed to resemble a petticoat spread on the ground, embroidered with figures of gold and silver.

His Imperial Majesty spoke often to me, and I returned answers, but neither of us could understand a syllable. There were several of his priests and lawyers present (as I conjectured by their habits) who were commanded to address themselves to me. I spoke to them in as many languages as I had the least smattering of, which were High and Low Dutch, Latin, French, Spanish, Italian, and Lingua Franca; but all to no purpose.

After about two hours the court retired, and I was left with a strong guard, to prevent the impertinence and probably the malice of the rabble, who were very impatient to crowd about me as near as they dared. Some of them had the impudence to shoot their arrows at me as I sat on the ground by the door of my house, whereof one very narrowly missed my left eye. But the colonel ordered six of the ringleaders to be seized, and thought no punishment so proper as to deliver them bound into my hands. Some of his soldiers accordingly did, pushing them forward with the butt ends of their pikes into my reach. I took them all in my right hand, put five of them into my coat pocket, and as to the sixth, I made a countenance as if I would eat him alive. The poor man squalled terribly, and the colonel and his officers were in much pain, especially when they saw me take out my penknife. But I soon put them out of fear; for immediately cutting the strings he was bound with, I set him gently on the ground, and away he ran. I treated the rest in the same manner, taking them one by one out of my pocket, and I observed both the soldiers and people were highly pleased of my clemency.

Toward night I with some difficulty got into my house, where I lay on the ground, and continued to do so about a fortnight; during which time the Emperor gave orders to have a bed prepared for me. Six hundred beds of the common measure were brought in carriages, and worked up in my house. A hundred and fifty of their beds sewn together made up the breadth and length, and these were four double, which however kept me but very indifferently from the hardness of the floor, that was of smooth stone. By the same computation they provided me with sheets, blankets, and coverlets.

As the news of my arrival spread through the kingdom, it brought prodigious numbers of rich, idle, and curious people to see me; so that the villages were almost emptied. Great neglect of tillage and household affairs must have ensued, if his Imperial Majesty had not provided, by several proclamations and orders of state, against this inconvenience. He directed that those who had already beheld me should return home, and not presume to come within fifty yards of my house without license from court, whereby the secretaries of state got considerable fees.

In the meantime, the Emperor held frequent councils to debate what course should be taken with me. I was afterward assured by a particular friend, a person of great quality, that the court was under many difficulties concerning me. They apprehended my breaking loose, that my diet would be very expensive, and might cause a famine. Sometimes they determined to starve me, or at least to shoot me in the face and hands with poisoned arrows, which would soon dispatch me. But again they considered that the stench of so large a carcass might produce a plague in the metropolis, and spread through the whole kingdom.

In the midst of these consultations, several army officers went to the door of the great council chamber. Two of them being admitted, they gave an account of my behavior to the six criminals above mentioned, which made so favorable an impression in the breast of his Majesty and the whole board in my behalf that an imperial commission was issued out, obliging all the villages nine hundred yards round the city, to deliver every morning six beeves, forty sheep, and other victuals for my sustenance; together with a proportionable quantity of bread, and wine, and other liquors for the due payment of which his Majesty gave assignments upon his treasury. For this prince lives chiefly upon his own demesnes, seldom raising any subsidies upon his subjects.

An establishment was also made of six hundred persons to be my domestics, who had board-wages allowed for their maintenance, and tents built for them very conveniently on each side of my door. It was likewise ordered that three hundred tailors should make me a suit of clothes after the fashion of the country; that six of his Majesty's greatest scholars should be employed to instruct me in their language; and, lastly, that the Emperor's horses, and those of the nobility and troops of guards, should be frequently exercised in my sight, to accustom themselves to me.

All these orders were duly put in execution, and in about three weeks I made great progress in learning their language; during which time the Emperor frequently honored me with his visits, and was pleased to assist my masters in teaching me.

We began already to converse together in some fashion; and the first words I learned were to express my desire that he would please give me my liberty, which I every day repeated on my knees. His answer, as I could apprehend it, was that this must be a work of time, not to be thought on without the advice of his council, and that first I must *Lumos kelmin pesso desmar lon Emposo;* that is, swear a peace with him and his kingdom. Meanwhile, I should be used with all kindness, and he advised me to acquire the good opinion of himself and his subjects.

He desired I would not take it ill if he gave orders to certain proper officers to search me; for probably I might carry about me several weapons, which must needs be dangerous things, if they answered the bulk of so prodigious a person. I said his Majesty should be satisfied, for I was ready to strip myself, and turn out my pockets before him. This I delivered part in words, and part in signs. He replied, that by the laws of the kingdom I must be searched by two of his officers. He said that he knew this could not be done without my consent and assistance; but that he had so good an opinion of my generosity and justice as to trust their persons in my hands. Whatever they took from me should be returned when I left the country, or paid for at the rate which I would set upon them.

I took up the two officers in my hands, put them into my coat pockets, and then into every other pocket about me, except my two fobs, and another secret pocket I had no mind should be searched, wherein I had some little necessaries that were of no consequence to any but myself. In one of my fobs there was a silver watch, and in the other a small quantity of gold in a purse. These gentlemen, having pen, ink, and paper about them, made an exact inventory of everything they saw; and when they were through, desired I would set them down, that they might deliver it to the Emperor. This inventory I afterward translated into English, and is word for word as follows:

In the right coat pocket of the Great Man-Mountain after the strictest search, we found only one great piece of coarse cloth, large enough to be a foot cloth for your Majesty's chief room of state. In the left pocket we saw a huge silver chest, with a cover of the same metal, which we the searchers were not able to lift. We desired it should be opened, and one of us stepping into it, found himself up to the midleg in a sort of dust, some part whereof flying up to our faces, set us both sneezing for several times together.

In his right waistcoat pocket we found a prodigious bundle of white thin substances, folded one over another, about the bigness of three men, tied with a strong cable, and marked with black figures; which we humbly conceive to be writings, every letter al-

most half as large as the palm of our hands. In the
left there was a sort of engine, from the back of which
were extended twenty long poles, resembling the
palisados before your Majesty's court; wherewith we
conjecture the Man-Mountain combs his head, for we
did not always trouble him with questions, because
we found it difficult to make him understand us.

In the large pocket on the right side of his breeches
we saw a hollow pillar of iron, about the length of a
man, fastened to a strong piece of timber, larger than
the pillar; and upon one side of the pillar were huge
pieces of iron sticking out, cut into strange figures,
which we know not what to make of. In the left
pocket, another engine of the same kind.

In the smaller pocket on the right side were several
round flat pieces of white and red metal, of different
bulk. Some of the white, which seemed to be silver,
were so large and heavy that my comrade and I
could hardly lift them. In the left pocket were two
black pillars irregularly shaped. We could not, without difficulty, reach the top of them as we stood at the
bottom of his pocket. One of them was covered, and
seemed all of a piece. But at the upper end of the
other, there appeared a white round substance, about
twice the bigness of our heads. Within each of these
was enclosed a prodigious plate of steel; which, by
our orders, we obliged him to show us, because we
apprehended they might be dangerous engines. He
took them out of their cases, and told us that in his
own country his practice was to shave his beard with
one of these, and to cut his meat with the other.

There were two pockets which we could not enter:
these he called his fobs.

Out of the right fob hung a great silver chain, with a wonderful kind of engine at the bottom. We directed him to draw out whatever was fastened to that chain; which appeared to be a globe, half silver, and half of some transparent metal. On the transparent side we saw certain strange figures circularly drawn, and thought we could touch them, till we found our fingers stopped by that lucid substance. He put this engine to our ears, which made an incessant noise like that of a watermill. We conjecture it is either some unknown animal, or the god that he worships; but we are more inclined to the latter opinion, because he assured us that he seldom did anything without consulting it. He called it his oracle, and said it pointed out the time for every action of his life.

From the left fob he took out a net almost large enough for a fisherman, but contrived to open and shut like a purse and serve him for the same use. We found therein several massy pieces of yellow metal, which, if they be real gold, must be of immense value.

Having thus, in obedience to your Majesty's commands, diligently searched all his pockets, we observed a girdle about his waist made of the hide of some prodigious animal; from which, on the left side, hung a sword of the length of five men; and on the right, a bag or pouch divided into two cells, each cell capable of holding three of your Majesty's subjects. In one of these cells were several globes or balls of a most ponderous metal, about the bigness of our heads, and requiring a strong hand to lift them. The other cell contained a heap of certain black grains, but of no great bulk or weight, for we could hold above fifty of them in the palms of our hands.

This is an exact inventory of what we found about the body of the Man-Mountain, who used us with great civility and due respect to your Majesty's commission. Signed and sealed on the fourth day of the eighty-ninth moon of your Majesty's auspicious reign.

CLEFREN FRELOCK
MARSI FRELOCK

When this inventory was read over to the Emperor, he directed me, although in very gentle terms, to deliver up the several particulars. He first called for my scimitar, which I took out, scabbard and all. In the meantime he ordered three thousand of his choicest troops to surround me at a distance, with their bows and arrows just ready to discharge: but I did not observe it, for my eyes were wholly fixed upon his Majesty.

He then desired me to draw my scimitar, which, although it had got some rust by the sea water, was in most parts exceeding bright. I did so, and immediately all the troops gave a shout between terror and surprise; for the sun shone clear, and the reflection dazzled their eyes as I waved the scimitar to and fro in my hand. His Majesty, who is a most magnanimous prince, was less daunted than I could expect. He ordered me to return it into the scabbard, and cast it on the ground as gently as I could, about six feet from the end of my chain.

The next thing he demanded was one of the hollow iron pillars, by which he meant my pocket pistols. I drew it out, and at his desire, as well as I could, expressed to him the use of it. Charging it only with powder, I first cautioned the Emperor not to be afraid, and then I let it off in the air. The astonishment here was much greater than at the sight of my scimitar. Hundreds fell down as if they had been struck dead; and even the Emperor, although he stood his ground, could scarcely recover himself.

I delivered up both my pistols in the same manner as I had done my scimitar, and then my pouch of powder and bullets; begging him that the former might be kept from the fire, for it would kindle with the smallest spark, and blow his Imperial palace into the air. I likewise delivered up my watch, which the Emperor was very curious to see, and commanded two of his tallest yeomen of the guards to bear it on a pole upon their shoulders, as draymen in England do a barrel of ale. He was amazed at the continual noise it made, and the motion of the minute hand, which he could easily discern. He asked the opinions of his learned men about him, which were various and remote, as the reader may well imagine; although indeed I could not very perfectly understand them. I then gave up my silver and copper money, my purse with nine large pieces of gold, and some smaller ones; my knife and razor, my comb and silver snuffbox, my handkerchief and journal book. My scimitar, pistols, and pouch were conveyed in carriages to his Majesty's stores; but the rest of my goods were returned me.

I had, as I before observed, one private pocket which escaped their search, wherein there was a pair of spectacles (which I sometimes use for the weakness of my eyes), a pocket perspective, and several other little conveniences. These being of no consequence to the Emperor, I did not think myself bound in honor to discover, and I apprehended they might be lost or spoiled if I ventured them out of my possession.

CHAPTER 3

Gulliver at the Court of Lilliput

M Y GENTLENESS and good behavior had gained so far on the Emperor and his court, and indeed upon the army and people in general, that I began to conceive hopes of getting my liberty in a short time. I took all possible methods to cultivate this favorable disposition. The natives came by degrees to be less apprehensive of any danger from me. I would sometimes lie down, and let five or six of them dance on my hand. And at last the boys and girls would venture to come and play at hide and seek in my hair. I had now made good progress in understanding and speaking their language. The Emperor had a mind one day to entertain me with several of the country shows, wherein they exceeded all nations I have known, for both dexterity and magnificence. I was diverted with none so much as that of the rope dancers, performed upon a slender white thread, extended about two feet, and twelve inches from the ground.

This diversion is practiced only by those persons who are candidates for great employments and high favors at court. They are trained in this art from

their youth, and are not always of noble birth or
liberal education. When a great office is vacant either
by death or disgrace, five or six of those candidates
petition the Emperor to entertain his Majesty and the
court with a dance on the rope, and whoever jumps
the highest without falling succeeds in the office.

Very often the chief ministers themselves are commanded to show their skill, and to convince the Emperor that they have not lost their faculty.[1] Flimnap,
the Treasurer, is allowed to cut a caper on the straight

[1] This makes fun of politicians' efforts to secure office.

rope, at least an inch higher than any other lord in the whole empire. I have seen him do the summerset several times together upon a trencher fixed on the rope, which is no thicker than a common packthread in England. My friend Reldresal, Principal Secretary for Private Affairs, is, in my opinion, if I am not partial, the second after the Treasurer; the rest of the great officers are much upon a par.

These diversions are often attended with fatal accidents. I myself have seen two or three candidates break a limb. But the danger is much greater when the ministers themselves are commanded to show their dexterity; for they strain so far that there is hardly one of them who has not received a fall, and some of them two or three. I was assured that a year or two before my arrival Flimnap would have inevitably broken his neck, if one of the King's cushions, that accidentally lay on the ground, had not weakened the force of his fall.

There is likewise another diversion, which is shown only before the Emperor and Empress and the first minister upon particular occasions. The Emperor lays on the table three fine silken threads of six inches long. One is blue, the other red, and the third green. These threads are proposed as prizes for those persons whom the Emperor has a mind to distinguish by a peculiar mark of his favor.[1] The ceremony is performed in his Majesty's great chamber of state, where the candidates are to undergo a trial of dexterity very different from the former, and such as I have not observed the least resemblance of in any other country of the Old or the New World. The Emperor holds a

[1] Reference is to the three orders of British knighthood.

stick in his hands, both ends parallel to the horizon, while the candidates, advancing one by one, sometimes leap over the stick, sometimes creep under it backward and forward several times, according as the stick is advanced or depressed. Sometimes the Emperor holds one end of the stick, and his first minister the other. Sometimes the minister has it entirely to himself. Whoever performs his part with most agility, and holds out the longest in leaping and creeping, is rewarded with the blue-colored silk. The red is given to the next, and the green to the third, which they all wear girt twice round about the middle. You see few great persons about this court who are not adorned with one of these girdles.

The horses of the army and those of the royal stables, having been daily led before me, were no longer shy, but would come up to my very feet without starting. The riders would leap them over my hand as I held it on the ground, and one of the Emperor's huntsmen, upon a large courser, took my foot, shoe and all; which was indeed a prodigious leap. I had the good fortune to divert the Emperor one day after a very extraordinary manner. I desired he would order several sticks two feet high, and the thickness of an ordinary cane, to be brought me; whereupon his Majesty commanded the master of his woods to give directions accordingly. The next morning six woodmen arrived with as many carriages, drawn by eight horses each. I took nine of these sticks, and fixing them firmly in the ground in a quadrangular figure, two feet and a half square, I took four other sticks, and tied them parallel at each corner, about two feet from the ground. Then I fastened my handkerchief

to the nine sticks that stood erect, and extended it on
all sides till it was as tight as the top of a drum; and
the four parallel sticks rising about five inches higher
than the handkerchief served as ledges on each side.
When I had finished my work, I desired the Emperor
to let a troop of his best horse, twenty-four in number, come and exercise upon this plain. His Majesty
approved of the proposal, and I took them up one by
one in my hands, ready mounted and armed, with the
proper officers to exercise them. As soon as they got
into order, they divided into two parties, performed
mock skirmishes, discharged blunt arrows, drew their
swords, fled and pursued, attacked and retired, and
in short discovered the best military discipline I ever
beheld. The parallel sticks secured them and their
horses from falling over the stage. The Emperor was
so much delighted that he ordered this entertainment
to be repeated several days, and once was pleased to
be lifted up and give the word of command. With
great difficulty, he persuaded even the Empress herself to let me hold her in her close chair within two
yards of the stage, from whence she was able to take a
full view of the whole performance. It was my good
fortune that no ill accident happened in these enter-
tainments, only once a fiery horse that belonged to
one of the captains pawing with his hoof struck a
hole in my handkerchief, and his foot slipping, he
overthrew his rider and himself. But I immediately
relieved them both, and covering the hole with one
hand, I set down the troop with the other, in the same
manner as I took them up. The horse that fell was
strained in the left shoulder, but the rider got no hurt,
and I repaired my handkerchief as well as I could.

However, I would not trust to the strength of it any more in such dangerous enterprises.

About two or three days before I was set at liberty, as I was entertaining the court with these feats, there arrived an express to inform his Majesty that some of his subjects riding near the place where I was first taken up had seen a great black substance lying on the ground, very oddly shaped, extending its edges round as wide as his Majesty's bedchamber, and rising up in the middle as high as a man. It was no living creature, as they at first apprehended, for it lay on the grass without motion, and some of them had walked round it several times. By mounting upon each other's shoulders, they had got to the top, which was flat and even, and stamping upon it they found it was hollow within. They humbly conceived it might be something belonging to the Man-Mountain, and if his Majesty pleased, they would undertake it to bring it with only five horses. I presently knew what they meant, and was glad at heart to receive this intelligence. It seems upon my first reaching the shore after our shipwreck I was in such confusion that before I came to the place where I went to sleep, my hat, which I had fastened with a string to my head while I was rowing, and had stuck on all the time I was swimming, fell off after I came to land. The string, as I conjecture, must have broken by some accident which I never observed, but thought my hat had been lost at sea. I entreated his Imperial Majesty to give orders it might be brought to me as soon as possible, describing to him the use and the nature of it. The next day the wagoners arrived with it, but not in a very good condition. They had bored two holes in

the brim, within an inch and a half of the edge, and
fastened two hooks in the holes; these hooks were
tied by a long cord to the harness, and thus my hat
was dragged along for above half an English mile.
But the ground in that country being extremely
smooth and level, it received less damage than I expected.

I had sent so many memorials and petitions for my
liberty, that his Majesty at length mentioned the matter, first in the cabinet, and then in a full council;
where it was opposed by none except Skyresh Bolgolam, who was pleased, without any provocation, to
be my mortal enemy. He was very much in his master's confidence, and a person well versed in affairs,
but of a morose and sour complexion. However, he
was at length persuaded to comply; but prevailed that
the articles and conditions upon which I should be set
free, and to which I must swear, should be drawn up
by himself. These articles were brought to me by
Skyresh Bolgolam in person, attended by two under-
secretaries, and several persons of distinction. After
they were read, I was demanded to swear to the performance of them; first in the manner of my own
country, and afterward in the method prescribed by
their laws; which was to hold my right foot in my left
hand, to place the middle finger of my right hand on
the crown of my head, and my thumb on the tip of my
right ear. But because the reader may perhaps be
curious to have some idea of the style and manner of
expression peculiar to that people, as well as to know
the articles upon which I recovered my liberty, I have
made a translation of the whole instrument word for
word, as near as I was able, which I here offer to the
public:

GOLBASTO MOMAREN EVLAME GURDILO SHEFIN MULLY ULLY GUE, most mighty Emperor of Lilliput, delight and terror of the universe, whose dominions extend five thousand *blustrugs* (about twelve miles in circumference) to the extremities of the globe; monarch of all monarchs, taller than the sons of men; whose feet press down to the center, and whose head strikes against the sun; at whose nod the princes of the earth shake their knees; pleasant as the spring, comfortable as the summer, fruitful as autumn, dreadful as winter. His most sublime Majesty proposes to the Man-Mountain, lately arrived to our celestial dominions, the following articles, which by a solemn oath he shall be obliged to perform:

I. The Man-Mountain shall not depart from our dominions without our license under our great seal.

II. He shall not presume to come into our metropolis without our express order; at which time the inhabitants shall have two hours' warning to keep within their doors.

III. The said Man-Mountain shall confine his walks to our principal highroads, and not offer to walk or lie down in a meadow or field of corn.

IV. As he walks the said roads, he shall take the utmost care not to trample upon the bodies of any of our loving subjects, their horses, or carriages, nor take any of our said subjects into his hands, without their own consent.

V. If an express requires extraordinary dispatch, the Man-Mountain shall be obliged to carry in his pocket the messenger and horse a six days' journey once in every moon, and return the said messenger back (if so required) safe to our Imperial Presence.

VI. He shall be our ally against our enemies in the

island of Blefuscu,[1] and do his utmost to destroy their fleet, which is now preparing to invade us.

VII. That the said Man-Mountain shall, at his times of leisure, be aiding and assisting to our workmen, in helping to raise certain great stones, toward covering the wall of the principal park, and other of our royal buildings.

VIII. That the said Man-Mountain shall, in two moons' time, deliver in an exact survey of the circumference of our dominions by a computation of his own paces round the coast.

Lastly, That upon his solemn oath to observe all the above articles, the said Man-Mountain shall have a daily allowance of meat and drink sufficient for the support of 1,728 of our subjects, with free access to our Royal Person, and other marks of our favor. Given at our palace at Belfaborac the twelfth day of the ninety-first moon of our reign.

I swore and subscribed to these articles with great cheerfulness and content, although some of them were not so honorable as I could have wished; whereupon my chains were immediately unlocked, and I was at full liberty. The Emperor himself in person did me the honor to be by at the whole ceremony. I made my acknowledgments by prostrating myself at his Majesty's feet: but he commanded me to rise. And after many gracious expressions, he added that he hoped I should prove a useful servant, and well deserve all the favors he had already conferred upon me, or might do for the future.

[1] Since Lilliput refers to England, this is probably France.

CHAPTER 4

The Emperor's Palace and His Principal Secretary

THE FIRST request I made after I had obtained my liberty was that I might have license to see Mildendo, the metropolis. This the Emperor easily granted me, but with a special charge to do no hurt either to the inhabitants or their houses. The people had notice by proclamation of my design to visit the town. The wall which encompassed it is two feet and a half high, and at least eleven inches broad, so that a coach and horses may be driven very safely round it; and it is flanked with strong towers at ten feet distance. I stepped over the great Western Gate, and passed very gently, and sidling through the two principal streets, only in my short waistcoat, for fear of damaging the roofs and eaves of the houses with the skirts of my coat.

I walked with the utmost circumspection, to avoid treading on any stragglers that might remain in the streets, although the orders were very strict that all people should keep in their houses at their own peril. The garret windows and tops of houses were so crowded with spectators that I thought in all my travels I had not seen a more populous place. The city is an exact square, each side of the wall being five hundred feet long. The two great streets, which run cross and divide it into four quarters, are five feet wide. The lanes and alleys, which I could not enter, but only viewed them as I passed, are from twelve to eighteen inches. The town is capable of holding five hundred thousand souls. The houses are from three to five stories; the shops and markets well provided.

The Emperor's palace is in the center of the city, where the two great streets meet. It is enclosed by a wall two feet high, and twenty feet distant from the buildings. I had his Majesty's permission to step over this wall; and the space being so wide between that and the palace, I could easily view it on every side. The outward court is a square of forty feet, and includes two other courts. In the inmost are the royal apartments, which I was very desirous to see, but found it extremely difficult; for the great gates, from one square into another, were but eighteen inches high and seven inches wide. Now the buildings of the outer court were at least five feet high, and it was impossible for me to stride over them without infinite damage to the pile, though the walls were strongly built of hewn stone, and four inches thick.

At the same time the Emperor had a great desire that I should see the magnificence of his palace. But this I was not able to do till three days after, which I spent in cutting down with my knife some of the largest trees in the royal park, about a hundred yards distant from the city. Of these trees I made two stools, each about three feet high, and strong enough to bear my weight. The people having received notice a second time, I went again through the city to the palace with my two stools in my hands. When I came to the side of the outer court, I stood upon one stool, and took the other in my hand: this I lifted over the roof, and gently set it down on the space between the first and second court, which was eight feet wide. I then stepped over the buildings very conveniently from one stool to the other, and drew up the first after me with a hooked stick. By this contrivance I got into the inmost court. Lying down upon my side, I applied my face to the windows of the middle stories, which were left open on purpose, and discovered the most splendid apartments that can be imagined.

There I saw the Empress and the young princes, in their several lodgings, with their chief attendants about them. Her Imperial Majesty was pleased to smile very graciously upon me, and gave me out of the window her hand to kiss.

One morning, about a fortnight after I had obtained my liberty, Reldresal, Principal Secretary of Private Affairs, came to my house attended only by one servant. He ordered his coach to wait at a distance, and desired I would give him an hour's audience; which I readily consented to, on account of his quality and personal merits, as well as the many good offices he had done me during my solicitations at court. I offered to lie down, that he might the more conveniently reach my ear; but he chose rather to let me hold him in my hand during our conversation. He began with compliments on my liberty; said he might pretend to some merit in it: but added that, if it had not been for the present situation of things at court, perhaps I might not have obtained it so soon. "For," said he, "as flourishing a condition as we may appear to be in to foreigners, we labor under two mighty evils: a violent faction at home, and the danger of an invasion by a most potent enemy from abroad. As to the first, you are to understand that for above seventy moons past there have been two struggling parties in this empire, under the names of *Tramecksan* and *Slamecksan*, from the high and low heels on their shoes, by which they distinguish themselves. It is alleged, indeed, that the high heels are most agreeable to our ancient constitution. But however this be, his Majesty has determined to make use of only low heels in the administration of the government and all offices in the gift of the Crown, as you cannot but observe; and particularly, that his Majesty's Imperial heels are lower at least by a *drurr* than any of his court (*drurr* is a measure about the fourteenth part of an inch). The animosities between these two parties run so high that they will neither eat nor drink, nor talk with each other.

"Now, in the midst of these domestic disquiets, we are threatened with an invasion from the island of Blefuscu, which is the other great empire of the universe, almost as large and powerful as this of his Majesty. For as to what we have heard you affirm, that there are other kingdoms and states in the world inhabited by human creatures as large as yourself, our philosophers are in much doubt and would rather conjecture that you dropped from the moon, or one of the stars;

because it is certain that a hundred mortals of your bulk would, in a short time, destroy all the fruits and cattle of his Majesty's dominions. Besides, our histories of six thousand moons make no mention of any other regions than the two great empires of Lilliput and Blefuscu. Which two mighty powers have, as I was going to tell you, been engaged in a most obstinate war for six and thirty moons past.

"It began upon the following occasion: It is allowed on all hands that the primitive way of breaking eggs before we eat them was upon the larger end: but his present Majesty's grandfather, while he was a boy, going to eat an egg, and breaking it according to the ancient practice, happened to cut one of his fingers. Whereupon the Emperor his father published an edict, commanding all his subjects, upon great penalties, to break the smaller end of their eggs. The people so highly resented this law that our histories tell us there have been six rebellions raised on that account; wherein one Emperor lost his life,[1] and another his crown.[2] These civil commotions were constantly fomented by the monarchs of Blefuscu; and when they were quelled, the exiles always fled for refuge to that empire. It is computed that eleven thousand persons have, at several times, suffered death, rather than submit to break their eggs at the smaller end. Many hundred large volumes have been published upon this controversy. But the books of the Big Endians have been long forbidden, and the whole party rendered incapable.

"Now, the Big Endian exiles have found so much

[1] Charles I of England.
[2] James II of England.

credit in the Emperor of Blefuscu's court, and so much
private assistance and encouragement from their party
here at home, that a bloody war has been carried on
between the two empires for six and thirty moons with
various success. During this time we have lost forty
capital ships, and a much greater number of smaller
vessels, together with thirty thousand of our best seamen and soldiers; and the damage received by the enemy is reckoned to be somewhat greater than ours.
However, they have now equipped a numerous fleet,
and are just preparing to make a descent upon us. His
Imperial Majesty, placing great confidence in your
valor and strength, has commanded me to lay this account of his affairs before you."

.. I desired the Secretary to present my humble duty
to the Emperor, and to let him know that I thought it
would not become me, who was a foreigner, to inter-
fere with parties; but I was ready, with the hazard of
my life, to defend his person and state against all in-
vaders.

CHAPTER 5

Gulliver Prevents an Invasion of Lilliput

T HE EMPIRE of Blefuscu is an island situated on the north-northeast side of Lilliput, from whence it is parted only by a channel of eight hundred yards wide. I had not yet seen it. And upon this notice of an intended invasion I avoided appearing on that side of the coast for fear of being discovered by some of the enemy's ships, who had received no intelligence of me, all intercourse between the two empires having been strictly forbidden during the war, upon pain of death, an embargo laid by our Emperor upon all vessels whatsoever. I communicated to his Majesty a project I had formed of seizing the enemy's whole fleet, which, as our scouts assured us, lay at anchor in the harbor ready to sail with the first fair wind.

I consulted the most experienced seamen upon the depth of the channel, which they had often plumbed. They told me that in the middle at high water it was seventy *glumgluffs* deep, which is about six feet of European measure; and the rest of it fifty *glumgluffs* at most. I walked toward the northeast coast over against Blefuscu; and lying down behind a hillock, took out my small pocket perspective glass and viewed the enemy's fleet at anchor, consisting of about fifty men-of-war and a great number of transports. I then came back to my house, and gave order (for which I had a warrant) for a great quantity of the strongest cable and bars of iron.

The cable was about as thick as packthread, and the bars of the length and size of a knitting needle. I trebled the cable to make it stronger, and for the same reason I twisted three of the iron bars together, binding the extremities into a hook. Having thus fixed fifty hooks to as many cables, I went back to the northeast coast, and putting off my coat, shoes, and stockings, walked into the sea in my leather jerkin, about half an hour before high water. I waded with what haste I could, and swam in the middle about thirty yards till I felt ground. I arrived at the fleet in less than half an hour.

The enemy was so frighted when they saw me that they leaped out of their ships, and swam to shore, where there could not be fewer than thirty thousand souls. I then took my tackling, and fastening a hook to a hole at the prow of each, I tied all the cords together at the end. While I was thus employed, the enemy discharged several thousand arrows, many of which stuck in my hands and face; and besides the excessive smart, gave me much disturbance in my work. My greatest apprehension was for my eyes, which I should certainly have lost if I had not suddenly thought of an expedient. I kept among other little necessaries a pair of spectacles in a private pocket, which, as I observed before, had escaped the Emperor's searchers. These I took out and fastened as strongly as I could upon my nose, and thus armed went on boldly with my work in spite of the enemy's arrows, many of which struck against the glasses of my spectacles, but without any other effect, further than a little to discompose them.

I now fastened all the hooks, and taking the knot in my hand, began to pull. But not a ship would stir, for they were all too fast held by their anchors, so that the boldest part of my enterprise remained. I therefore let go the cord, and leaving the hooks fixed to the ships, I resolutely cut with my knife the cables that fastened the anchors, receiving above two hundred shots in my face and hands. Then I took up the knotted end of the cables to which my hooks were tied, and with great ease drew fifty of the enemy's largest men-of-war after me.

The Blefuscudians, who had not the least imagination of what I intended, were at first confounded with astonishment. They had seen me cut the cables, and thought my design was only to let the ships run adrift or fall foul on each other, but when they perceived the whole fleet moving in order, and saw me pulling at the end, they set up such a scream of grief and despair that it is almost impossible to describe or conceive. When I had got out of danger, I stopped awhile to pick out the arrows that stuck in my hands and face, and rubbed on some of the same ointment that was given me at my first arrival. I then took off my spectacles, and waiting about an hour, till the tide was a little fallen, I waded through the middle with my cargo, and arrived safe at the royal port of Lilliput. The Emperor and his whole court stood on the shore awaiting the issue of this great adventure. They saw the ships move forward in a large half moon, but could not discern me, who was up to my breast in water. When I advanced to the middle of the channel, they were yet in more pain, because I was under water to my neck. The Emperor concluded me to be drowned, and that the enemy's fleet was approaching in a hostile manner. But he was soon eased of his fears, for the channel growing shallower every step I made, I came in a short time within hearing, and holding up the end of the cable by which the fleet was fastened, I cried in a loud voice, "Long live the most puissant Emperor of Lilliput!" This great prince received me at my landing with all possible encomiums, and created me a *nardac* upon the spot, which is the highest title of honor among them.

His Majesty desired I would take some other opportunity of bringing all the rest of his enemy's ships into his ports. And so unmeasurable is the ambition of princes that he seemed to think of nothing less than reducing the whole empire of Blefuscu into a province, and governing it by a viceroy; of destroying the Big Endian exiles, and compelling that people to break the smaller end of their eggs, by which he would remain the sole monarch of the whole world. But I endeavored to divert him from this design by many arguments drawn from the topics of policy as well as justice; and I plainly protested that I would never be an instrument of bringing a free and brave people into slavery. And when the matter was debated in council, the wisest part of the ministry were of my opinion.

About three weeks after this exploit there arrived a solemn embassy from Blefuscu with humble offers of a peace, which was soon concluded upon conditions very advantageous to our Emperor. There were six ambassadors with a train of about five hundred persons, and their entry was very magnificent, suitable to

the grandeur of their master and the importance of their business. When their treaty was finished, wherein I did them several good offices by the credit I now had, or at least appeared to have at court, their Excellencies, who were privately told how much I had been their friend, made me a visit in form. They began with many compliments upon my valor and generosity, invited me to that kingdom in their Emperor's name, and desired me to show them some proofs of my prodigious strength, of which they had heard so many wonders.

When I had for some time entertained their Excellencies, to their infinite satisfaction and surprise, I desired they would do me the honor to present my most humble respects to the Emperor their master, the renown of whose virtues had so justly filled the whole world with admiration, and whose royal person I resolved to attend before I returned to my own country. Accordingly, the next time I had the honor to see our Emperor, I desired his general license to wait on the Blefuscudian monarch, which he was pleased to grant me, as I could plainly perceive, in a very cold manner. But I could not guess the reason, till I had a whisper from a certain person, that Flimnap and Bolgolam had represented my intercourse with those ambassadors as a mark of disaffection, from which I am sure my heart was wholly free. And this was the first time I began to conceive some imperfect idea of courts and ministers.

It is to be observed that these ambassadors spoke to me by an interpreter, the languages of both empires differing as much from each other as any two in Europe, and each nation priding itself upon the antiquity, beauty, and energy of their own tongues, with an avowed contempt for that of their neighbor. Yet our Emperor, standing upon the advantage he had got by the seizure of their fleet, obliged them to deliver their credentials and make their speech in the Lilliputian tongue. And it must be confessed that from the great intercourse of trade and commerce between both realms, and from the custom in each empire to send their young nobility and richer gentry to the other, there are few persons of distinction, or merchants, or seamen but what can hold conversation in both tongues. This I discovered some weeks after, when I went to pay my respects to the Emperor of Blefuscu, which, through the malice of my enemies, proved a very happy adventure to me.

CHAPTER 6

Lilliput's Laws, Customs, and Educational Methods

ALTHOUGH I intend to leave the description of this empire to a particular treatise, yet in the meantime I am content to gratify the curious reader with some general ideas. As the common size of the natives is somewhat under six inches high, so there is an exact proportion in all other animals, as well as plants and trees. For instance, the tallest horses and oxen are between four and five inches in height, the sheep an inch and a half, more or less: their geese about the bigness of a sparrow. And so the several gradations downward till you come to the smallest, which, to my sight, were almost invisible. But nature had adapted the eyes of the Lilliputians to all objects proper for their view. They see with great exactness, but at no great distance. And to show the sharpness of their sight toward objects that are near, I have been much pleased with observing a cook pulling a lark, which was not so large as a common fly; and a young girl threading an invisible needle with invisible silk. Their tallest trees are about seven feet high; I mean some of those in the great royal park, the tops whereof I could but just reach with my fist clenched. The other vegetables are in the same proportion.

I shall say but little at present of their learning, which for many ages had flourished in all its branches among them. But their manner of writing is very peculiar, being neither from the left to the right, like the Europeans; nor from the right to the left, like the Arabians; nor from up to down, like the Chinese; nor from down to up, like the Cascagians; but aslant from one corner of the paper to the other.

They bury their dead with their heads directly downward, because they hold an opinion that in eleven thousand moons they are all to rise again, in which period the earth (which they conceive to be flat) will turn upside down. By this means they shall, at their resurrection, be found ready standing on their feet. The learned among them confess the absurdity of this doctrine, but the practice still continues.

There are some laws and customs in this empire very peculiar; and if they were not so directly contrary to those of my own dear country, I should be tempted to say a little in their justification. It is only to be wished that they were as well executed. The first I shall mention relates to informers. All crimes against the state are punished here with the utmost severity; but if the person accused makes his innocence plainly to appear upon his trial, the accuser is immediately put to an ignominious death. And out of his goods or lands the innocent person is quadruply recompensed for the loss of his time, for the danger he underwent, for the hardship of his imprisonment, and for all the charges he had been at in making his defense. Or, if that fund be deficient, it is largely supplied by the Crown. The Emperor does also confer on him some public mark of his favor, and proclamation is made of his innocence through the whole city.

They look upon fraud as a greater crime than theft, and therefore seldom fail to punish it with death. For they allege that care and vigilance, with a very common understanding, may preserve a man's goods from thieves, but honesty has no fence against superior cunning. And since it is necessary that there should be a perpetual intercourse of buying and selling, and dealing upon credit, where fraud is permitted and connived at, or has no law to punish it, the honest dealer is always undone, and the knave gets the advantage.

Whoever can bring sufficient proof that he has strictly observed the laws of his country for seventy-three moons has a claim to certain privileges, according to his quality and condition of life, with a proportionate sum of money out of a fund appropriated for that use.

In choosing persons for all employments they have more regard to good morals than to great abilities; for, since government is necessary to mankind, they believe that the common size of human understanding is fitted to some station or other, and that Providence never intended to make the management of public affairs a mystery, to be comprehended only by a few persons of sublime genius, of which there seldom are three born in an age. They suppose truth, justice, temperance, and the like, to be in every man's power; the practice of which virtues, assisted by experience and a good intention, would qualify any man for the service of his country, except where a course of study is required.

Ingratitude is among them a capital crime. They

reason thus: whoever makes ill returns to his bene-
factor must needs be a common enemy to the rest of
mankind, from whom he has received no obligation,
and therefore such a man is not fit to live.

Their notions relating to the duties of parents and
children differ extremely from ours. They will
never allow, for instance, that a child is under any obligation to his father for begetting him, or his mother
for bringing him into the world; which, considering
the miseries of human life, was neither a benefit in
itself nor intended so by his parents. Upon these and
the like reasonings their opinion is that parents are the
last of all others to be trusted with the education of
their own children. And therefore they have in every
town public nurseries, where all parents, except cottagers and laborers, are obliged to send their infants of
both sexes to be reared and educated when they come
to the age of twenty moons, at which time they are
supposed to have some rudiments of docility. These
schools are of several kinds, suited to different qualities
and to both sexes. They have certain professors well
skilled in preparing children for such a condition of
life as befits the rank of their parents, and their own
capacities.

The nurseries for males of noble or eminent birth
are provided with grave and learned professors and
their several deputies. The clothes and food of the
children are plain and simple. They are bred up in the
principles of honor, justice, courage, modesty, clemency, religion, and love of their country. They are
always employed in some business, except in the
times of eating and sleeping, which are very short,
and two hours for diversions, consisting of bodily exercises. They are dressed by men till four years of

age, and then are obliged to dress themselves, although their quality be ever so great. And the women attendants, who are aged proportionately to ours at fifty, perform only the most menial offices. They are never suffered to converse with servants, but go together in small or greater numbers to take their diversions. Their parents are suffered to see them only twice a year; the visit is to last but an hour. They are allowed to kiss the child at meeting and parting; but a professor, who always stands by on those occasions, will not suffer them to whisper, or use any fondling expressions, or bring any presents of toys, sweetmeats, and the like.

The nurseries for children of ordinary gentlemen, merchants, traders, and handicrafts are managed after the same manner. Those designed for trades are put out as apprentices at eleven years old, whereas those of persons of quality continue in their exercises till fifteen, which answers to one and twenty with us. But the confinement is gradually lessened for the last three years.

In the female nurseries the young girls of quality are educated much like the males, only they are dressed by orderly servants of their own sex; but always in the presence of a professor or deputy, till they come to dress themselves, which is at five years old. And if it be found that these nurses ever presume to entertain the girls with frightful or foolish stories, they are publicly whipped thrice about the city, imprisoned for a year, and banished for life to the most desolate part of the country. Thus the young ladies there are as much ashamed of being cowards and fools as the men, and despise all personal ornaments beyond decency and cleanliness.

Neither did I perceive any difference in their education, made by their difference of sex, only that the exercises of the females were not altogether so robust; and that some rules were given them relating to domestic life, and a smaller compass of learning was enjoined them. For their maxim is that among people of quality a wife should be always a reasonable and agreeable companion, because she cannot always be young. When the girls are twelve years old, which among them is the marriageable age, their parents or guardians take them home, with great expressions of gratitude to the professors, and seldom without tears of the young lady and her companions.

In the nurseries of females of the meaner sort the children are instructed in all kinds of work proper for their sex and their several degrees. Those intended for apprentices are dismissed at nine years old, the rest are kept to thirteen.

The poorer families who have children at these nurseries are obliged, besides their annual pension, which is as low as possible, to return to the steward of the nursery a small monthly share of their earnings, to be a portion for the child; and therefore all parents are limited in their expenses by the law. For the Lilliputians think nothing can be more unjust than for people, in subservience to their own appetites, to bring children into the world and leave the burden of supporting them on the public. As to persons of quality, they give security to appropriate a certain sum for each child, suitable to their condition; and these funds are always managed with good husbandry and the most exact justice.

The cottagers and laborers keep their children at home, their business being only to till and cultivate the

earth, and therefore their education is of little consequence to the public. But the old and diseased among
them are supported by hospitals, for begging is a trade
unknown in this kingdom.

And here it may perhaps divert the curious reader to
give some account of my domestics, and my manner
of living in this country, during a residence of nine
months and thirteen days. Having a head mechanically turned, and being likewise forced by necessity,
I had made for myself a table and chair out of the
largest trees in the royal park. Two hundred seamstresses were employed to make me shirts and linen for
my bed and table, all of the strongest and coarsest
kind they could get; which, however, they were
forced to quilt together in several folds, for the thickest was some degrees finer than lawn. Their linen is
usually three inches wide, and three feet make a piece.

The seamstresses took my measure as I lay on the
ground, one standing at my neck, and another at my
midleg, with a strong cord extended, that each held by
the end, while the third measured the length of the
cord with a rule an inch long. Then they measured
my right thumb, and desired no more. For by a mathematical computation, that twice round the thumb is
once round the wrist, and so on to the neck and the
waist, and by the help of my old shirt, which I displayed on the ground before them for a pattern, they
fitted me exactly.

Three hundred tailors were employed in the same
manner to make me clothes. But they had another
contrivance for taking my measure. I knelt down,
and they raised a ladder from the ground to my neck.
Upon this ladder one of them mounted, and let fall a
plumb line from my collar to the floor, which just an-

swered the length of my coat. But my waist and arms I measured myself. When my clothes were finished, which was done in my house (for the largest of theirs would not have been able to hold them) they looked like the patchwork made by the ladies in England, only that mine were all of a color.

I had three hundred cooks to dress my victuals in little convenient huts built about my house, where they and their families lived, and prepared me two dishes apiece. I took up twenty waiters in my hand, and placed them on the table. A hundred more attended below on the ground, some with dishes of meat, and some with barrels of wine, and other liquors, slung on their shoulders; all of which the waiters above drew up as I wanted, in a very ingenious manner, by certain cords, as we draw the bucket up a well in Europe. A dish of their meat was a good mouthful and a barrel of their liquor a reasonable draught. Their mutton yields to ours, but their beef is excellent. I have had a sirloin so large that I have been forced to make three bites of it. But this is rare. My servants were astonished to see me eat it bones and all, as in our country we do the leg of a lark. Their geese and turkeys I usually ate at a mouthful, and I must confess they far exceed ours. Of their smaller fowl I could take up twenty or thirty at the end of my knife.

One day his Imperial Majesty, being informed of my way of living, desired that himself and his Royal Consort, with the young princes of the blood of both sexes, might have the happiness of dining with me. They came accordingly, and I placed them upon chairs of state on my table, just over against me, with their guards about them. Flimnap, the Lord High Treasurer, attended there likewise with his white staff. And

I observed he often looked on me with a sour countenance, which I would not seem to regard, but ate more
than usual, in honor to my dear country as well as to
fill the court with admiration. I have some private reasons to believe that this visit from his Majesty gave
Flimnap an opportunity of doing me ill offices to his
master. That minister had always been my secret enemy, though he outwardly caressed me more than was
usual to the moroseness of his nature. He represented
to the Emperor the low condition of his treasury; that
he was forced to take up money at great discount;
that exchequer bills would not circulate under nine
per cent below par; that in short I had cost his Majesty
above a million and a half of *sprugs* (their greatest
gold coin, about the bigness of a spangle); and upon
the whole, that it would be advisable in the Emperor
to take the first fair occasion of dismissing me.

The ladies and gentlemen of the court often came to
call on me. On those occasions, it was my custom to
go immediately to the door; and, after paying my respects, to take up the coach and two horses very carefully in my hands (for if there were six horses, the
postillion always unharnessed four) and place them on
a table, where I had fixed a movable rim quite round,
of five inches high, to prevent accidents. And I have
often had four coaches and horses at once on my table
full of company, while I sat in my chair leaning my
face toward them. And when I was engaged with one
set, the coachmen would gently drive the others
round my table. I have passed many an afternoon very
agreeably in these conversations.

CHAPTER 7

Escape to Blefuscu

W<small>HEN</small> I was just preparing to pay my attendance on the Emperor of Blefuscu, a considerable person at court (to whom I had been very serviceable at a time when he lay under the highest displeasure of his Imperial Majesty) came to my house very privately at night in a close chair, and without sending his name, desired admittance. The chairmen were dismissed. I put the chair, with his Lordship in it, into my coat pocket, and giving orders to a trusty servant to say I was indisposed and gone to sleep, I fastened the door of my house, placed the chair on the table, according to my usual custom, and sat down by it. After the common salutations were over, observing his Lordship's countenance full of concern, and inquiring into the reason, he desired I would hear him with patience in a matter that highly concerned my honor and my life. His speech was to the following effect, for I took notes of it as soon as he left me.

"You are to know," said he, "that several committees of council have been lately called in the most private manner on your account; and it is but two days since his Majesty came to a full resolution.

"You are very sensible that Skyresh Bolgolam has been your mortal enemy almost ever since your arrival. His original reasons I know not, but his hatred is much increased since your great success against Blefuscu, by which his glory as admiral is obscured. This lord, in conjunction with Flimnap, the High Treasurer, and several others have prepared articles of impeachment against you for treason and other capital crimes."

This preface made me so impatient, being conscious of my own merits and innocence, that I was going to interrupt; but he entreated me to be silent, and thus proceeded.

"Out of gratitude for the favors you have done me, I procured information of the whole proceedings, and a copy of the articles, wherein I venture my head for your service."

Articles of Impeachment against Quinbus Flestrin (the Man-Mountain)

ARTICLE I

That the said Quinbus Flestrin, having brought the Imperial fleet of Blefuscu into the royal port, and being afterward commanded by his Imperial Majesty to seize all the other ships of the said empire of Blefuscu, and reduce that empire to a province, to be governed by a viceroy from hence, and to destroy and put to death not only all the Big Endian exiles, but likewise all the people of that empire, who would not immediately forsake the Big Endian heresy: he, the said Flestrin, like a false traitor against his most Auspicious, Serene, Imperial Majesty, did petition to be excused from the said service upon pretense of unwillingness to force the consciences or destroy the liberties and lives of an innocent people.

ARTICLE II

That, whereas certain ambassadors arrived from the court of Blefuscu, to sue for peace in his Majesty's court: he, the said Flestrin, did, like a false traitor, aid, abet, comfort, and divert the said ambassadors, although he knew them to be servants to a prince who was lately an open enemy to his Imperial Majesty, and in open war against his said Majesty.

ARTICLE III

That the said Quinbus Flestrin, contrary to the duty of a faithful subject, is now preparing to make a voyage to the court and empire of Blefuscu, for which he had received only verbal license from his Imperial Majesty; and under color of the said license, doth falsely and traitorously intend to take the said voyage, and thereby to aid, comfort, and abet the Emperor of Blefuscu, so late an enemy, and in open war with his Imperial Majesty aforesaid.

"There are some other articles, but these are the most important, of which I have read you an abstract.

"In the several debates upon this impeachment, it must be confessed that his Majesty gave many marks of his great leniency, often urging the services you had done him and endeavoring to extenuate your crimes. The Treasurer and Admiral insisted that you should be put to the most painful and ignominious death, by setting fire on your house at night, and the General was to attend with twenty thousand men armed with poisoned arrows to shoot you on the face and hands. Some of your servants were to have private orders to strew a poisonous juice on your shirts, which would

soon make you tear your own flesh, and die in the utmost torture. The General came into the same opinion, so that for a long time there was a majority against
you.

"Upon this incident, Reldresal, Principal Secretary
for Private Affairs, who always approved himself
your true friend, was commanded by the Emperor to
deliver his opinion, which he accordingly did; and
therein justified the good thoughts you have of him.
He allowed your crimes to be great, but that still there
was room for mercy, the most commendable virtue in
a prince, and for which his Majesty was so justly cele-
brated. He said, the friendship between you and him
was so well known to the world that perhaps the most
honorable board might think him partial. However,
in obedience to the command he had received, he
would freely offer his sentiments. That if his Majesty,
in consideration of your services, and pursuant to his
own merciful disposition, would please to spare your
life, and only give order to put out both your eyes,
he humbly conceived that by this expedient justice
might in some measure be satisfied, and all the world
would applaud the leniency of the Emperor, as well as
the fair and generous proceedings of those who have
the honor to be his counselors. That the loss of your
eyes would be no impediment to your bodily
strength, by which you might still be useful to his Majesty. That blindness is an addition to courage, by concealing dangers from us; that the fear you had for your
eyes was the greatest difficulty in bringing over the
enemy's fleet, and it would be sufficient for you to see
by the eyes of the ministers, since the greatest princes
do no more.

"This proposal was received with the utmost disapprobation by the whole board. Bolgolam, the Admiral, could not preserve his temper, but rising up in fury, said he wondered how the Secretary dared presume to give his opinion for preserving the life of a traitor; that the services you had performed were, by all true reasons of state, the great aggravation of your crimes; and the same strength which enabled you to bring over the enemy's fleet might serve, upon the first discontent, to carry it back; that he had good reasons to think you were a Big Endian in your heart; and as treason begins in the heart, before it appears in overt acts, so he accused you as a traitor on that account, and therefore insisted you should be put to death.

"The Treasurer was of the same opinion. He showed to what straits his Majesty's revenue was reduced by the charge of maintaining you, which would soon grow insupportable; that the Secretary's expedient of putting out your eyes was so far from being a remedy against this evil, it would probably increase it, as it is manifest from the common practice of blinding some kind of fowl, after which they fed the faster, and grew sooner fat; that his sacred Majesty and the Council, who are your judges, were in their own consciences fully convinced of your guilt, which was a sufficient argument to condemn you to death, without the formal proofs required by the strict letter of the law.

"But his Imperial Majesty, fully determined against capital punishment, was graciously pleased to say that since the Council thought the loss of your eyes too easy a censure, some other may be inflicted hereafter. And your friend the Secretary, humbly desiring to be heard again in answer to what the Treasurer had objected concerning the great charge his Majesty was at in maintaining you, said that his Excellency, who had the sole disposal of the Emperor's revenue, might easily provide against that evil by gradually lessening your establishment; by which, for want of sufficient food, you would grow weak and faint, and lose your appetite, and consequently decay and consume in a few months. Thus by the great friendship of the Secretary, the whole affair was compromised.

"In three days your friend the Secretary will be directed to come to your house, and read before you the articles of impeachment; and then to signify the great leniency and favor of his Majesty and Council, whereby you are only condemned to the loss of your eyes, which his Majesty does not question you will gratefully and humbly submit to. And twenty of his Majesty's surgeons will attend, in order to see the operation well performed, by discharging very sharp-pointed arrows into the balls of your eyes, as you lie on the ground.

"I leave to your prudence what measures you will take; and to avoid suspicion, I must immediately return in as private a manner as I came."

His Lordship did so, and I remained alone, under many doubts and perplexities of mind. I must confess that, having never been designed for a courtier either by my birth or education, I was so ill a judge of things that I could not discover the leniency and favor of the sentence, but conceived it rather to be rigorous than gentle. I sometimes thought of standing my trial, for although I could not deny the facts alleged in the several articles, yet I hoped they would admit of some extenuations.

At last I fixed upon a resolution, and to it I owe the preserving of my eyes, and consequently my liberty. Having his Imperial Majesty's license to pay my attendance upon the Emperor of Blefuscu, I took this opportunity, before the three days were elapsed, to send a letter to my friend the Secretary, signifying my resolution of setting out that morning for Blefuscu, and without waiting for an answer, I went to that side of the island where our fleet lay. I seized a large man-of-war, tied a cable to the prow, and, lifting up the anchors, I stripped myself, put my clothes (together with my coverlet, which I carried under my arm) into the vessel, and drawing it after me between wading and swimming, arrived at the royal port of Blefuscu, where the people had long expected me. They lent me two guides to direct me to the capital city, which is of the same name. I held them in my hands till I came within two hundred yards of the gate, and desired them to signify my arrival to one of the secretaries, and let him know I there waited his Majesty's commands.

I had an answer in about an hour, that his Majesty, attended by the Royal Family and great officers of the court, was coming out to receive me. I advanced a hundred yards. The Emperor and his train alighted from their horses, the Empress and ladies from their coaches, and I did not perceive they were in any fright or concern. I lay on the ground to kiss his Majesty's and the Empress's hand. I told his Majesty that I had come according to my promise, and with the license of the Emperor, my master, to have the honor of seeing so mighty a monarch, and to offer him any service in my power, consistent with my duty to my own prince. I did not mention a word about my disgrace.

I shall not trouble the reader with the particular account of my reception at this court, which was suitable to the generosity of so great a prince; [1] nor of the difficulties I was in for want of a house and bed, being forced to lie on the ground, wrapped up in my coverlet.

[1] Louis XIV.

CHAPTER 8

Gulliver Returns to His Native Country

THREE DAYS after my arrival, walking out of curiosity to the northeast coast of the island, I observed, about half a league off, in the sea, something that looked like a boat overturned. I pulled off my shoes and stockings, and wading two or three hundred yards, I found the object to approach nearer by force of the tide. And then I plainly saw it to be a real boat, which I supposed might, by some tempest, have been driven from a ship. Whereupon I returned immediately toward the city, and desired his Imperial Majesty to lend me twenty of the tallest vessels he had left after the loss of his fleet, and three thousand seamen under the command of his Vice-Admiral. This fleet sailed round, while I went back the shortest way to the coast where I first discovered the boat. I found the tide had driven it still nearer.

The seamen were all provided with cordage, which I had beforehand twisted to a sufficient strength. When the ships came up, I stripped myself, and waded till I came within a hundred yards of the boat, after which I was forced to swim till I got up to it. The seamen threw me the end of the cord, which I fastened to a hole in the forepart of the boat, and the other end to a man-of-war. But I found all my labor to little purpose; for being out of my depth, I was not able to work. In this necessity, I was forced to swim behind, and push the boat forward as often as I could, with one of my hands. And the tide favoring me, I advanced so far that I could just hold up my chin and feel the ground. I rested two or three minutes, and then gave the boat another shove, and so on till the sea was no higher than my armpits. Now, the most laborious part being over, I took out my other cables, which were stowed in one of the ships, and fastened them first to the boat and then to nine of the vessels which attended me. The wind being favorable, the seamen towed and I shoved till we arrived within forty yards of the shore. Then waiting till the tide was out, I got dry to the boat, and by the assistance of two thousand men, with ropes and engines, I made a

shift to turn it on its bottom, and found it was but little damaged.

After great difficulties, I was by the help of certain paddles, which cost me ten days' making, able to get my boat to the royal port of Blefuscu, where a mighty concourse of people appeared upon my arrival, full of

wonder at the sight of so prodigious a vessel. I told the Emperor that my good fortune had thrown this boat in my way to carry me to some place from whence I might return into my native country, and begged his Majesty's orders for getting materials to fit it up, together with his license to depart; which, after some kind expostulations, he was pleased to grant.

I did very much wonder, in all this time, not to have heard of any express relating to me from our Emperor to the court of Blefuscu. But I was afterward given privately to understand that his Imperial Majesty, never imagining I had the least notice of his designs, believed I was only gone to Blefuscu in performance of my promise, according to the license he had given me, which was well known at our court, and would return in a few days when that ceremony was ended. But he was at last in pain at my long absence. And after consulting with the Treasurer and the rest of that cabal, a person of quality was dispatched with the copy of the articles against me. This envoy had instructions to represent to the monarch of Blefuscu the great leniency of his master, who was content to punish me no further than with the loss of my eyes; that I had fled from justice, and if I did not return in two hours, I should be deprived of my title of *nardac*, and declared a traitor. The envoy further added that, in order to maintain the peace and amity between both empires, his master expected that his brother of Blefuscu would give orders to have me sent back to Lilliput, bound hand and foot, to be punished as a traitor.

The Emperor of Blefuscu, having taken three days to consult, returned an answer consisting of many civilities and excuses. He said that, as for sending me bound, his brother knew it was impossible; that although I had deprived him of his fleet, yet he owed great obligations to me for many good offices I had done him in making the peace. That, however, both their Majesties would soon be made easy; for I had found a prodigious vessel on the shore, able to carry me on the sea, which he had given order to fit up with my own assistance and direction; and he hoped in a few weeks both empires would be freed from so insupportable an encumbrance.

With this answer the envoy returned to Lilliput, and the monarch of Blefuscu related to me all that had passed, offering me at the same time (but under the strictest confidence) his gracious protection, if I would continue in his service. Although I believed him sincere, yet I resolved never more to put any confidence in princes or ministers, where I could possibly avoid it. And therefore, with all due acknowledgments for his favorable intentions, I humbly begged to be excused. I told him that since fortune, whether good or evil, had thrown a vessel in my way, I was resolved to venture myself in the ocean, rather than be an occasion of difference between two such mighty monarchs. Neither did I find the Emperor at all displeased; and I discovered by a certain accident that he was very glad of my resolution, and so were most of his ministers.

These considerations moved me to hasten my departure; to which the court, impatient to have me gone, very readily contributed. Five hundred workmen were employed to make two sails to my boat, according to my directions, by quilting thirteen folds of their strongest linen together. I was at the pains of making ropes and cables, by twisting ten, twenty or thirty of the thickest and strongest of theirs. A great stone that I happened to find, after a long search, by the seashore, served me for an anchor. I had the tallow of three hundred cows for greasing my boat, and other uses. I was at incredible pains in cutting down some of the largest timber trees for oars and masts, wherein I was, however, much assisted by his Majesty's ship carpenters, who helped me in smoothing them, after I had done the rough work.

In about a month, when all was prepared, I sent to receive his Majesty's commands, and to take my leave. The Emperor and Royal Family came out of the palace. I lay down on my face to kiss his hand, which he very graciously gave me. So did the Empress and young princes of the blood. His Majesty presented me with fifty purses of two hundred *sprugs* apiece, together with his picture at full length, which I put immediately into one of my gloves to keep it from being hurt. The ceremonies at my departure were too many to trouble the reader with at this time.

I stored the boat with the carcasses of a hundred oxen, and three hundred sheep, with bread and drink and as much meat ready dressed as four hundred cooks could provide. I took with me six cows and two bulls alive, with as many ewes and rams, intending to carry them into my own country and propagate the breed. And to feed them on board I had a good bundle of hay and a bag of corn. I would gladly have taken a dozen of the natives, but this was a thing the Emperor would by no means permit. And besides a diligent search into my pockets, his Majesty engaged my honor not to carry away any of his subjects, although with their own consent and desire.

Having thus prepared all things as well as I was able, I set sail on the 24th day of September, 1701, at six in the morning. And when I had gone about four leagues to the northward, the wind being at southeast, at six in the evening I descried a small island about half a league to the northwest. I advanced forward, and cast anchor on the lee side of the island, which seemed to be uninhabited. I then took some refreshment, and went to my rest. I slept well, and I conjecture at least six hours, for I found the day broke in two hours after I awaked. It was a clear night. I ate my breakfast before the sun was up. And heaving anchor, the wind being favorable, I steered the same course that I had done the day before, wherein I was directed by my pocket compass.

My intention was to reach, if possible, one of those islands which I had reason to believe lay to the northeast of Van Diemen's Land. I discovered nothing all that day. But upon the next, about three in the afternoon, when I had by my computation made twenty-four leagues from Blefuscu, I descried a sail steering to the southeast. My course was due east. I hailed her, but could get no answer; yet I found I gained upon her, for the wind slackened. I made all the sail I could, and in half an hour she spied me, then hung out her ancient, and discharged a gun.

It is not easy to express the joy I was in upon the unexpected hope of once more seeing my beloved country, and the dear pledges I had left in it. The ship slackened her sails, and I came up with her between five and six in the evening, September 26. My heart leapt within me to see her English colors. I put my cows and sheep into my coat pockets, and got on board with all my little cargo of provisions.

The vessel was an English merchantman, returning from Japan by the North and South Seas; the captain, Mr. John Biddle of Deptford, a very civil man, and an excellent sailor. There were about fifty men in the ship; and here I met an old comrade of mine, one Peter Williams, who gave me a good character to the captain. This gentleman treated me with kindness, and desired I would let him know what place I came from last, and whither I was bound. I answered in a few words, but he thought I was raving, and that the dangers I underwent had disturbed my head; whereupon I took my black cattle and sheep out of my pocket, which, after great astonishment, clearly convinced him of my veracity. I then showed him the gold given me by the Emperor of Blefuscu, together with his Majesty's picture at full length, and some other rarities of that country. I gave him two purses of two hundred *sprugs* each, and promised, when we arrived in England, to make him a present of a cow and a sheep.

We arrived in the Downs on the 13th of April, 1702. I had only one misfortune: the rats on board carried away one of my sheep. I found her bones in a hole, picked clean from the flesh. The rest of my cattle I got safe on shore, and set them grazing in a bowling green at Greenwich, where the fineness of the grass made them feed very heartily, though I had always preserved them in so long a voyage if the captain had feared the contrary. Neither could I possibly have not allowed me some of his best biscuit, which, rubbed to powder and mingled with water, was their constant food.

The short time I continued in England I made considerable profit by showing my cattle to many persons of quality, and others. And before I began my second voyage, I sold them for six hundred pounds. Since my last return, I find the breed is considerably increased, especially the sheep; which I hope will prove much to the advantage of the woolen manufacture, by the fineness of the fleeces.

I stayed but two months with my wife and family; for my insatiable desire of seeing foreign countries would suffer me to continue no longer. I left fifteen hundred pounds with my wife, and fixed her in a good house at Redriff. My remaining stock I carried with me, part in money and part in goods, in hopes to improve my fortunes. My eldest uncle John had left me an estate in land, near Epping, of about thirty pounds a year; and I had a long lease of the Black Bull in Fetter Lane, which yielded me as much more; so that I was not in any danger of leaving my family upon the parish. My son Johnny, named so after his uncle, was at the Grammar School, and a towardly child. My daughter Betty (who is now well married, and has children) was then at her needlework. I took leave of my wife, and boy and girl, with tears on both sides, and went on board the *Adventure*, a merchant ship of three hundred tons, bound for Surat, India, Captain John Nicholas of Liverpool, commander.

PART II

A Voyage
to Brobdingnag

CHAPTER 9

Gulliver Is Captured by a Native

W E SET sail in the *Adventure* on June 20, 1702, and
had a good voyage till we arrived at the Cape of
Good Hope. We landed for fresh water, but dis-
covering a leak, we unshipped our goods and wintered
there. Toward the end of March we sailed again.
North of the island of Madagascar we ran into a terrible storm which lasted for twenty days and carried
us far off our course.

After two days of perfect calm, the southern mon-
soon began to set in. It was a very fierce storm; the
sea broke strange and dangerous. When it was over
we brought the ship to. Our course was east-
northeast, the wind was at southwest.

During this storm, we had been carried by my computation about five hundred leagues to the east, so that
the oldest sailor on board could not tell in what part
of the world we were. Our provisions held out well,
our ship was stanch, and our crew all in good health;
but we lay in the utmost distress for water.

On the 16th day of June, 1703, a boy on the topmast discovered land. On the 17th we came in full view of a great island or continent (for we knew not which) on the south side whereof was a small neck of land jutting out into the sea, and a creek too shallow to hold a ship of above one hundred tons. We cast anchor within a league of this creek, and our captain sent a dozen of his men well armed in the longboat with vessels for water if any could be found. I desired his leave to go with them, that I might see the country and make what discoveries I could.

When we came to land we saw no river or spring, nor any sign of inhabitants. Our men therefore wandered on the shore to find out some fresh water near the sea, and I walked alone about a mile on the other side, where I observed the country all barren and rocky. I now began to be weary, and seeing nothing to entertain my curiosity, I returned gently down toward the creek; and the sea being full in my view, I saw our men already got into the boat, and rowing for life to the ship. I was going to halloo after them, although it had been to little purpose, when I observed a huge creature walking after them in the sea, as fast as he could. He waded not much deeper than his knees, and took prodigious strides, but our men had the start of him half a league, and the sea thereabouts being full of sharp-pointed rocks, the monster was not able to overtake the boat.

I did not stay to see the issue of that adventure, but ran as fast as I could the way I first went, and then climbed up a steep hill, which gave me some prospect of the country. I found it fully cultivated; but that which first surprised me was the length of the grass, which in those grounds that seemed to be kept for hay was about twenty feet high.

I came upon a highroad, for so I took it to be, though it served to the inhabitants only as a footpath through a field of barley. Here I walked on for some time, but could see little on either side, it being now near harvest and the corn rising at least forty feet. I was an hour walking to the end of this field, which was fenced in with a hedge of at least one hundred and twenty feet high, and the trees so lofty that I could make no computation of their altitude. There was a stile to pass from this field into the next. It had four steps, and a stone to cross over when you came to the uppermost. It was impossible for me to climb this stile, because every step was six feet high, and the upper stone above twenty.

I was endeavoring to find some gap in the hedge when I discovered one of the inhabitants in the next field, advancing toward the stile, of the same size as the one I saw in the sea pursuing our boat. He appeared as tall as an ordinary spire steeple, and took about ten yards at every stride, as near as I could guess. I was struck with the utmost fear and astonishment, and ran to hide myself in the corn, from whence I saw him at the top of the stile, looking back into the next field on the right hand, and heard him call in a voice many degrees louder than a speaking trumpet. But the noise was so high in the air that at first I certainly thought it was thunder. Whereupon seven monsters like himself came toward him with reaping hooks in their hands, each hook about the size of six scythes.

These people were not so well clad as the first, whose servants or laborers they seemed to be. For

upon some words he spoke, they went to reap the
corn in the field where I lay. I kept at as great a distance from them as I could, but was forced to move
with extreme difficulty, for the stalks of the corn were
sometimes not above a foot distant, so that I could
hardly squeeze my body between them. However, I
made a shift to go forward till I came to a part of the
field where the corn had been laid by the rain and
wind. Here it was impossible for me to advance a step;
for the stalks were so interwoven that I could not
creep through, and the beards of the fallen ears so
strong and pointed that they pierced through my
clothes into my flesh. At the same time I heard the
reapers not above a hundred yards behind me.

Being quite dispirited with toil and wholly over-
come by grief and despair, I lay down between two
ridges and heartily wished I might there end my days.
I bemoaned my desolate widow and fatherless children. I lamented my own folly and willfulness in attempting a second voyage against the advice of all my
friends and relations. In this terrible agitation of mind
I could not forbear thinking of Lilliput, whose inhabitants looked upon me as the greatest prodigy that
ever appeared in the world; where I was able to draw
an imperial fleet in my hand and perform those other
actions which will be recorded forever in the chroni-
cles of that empire, while posterity shall hardly believe
them, although attested by millions. I reflected what
a mortification it must prove to me to appear as inconsiderable in this nation as one single Lilliputian
would be among us.

But this I conceived was to be the least of my misfortunes. For as human creatures are observed to be

more savage and cruel in proportion to their bulk, what could I expect but to be a morsel in the mouth of the first among these enormous barbarians that should happen to seize me?

One of the reapers approached within ten yards of the ridge where I lay, and I feared that with the next step I should be squashed to death under his foot or cut in two with his reaping hook. And therefore when he was again about to move, I screamed as loud as fear could make me. Whereupon the huge creature trod short, and looking round about under him for some time, at last espied me as I lay on the ground. He considered awhile with the caution of one who endeavors to lay hold on a small dangerous animal in such a manner that it shall not be able either to scratch or to bite him, as I myself have sometimes done with a weasel in England.

At length he ventured to take me up behind by the middle between his forefinger and thumb, and brought me within three yards of his eyes, that he might behold my shape more perfectly. I guessed his meaning, and my good fortune gave me so much presence of mind that I resolved not to struggle in the least as he held me in the air about sixty feet from the ground, although he grievously pinched my sides, for fear I should slip through his fingers. All I ventured was to raise my eyes toward the sun, and place my hands together in a supplicating posture, and to speak some words in a humble melancholy tone, suitable to the condition I then was in. I feared every moment that he would dash me against the ground, as we usually do any little hateful animal which we have a mind to destroy.

But my good star would have it that he appeared pleased with my voice and gestures, and began to look upon me as a curiosity, much wondering to hear me pronounce articulate words, although he could not understand them. In the meantime I was not able to forbear groaning and shedding tears, and turning my head toward my sides, letting him know, as well as I could, how cruelly I was hurt by the pressure of his thumb and finger. He seemed to get my meaning; for, lifting up the lappet of his coat, he put me gently into it, and immediately ran along with me to his master, who was a substantial farmer and the same person I had first seen in the field.

The farmer, having received such an account of me as his servant could give him, took a piece of a small straw, about the size of a walking staff, and therewith lifted up the lappets of my coat; which it seems he thought to be some kind of covering that nature had given me. He blew my hair aside to take a better view of my face. He called his hinds about him and asked them, as I afterward learned, whether they had ever seen in the fields any little creature that resembled me. He then placed me softly on the ground upon all four, but I got immediately up, and walked slowly backward and forward, to let those people see I had no intent to run away.

They all sat down in a circle about me, the better to observe my motions. I pulled off my hat, and made a low bow toward the farmer. I fell on my knees, and lifted up my hands and eyes, and spoke several words as loud as I could; I took a purse of gold out of my pocket, and humbly presented it to him. He received it on the palm of his hand, then applied it close to his eye, to see what it was, and afterward turned it several times with the point of a pin but could make nothing of it. Whereupon I made a sign that he should place his hand on the ground. I took the purse, and opening it poured all the gold into his palm. There were six Spanish pieces of four pistoles each, besides twenty or thirty smaller coins. I saw him wet the tip of his little finger upon his tongue and take up one of my largest pieces, and then another, but he seemed to be wholly ignorant what they were. He made me a sign to put them again into my purse, and the purse again into my pocket, which, after offering to him several times, I thought it best to do.

The farmer by this time was convinced I must be a rational creature. He spoke often to me, but the sound of his voice pierced my ears like that of a water mill, yet his words were articulate enough. I answered as loud as I could, in several languages, and he often laid his ear within two yards of me, but all in vain, for we were wholly unintelligible to each other. He then sent his servants to their work, and taking his handkerchief out of his pocket, he doubled and spread it on his left hand, which he placed flat on the ground, with the palm upward, making me a sign to step into it, as I could easily do, for it was not above a foot in thickness. I thought it my part to obey, and for fear of falling, laid myself at length upon the handkerchief, with the remainder of which he lapped me up to the head for further security, and in this manner carried me home to his house. There he called his wife, and showed me to her. But she screamed and ran back, as women in England do at the sight of a toad or a spider. However, when she had awhile seen my behavior, and how well I observed the signs her husband made, she was soon reconciled, and by degrees grew extremely tender of me.

It was about twelve at noon, and a servant brought in dinner. It was only one substantial dish of meat (fit for the plain condition of an husbandman) in a dish of about twenty-four feet in diameter. The company were the farmer and his wife, three children, and an old grandmother. When they sat down, the farmer placed me at some distance from him on the table, which was thirty feet high from the floor. I was in a terrible fright, and kept as far as I could from the edge for fear of falling.

The wife minced a bit of meat, then crumbled some bread on a trencher, and placed it before me. I made her a low bow, took out my knife and fork, and fell to eating, which gave them exceeding delight. The mistress sent her maid for a small dram cup, which held about three gallons, and filled it with drink. I took up the vessel with much difficulty in both hands, and in a most respectful manner drank to her Ladyship's health, expressing the words as loud as I could in English, which made the company laugh so heartily that I was almost deafened with the noise. This liquor tasted like a small cider, and was not unpleasant.

Then the master made me a sign to come to his trencher side; but as I walked on the table, I happened to stumble against a crust, and fell flat on my face, but received no hurt. I got up immediately, and observing the good people to be in much concern, I took my hat (which I held under my arm out of good manners) and waving it over my head, made three huzzas, to show I had got no mischief by my fall. But advancing forward toward my master (as I shall henceforth call him), his youngest son who sat next him, an arch boy of about ten years old, took me up by the legs, and held me so high in the air that I trembled in every limb. But his father snatched me from him, and at the same time gave him such a box on the left ear as would have felled an European troop of horse to the earth, ordering him to be taken from the table. But being afraid the boy might owe me a spite, and well remembering how mischievous all children among us naturally are to sparrows, rabbits, young kittens, and puppy dogs, I fell on my knees, and pointing to the boy, made my master to understand, as well as I could, that I desired his son might be pardoned. The father complied, and the lad took his seat again; whereupon I went to him and kissed his hand, which my master took, and made him stroke me gently with it.

In the midst of dinner, my mistress's favorite cat leaped into her lap. I heard a noise behind me like that of a dozen stocking weavers at work. Turning my head, I found it proceeded from the purring of this animal, who seemed to be three times larger than an ox, as I computed by the view of her head, and one of her paws, while her mistress was feeding and stroking her. The fierceness of this creature's countenance altogether discomposed me; though I stood at the farther end of the table, above fifty feet off, and although my mistress held her fast for fear she might give a spring and seize me in her talons. But it happened there was no danger; for the cat took not the least notice of me when my master placed me within three yards of her. And as I have been always told, and found true by experience in my travels, that flying or displaying fear before a fierce animal is a certain way to make it pursue or attack you, so I resolved in this dangerous juncture to show no manner of concern. I walked with intrepidity five or six times before the very head of the cat, and came within half a yard of her; whereupon she drew herself back, as if she were more afraid of me. I had less apprehension concerning the dogs, whereof three or four came into the room, as it is usual in farmers' houses. One of them was a mastiff, equal in bulk to four elephants, and a greyhound, somewhat taller than the mastiff but not so large.

When dinner was almost done, the nurse came in carrying a child of a year old who immediately spied me and began a squall that you might have heard from London Bridge to Chelsea, after the usual oratory of infants, to get me for a plaything. The mother out of pure indulgence took me up and put me toward the child, who presently seized me by the middle and got my head in his mouth, where I roared so loud that the urchin was frightened and let me drop; and I should certainly have broken my neck if the mother had not held her apron under me. The nurse to quiet her babe made use of a rattle, which was a kind of hollow vessel filled with great stones, and fastened by a cable to the child's waist: but all in vain, so that she was forced to apply the last remedy by giving it milk.

When dinner was done, my master went out to his laborers, and as I could discover by his voice and gesture, gave his wife a strict charge to take care of me. I was very much tired, and disposed to sleep, which my mistress perceiving, she put me on her own bed, and covered me with a clean white handkerchief, but larger and coarser than the mainsail of a man-of-war.

I slept about two hours, and dreamed I was at home with my wife and children, which aggravated my sorrows when I awakened and found myself alone in a vast room, between two and three hundred feet wide, and above two hundred high, lying in a bed twenty yards wide. My mistress was gone about her household affairs, and had locked me in. The bed was eight yards from the floor. Although desiring to get down, I dared not call; and it would have been in vain at so great a distance from the room where I lay to the kitchen where the family kept.

While I was under these circumstances, two rats crept up the curtains, and ran smelling backward and forward on the bed. One of them came up almost to my face, whereupon I rose in a fright, and drew out my sword to defend myself. These horrible animals had the boldness to attack me on both sides, and one of them held his forefeet at my collar. But I had the good fortune to rip up his belly before he could do me any mischief. He fell down at my feet, and the other, seeing the fate of his comrade, made his escape, but not without one good wound on the back, which I gave him as he fled, and made the blood run trickling from him.

After this exploit, I walked gently to and fro on the bed, to recover my breath and loss of spirits. These creatures were of the size of a large mastiff, but infinitely more nimble and fierce, so that if I had taken off my belt before I went to sleep I must have been torn to pieces and devoured. I measured the tail of the dead rat, and found it to be two yards long, wanting an inch. But it went against my stomach to drag the carcass off the bed, where it lay still bleeding; I observed it had yet some life, but with a strong slash across the neck, I dispatched it.

Soon after, my mistress came into the room, and seeing me all bloody, ran and took me up in her hand. I pointed to the dead rat, smiling and making other signs to show I was not hurt, whereat she was extremely rejoiced, calling the maid to take up the dead rat with a pair of tongs, and throw it out of the window. Then she set me on a table, where I showed her my sword all bloody; then wiping it on the lappet of my coat, I returned it to the scabbard.

CHAPTER 10

Gulliver is Taken to the City

M Y MISTRESS had a daughter of nine years old, a child mature for her age, very dexterous at her needle, and skillful in dressing her doll. Her mother and she contrived to fit up the doll's cradle for me against night. The cradle was put into a small drawer of a cabinet, and the drawer placed upon a hanging shelf for fear of the rats. This was my bed all the time I stayed with those people, though made more convenient by degrees, as I began to learn their language and make my wants known. This young girl was so handy that after I had once or twice pulled off my clothes before her, she was able to dress and undress me, though I never gave her that trouble when she would let me do either myself.

She made me seven shirts, and some other linen, of as fine cloth as could be got, which indeed was coarser than sackcloth; and these she constantly washed for me with her own hands. She was likewise my school-mistress to teach me the language. When I pointed to anything, she told me the name of it in her own tongue, so that in a few days I was able to call for whatever I had a mind to. She was very good-natured, and not above forty feet high, being little for her age. She gave me the name of *Grildrig*, which the family took up, and afterward the whole kingdom. The word imports what the Latins call *nanunculus*, the Italians *homunceletino*, and the English *mannikin*. To her I chiefly owe my preservation in that country: we never parted while I was there; I called her my *glumdalclitch*, or little nurse: and I should be guilty of great ingratitude if I omitted this honorable mention of her care and affection toward me.

It now began to be known and talked of in the neighborhood that my master had found a strange animal in the field, about the bigness of a *splacknuck*, but exactly shaped in every part like a human creature; which it likewise imitated in all its actions; seemed to speak in a little language of its own, had already learned several words of theirs, went erect upon two legs, was tame and gentle, would come when it was called, do whatever it was bid, had the finest limbs in the world, and a complexion fairer than a nobleman's daughter of three years old.

Another farmer who lived hard by, and was a particular friend of my master, came on a visit on purpose to inquire into the truth of this story. I was immediately produced, and placed upon a table, where I walked as I was commanded, drew my sword, put it up again, made my reverence to my master's guest, asked him in his own language how he did, and told him he was welcome, just as my little nurse had instructed me. This man, who was old and dimsighted, put on his spectacles to behold me better, at which I could not forbear laughing very heartily, for his eyes appeared like the full moon shining into a chamber at two windows. Our people, who discovered the cause of my mirth, bore me company in laughing, at which the old fellow was fool enough to be angry and out of countenance.

He had the character of a great miser, and to my misfortune he well deserved it, by the cursed advice he gave my master to show me as a sight upon a market day in the next town, which was half an hour's riding, about twenty-two miles from our house. I guessed there was some mischief contriving, when I observed my master and his friend whispering long together, sometimes pointing at me. And my fears made me fancy that I overheard and understood some of their words.

But the next morning Glumdalclitch, my little nurse, told me the whole matter, which she had cunningly picked out from her mother. The poor girl laid me on her bosom, and fell weeping with shame and grief. She apprehended some mischief would happen to me from rude vulgar folks, who might squeeze me to death or break one of my limbs by taking me in their hands. She had also observed how modest I was in my nature, how nicely I regarded my honor, and what an indignity I should conceive it to be exposed for money as a public spectacle to the meanest of the people. She said her papa and mamma had promised that Grildrig should be hers, but now she found they meant to serve her as they did last year, when they pretended to give her a lamb, and yet, as soon as it was fat, sold it to a butcher.

For my own part, I may truly affirm that I was less concerned than my nurse. I had a strong hope which never left me, that I should one day recover my liberty. And as to the ignominy of being carried about for a monster, I considered myself to be a perfect stranger in the country, and that such a misfortune could never be charged upon me as a reproach, if ever I should return to England; since the King of Great Britain himself, in my condition, must have undergone the same distress.

My master, pursuant to the advice of his friend, carried me in a box the next market day to the neighboring town, and took along with him his little daughter, my nurse, upon a pillion behind him. The box was close on every side, with a little door for me to go in and out, and a few gimlet holes to let in air. The girl had been so careful to put the quilt of her doll's bed into it, for me to lie down on. However, I was terribly shaken and discomposed in this journey, though it were but of half an hour. For the horse went about forty feet at every step, and trotted so high that the agitation was equal to the rising and falling of a ship in a great storm, but much more frequent.

Our journey was somewhat farther than from London to St. Albans. My master alighted at an inn which he used to frequent. And after consulting awhile with the innkeeper, and making some necessary preparations, he hired the *grultrud*, or crier, to give notice through the town of a strange creature to be seen at the Sign of the Green Eagle, not so big as a *splacknuck* (an animal in that country very finely shaped, about six feet long) and in every part of the body resembling a human creature, could speak several words, and perform a hundred diverting tricks.

I was placed upon a table in the largest room of the inn, which might be near three hundred feet square. My little nurse stood on a low stool close to the table, to take care of me and direct what I should do. My master, to avoid a crowd, would suffer only thirty people at a time to see me. I walked about on the table as the girl commanded. She asked me questions as far as she knew my understanding of the language reached, and I answered them as loud as I could. I turned about several times to the company, paid my humble respects, said they were welcome, and used some other speeches I had been taught. I took up a thimble filled with liquor, which Glumdalclitch had given me for a cup, and drank their health. I drew out my sword, and flourished it after the manner of fencers in England. My nurse gave me part of a straw, which I exercised as a pike, having learned the art in my youth.

I was that day shown to twelve sets of company, and as often forced to go over again with the same fopperies till I was half dead with weariness and vexation. For those who had seen me made such wonderful reports that the people were ready to break down the doors to come in. My master for his own interest would not suffer anyone to touch me except my nurse. And, to prevent danger, benches were set around the table at such a distance as put me out of everybody's reach. However, an unlucky schoolboy aimed a hazelnut directly at my head, which very narrowly missed me. Otherwise, it came with so much violence that it would have knocked out my brains, for it was almost as large as a small pumpion.[1] But I had the satisfaction to see the young rogue well beaten, and turned out of the room.

My master gave public notice that he would show me again the next market day, and in the meantime he prepared a more convenient vehicle for me, which he had reason enough to do, for I was so tired with my first journey and with entertaining company for eight hours together that I could hardly stand upon my legs or speak a word. It was at least three days before I recovered my strength. And that I might have no rest at home, all the neighboring gentlemen from a hundred miles around, hearing of my fame, came to see me at my master's own house. There could not be fewer than thirty persons with their wives and children (for the country is very populous); and my master demanded the rate of a full room whenever he showed me at home, although it were only to a single family. So that for some time I had but little ease every day of the week (except Wednesday, which is their Sabbath) although I was not carried to the town.

My master, finding how profitable I was likely to be, resolved to carry me to the most considerable cities of the kingdom. Having therefore provided himself with all things necessary for a long journey, and settled his affairs at home, he took leave of his wife, and upon the 17th of August, 1703, about two months after my arrival, we set out for the metropolis, situated near the middle of that empire, and about three thousand miles distance from our house. My master made his daughter Glumdalclitch ride behind

[1] Pumpkin.

him. She carried me on her lap in a box tied about her waist. The girl had lined it on all sides with the softest cloth she could get, well quilted underneath, furnished it with her doll's bed, provided me with linen and other necessaries, and made everything as convenient as she could. We had no other company but a boy of the house, who rode after us with the luggage.

My master's design was to show me in all the towns by the way, and to step out of the road for fifty or a hundred miles, to any village or person of quality's house where he might expect custom. We made easy journeys of not above seven or eight score miles a day. Glumdalclitch, on purpose to spare me, complained she was tired with the trotting of the horse. She often took me out of my box at my own desire, to give me air and show me the country, but always held me fast by a leading string. We passed over five or six rivers many degrees broader and deeper than the Nile or the Ganges; and there was hardly a rivulet so small as the Thames at London Bridge. We were ten weeks in our journey, and I was shown in eighteen large towns besides many villages and private families.

On the 26th day of October, we arrived at the metropolis, called in their language *Lorbrulgrud,* or Pride of the Universe. My master took a lodging in the principal street of the city, not far from the royal palace, and put out bills in the usual form, containing an exact description of my person and parts. He hired a large room between three and four hundred feet wide. He provided a table sixty feet in diameter, upon which I was to act my part, and palisadoes it around three feet from the edge, and as many high, to prevent my falling over. I was shown ten times a day, to the wonder and satisfaction of all people. I could now speak the language tolerably well, and perfectly understood every word that was spoken to me. Besides, I had learned their alphabet, and could make a shift to explain a sentence here and there; for Glumdalclitch had been my instructor while we were at home, and at leisure hours during our journey. She carried a little book in her pocket, not much larger than a Sanson's Atlas. It was a common treatise for the use of young girls, giving a short account of their religion. Out of this she taught me my letters, and interpreted the words.

CHAPTER 11

The Queen Buys Gulliver from the Farmer

THE FREQUENT labors I underwent every day made in a few weeks a very considerable change in my health. The more my master got by me, the more insatiable he grew. I had quite lost my appetite, and was almost reduced to a skeleton. The farmer observed it, and concluding I soon must die, resolved to make as good a hand of me as he could. While he was thus reasoning and resolving with himself, a *slardral*, or gentleman usher, came from court, commanding my master to carry me immediately thither for the diversion of the Queen and her ladies. Some of the latter had already been to see me, and reported strange things of my beauty, behavior, and good sense.

Her Majesty and those who attended her were beyond measure delighted with my demeanor. I fell on my knees, and begged the honor of kissing her Imperial foot. But this gracious princess held out her little finger toward me (after I was set on a table), which I embraced in both my arms, and put the tip of it with the utmost respect to my lip. She made me some general questions about my country and my travels, which I answered as distinctly and in as few words as I could. She asked whether I would be content to live at court. I bowed down to the board of the table, and humbly answered that I was my master's slave, but if I were at my own disposal I should be proud to devote my life to her Majesty's service. She then asked my master whether he were willing to sell me at a good price. He, who apprehended I could not live a month, was ready enough to part with me, and demanded a thousand pieces of gold, which were ordered him on the spot, each piece being about the bigness of eight hundred moidores. But, allowing for the proportion of all things between that country and Europe, and the high price of gold among them, this was hardly so great a sum as a thousand guineas would be in England.

I then said to the Queen, since I was now her Majesty's most humble creature and vassal, I must beg the favor that Glumdalclitch, who had always tended me with so much care and kindness, and understood to do it so well, might be admitted into her service, and continue to be my nurse and instructor. Her Majesty agreed to my petition, and easily got the farmer's consent, who was glad enough to have his daughter preferred at court. The poor girl herself was not able to hide her joy. My late master withdrew, bidding me farewell, and saying he had left me in a good service; to which I replied not a word, only making him a slight bow.

The Queen observed my coldness, and when the farmer was gone out of the apartment, asked me the reason. I made bold to tell her Majesty that I owed no other obligation to my late master, than his not dashing out the brains of a poor harmless creature found by chance in his field; which obligation was amply recompensed by the gain he had made in showing me through half the kingdom, and the price he had now sold me for. That the life I had since led was laborious enough to kill an animal of ten times my strength. That my health was much impaired by the continual drudgery of entertaining the rabble every hour of the day, and that if my master had not thought my life in danger, her Majesty perhaps would not have got so cheap a bargain. But as I was out of all fear of being ill treated under the protection of so great and good an Empress, the Ornament of Nature, the Darling of the World, the Delight of her Subjects, the Phoenix of the Creation, so I hoped my late master's apprehensions would appear to be groundless, for I already found my spirits to revive by the influence of her most august presence.

This was the sum of my speech, delivered with great hesitation. The latter part was altogether framed in the style peculiar to that people, whereof I learned some phrases from Glumdalclitch, while she was carrying me to court.

The Queen, giving great allowance for my defectiveness in speaking, was, however, surprised at so much wit and good sense in so diminutive an animal. She took me in her own hand, and carried me to the King, who was then retired to his cabinet. His Majesty, a prince of much gravity and austere countenance, not well observing my shape at first view, asked the Queen after a cold manner how long it was since she grew fond of a *splacknuck;* for such it seems he took me to be as I lay upon my breast in her Majesty's right hand. But this princess, who has an infinite deal of wit and humor, set me gently on my feet upon the desk, and commanded me to give his Majesty an account of myself. This I did in a very few words, and Glumdalclitch, who attended at the cabinet door and could not endure I should be out of her sight, being admitted, confirmed all that had passed from my arrival at her father's house.

The King, although he be as learned a person as any in his dominions, and had been educated in the study of philosophy, and particularly mathematics, yet when he observed my shape exactly, and saw me walk erect, before I began to speak, conceived I might be a piece of clockwork (which is in that country arrived to a very great perfection) contrived by some ingenious artist. But when he heard my voice and found what I delivered to be regular and rational he could not conceal his astonishment. He was by no means satisfied with the relation I gave him of the manner I came into his kingdom, but thought it a story concerted between Glumdalclitch and her father, who had taught me a set of words to make me sell at a higher price. Upon this imagination he put several other questions to me, and still received rational answers, no otherwise defective than by a foreign accent and an imperfect knowledge in the language, with some rustic phrases which I had learned at the farmer's house and did not suit the polite style of a court.

His Majesty sent for three great scholars who were

then in their weekly waiting, according to the custom in that country. These gentlemen, after they had awhile examined my shape with much nicety, were of different opinions concerning me. They all agreed that I could not be produced according to the regular laws of nature, because I was not framed with a capacity of preserving my life, either by swiftness, or climbing of trees, or digging holes in the earth.

They observed by my teeth, which they viewed with great exactness, that I was a carnivorous animal; yet most quadrupeds being an overmatch for me, and field mice, with some others, too nimble, they could not imagine how I should be able to support myself, unless I fed upon snails and other insects, which they offered, by many learned arguments, to evince that I could not possibly do. They would not allow me to be a dwarf, because my littleness was beyond all degrees of comparison; for the Queen's favorite dwarf, the smallest every known in that kingdom, was nearly thirty feet high. After much debate, they concluded unanimously that I was a freak of nature.

After this decisive conclusion, I entreated to be heard a word or two. I applied myself to the King, and assured his Majesty that I came from a country which abounded with several millions of both sexes, and of my own stature; where the animals, trees, and houses were all in proportion, and where by consequence I might be as able to defend myself, and to find sustenance, as any of his Majesty's subjects could do here; which I took for a full answer to those gentlemen's arguments. To this they only replied with a smile of contempt, saying that the farmer had instructed me very well in my lesson. The King, who

had a much better understanding, dismissed his learned
men and sent for the farmer, who by good fortune was
not yet gone out of town. Having therefore first
examined him privately, and then confronted him with
me and the young girl, his Majesty began to think that
what we told him might possibly be true. He desired
the Queen to order that a particular care should be
taken of me, and was of opinion that Glumdalclitch
should still continue in her office of tending me, because he observed we had a great affection for each
other. A convenient apartment was provided for her
at court. She had a sort of governess appointed to
take care of her education, a maid to dress her, and
two other servants for menial offices; but the care of
me was wholly appropriated to herself.

The Queen commanded her own cabinetmaker to
contrive a box that might serve me for a bedchamber,
after the model that Glumdalclitch and I should agree
upon. This man was a most ingenious artist, and according to my directions, in three weeks finished for
me a wooden chamber of sixteen feet square, and
twelve high, with sash windows, a door, and two
closets, like a London bedchamber. The board that
made the ceiling was to be lifted up and down by two
hinges, to put in a bed ready furnished by her Majesty's upholsterer, which Glumdalclitch took out
every day to air, made it with her own hands, and
letting it down at night, locked up the roof over me.
A nice workman, who was famous for little curiosities,
undertook to make me two chairs, with backs and
frames, of a substance not unlike ivory, and two
tables, with a cabinet to put my things in.

The room was quilted on all sides, as well as the

floor and the ceiling, to prevent any accident from the carelessness of those who carried me, and to break the force of a jolt when I went in a coach. I desired a lock for my door, to prevent rats and mice from coming in. The smith, after several attempts, made the smallest that ever was seen among them, for I have known a larger at the gate of a gentleman's house in England. I made a shift to keep the key in a pocket of my own, fearing Glumdalclitch might lose it.

The Queen likewise ordered the thinnest silks that could be got, to make me clothes, not much thicker than an English blanket, very cumbersome till I was accustomed to them. They were after the fashion of the kingdom, partly resembling the Persian, and partly the Chinese, and are a very grave and decent habit.

The Queen became so fond of my company that she could not dine without me. I had a table placed upon the same at which her Majesty ate, just at her left elbow, and a chair to sit on. Glumdalclitch stood upon a stool on the floor, near my table, to assist and take care of me. I had an entire set of silver dishes and plates, and other necessaries, which, in proportion to those of the Queen, were not much bigger than what I have seen of the same kind in a London toy shop, for the furniture of a dollhouse. These my little nurse kept in her pocket in a silver box, and gave me at meals as I wanted them, always cleaning them herself.

No person dined with the Queen but the two Princesses Royal, the elder sixteen years old and the younger at that time thirteen and a month. Her Majesty used to put a bit of meat upon one of my dishes, out of which I carved for myself, and her diversion was to see me eat in miniature. For the Queen (who had indeed but a weak stomach) took up at one mouthful as much as a dozen English farmers could eat at a meal, which to me was for some time a very nauseous sight. She would crunch the wing of a lark, bones and all, between her teeth, although it were nine times as large as that of a full-grown turkey; and put a bit of bread into her mouth, as big as two twelve-penny loaves. She drank out of a golden cup, above a hogshead at a draught. Her knives were twice as long as a scythe set straight upon the handle. The spoons, forks, and other instruments were all in the same proportion. I remember when Glumdalclitch carried me out of curiosity to see some of the tables at court, where ten or a dozen of these enormous knives and forks were lifted up together, I thought I had never till then beheld so terrible a sight.

It is the custom that every Wednesday (which, as I have before observed, was their Sabbath) the King and Queen, with the royal issue of both sexes, dine to-gether in the apartment of his Majesty, to whom I was now become a great favorite. And at these times my little chair and table were placed at his left hand, be-fore one of the salt cellars. This prince took a pleasure in conversing with me, inquiring into the manners, religion, laws, government, and learning of Europe; wherein I gave him the best account I was able. His apprehension was so clear and his judgment so exact that he made very wise reflections and observations upon all I said.

But, I confess that after I had been a little too co-pious in talking of my own beloved country, of our trade, and wars by sea and land, of our schisms in religion, and parties in the state, the prejudices of his education prevailed so far that he could not forbear taking me up in his right hand and stroking me gently with the other, after an hearty fit of laughing, asked me whether I were a Whig or a Tory. Then turning to his first minister, who waited behind him with a white staff, near as tall as the mainmast of the *Royal Sovereign*, he observed how contemptible a thing was human grandeur, which could be mimicked by such diminutive insects as I. "And yet," said he, "I dare engage, these creatures have their titles and distinctions of honor, they contrive little nests and burrows, that they call houses and cities; they make a figure in dress and equipage; they love, they fight, they dispute, they cheat, they betray."

And thus he continued on, while my color came and went several times with indignation to hear our noble country—the mistress of arts and arms, the scourge of France, the arbitress of Europe, the seat of virtue, piety, honor and truth, the pride and envy of the world—so contemptuously treated.

But as I was not in a condition to resent injuries, so, upon mature thoughts, I began to doubt whether I were injured or not. For, after having been accustomed several months to the sight and converse of this people, and observed every object upon which I cast my eyes to be of proportionate magnitude, the horror I had first conceived from their bulk and aspect was so far worn off that if I had then beheld a company of English lords and ladies in their finery and best day clothes, acting their several parts in the most courtly manner, of strutting, and bowing, and prating, to say the truth, I should have been strongly tempted to laugh as much at them as the King and his grandees did at me. Neither indeed could I forbear smiling at myself, when the Queen used to place me upon her hand toward a looking glass, by which both our persons appeared before me in full view together! And there could be nothing more ridiculous than the comparison; so that I really began to imagine myself dwindled many degrees below my usual size.

Nothing angered and mortified me so much as the Queen's dwarf, who being of the lowest stature that was ever in that country, became insolent at seeing a creature so much beneath him that he would always affect to swagger and look big as he passed by me in the Queen's antechamber, while I was standing on some table talking with the lords or ladies of the court. And he seldom failed of a smart word or two upon my littleness; against which I could only revenge myself by calling him brother, challenging him to wrestle, and such repartees as are usual in the mouths of court pages.

One day at dinner this malicious little cub was so nettled with something I had said to him that raising himself upon the frame of her Majesty's chair he took me up by the middle, as I was sitting down, not thinking any harm, and let me drop into a large silver bowl of cream, and then ran away as fast as he could. I fell over head and ears, and if I had not been a good swimmer, it might have gone very hard with me. For Glumdalclitch in that instant happened to be at the other end of the room and the Queen was in such a fright that she wanted presence of mind to assist me. But my little nurse ran to my relief, and took me out, after I had swallowed above a quart of cream. I was put to bed, but I received no other damage than the loss of a suit of clothes, which was utterly spoiled. The dwarf was soundly whipped, and as a further punishment, forced to drink up the bowl of cream into which he had thrown me. Neither was he ever restored to favor. Soon after, the Queen bestowed him to a lady of high quality, so that I saw him no more, to my very great satisfaction, for I could not tell to what extremity such a malicious urchin might have carried his resentment.

He had before served me a scurvy trick, which set the Queen a-laughing, although at the same time she was heartily vexed and would have immediately cashiered him if I had not been so generous as to intercede. Her Majesty had taken a marrow bone upon her plate, and after knocking out the marrow, placed the bone again in the dish erect as it stood before. The dwarf, watching his opportunity, while Glumdalclitch was gone to the sideboard, mounted upon the stool she stood on to take care of me at meals, took me up in both hands, and squeezing my legs together, wedged them into the marrow bone above my waist, where I stuck for some time and made a very ridiculous figure. I believe it was near a minute before anyone knew what was become of me, for I thought it below me to cry out. But, as princes seldom get their meat hot, my legs were not scalded, only my stockings and breeches in a sad condition. The dwarf at my entreaty had no other punishment than a sound whipping.

I was frequently rallied by the Queen upon account of my fearfulness, and she used to ask me whether the people of my country were as great cowards as myself. The occasion was this. The kingdom is much

I dispatched four of them

pestered with flies in summer. And these odious insects, each of them as big as a Dunstable lark, hardly gave me any rest while I sat at dinner, with their continual humming and buzzing about my ears. They would sometimes alight upon my victuals and sometimes would fix upon my nose or forehead, where they stung me to the quick. I had much ado to defend myself against these detestable animals, and could not forbear starting when they came on my face. It was the common practice of the dwarf to catch a number of these insects in his hand, as schoolboys do among us, and let them out suddenly under my nose, on purpose to frighten me, and divert the Queen.

I remember one morning when Glumdalclitch had set me in my box upon a window, as she usually did in fair days, to give me air after I had lifted up one of my sashes and sat down at my table to eat a piece of sweet cake for my breakfast, above twenty wasps, allured by the smell, came flying into the room, humming louder than the drones of as many bagpipes. Some of them seized my cake, and carried it piecemeal away, others flew about my head and face, confounding me with the noise and putting me in the utmost terror of their stings. However, I had the courage to rise and draw my sword, and attack them in the air. I dispatched four of them, but the rest got away, and I presently shut my window.

These insects were as large as partridges: I took out their stings, found them an inch and a half long, and as sharp as needles. I carefully preserved them all, and having since shown them with some other curiosities in several parts of Europe, upon my return to England I gave three of them to Gresham College, and kept the fourth for myself.

CHAPTER 12

Gulliver Shows His Skill in Navigation

I NOW INTEND to give the reader a short description of this country, as far as I traveled in it, which was not above two thousand miles round Lorbrulgrud, the metropolis. For the Queen, whom I always attended, never went farther when she accompanied the King in his progresses, and there stayed until his Majesty returned from viewing his frontiers. The whole extent of this prince's dominions reaches about six thousand miles in length, and from three to five in breadth. From this I cannot but conclude that our geographers of Europe are in a great error, by supposing nothing but sea between Japan and California. They ought to correct their maps and charts, by joining this vast tract of land to the northwest parts of America.

The kingdom is a peninsula, terminated to the northeast by a ridge of mountains thirty miles high, which are altogether impassable by reason of the volcanoes upon the tops. Neither do the most learned know what sort of mortals inhabit beyond those

mountains, or whether they be inhabited at all. On the
three other sides it is bounded by the ocean. There is
not one seaport in the whole kingdom, and those parts
of the coasts into which the rivers issue are so full of
pointed rocks, and the sea generally so rough, that
there is no venturing with the smallest of their boats,
so that these people are wholly excluded from any
commerce with the rest of the world.

But the large rivers are full of vessels, and abound
with excellent fish, for they seldom get any from the
sea because the sea fish are of the same size with those
in Europe, and consequently not worth catching.
Whereby it is manifest that nature, in the production
of plants and animals of so extraordinary a bulk, is
wholly confined to this continent. However, now and
then they take a whale that happens to be dashed
against the rocks, which the common people feed on
heartily. These whales I have known so large that a
man could hardly carry one upon his shoulders. And
sometimes for curiosity they are brought in hampers
to Lorbrulgrud. I saw one of them in a dish at the
King's table, which passed for a rarity, but I did not
observe he was fond of it; for I think indeed the bigness disgusted him, although I have seen one somewhat larger in Greenland.

The country is well inhabited, for it contains fifty-
one cities, near a hundred walled towns, and a great
number of villages. Lorbrulgrud stands upon almost
two equal parts on each side the river that passes
through. It contains above eighty thousand houses
and about six hundred thousand inhabitants. It is in
length three *glonglungs* (which make about fifty-
four English miles) and two and a half in breadth, as I

measured it myself in the royal map made by the
King's order, which was laid on the ground on purpose for me, and extended a hundred feet. I paced
the diameter and circumference several times bare-
foot and, computing by the scale, measured it pretty
exactly.

The King's palace is no regular edifice, but a heap of
buildings about seven miles around: the chief rooms
are generally two hundred and forty feet high, and
broad and long in proportion. A coach was allowed
to Glumdalclitch and me, wherein her governess frequently took her out to see the town or go among the
shops. I was always of the party, carried in my box;
although the girl at my own desire would often take
me out, and hold me in her hand, that I might more
conveniently view the houses and the people as we
passed along the streets. I reckoned our coach to be
about a square of Westminster Hall, but not altogether
so high; however, I cannot be very exact.

Besides the large box in which I was usually carried, the Queen ordered a smaller one to be made for
me, of about twelve feet square, and ten high, for the
convenience of traveling, because the other was somewhat too large for Glumdalclitch's lap, and cumbersome in the coach. It was made by the same artist,
whom I directed in the whole contrivance. This traveling closet was an exact square with a window in
the middle of three of the squares, and each window
was latticed with iron wire on the outside, to prevent
accidents in long journeys. On the fourth side, which
had no window, two strong staples were fixed,
through which the person that carried me, when I had
a mind to be on horseback, put in a leathern belt, and

buckled it about his waist. This was always the office
of some grave trusty servant in whom I could confide,
whether I attended the King and Queen in their progresses, or were disposed to see the gardens, or pay a
visit to some great lady or minister of state in the
court, when Glumdalclitch happened to be out of order. I soon began to be known and esteemed among
the greatest officers, I suppose more upon account of
their Majesties' favor than any merit of my own.

In journeys, when I was weary of the coach, a servant on horseback would buckle my box and place it
on a cushion before him, and there I had a full prospect
of the country on three sides from my three windows.
I had in this closet a field bed and a hammock hung
from the ceiling, two chairs and a table, neatly
screwed to the floor, to prevent being tossed about
by the agitation of the horse or the coach. And having
been long used to sea voyages, those motions, although
sometimes very violent, did not much discompose me.

Whenever I had a mind to see the town, it was always in my traveling closet, which Glumdalclitch held
in her lap in a kind of open sedan, after the fashion of
the country, borne by four men, and attended by two
others in the Queen's livery. The people, who had
often heard of me, were very curious to crowd about
the sedan, and the girl was complaisant enough to
make the bearers stop, and to take me in her hand that
I might be more conveniently seen.

I was very desirous to see the chief temple, and particularly the tower belonging to it, which is reckoned
the highest in the kingdom. Accordingly, one day my
nurse carried me thither, but I may truly say I came
back disappointed. For the height is not above three

thousand feet, reckoning from the ground to the high-est pinnacle top, which, allowing for the difference between the size of those people and us in Europe, is no great matter for admiration, nor at all equal in proportion (if I rightly remember) to Salisbury steeple. But, not to detract from a nation to which during my life I shall acknowledge myself extremely obliged, it must be allowed that whatever this famous tower wants in height is amply made up in beauty and strength. For the walls are near a hundred feet thick, built of hewn stone, whereof each is about forty feet square, and adorned on all sides with statues of gods and emperors cut in marble larger than the life, placed in their several niches. I measured a little finger which had fallen down from one of these statues, and lay un-perceived among some rubbish, and found it exactly four feet and an inch in length. Glumdalclitch wrapped it up in a handkerchief, and carried it home in her pocket to keep among other trinkets, of which the girl was very fond, as children at her age usually are.

The King's kitchen is indeed a noble building, vaulted at top, and about six hundred feet high. The great oven is not so wide by ten yards as the cupola at St. Paul's, for I measured the latter on purpose after my return. But if I should describe the kitchen grate, the prodigious pots and kettles, the joints of meat turning on the spits, with many other particulars, per-haps I should be hardly believed.

His Majesty seldom keeps above six hundred horses in his stables; they are generally from fifty-four to sixty feet high. But when he goes abroad on solemn days he is attended for state by a militia guard of five hundred horse, which indeed I thought was the most splendid sight that could be ever beheld, till I saw part of his army in battalions.

I should have lived happily enough in that country if my littleness had not exposed me to several ridiculous and troublesome accidents, some of which I shall venture to relate.

Glumdalclitch often carried me into the gardens of the court in my smaller box, and would sometimes take me out of it and hold me in her hand or set me down to walk. I remember, before the dwarf left the Queen, he followed us one day into those gardens, and my nurse having set me down, he and I being close together, near some dwarf apple trees, I must needs show my wit by a silly allusion between him and the trees, which happens to hold in their language as it does in ours. Whereupon the malicious rogue, watching his opportunity, when I was walking under one of them, shook it directly over my head, by which a dozen apples, each of them near as large as a Bristol barrel, came tumbling about my ears. One of them hit me on the back as I chanced to stoop, and knocked me down flat on my face, but I received no other hurt, and the dwarf was pardoned at my desire.

Another day Glumdalclitch left me on a smooth grass plot to divert myself while she walked at some distance with her governess. In the meantime there suddenly fell such a violent shower of hail that I was immediately by the force of it struck to the ground, and when I was down, the hailstones gave me such cruel bangs all over the body as if I had been pelted with tennis balls. However, I made a shift to creep on all fours, and shelter myself by lying flat on my face on the lee side of a border of lemon thyme, but so

bruised from head to foot that I could not go abroad
in ten days. Neither is this at all to be wondered at
because in that country a hailstone is near eighteen
hundred times as large as one in Europe, which I can
assert upon experience, having been so curious as to
weigh and measure them.

But a more dangerous accident happened to me in
the same garden, when my little nurse believing she
had put me in a secure place, which I often entreated
her to do, that I might enjoy my own thoughts, and
having left my box at home to avoid the trouble of
carrying it, went to another part of the garden with
her governess and some ladies of her acquaintance.

While she was absent and out of hearing, a small
white spaniel belonging to one of the chief gardeners,
having got by accident into the garden, happened to
range near the place where I lay. The dog, following
the scent, came directly up, and taking me in his
mouth, ran straight to his master, wagging his tail, and
set me gently on the ground. By good fortune he had
been so well taught that I was carried between his
teeth without the least hurt, or even tearing my
clothes.

But the poor gardener, who knew me well and had a
great kindness for me, was in a terrible fright. He
gently took me up in both his hands and asked me
how I did. But I was so amazed and out of breath that
I could not speak a word. In a few minutes I came to
myself, and he carried me safe to my little nurse, who
by this time had returned to the place where she left
me and was in cruel agonies when I did not appear, nor
answer when she called. She severely reprimanded
the gardener on account of his dog. But the thing was

hushed up, and never known at court; for the girl was afraid of the Queen's anger and truly, as to myself, I thought it would not be for my reputation that such a story should go about.

This accident absolutely determined Glumdalclitch never to trust me abroad out of her sight. I had been long afraid of this resolution, and therefore concealed from her some little unlucky adventures that happened in those times when I was left by myself. Once a hawk hovering over the garden made a swoop at me, and if I had not resolutely drawn my sword, and run under a thick trellis, he would have certainly carried me away in his claws. Another time, walking to the top of a fresh molehill, I fell to my neck in the hole through which that animal had cast up the earth. I coined some lie, not worth remembering, to excuse myself for spoiling my clothes. I likewise broke my right shin against the shell of a snail, which I happened to stumble over, as I was walking alone and thinking on poor England.

I cannot tell whether I was more pleased or mortified to observe in those solitary walks that the smaller birds did not appear to be at all afraid of me, but would hop about within a yard's distance, looking for worms and other food with as much indifference and security as if no creature at all were near them. I remember a thrush had the confidence to snatch out of my hand with his bill a piece of cake that Glumdalclitch had just given me for my breakfast. When I attempted to catch any of these birds, they would boldly turn against me, endeavoring to pick my fingers, which I dared not venture within their reach. And then they would hop back unconcerned to hunt for worms or snails, as they did before. But one day I took a thick cudgel, and threw it with all my strength so luckily at a linnet that I knocked him down, and seizing him by the neck with both my hands, ran with him in triumph to my nurse. However, the bird, who had only been stunned, recovered himself and gave me so many boxes with his wings on both sides of my head and body, though I held him at arm's length, and was out of the reach of his claws, that I was twenty times thinking to let him go. But I was soon relieved by one of our servants, who wrung off the bird's neck, and I had him next day for dinner, by the Queen's command. This linnet, as near as I can remember, seemed to be somewhat larger than an English swan.

The Queen, who often used to hear me talk of my sea voyages, and took all occasions to divert me when I was melancholy, asked me whether I understood how to handle a sail or an oar, and whether a little exercise of rowing might not be convenient for my health. I answered that I understood both very well. For, although my proper employment had been to be surgeon or doctor to the ship, yet often, upon a pinch, I was forced to work like a common mariner. But I could not see how this could be done in their country, where the smallest wherry was equal to a first-rate man-of-war among us, and such a boat as I could manage would never live in any of their rivers. Her Majesty said, if I would contrive a boat, her own joiner should make it and she would provide a place for me to sail in.

The fellow was an ingenious workman, and by my instructions in ten days finished a pleasure boat with all its tackling, able conveniently to hold eight Europeans. When it was finished, the Queen was so delighted that she ran with it in her lap to the King, who ordered it to be put in a cistern full of water where I could not manage my two sculls, or little oars, for want of room. But the Queen had before contrived another project. She ordered the joiner to make a wooden trough of three hundred feet long, fifty broad, and eight deep; which, being well pitched to prevent leaking, was placed on the floor along the wall, in an outer room of the palace. It had a cock near the bottom to let out the water when it began to grow stale, and two servants could easily fill it in half an hour.

Here I often used to row for my own diversion, as well as that of the Queen and her ladies, who thought themselves well entertained with my skill and agility. Sometimes I would put up my sail, and then my business was only to steer, while the ladies gave me a gale with their fans. And when they were weary, some of the pages would blow my sail forward with their breath, while I showed my art by steering starboard or larboard as I pleased. When I had done, Glumdalclitch always carried my boat into her closet, and hung it on a nail to dry.

In this exercise I once met an accident which had like to have cost me my life. One of the pages having put my boat into the trough, the governess who attended Glumdalclitch very officiously lifted me up to place me in the boat, but I happened to slip through her fingers and should have fallen down forty feet upon the floor if by the luckiest chance in the world I had not been stopped by a large pin that stuck in the good gentlewoman's stomacher. The head of the pin passed between my shirt and the waistband of my breeches, and thus I was held by the middle in the air till Glumdalclitch ran to my relief.

Another time, one of the servants, whose office it was to fill my trough every third day with fresh water, was so careless to let a huge frog slip out of his pail. The frog lay concealed till I was put into my boat, but then seeking a resting place, climbed up, and made it lean so much on one side that I was forced to balance it with all my weight on the other to prevent overturning. When the frog got in, it hopped at once half the length of the boat, and then over my head, backward and forward. The largeness of its features made it appear the most deformed animal that can be conceived. However, I desired Glumdalclitch to let me deal with it alone. I banged it a good while with one of my sculls, and at last forced it to leap out of the boat.

But the greatest danger I ever underwent in that kingdom was from a monkey, who belonged to one of the clerks of the kitchen. Glumdalclitch had locked me up in her closet, while she went somewhere upon business or a visit. The weather being very warm, the closet window was left open, as well as the windows and the door of my bigger box, in which I usually lived. As I sat quietly meditating at my table, I heard something bounce in at the closet window and skip about from one side to the other; whereat, although I was much alarmed, yet I ventured to look out, but stirred not from my seat. And then I saw this frolicsome animal, frisking and leaping up and down, till at last he came to my box, which he seemed to view with great pleasure and curiosity, peeping in at the door and every window. I retreated to the farther corner of my room, or box, but the monkey put me into such a fright that I wanted presence of mind to conceal myself under the bed, as I might easily have done. After some time spent in peeping, grinning, and chattering, he at last espied me, and reaching one of his paws in at the door, as a cat does when she plays with a mouse, although I often shifted place to avoid him, he at length seized the lappet of my coat and dragged me out.

He took me up in his right forefoot just as I have seen the same sort of creature do with a kitten in Europe. And when I offered to struggle, he squeezed me so hard that I thought it more prudent to submit. I have good reason to believe that he took me for a young one of his own species, by his often stroking my face very gently with his other paw. In these diversions he was interrupted by a noise at the closet door, as if somebody were opening it. Whereupon he suddenly leaped up to the window at which he had come in, and thence upon the leads and gutters, walking upon three legs, and holding me in the fourth, till he clambered up to a roof that was next to ours.

I heard Glumdalclitch give a shriek at the moment he was carrying me out. The poor girl was almost distracted. That quarter of the palace was all in an uproar. The servants ran for ladders. The monkey was seen by hundreds in the court, sitting upon the ridge of a building, holding me like a baby in one of his forepaws, and feeding me with the other, by cramming into my mouth some victuals he had squeezed out of the bag on one side of his chaps, and patting me when I would not eat. Many of the rabble below could not forbear laughing at this, neither do I think they justly ought to be blamed, for without question the sight was ridiculous enough to everybody but myself. Some of the people threw up stones, hoping to drive the monkey down; but this was strictly forbidden, or else very probably my brains had been dashed out.

The ladders were now applied, and mounted by several men. The monkey, observing this and not being able to make speed enough with his three legs, let me drop on a ridge tile and made his escape. Here I sat for some time three hundred yards from the ground, expecting every moment to be blown down by the wind, or to fall by my own giddiness, and come tumbling over and over from the ridge to the eaves. But an honest lad, one of my nurse's footmen, climbed up, and putting me into his breeches pocket, brought me down safe.

I was so weak and bruised in the sides with the squeezes given me by this odious animal that I was forced to keep my bed a fortnight. The King, Queen, and all the court sent every day to inquire after my health, and her Majesty made me several visits during my sickness. The monkey was killed, and an order issued that no such animal should be kept about the palace.

When I attended the King after my recovery, to return him thanks for his favors, he was pleased to rally me a good deal upon this adventure. He asked me what my thoughts and speculations were while I lay in the monkey's paw, how I liked the victuals he gave me, his manner of feeding, and whether the fresh air on the roof had sharpened my appetite. He desired to know what I would have done upon such an occasion in my own country. I told his Majesty that in Europe we had no monkeys, except such as were brought for curiosities from other places, and so small that I could deal with a dozen of them together if they presumed to attack me. And as for that monstrous animal with whom I was so lately engaged (it was indeed as large as an elephant), if my fears had suffered me to think so far as to make use of my sword (looking fiercely and clapping my hand upon the hilt as I spoke) when he poked his paw into my chamber, perhaps I should have given him such a wound as would have made him glad to withdraw it with more haste than he put it in. This I delivered in a firm tone, like a person who was jealous lest his courage be called in question. However, my speech produced nothing but loud laughter, which all the respect due to his Majesty from those about him could not make them contain. This made me reflect how vain an attempt it is for a man to endeavor doing himself honor among those who are out of all degree of equality or comparison with him. Frequently, in England, a contemptible varlet, without the least title to birth, person, wit, or common sense, shall presume to look with importance, and put himself upon a foot with the greatest persons of the kingdom.

CHAPTER 13

Gulliver Amuses the King and Queen

THE KING had frequent concerts at court, to which I was sometimes carried, and set in my box on a table to hear them. But the noise was so great that I could hardly distinguish the tunes. I am confident that all the drums and trumpets of a royal army, beating and sounding together just at your ears, could not equal it. My practice was to have my box removed as far as I could from the places where the performers sat, then to shut the doors and windows, and draw the window curtains; after which I found their music not disagreeable.

I had learned in my youth to play a little upon the spinet. Glumdalclitch kept one in her chamber, and a master attended twice a week to teach her. I call it a spinet, because it somewhat resembled that instrument and was played upon in the same manner. A fancy came into my head that I would entertain the King and Queen with an English tune upon this instrument. But this appeared extremely difficult; for the spinet was near sixty feet long, each key being almost a foot wide, so that, with my arms extended, I could not reach to above five keys, and to press them down required a good smart stroke with my fist, which would be too great a labor, and to no purpose. The method I contrived was this:

I prepared two round sticks about the bigness of common cudgels. They were thicker at one end than the other, and I covered the thicker ends with a piece of a mouse's skin, so that by rapping on them I might neither damage the tops of the keys nor interrupt the sound. Before the spinet a bench was placed, about four feet below the keys, and I was put upon the bench. I ran sidling upon it that way and this, as fast as I could, banging the proper keys with my two sticks, and made a shift to play a jig, to the great satisfaction of both their Majesties. It was the most violent exercise I ever underwent, and yet I could not strike above sixteen keys, nor, consequently, play the bass and treble together, as other artists do; which was a great disadvantage to my performance.

The King, who, as I before observed, was a prince of excellent understanding, would frequently order that I should be brought in my box and set upon the table in his room. He would then command me to bring one of my chairs out of the box, and sit down within three yards' distance upon the top of the cabinet, which brought me almost to a level with his face. In this manner I had several conversations with him. I one day took the freedom to tell his Majesty that the contempt he showed toward Europe, and the rest of the world, did not seem answerable to those excellent qualities of the mind he was master of. That reason did not extend itself with the bulk of the body; on the contrary, we observed in our country that the tallest persons were usually least provided with it. That among other animals, bees and ants had the reputation of more industry, art and sagacity, than many of the larger kinds. And that, inconsiderable as he took me to be, I hoped I might live to do his Majesty some signal service. The King heard me with attention, and began to conceive a much better opinion of me than he had ever before. He desired I would give him as exact an account of the government of England as I possibly could; because, fond as princes commonly are of their own customs, he should be glad to hear of anything that might deserve imitation.

I began my discourse by informing his Majesty that our dominions consisted of two islands, which composed three mighty kingdoms under one sovereign, besides our plantations in America. I dwelt long upon the fertility of our soil and the temperature of our climate. I then spoke at large upon the constitution of an English Parliament, partly made up of an illustrious body called the House of Peers, persons of the noblest blood, and of the most ancient and ample patrimonies.

I described that extraordinary care always taken of their education in arts and arms, to qualify them for being counselors born to the king and kingdom, to have a share in the legislature, to be members of the highest court, whence there could be no appeal, and to be champions always ready for the defense of their prince and country, by their valor, conduct, and fidelity. That these were the ornament and bulwark of the kingdom, worthy followers of their most renowned ancestors, whose honor had been the reward of their virtue, from which their posterity were never once known to degenerate. To these were joined several holy persons, as part of that assembly, under the title of bishops, whose peculiar business it is to take care of religion, and of those who instruct the people therein.

The other part of Parliament consisted of an assembly called the House of Commons, who were all principal gentlemen, freely picked and culled out by the people themselves, for their great abilities and love of their country, to represent the wisdom of the whole nation. And these two bodies make up the most august assembly in Europe, to whom, in conjunction with the prince, the whole legislature is committed.

I then descended to the courts of justice, over which the judges, those venerable sages and interpreters of the law, presided, for determining the disputed rights and properties of men, as well as for the punishment of vice and the protection of innocence. I mentioned the prudent management of our treasury; the valor and achievements of our forces by sea and land. I computed the number of our people, by reckoning how many millions there might be of each religious sect or political party among us. I did not omit even our sports and pastimes, or any other particular which I thought might redound to the honor of my country. And I finished all with a brief historical account of affairs and events in England for about a hundred years past.

This conversation was not ended under five audiences, each of several hours, and the King heard the whole with great attention, frequently taking notes of what I spoke, as well as memorandums of several questions he intended to ask me.

When I had put an end to these long discourses, his Majesty in a sixth audience, consulting his notes, proposed many doubts, queries, and objections upon every article. He asked what methods were used to cultivate the minds and bodies of our young nobility, and in what kind of business they commonly spent the first and teachable part of their lives; what course was taken to supply that assembly when any noble family became extinct; what qualifications were necessary in those who were to be created new lords; whether the humor of the prince, a sum of money to a court lady or a prime minister, or a design of strengthening a party opposite to the public interest, ever happened to be motives in those advancements; what share of knowledge these lords had in the laws of their country; whether they were always so free from avarice that they would not accept a bribe.

He then desired to know what arts were practiced in electing those whom I called commoners; whether a stranger with a strong purse might not influence the vulgar voters to choose him before their own landlord, or the most considerable gentleman in the neighborhood; how it came to pass that people were so violently bent upon getting into this assembly, without any salary or pension. This appeared such an exalted strain of public spirit that his Majesty seemed to doubt it might possibly not be always sincere.

Upon what I said in relation to our courts of justice, his Majesty desired to be satisfied in several points. And this I was the better able to do, having been formerly almost ruined by a long suit in chancery, which was decreed for me with costs. He asked what time was usually spent in determining between right and wrong, and what degree of expense; whether advocates and orators had liberty to plead in causes manifestly known to be unjust, vexatious, or oppressive; whether party, in religion or politics, was observed to be of any weight in the scale of justice.

He was amazed to hear me talk of such serious and expensive wars: that certainly we must be a quarrelsome people, or live among very bad neighbors, and that our generals must needs be richer than our kings. He asked what business we had out of our own islands, unless upon the score of trade or treaty or to defend the coasts with our fleet. Above all, he was amazed to hear me talk of a mercenary standing army in the midst of peace, and among a free people. He said, if we were governed by our own consent in the persons of our representatives, he could not imagine of whom we were afraid, or against whom we were to fight. And he would like my opinion, whether a private man's house might not better be defended by himself, his children, and his family than by half a dozen rascals picked up at a venture in the streets, for small wages, who might get a hundred times more by cutting their throats.

He observed that among the diversions of our nobility and gentry I had mentioned gaming. He desired to know at what age this entertainment was usually taken up, and when it was laid down; how much of their time it employed; whether it ever went so high as to affect their fortunes; whether mean, vicious people, by their dexterity in that art, might not arrive at great riches, and sometimes keep our very nobles in dependence, as well as habituate them to vile companions, wholly take them from the improvement of their minds, and force them, by the losses they have received, to learn and practice that infamous dexterity upon others.

His Majesty in another audience was at pains to recapitulate the sum of all I had spoken. He compared the questions he made with the answers I had given, then taking me into his hands, and stroking me gently, delivered himself in these words, which I shall never forget nor the manner he spoke them in: "My little friend Grildrig, you have made a most admirable panegyric upon your country; you have clearly proved that ignorance, idleness, and vice may be sometimes the only ingredients for qualifying a legislator; that laws are best explained, interpreted, and applied by those whose interest and abilities lie in perverting, confounding, and eluding them. I observe among you some lines of an institution, which in its original might have been tolerable, but these half erased, and the rest wholly blurred and blotted by corruptions. It does not appear, from all you have said, how any one virtue is required toward the procurement of any one station among you; much less that men are ennobled on account of their virtue, that priests are advanced for their piety or learning, soldiers for their conduct or valor, judges for their integrity, senators for the love of their country, or counselors for their wisdom. As for yourself," continued the King, "who have spent the greatest part of your life in traveling, I am well disposed to hope you may hitherto have escaped many vices of your country. But by what I have gathered from your own relation, and the answers I have with much pains wrung and extorted from you, I cannot but conclude the bulk of your natives to be the most pernicious race of little odious vermin that nature ever suffered to crawl upon the surface of the earth."

Nothing but an extreme love of truth could have hindered me from concealing this part of my story. It was in vain to show my resentments, which were always turned into ridicule; and I was forced to rest with patience while my noble and most beloved country was so injuriously treated. But this prince happened to be so curious and inquisitive upon every particular, that it could not consist with either gratitude or good manners to refuse giving him what satisfaction I was able. Yet thus much I may be allowed to say in my own vindication, that I artfully eluded many of his questions and gave to every point a more favorable turn than the strictness of truth would allow. I would hide the frailties and deformities of my political mother, and place her virtues and beauties in the most advantageous light. This was my sincere endeavor in those many discourses I had with that mighty monarch, although it unfortunately failed of success.

But great allowances should be made for a King who lives wholly secluded from the rest of the world, and must therefore be altogether unacquainted with the manners and customs that most prevail in other nations. The want of this knowledge will ever produce many prejudices, and a certain narrowness of thinking. And it would be hard, indeed, if so remote a prince's notions of virtue and vice were to be offered as a standard for all mankind.

To confirm what I have now said and, further, to show the miserable effects of a confined education, I shall here insert a passage which will hardly obtain belief. In the hope of ingratiating myself further into his Majesty's favor, I told him of an invention discovered between three and four hundred years ago— the uses of gunpowder. A proper quantity of this powder rammed into a hollow tube of brass or iron would drive a ball of iron or lead with such violence and speed that nothing was able to sustain its force. The largest balls would not only destroy whole ranks of an army, but batter the strongest walls to the ground, sink down ships to the bottom of the sea; and, when linked together by a chain, would cut through masts and rigging and lay all waste before them. That this powder put into large hollow balls of iron and discharged by an engine into some city would rip up the pavements, tear the houses to pieces, burst and throw splinters on every side, and kill all who came near.

The King was struck with horror at the description I had given of those terrible engines. He was amazed how so impotent and groveling an insect as I (these were his expressions) could entertain such inhuman ideas, and in so familiar a manner as to appear wholly unmoved at all the scenes of blood and desolation, which I had painted as the common effects of those destructive machines, whereof he said some evil genius, enemy to mankind, must have been the first contriver. As for himself, he protested that, although few things delighted him so much as new discoveries in art or in nature, he would rather lose half his kingdom than be privy to such a secret, which he commanded me, as I valued my life, never to mention any more.

I remember very well, in a discourse one day with the King, when I happened to say there were several thousand books among us written upon the art of government, it gave him a very mean opinion of our understandings. He could not tell what I meant by secrets of state, where an enemy or some rival nation was not in the case. And he gave it for his opinion, that whoever could make two ears of corn or two blades of grass to grow upon a spot of ground where only one grew before would deserve better of mankind and do more essential service to his country than the whole race of politicians put together.

The learning of this people is very defective, consisting only in morality, history, poetry, and mathematics, wherein they must be allowed to excel. But the last of these is wholly applied to what may be useful in life, to the improvement of agriculture, and all mechanical arts; so that among us it would be little esteemed.

No law of that country must exceed in words the number of letters in their alphabet, which consists of only twenty-two. But indeed few of them extend even to that length, and they are expressed in the most plain and simple terms.

They, as well as the Chinese, have had the art of printing time out of mind. But their libraries are not very large. That of the King, which is reckoned the biggest, does not amount to above a thousand volumes, placed in a gallery twelve hundred feet long, from which I had liberty to borrow what books I pleased. The Queen's joiner had contrived in one of Glumdalclitch's rooms a kind of wooden machine twenty-five feet high, formed like a standing ladder. The steps were each fifty feet long. It was indeed a movable pair of stairs, the lowest end placed at ten feet distance from the wall of the chamber.

The book I had a mind to read was put up leaning against the wall. I first mounted to the upper step of the ladder, and turning my face toward the book, began at the top of the page, and so walking to the right and left about eight or ten yards, according to the length of the lines, till I had got a little below the level of my eyes, and then descending gradually till I came to the bottom; after which I mounted again and began the other page in the same manner, and so turned over the leaf, which I could easily do with both my hands, for it was as thick and stiff as pasteboard, and in the largest folios not above eighteen or twenty feet long.

CHAPTER 14

Gulliver Returns
to England

I HAD ALWAYS a strong impulse that I should some time recover my liberty, though it was impossible to conjecture by what means or to form any project with the least hope of succeeding. The ship in which I sailed was the first ever known to be driven within sight of that coast, and the King had given strict orders that if at any time another appeared it should be taken ashore, and all its crew and passengers brought to Lorbrulgrud.

Meanwhile I was, indeed, treated with much kindness. I was the favorite of a great King and Queen, and the delight of the whole court, but it was upon such a foot as ill became the dignity of human kind. I could never forget those domestic pledges I had left behind me. I wanted to be among people with whom I could converse upon even terms, and walk about the streets and fields without fear of being trod to death like a frog or a young puppy. But my deliverance came sooner than I expected, and in a manner not very common; the whole story and circumstances of which I shall faithfully relate.

I had now been two years in this country; and about the beginning of the third, Glumdalclitch and I attended the King and Queen in a progress to the south coast. I was carried, as usual, in my traveling box, which, as I have already described, was a very convenient closet twelve feet wide. And I had ordered a hammock to be fixed by silken ropes from the four corners at the top, to break the jolts, when a servant carried me before him on horseback, as I sometimes desired, and would often sleep in my hammock while we were upon the road. On the roof of my closet, just over the middle of the hammock, I ordered the joiner to cut out a hole a foot square, to give me air in hot weather as I slept, which hole I shut at pleasure with a board that drew backward and forward through a groove.

When we came to our journey's end, the King thought proper to pass a few days at a palace he has near Flanflasnic, a city within eighteen English miles of the seaside. Glumdalclitch and I were much fatigued. I had got a small cold, but the poor girl was so ill as to be confined to her chamber. I longed to see the ocean, which must be the only scene of my escape, if ever it should happen. I pretended to be worse than I really was, and desired leave to take the fresh air of the sea, with a page whom I was very fond of and who had sometimes been trusted with me. I shall never forget with what unwillingness Glumdalclitch consented, nor the strict charge she gave the page to be careful of me, bursting at the same time into a flood of tears as if she had some foreboding of what was to happen.

The boy took me out in my box about half an hour's walk from the palace, toward the rocks on the seashore. I ordered him to set me down, and lifting up one of my sashes, cast many a wistful, melancholy look toward the sea. I found myself not very well, and told the page that I had a mind to take a nap in my hammock, which I hoped would do me good. I got in, and the boy shut the window close down to keep out the cold.

I soon fell asleep, and all I can conjecture is that while I slept the page, thinking no danger could happen, went among the rocks to look for birds' eggs, having before observed him from my window searching about, and picking up one or two in the clefts. Be that as it will, I found myself suddenly awaked with a violent pull upon the ring which was fastened at the top of my box for the convenience of carriage. I felt my box raised very high in the air, and then borne forward with prodigious speed. The first jolt had like to have shaken me out of my hammock, but afterward the motion was easy enough. I called out several times as loud as I could raise my voice, but all to no purpose. I looked toward my windows and could see nothing but the clouds and sky.

I heard a noise just over my head like the beating of wings, and then began to perceive the woeful condition I was in. Some eagle had got the ring of my box in his beak, with an intent to let it fall on a rock like a tortoise in a shell, and then pick out my body, and devour it.

In a little time I observed the noise of the flutter of wings to increase very fast, and my box was tossed up and down, like a signpost on a windy day. I heard

several bangs or buffets, as I thought, given to the
eagle and then all of a sudden felt myself falling per-
pendicularly down for above a minute, but with such
incredible swiftness that I almost lost my breath. My
fall was stopped by a terrible squash, that sounded
louder to my ears than the cataract of Niagara. After
that I was quite in the dark for another minute, and
then my box began to rise so high that I could see light
from the tops of my windows. I now perceived that I
had fallen into the sea.

My box, by the weight of my body, the goods that
were in it, and the broad plates of iron fixed for
strength at the four corners of the top and bottom,
floated five feet deep in water. I did then, and do now,
suppose that the eagle which flew away with my box
was pursued by two or three others, and forced to let
me drop while he was defending himself against the
rest, who hoped to share in the prey.

The plates of iron fastened at the bottom of the box
preserved the balance while it fell, and hindered it
from being broken on the surface of the water.
Every joint of it was well grooved, and the door did
not move on hinges, but up and down like a sash,
which kept my closet so tight that very little water
came in. I got with much difficulty out of my hammock, having first ventured to draw back the slip-
board on the roof already mentioned, contrived on
purpose to let in air, for want of which I found myself almost stifled.

How often did I then wish myself with my dear
Glumdalclitch, from whom one single hour had so
far divided me! And I may say with truth that in the
midst of my own misfortunes I could not forbear la-

menting my poor nurse, the grief she would suffer for my loss, the displeasure of the Queen, and the ruin of her fortune. Perhaps many travelers have not been under greater difficulties and distress than I was at this juncture, expecting every moment to see my box dashed in pieces, or at least overset by the first violent blast or a rising wave.

A breach in one single pane of glass would have been immediate death: nor could anything have preserved the windows, but the strong lattice wires placed on the outside against accidents in traveling. I saw the water ooze in at several crannies, although the leaks were not considerable, and I endeavored to stop them as well as I could. I was not able to lift up the roof, which otherwise I certainly should have done and sat on the top of it, where I might at least preserve myself some hours longer than by being shut up, as I may call it, in the hold. Or, if I escaped these dangers for a day or two, what could I expect but a miserable death from cold and hunger! I was four hours under these circumstances, expecting and indeed wishing every moment to be my last.

I have already told the reader that there were two strong staples fixed upon that side of my box which had no window, and into which the servant who used to carry me on horseback would put a leathern belt, and buckle it about his waist. Being in this disconsolate state, I heard or at least thought I heard some kind of grating noise on that side of my box where the staples were fixed, and soon after I began to fancy that the box was pulled or towed along in the sea; for I now and then felt a sort of tugging, which made the waves rise near the tops of my windows, leaving me almost in the dark. This gave me some faint hopes of relief, although I was not able to imagine how it could be brought about.

I ventured to unscrew one of my chairs, which were always fastened to the floor; and having made a hard shift to screw it down again directly under the slipping board that I had lately opened, I mounted on the chair, and putting my mouth as near as I could to the hole, I called for help in a loud voice, and in all the languages I understood. I then fastened my handkerchief to a stick I usually carried, and thrusting up the hole, waved it several times in the air, so that if any boat or ship were near, the seamen might conjecture some unhappy mortal to be shut up in the box.

I found no effect from all I could do, but plainly perceived myself to be moved along. And in the space of an hour, or better, that side of the box where the staples were, and had no window, struck against something that was hard. I apprehended it to be a rock, and found myself tossed more than ever. I plainly heard a noise upon the cover of my closet, like that of a cable, and the grating of it as it passed through the ring. I then found myself hoisted up by degrees at least three feet higher than I was before. Whereupon I again thrust up my stick and handkerchief, calling for help till I was almost hoarse. In return to which I heard a great shout repeated three times, giving me such transports of joy as are not to be conceived but by those who feel them.

I now heard a trampling over my head, and somebody calling through a hole with a loud voice in the English tongue: "If there be anybody below, let them speak." I answered that I was an Englishman, drawn by ill fortune into the greatest clamity that ever any creature underwent, and begged, by all that is moving, to be delivered out of the dungeon I was in. The voice replied that I was safe, for my box was fastened to their ship; and the carpenter should immediately come and saw an hole in the cover, large enough to pull me out. I said that was needless and would take up too much time, for there was no more to be done, but let one of the crew put his finger into the ring, and take the box out of the sea into the ship, and so into the captain's cabin. Some of them, upon hearing me talk so wildly, thought I was mad; others laughed. It never came into my head that I was now among people of my own stature and strength.

The carpenter came, and in a few minutes sawed a passage about four feet square, then let down a small ladder, upon which I mounted, and from thence was taken into the ship in a very weak condition.

The sailors were all in amazement and asked me a thousand questions, which I had no inclination to answer. I was equally confounded at the sight of so many pygmies, for such I took them to be, after having so long accustomed my eyes to the monstrous objects I had left. But the captain, Mr. Thomas Wilcocks, an honest, worthy Shropshire man, observing I was ready to faint, took me into his cabin, gave me a cordial to comfort me, and made me turn in upon his own bed, advising me to take a little rest, of which I had great need.

Before I went to sleep I gave him to understand that I had some valuable furniture in my box, too good to be lost, a fine hammock, a handsome field bed, two chairs, a table, and a cabinet; that my closet was hung on all sides, or rather quilted, with silk and cotton; that if he would let one of the crew bring my closet into his cabin, I would open it there before him, and show him my goods. The captain, hearing me utter these absurdities, concluded I was raving. However (I suppose to pacify me), he promised to give orders as I desired, and going upon deck sent some of his men down into my closet whence (as I afterward found) they drew up all my goods, and stripped off the quilting; but the chairs, cabinet, and bedstead, being screwed to the floor, were much damaged by the ignorance of the seamen, who tore them up by force. Then they knocked off some of the boards for the use of the ship, and when they had got all they had a mind for, let the hull drop into the sea, which by reason of many breaches made in the bottom and sides, sank at once. And indeed I was glad not to have been a spectator of the havoc they made; because I am confident it would have sensibly touched me, by bringing former passages into my mind, which I had rather forget.

I slept some hours, but perpetually disturbed with dreams of the place I had left, and the dangers I had escaped. However, upon waking I found myself much recovered. It was now about eight o'clock at night, and the captain ordered supper immediately, thinking I had already fasted too long. He entertained me with great kindness, observing me not to look wildly or talk inconsistently. And when we were left alone, he desired I would give him a relation of my travels, and by what accident I came to be set adrift in that monstrous wooden chest.

He said that about twelve o'clock at noon, as he was looking through his glass, he spied it at a distance, and thought it was a sail. Upon coming nearer, and finding his error, he sent out his longboat to discover what it was; but his men came back in a fright, swearing they had seen a swimming house. He laughed at their folly, and went himself in the boat, ordering his men to take a strong cable along with them. The weather being calm, he rowed round me several times, observed my windows, and the wire lattices that defended them, and he discovered two staples upon one side, which was all of boards without any passage for light. He then commanded his men to row up to that side, and fastening a cable to one of the staples, ordered them to tow my chest (as he called it) toward the ship.

When it was there, he gave directions to fasten another cable to the ring fixed in the cover, and to raise up my chest with pulley, which all the sailors were not able to do above two or three feet. He said they saw my stick and handkerchief thrust out of the hole, and concluded that some unhappy men must be shut up in the cavity. I asked whether he or the crew had seen any prodigious birds in the air about the time he first discovered me. To this he answered that, discussing this matter with the sailors while I was asleep, one of them said he had observed three eagles flying toward the north, but remarked nothing of their being larger than the usual size, which I suppose must be imputed to the great height they were flying. He could not guess the reason of my question.

I then asked the captain how far he reckoned we might be from land. He said, by the best computation he could make, we were at least a hundred leagues. I assured him that he must be mistaken by almost half, for I had not left the country from where I came above two hours before I dropped into the sea. Whereupon he began again to think that my brain was disturbed, of which he gave me a hint and advised me to go to bed in a cabin he had provided. I assured him I was well refreshed with his good entertainment and company, and as much in my senses as ever I was in my life.

He then grew serious, and desired to ask me freely whether I were not troubled in mind by the consciousness of some enormous crime, for which I was punished at the command of some prince, by exposing me in that chest, as great criminals in other countries have been forced to sea in a leaky vessel without provisions. Although he should be sorry to have taken so ill a man into his ship, yet he would engage his word to set me safe on shore in the first port where we arrived. He added that his suspicions were much increased by some very absurd speeches I had delivered at first to the sailors, and afterward to himself, in relation to my closet, or chest, as well as by my odd looks and behavior while I was at supper.

I begged his patience to hear me tell my story, which I faithfully did from the last time I left England to the moment he first discovered me. And as truth always forces its way into rational minds, so this honest, worthy gentleman, who had some tincture of learning and very good sense, was immediately convinced of my candor and veracity. But further to confirm all I had said, I entreated him to give order that my cabinet should be brought, of which I had the key in my pocket. I opened it in his presence and showed him the small collection of rarities I made in the country from where I had been so strangely delivered.

There was a collection of needles and pins from a foot to half a yard long; four wasp stings, like joiners' tacks; a lock of the Queen's hair; a gold ring which one day she made me a present of in a most obliging manner, taking it from her little finger, and throwing it over my head like a collar. I desired the captain would please to accept this ring in return of his civilities, which he absolutely refused. Lastly, I showed him the breeches I had then on, which were made of a mouse's skin.

He said he wondered at one thing very much, which was to hear me speak so loud, asking me whether the King or Queen of that country were hard of hearing. I told him it was what I had been used to for above two years past, and that I wondered as much at the voices of him and his men, who seemed to me only to whisper, and yet I could hear them well enough. But when I spoke in that country, it was like a man talking in the street to another looking out from the top of a steeple, unless when I was placed on a table or held in any person's hand. I told him I had likewise observed another thing, that when I first got into the ship, and the sailors stood all about me, I thought they were the most little contemptible creatures I had ever beheld. For, indeed, while I was in that prince's country, I could never endure to look in a glass after my eyes had been accustomed to such prodigious objects, because the comparison gave me so despicable an opinion of myself.

The captain said that while we were at supper he

observed me look at everything with a sort of wonder, and that I often seemed hardly able to contain my laughter, which he knew not well how to take, but imputed it to some disorder in my brain. I answered that it was very true; and I wondered how I could forbear, when I saw his dishes of the size of a silver threepence, a leg of pork hardly a mouthful, a cup not so big as a nutshell. And so I went on, describing the rest of his household stuff and provisions after the same manner. For, although the Queen had ordered a little equipage of all things necessary for me while I was in her service, yet my ideas were wholly taken up with what I saw on every side of me, and I winked at my own littleness as people do at their own faults.

Our voyage to England was very prosperous, but I shall not trouble the reader with a journal of it. The captain called in at one or two ports, and sent in his longboat for provisions and fresh water, but I never went out of the ship till we came into the Downs, which was on the 3rd of June, 1706, about nine months after my escape. I offered to leave my goods in security for payment of my passage, but the captain protested he would not receive one farthing. We took kind leave of each other, and I made him promise he would come to see me at my house in Redriff. I hired a horse and guide for five shillings, which I borrowed of the captain.

As I was on the road, observing the littleness of the houses, the trees, the cattle, and the people, I began to think myself in Lilliput. I was afraid of trampling on every traveler I met, and often called aloud to have them stand out of the way, so that I had like to have got one or two broken heads for my impertinence.

When I came to my own house, for which I was forced to inquire, one of the servants opening the door, I bent down to go in (like a goose under a gate) for fear of striking my head. My wife ran out to embrace me, but I stooped lower than her knees, thinking she could otherwise never be able to reach my mouth. My daughter kneeled to ask my blessing, but I could not see her till she arose, having been so long used to stand with my head and eyes erect to above sixty feet; and then I went to take her up with one hand, by the waist. I looked down upon the servants and one or two friends who were in the house, as if they had been pygmies and I a giant. I told my wife she had been too thrifty, for I found she had starved herself and her daughter to nothing. In short, I behaved myself so unaccountably that they were all of the captain's opinion when he first saw me, and concluded I had lost my wits. This I mention as an instance of the great power of habit and prejudice.

In a little time, I and my family and friends came to a right understanding, but my wife protested I should never go to sea any more. Although my evil destiny so ordered that she had not power to hinder me.

PART III

Voyages to Laputa and the Country of the Houyhnhnms

CHAPTER 15

A Flying Island

I HAD NOT been at home above ten days, when Captain William Robinson, a Cornish man, commander of the *Hopewell*, a stout ship of three hundred tons, came to my house. I had formerly been surgeon of another ship where he was master, and a fourth part owner, in a voyage to the Levant. He had always treated me more like a brother than an inferior officer, and hearing of my arrival made me a visit, as I apprehended only out of friendship, for nothing passed more than what is usual after long absences.

But repeating his visits often, expressing his joy to find me in good health, asking whether I were now settled for life, adding that he intended a voyage to the East Indies in two months; at last he plainly invited me, though with some apologies, to be surgeon of the ship. He told me that I should have another surgeon under me besides our two mates; that my salary should be double the usual pay; and that having experienced my knowledge in sea affairs to be at least equal to his, he would enter into any engagement to follow my advice, as much as if I had share in the command.

He said so many other obliging things, and I knew him to be so honest a man, that I could not reject his proposal. The thirst I had of seeing the world, notwithstanding my past misfortunes, continuing as violent as ever. The only difficulty that remained was to persuade my wife, whose consent I at last obtained by the prospect of advantage she proposed to her children.

We set out the 5th of August, 1706, and arrived at Fort St. George [Madras, India] the 11th of April, 1707. We stayed there three weeks to refresh our crew, many of whom were sick. From there we went to Tonquin [Indo-China], where the captain resolved to continue some time, because many of the goods he intended to buy were not ready, nor could he expect to be dispatched in some months. Therefore, in hopes to defray some of the charges he must be at, he bought a sloop, loaded it with several sorts of goods, wherewith the Tonquinese usually trade to the neighboring islands, and putting fourteen men on board, whereof three were of the country, he appointed me master of the sloop, and gave me power to traffic for two months, while he transacted his affairs at Tonquin.

We had not sailed more than three days when a great storm arose and we were driven five days to the north-northeast, and then to the east; after which we had fair weather, but still with a pretty strong gale from the west. Upon the tenth day we were chased by two pirates, who soon overtook us, for my sloop was so deep loaden that she sailed very slowly. Neither were we in a condition to defend ourselves.

We were boarded about the same time by both the pirates, who entered furiously at the head of their men, but finding us all prostrate upon our faces (for so I gave order) they pinioned us with strong ropes, and setting a guard upon us, went to search the sloop.

I observed among them a Dutchman, who seemed to be of some authority, though he was not commander of either ship. He knew us by our countenances to be Englishmen, and jabbering to us in his own language swore we should be tied back to back, and thrown into the sea. I spoke Dutch tolerably well. I told him who we were, and begged him in consideration of our being Christians and Protestants, of neighboring countries in strict alliance, that he would move the captains to take some pity on us. This only inflamed his rage. He repeated his threatenings, and turning to his companions, spoke with great vehemence, in the Japanese language, as I suppose, often using the word *Christianos*.

The largest of the two pirate ships was commanded by a Japanese captain, who spoke a little Dutch, but very imperfectly. He came up to me and after several questions, which I answered in great humility, he said we should not die. I made the captain a very low bow, and then turning to the Dutchman, said I was sorry to find more mercy in a heathen than in a brother Christian. But I had soon reason to repent those foolish words; for that malicious reprobate, having often endeavored in vain to persuade both the captains that I might be thrown into the sea (which they would not yield to after the promise made me, that I should not die), prevailed so far as to have a punishment inflicted on me, worse in all human appearance than death itself.

My men were sent by an equal division into both the

pirate ships and my sloop new manned. As to myself, it was determined that I should be set adrift in a small canoe, with paddles and a sail, and four days' provisions, which last the Japanese captain was so kind to double out of his own stores, and would permit no man to search me. I got down into the canoe, while the Dutchman, standing upon the deck, loaded me with all the curses and injurious terms his language could afford.

When I was at some distance from the pirates, I discovered by my pocket glass several islands to the southeast. I set up my sail, the wind being fair, with a design to reach the nearest of those islands, which I made a shift to do in about three hours. It was all rocky. However, I got many birds' eggs, and striking fire, I kindled some heath and dry seaweed, by which I roasted my eggs. I ate no other supper, being resolved to spare my provisions as much as I could. I passed the night under the shelter of a rock, strewing some heath under me, and slept pretty well.

The next day I sailed to another island, and then to a third and fourth, sometimes using my sail and sometimes my paddles. But not to trouble the reader with a particular account of my distresses, let it suffice that on the fifth day I arrived at the last island in my sight, which lay south-southeast to the former.

This island was at a greater distance than I expected and I did not reach it in less than five hours. I encompassed it almost around before I could find a convenient place to land in, which was a small creek about three times the wideness of my canoe.

I found the island to be all rocky, only a little inter-

mingled with tufts of grass and sweet-smelling herbs.
I took out my small provisions, and after having refreshed myself, I secured the remainder in a cave,
whereof there were great numbers. I gathered plenty
of eggs upon the rocks, and got a quantity of dry seaweed and parched grass, which I designed to kindle
the next day, and roast my eggs as well as I could.
(For I had about me my flint, steel, match, and burning glass.) I lay all night in the cave where I had
lodged my provisions. My bed was the same dry grass
and seaweed which I intended for fuel.

I slept very little, for the disquiets of my mind prevailed over my weariness, and kept me awake. I considered how impossible it was to preserve my life in so
desolate a place and how miserable my end must be.
Yet I found myself so listless and desponding that I
had not the heart to rise, and before I could get spirits
enough to creep out of my cave the day was far advanced.

I walked awhile among the rocks. The sky was perfectly clear, and the sun so hot that I was forced to
turn my face from it. Then all of a sudden it became
obscured, as I thought, in a manner very different
from what happens by the interposition of a cloud. I
turned back, and perceived a vast opaque body between me and the sun, moving forward toward the
island: it seemed to be about two miles high, and hid
the sun six or seven minutes, but I did not observe the
air to be much colder or the sky more darkened than
if I had stood under the shade of a mountain. As it
approached nearer over the place where I was it appeared to be a firm substance, the bottom flat, smooth,

and shining very bright from the reflection of the sea below.

I stood upon a height about two hundred yards from the shore, and saw this vast body descending almost to a parallel with me, at less than an English mile distance. I took out my pocket perspective, and could plainly discover numbers of people moving up and down the sides of it, which appeared to be sloping, but what those people were doing I was not able to distinguish.

The natural love of life gave me some inward motions of joy, and I was ready to entertain a hope that this adventure might some way or other help to deliver me from the desolate place and condition I was in. But at the same time the reader can hardly con-

ceive my astonishment, to behold an island in the air,
inhabited by men, who were able (as it would seem)
to raise or sink, or put it into a progressive motion, as
they pleased.

But not being at that time in a disposition to phi-
losophize upon this phenomenon, I rather chose to observe what course the island would take, because it
seemed for a while to stand still. Yet soon after it advanced nearer, and I could see the sides of it, encompassed with several gradations of galleries, and stairs
at certain intervals, to descend from one to the other.
In the lowest gallery I beheld some people fishing with
long angling rods, and others looking on.

I waved my cap (for my hat was long since worn
out) and my handkerchief toward the island. And
upon its nearer approach, I called and shouted with
the utmost strength of my voice; and then looking circumspectly, I beheld a crowd gather to that side which
was most in my view. I found by their pointing toward me and to each other that they plainly discovered me, although they made no return to my shouting. But I could see four or five men running in great
haste up the stairs to the top of the island and then dis-
appear. I happened rightly to conjecture that these

were sent for orders to some person in authority upon this occasion.

The number of people increased, and in less than half an hour the island was moved and raised in such a manner that the lowest gallery appeared in a parallel of less than a hundred yards distance from the height where I stood. I then put myself into the most supplicating postures, and spoke in the humblest accent but received no answer. Those who stood nearest over against me seemed to be persons of distinction, as I supposed by their habit. They conferred earnestly with each other, looking often upon me. At length one of them called out in a clear, polite, smooth dialect, not unlike in sound to the Italian. Therefore I returned an answer in that language, hoping at least that the cadence might be more agreeable to his ears. Although neither of us understood the other, yet my meaning was easily known, for the people saw the distress I was in.

They made signs for me to come down from the rock and go toward the shore, which I accordingly did. The flying island being raised to a convenient height, the verge directly over me, a chain was let down from the lowest gallery, with a seat fastened to the bottom, to which I fixed myself and was drawn up by pulleys.

CHAPTER 16

Laputa and Its People

A<small>T MY</small> alighting I was surrounded by a crowd of people, but those who stood nearest seemed to be of better quality. They beheld me with all the marks and circumstances of wonder. Neither indeed was I much in their debt, having never till then seen a race of mortals so singular in their shapes, habits, and countenances. Their heads were all reclined either to the right or the left; one of their eyes turned inward, and the other directly up to the zenith. Their outward garments were adorned with the figures of suns, moons, and stars, interwoven with those of fiddles, flutes, harps, trumpets, guitars, harpsichords, and many other instruments of music unknown to us in Europe.

I observed here and there many in the habit of servants, with a blown bladder fastened like a flail to the end of a short stick, which they carried in their hands. In each bladder was a small quantity of dried peas, or little pebbles (as I was afterward informed). With these bladders they now and then flapped the mouths and ears of those who stood near them, of which practice I could not then conceive the meaning.

It seems the minds of these people are so taken up with intense speculations that they neither can speak nor attend to the discourses of others without being roused by some external taction upon the organs of speech and hearing; for which reason those persons who are able to afford it always keep a flapper in their family, as one of their domestics, nor ever walk abroad or make visits without him. And the business of this officer is, when two or more persons are in company, gently to strike with his bladder the mouth of him who is to speak, and the right ear of him or them to whom the speaker addresses himself. This flapper is likewise employed diligently to attend his master in his walks, and upon occasion to give him a soft flap on his eyes, because he is always so wrapped up in cogitation that he is in manifest danger of falling down every precipice, and bouncing his head against every post, and in the streets, of jostling others, or being jostled himself into the kennel.

It was necessary to give the reader this information, without which he would be at the same loss with me to understand the proceedings of these people, as they conducted me up the stairs, to the top of the island, and from there to the royal palace. While we were ascending, they forgot several times what they were about, and left me to myself, till their memories were again roused by their flappers. For they appeared altogether unmoved by the sight of my foreign habit and countenance, and by the shouts of the vulgar, whose thoughts and minds were more disengaged.

At last we entered the palace, and proceeded into

the chamber of presence, where I saw the King seated on his throne, attended on each side by persons of prime quality. Before the throne was a large table filled with globes and spheres, and mathematical instruments of all kinds. His Majesty took not the least notice of us, although our entrance was not without sufficient noise, by the concourse of all persons belonging to the court. But he was then deep in a problem, and we attended at least an hour before he could solve it.

There stood by him on each side a young page, with flaps in their hands, and when they saw he was at leisure one of them gently struck his mouth, and the other his right ear. Thereupon he started like one awakened on the sudden, and looking toward me and the company I was in, recollected the occasion of our coming, whereof he had been informed before. He spoke some words, whereupon immediately a young man with a flap came up to my side, and flapped me gently on the right ear. But I made signs, as well as I could, that I had no occasion for such an instrument; which, as I afterward found, gave his Majesty and the whole court a mean opinion of my understanding.

The King, as far as I could conjecture, asked me several questions, and I addressed myself to him in all the languages I had. When it was found that I could neither understand nor be understood, I was conducted by the King's order to an apartment in his palace where two servants were appointed to attend me.

My dinner was brought, and four persons of quality, whom I remembered to have seen very near the King's person, did me the honor to dine with me. We had two courses of three dishes each. In the first course there was a shoulder of mutton, cut into an equilateral triangle, a piece of beef into a rhomboid, and a pudding into a cycloid. The second course was two ducks, trussed up into the form of fiddles; sausages and puddings resembling flutes and hautboys, and a breast of veal in the shape of a harp. The servants cut our bread into cones, cylinders, parallelograms, and several other mathematical figures.

While we were at dinner I made bold to ask the names of several things in their language. And those noble persons, by the assistance of their flappers, delighted to give me answers, hoping to raise my admiration of their great abilities, if I could be brought to converse with them. I was soon able to call for bread and drink, or whatever else I wanted.

After dinner my company withdrew, and a person was sent to me by the King's order, attended by a flapper. He brought with him pen, ink, and paper, and three or four books, giving me to understand by signs that he was sent to teach me the language. We sat together four hours, in which time I wrote down a great number of words in columns, with the translations over against them. I likewise made a shift to learn several short sentences. For my tutor would order one of my servants to fetch something, to turn about, to make a bow, to sit, or stand, or walk, and the like. Then I took down the sentence in writing.

He showed me also in one of his books the figures of the sun, moon, and stars, the zodiac, the tropics, and polar circles, together with the denominations of many figures of planes and solids. He gave me the names and descriptions of all the musical instruments, and the general terms of art in playing on each of them. After he had left me, I placed all my words with their interpretations in alphabetical order. And thus in a few days, by the help of a very faithful memory, I got some insight into their language.

Those to whom the King had entrusted me, observing how ill I was clad, ordered a tailor to come next morning and take my measure for a suit of clothes. This operator did his office after a different manner from those of his trade in Europe. He first took my height by a quadrant, and then with a rule and compasses described the dimensions and outlines of my whole body, all which he entered upon paper, and in six days brought my clothes very ill made, and quite out of shape, by happening to mistake a figure in the calculation. But my comfort was that I observed such accidents very frequent, and little regarded.

During my confinement for want of clothes, and by an indisposition that held me some days longer, I much enlarged my dictionary. When I went next to court I was able to understand many things the King spoke, and to return him some kind of answers. His Majesty had given orders that the island should move northeast and by east, to the vertical point over Lagado, the metropolis of the whole kingdom below upon the firm earth. It was about ninety leagues distant, and our voyage lasted four days and an half. I was not in the least sensible of the progressive motion made in the air by the island.

On the second morning about eleven o'clock, the King himself in person, attended by his nobility, courtiers, and officers, having prepared all their musical instruments, played on them for three hours without intermission, so that I was quite stunned with the noise.

Neither could I possibly guess the meaning, till my tutor informed me. He said that the people of their island had their ears adapted to hear the music of the spheres, which always played at certain periods, and the court was now prepared to bear their part in whatever instrument they most excelled.

In our journey toward Lagado, the capital city, his Majesty ordered that the island should stop over certain towns and villages, from whence he might receive the petitions of his subjects. And to this purpose several packthreads were let down with small weights at the bottom. On these packthreads the people strung their petitions, which mounted up directly like the scraps of paper fastened by schoolboys at the end of the string that holds their kite. Sometimes we received wine and victuals from below, which were drawn up by pulleys.

The knowledge I had in mathematics gave me great assistance in acquiring their phraseology, which depended much upon that science and music; and in the latter I was not unskilled. Their ideas are perpetually conversant in lines and figures. If they would, for example, praise the beauty of a woman, or any other animal, they describe it by rhombs, circles, parallelograms, ellipses, and other geometrical terms, or by words of art drawn from music. I observed in the King's kitchen all sorts of mathematical and musical instruments, after the figures of which they cut up the joints that were served to his Majesty's table.

Their houses are very ill built, the walls bevel without one right angle in any apartment. This defect arises from the contempt they bear to practical geometry, which they despise as vulgar and mechanic, those instructions they give being too refined for the minds of their workmen, which occasions perpetual mistakes. And although they are dexterous enough upon a piece of paper in the management of the rule, the pencil, and the divider, yet in the common actions and behavior of life, I have not seen a more clumsy, awkward, and unhandy people, nor so slow and perplexed in their conceptions upon all other subjects except those of mathematics and music. They are very bad reasoners, and vehemently given to opposition, unless when they happen to be of the right opinion, which is seldom their case. Imagination, fancy, and invention, they are wholly strangers to, nor have any words in their language by which those ideas can be expressed.

These people are under continual disquietudes, never enjoying a minute's peace of mind. Their apprehensions arise from several changes they dread in the celestial bodies. For instance, they fear that the earth, by the continual approaches of the sun toward it, must in course of time be absorbed or swallowed up; and that the earth very narrowly escaped a brush from the tail of the last comet, which would have reduced it to ashes; and that the next, which they have calculated for thirty-one years hence, will probably destroy us. They believe the sun, by daily spending its rays without any fresh nutriment to supply them, will at last be wholly consumed and annihilated.

They are so alarmed with the apprehensions of these and the like impending dangers that they can neither sleep quietly in their beds nor have any relish for the common pleasures or amusements of life. When they meet an acquaintance in the morning, the first question is about the sun's health, how he looked at his setting and rising, and what hopes they have to avoid the stroke of the approaching comet. This conversation they are apt to run into with the same temper that boys show in listening to terrible stories of sprites and hobgoblins and then dare not go to bed for fear.

The wives and daughters lament their confinement to the island, although I think it the most delicious spot of ground in the world. Although they live here in the greatest plenty and magnificence, and are allowed to do whatever they please, they long to see the world, and take the diversions of the metropolis, which they are not allowed to do without a particular license from the King. This is not easy to be obtained, because the people of quality have found by frequent experience how hard it is to persuade their women to return from below.

In about a month's time I had learned their language fairly well and was able to answer most of the King's questions, when I had the honor to attend him. His Majesty showed not the least curiosity about the laws, government, history, religion, or manners of the countries where I had been, but confined his questions to the state of mathematics, and received the account I gave him with great contempt and indifference, though often roused by his flapper on each side.

The King graciously allowed me to look about the island, attended by my tutor. I chiefly wanted to know to what cause in art or in nature it owed its several motions.

The Flying, or Floating, Island is exactly circular, about four and a half miles in diameter, and consequently contains ten thousand acres. It is three hundred yards thick. The under surface, which appears to those who view it from below, is one even regular plate of adamant,[1] shooting up to the height of about two hundred yards. Above it lie the several minerals in their usual order, and over all is a coat of rich mold, ten or twelve feet deep. The slope of the upper surface, from the circumference to the center, causes all the dews and rains to be conveyed in small rivulets toward the middle, where they are emptied into four large basins, each of about half a mile in circuit and two hundred yards distant from the center. From these basins the water is continually exhaled by the sun in the daytime, which prevents their overflowing. Besides, as it is in the power of the monarch to raise the island above the region of clouds and vapors, he can prevent the falling of dews and rains whenever he pleases.

At the center of the island there is a chasm about fifty yards in diameter, from whence the astronomers descend into a large dome, called the astronomer's cave, situated at the depth of a hundred yards beneath the upper surface of the adamant. In this cave twenty lamps are continually burning, thus casting a strong light into every part. The place is stored with great variety of sextants, telescopes, and other astronomical instruments.

But the greatest curiosity, upon which the fate of the island depends, is a loadstone of a prodigious size, in shape resembling a weaver's shuttle. It is in length six yards, and in the thickest part at least three yards over. This magnet is sustained by a very strong axle of adamant passing through its middle, upon which it

---

[1] An imaginary stone so hard as to be impenetrable.

plays, and is poised so exactly that the weakest hand can turn it.

By means of this loadstone, the island is made to rise and fall, and move from one place to another. One side of the stone is endowed with an attracting power, and the other with a repelling. Upon placing the magnet erect with its attracting end toward the earth, the island descends; but when the repelling extremity points downward, the island mounts directly upward. When the position of the stone is oblique, the motion of the island is so too. By this oblique motion the island is conveyed to different parts of the monarch's dominions. But it must be observed that this island cannot move beyond the extent of the dominions below, nor can it rise above the height of four miles.

When the stone is put parallel to the plane of the horizon, the island stands still; for in that case the extremities of it being at equal distance from the earth, act with equal force, the one in drawing downward, the other in pushing upward, and consequently no motion can ensue.

If any town should engage in rebellion, fall into violent factions, or refuse to pay the usual tribute, the King has two methods of reducing them to obedience. The first and the mildest course is by keeping the island hovering over such a town, and the lands about it, whereby he can deprive them of the benefit of the sun and the rain, and consequently afflict the inhabitants with dearth and diseases. And if the crime deserve it, they are at the same time pelted from above with great stones, against which they have no defense but by creeping into cellars or caves, while the roofs of their houses are beaten to pieces. But if they still continue obstinate or offer to raise insurrections, he proceeds to the last remedy: by letting the island drop directly upon their heads, which makes a universal destruction both of houses and men. However, this is an extremity to which the prince is seldom driven, neither indeed is he willing to put it in execution.

But there is still a more weighty reason why the kings of this country have always avoided so terrible an action. For if the town intended to be destroyed should have in it any tall rocks or high spires of stone, a sudden fall might endanger the bottom or under surface of the island. Although it consist, as I have said, of one entire adamant two hundred yards thick, it might happen to crack by too great a shock, or burst by approaching too near the fires from the houses below, as the backs both of iron and stone will often do in our chimneys. Of all this the people are well apprised, and understand how far to carry their obstinacy, where their liberty or property is concerned.

CHAPTER 17

The Grand Academy at Lagado

A<small>LTHOUGH</small> I cannot say that I was ill treated in this island, yet I must confess I thought myself too much neglected. For neither prince nor people appeared to be curious in any part of knowledge, except mathematics and music, wherein I was far their inferior, and upon that account very little regarded.

On the other side, after having seen all the curiosities of the island, I was very desirous to leave it, being heartily weary of those people. They were indeed excellent in two sciences for which I have great esteem, and wherein I am not unversed. But at the same time they are so abstracted and involved in speculation that I never met with such disagreeable companions. I conversed only with women, tradesmen, flappers, and court pages, during two months of my abode there, by which at last I rendered myself extremely contemptible. Yet these were the only people from whom I could ever receive a reasonable answer.

I had obtained by hard study a good degree of

knowledge in their language. I was weary of being confined to an island where I received so little countenance, and resolved to leave it with the first opportunity.

There was a great lord at court, nearly related to the King, and for that reason alone used with respect. He was universally reckoned the most ignorant and stupid person among them. He had performed many eminent services for the Crown, had great natural and acquired parts, adorned with integrity and honor, but so ill an ear for music that his detractors reported he had been often known to beat time in the wrong place. Neither could his tutors without extreme difficulty teach him to demonstrate the most easy proposition in mathematics. He was pleased to show me many marks of favor, often did me the honor of a visit, desired to be informed in the affairs of Europe, the laws and customs, the manners and learning of the several countries where I had traveled. He listened to me with great attention, and made very wise observations on all I spoke. He had two flappers attending him for state, but never made use of them except at court and in visits of ceremony, and would always command them to withdraw when we were alone together.

I entreated this illustrious person to intercede in my behalf with his Majesty for leave to depart, which he accordingly did, as he was pleased to tell me, with regret. For, indeed, he had made me several offers very advantageous, which however I refused with expressions of the highest acknowledgment.

On the 16th day of February I took leave of his Majesty and the court. The King made me a present to the value of about two hundred pounds English, and my protector his kinsman as much more, together with a letter of recommendation to a friend of his in Lagado, the metropolis. The island being then hovering over a mountain about two miles from it, I was let down from the lowest gallery, in the same manner as I had been taken up.

The continent, as far as it is subject to the monarch of the Flying Island, passes under the general name of Balnibarbi, and the metropolis, as I said before, is called Lagado. I felt some little satisfaction in finding myself on firm ground. I walked to the city without any concern, being clad like one of the natives, and sufficiently instructed to converse with them. I soon found out the person's house to whom I was recommended, presented my letter from his friend the grandee in the island, and was received with much kindness. This great lord, whose name was Munodi, ordered me an apartment in his own house, where I continued during my stay, and was entertained in a most hospitable manner.

The next morning after my arrival, he took me in his chariot to see the town, which is about half the size of London, but the houses very strangely built, and most of them out of repair. The people in the streets walked fast, looked wild, their eyes fixed, and were generally in rags. We passed through one of the town gates, and went about three miles into the country, where I saw many laborers working with several sorts of tools in the ground, but was not able to conjecture what they were about. Neither did I observe any expectation either of corn or grass, although the soil appeared to be excellent. I could not forbear wondering at these odd appearances both in town and country, and I made bold to desire my conductor that he would be pleased to explain to me what could be meant by so many busy heads, hands, and faces, both in the streets and the fields, because I did not discover any good effects they produced; but on the contrary, I never knew a soil so unhappily cultivated, houses so ill contrived and so ruinous, or a people whose countenances and habit expressed so much misery and want.

When I gave that free censure of the country and its inhabitants, he made no further answer than by telling me that I had not been long enough among them to form a judgment, and that the different nations of the world had different customs, with other common topics to the same purpose. But when we returned to his palace, he asked me how I liked the building, what absurdities I observed, and what quarrel I had with the dress or looks of his domestics. This he might safely do, because everything about him was magnificent, regular, and polite. I answered that his Excellency's prudence, quality, and fortune had exempted him from those defects which folly and beggary had produced in others. He said if I would go with him to his country house, about twenty miles distant, where his estate lay, there would be more leisure for this kind of conversation. I told his Excellency that I was entirely at his disposal, and accordingly we set out next morning.

During our journey he made me observe the several methods used by farmers in managing their lands, which to me were wholly unaccountable. For except in some very few places I could not discover one ear of corn or blade of grass. But in three hours' traveling the scene was wholly altered. We came into a most beautiful country: farmers' houses at small distances, neatly built; the fields enclosed, containing vineyards, corn grounds, and meadows. Neither do I remember to have seen a more delightful prospect. His Excellency observed my countenance to clear up. He told me with a sigh that there his estate began, and would continue the same till we should come to his house. He said that his countrymen ridiculed and despised him for managing his affairs no better, and for setting so ill an example to the kingdom, which however was followed by very few, such as were old, and willful, and weak like himself.

We came at length to the house, which was indeed a noble structure, built according to the best rules of ancient architecture. The fountains, gardens, walks, avenues, and groves were all disposed with exact judgment and taste. I gave due praises to everything I saw, whereof his Excellency took not the least notice till after supper, when, there being no third companion, he told me with a very melancholy air that he doubted he must throw down his houses in town and country, to rebuild them after the present mode, destroy all his plantations, and cast others into such a form as modern usage required, and give the same directions to all his tenants, unless he would submit to incur the censure of pride, singularity, affectation, ignorance, caprice, and perhaps increase his Majesty's displeasure.

The sum of his discourse was to this effect. That about forty years ago certain persons went up to Laputa, either upon business or diversion, and after five months' continuance came back with a very little smattering in mathematics, but full of volatile spirits acquired in that airy region. That these persons upon their return began to dislike the management of everything below, and fell into schemes of putting all arts, sciences, languages, and mechanics upon a new foot. To this end they procured a royal patent for erecting an Academy of Projectors in Lagado. And the humor prevailed so strongly among the people that there is not a town of any consequence in the kingdom without such an academy.

In these colleges the professors contrive new rules and methods of agriculture and building, and new instruments and tools for all trades and manufactures, whereby, as they undertake, one man shall do the work of ten. A palace may be built in a week, of materials so durable as to last forever without repairing. All the fruits of the earth shall come to maturity at whatever season we think fit to choose, and increase a hundredfold more than they do at present, with innumerable other happy proposals. The only inconvenience is that none of these projects are yet brought to perfection, and in the meantime the whole country lies miserably waste, the houses in ruins, and the people without food or clothes. By all which, instead of being discouraged, they are fifty times more violently bent upon prosecuting their schemes, driven equally on by hope and despair; that as for himself, being not of an enterprising spirit, he was content to go on in the old forms, to live in the houses his ancestors had built, and act as they did in every part of life without innovation. That some few other persons of quality and gentry had done the same, but were looked on with an eye of contempt and ill will, as enemies to art, ignorant, and ill commonwealth's-men, preferring their own ease and sloth before the general improvement of their country.

In a few days we came back to town, and his Excellency, considering the bad character he had in the Academy, would not go with me himself, but recommended me to a friend of his to bear me company thither. My lord was pleased to represent me as a great admirer of projects, and a person of much curiosity and easy belief; which, indeed, was not without truth, for I had myself been a sort of projector in my younger days.

This Academy is not an entire single building, but a continuation of several houses on both sides of a street, which going to waste was purchased and applied to that use.

I was received very kindly by the warden, and went for many days to the Academy. Every room has in it one or more projectors, and I believe I could not have been in fewer than five hundred rooms.

The first man I saw was of a meager aspect, with sooty hands and face, his hair and beard long, ragged, and singed in several places. His clothes, shirt, and skin were all of the same color. He had been eight years upon a project for extracting sunbeams out of cucumbers, which were to be put into vials hermetically sealed, and let out to warm the air in raw inclement summers. He told me he did not doubt in eight years more he should be able to supply the Governor's gardens with sunshine at a reasonable rate. But he complained that his stock was low, and entreated me to give him something as an encouragement to ingenuity, especially since this had been a very dear season for cucumbers. I made him a small present, for my lord had furnished me with money on purpose, because he knew their practice of begging from all who go to see them.

There was a most ingenious architect who had contrived a new method for building houses, by beginning at the roof, and working downward to the foundation, which he justified to me by the like practice of those two prudent insects, the bee and the spider.

There was a man born blind, who had several apprentices in his own condition. Their employment was to mix colors for painters, which their master taught them to distinguish by feeling and smelling. It was indeed my misfortune to find them at that time not very perfect in their lessons, and the professor himself happened to be generally mistaken. This artist is much encouraged and esteemed by the whole fraternity.

I went into another room, where the walls and ceiling were all hung round with cobwebs, except a narrow passage for the artist to go in and out. At my entrance he called aloud to me not to disturb his webs. He lamented the fatal mistake the world had been so long in of using silkworms, while we had such plenty of domestic insects, who infinitely excelled the former because they understood how to weave as well as spin. And he proposed further that by employing spiders the charge of dyeing silks should be wholly saved, whereof I was fully convinced when he showed me a vast number of flies most beautifully colored, wherewith he fed his spiders, assuring us that the webs would take a tincture from them. And as he had them of all hues, he hoped to fit everybody's fancy, as soon as he could find proper food for the flies, of certain gums, oils, and other glutinous matter to give a strength and consistence to the threads.

I had hitherto seen only one side of the Academy, the other being appropriated to the advancers of speculative learning, of which I shall say something when I have mentioned one illustrious person more, who is called among them *the universal artist*. He told us he had been thirty years employing his thoughts for the improvement of human life. He had two large rooms full of wonderful curiosities, and fifty men at work.

Some were condensing air into a dry tangible substance, by extracting the niter, and letting the aqueous or fluid particles percolate. Others were softening marbles for pillows and pincushions; others petrifying the hoofs of a living horse to preserve them from foundering. The artist himself was at that time busy upon two great designs: the first, to sow land with chaff, wherein he affirmed the true seminal virtue to be contained, as he demonstrated by several experiments which I was not skillful enough to comprehend. The other was, by a certain composition of gums, minerals, and vegetables outwardly applied, to prevent the growth of wool upon two young lambs. He hoped in a reasonable time to propagate the breed of naked sheep all over the kingdom.

We crossed a walk to the other part of the Academy, where, as I have already said, the projectors in speculative learning resided.

The first professor I saw was in a very large room, with forty pupils about him. After salutation, observing me to look earnestly upon a frame which took up the greatest part of both the length and breadth of the room, he said perhaps I might wonder to see him employed in a project for improving speculative knowledge by practical and mechanical operations. But the world would soon be sensible of its usefulness, and he flattered himself that a more noble exalted thought never sprang in any other man's head. Everyone knew how laborious the usual method is of attaining to arts and sciences; whereas by his contrivance the most ignorant person at a reasonable charge, and with a little bodily labor, may write books in philosophy, poetry, politics, law, mathematics, and theology, without the least assistance from genius or study.

He then led me to the frame, about the sides whereof all his pupils stood in ranks. It was twenty feet square, placed in the middle of the room. The surface was composed of several bits of wood, about the bigness of a die, but some larger than others. They were all linked together by slender wires. These bits of wood were covered on every square with paper pasted on them, and on these papers were written all the words of their language, in their several moods, tenses, and declensions, but without any order.

The professor then desired me to observe, for he was going to set his engine at work. The pupils at his command took each of them hold of an iron handle, whereof there were forty fixed round the edges of the frame, and giving them a sudden turn, the whole disposition of the words was entirely changed. He then commanded thirty-six of the lads to read the several lines softly as they appeared upon the frame. And where they found three or four words together that might make part of a sentence, they dictated to the four remaining boys, who were scribes. This work was repeated three or four times, and at every turn the engine was so contrived that the words shifted into new places, as the square bits of wood moved upside down.

Six hours a day the young students were employed in this labor, and the professor showed me several volumes in large folio already collected, of broken sentences which he intended to piece together, and out of those rich materials to give the world a complete body of all arts and sciences.

We next went to the school of languages, where three professors sat in consultation upon improving that of their own country.

The first project was to shorten discourse by cutting polysyllables into one, and leaving out verbs and participles, because in reality all things imaginable are but nouns.

The other project was a scheme for entirely abolishing all words whatsoever. This was urged as a great advantage in point of health as well as brevity. For it is plain that every word we speak is in some degree a diminution of our lungs by corrosion, and consequently contributes to the shortening of our lives. An expedient was therefore offered: since words are only names for *things*, it would be more convenient for all men to carry about them such things as were necessary to express the particular business they are to discourse on.

And this invention would certainly have taken place, to the great ease as well as health of the subject, if the women, in conjunction with the vulgar and illiterate, had not threatened to raise a rebellion, unless they might be allowed the liberty to speak with their tongues, after the manner of their ancestors. Such constant irreconcilable enemies to science are the common people. However, many of the most learned and wise adhere to the new scheme of expressing themselves by things, which has only this inconvenience attending it, that if a man's business be very great, and of various kinds, he must be obliged in proportion to carry a greater bundle of things upon his back, unless he can afford one or two strong servants to attend him.

I have often beheld two of those sages almost sinking under the weight of their packs, like peddlers among us; who, when they met in the streets, would lay down their loads, open their sacks, and hold conversation for an hour together; then put up their implements, help each other to resume their burdens, and take their leave.

But for short conversations a man may carry implements in his pockets and under his arms, enough to supply him, and in his house he cannot be at a loss. Therefore the room where company meet who practice this art is full of all things ready at hand requisite to furnish matter for this kind of artificial converse.

I was at the mathematical school, where the master taught his pupils after a method scarce imaginable to us in Europe. The proposition and demonstration was fairly written on a thin wafer, with a special kind of ink. This the student was to swallow upon a fasting stomach, and for three days following eat nothing but bread and water. As the wafer digested, the ink mounted to his brain bearing the proposition along with it. But the success has not hitherto been answerable, partly by some error in the composition of the ink and partly by the perverseness of lads, to whom this pill is so nauseous that they generally steal aside and only pretend to swallow it; also they have not yet been persuaded to use so long an abstinence as the prescription requires.

I saw nothing in this country that could invite me to a longer continuance, and began to think of returning home to England.

CHAPTER 18

The Land of Magic—
Japan—Then Home

THE CONTINENT of which this kingdom is a part extends itself, as I have reason to believe, eastward to that unknown tract of America, westward to California, and north to the Pacific Ocean, which is not above a hundred and fifty miles from Lagado, where there is a good port and much commerce with the great island of Luggnagg. The island of Luggnagg stands southeastward of Japan, about a hundred leagues distant. There is a strict alliance between the Japanese Emperor and the King of Luggnagg, which affords frequent opportunities of sailing from one island to the other.

I determined therefore to direct my course this way, in order to return to Europe. I hired two mules with a guide to show me the way, and carry my small baggage. I took leave of my noble protector, who had shown me so much favor and made me a generous present at my departure.

When I arrived at the port of Maldonada there was no ship in the harbor bound for Luggnagg, nor likely to be in some time. I soon fell into some acquaintance, and was very hospitably received. A gentleman of distinction said to me that since the ship bound for Luggnagg could not be ready in less than a month, it might be no disagreeable amusement for me to take a trip to the little island of Glubbdubdrib, about five leagues off to the southwest. He offered himself and a friend to accompany me, and that I should be provided with a small convenient barque for the voyage.

Glubbdubdrib, as nearly as I can interpret the word, signifies the Island of Sorcerers or Magicians. It is about one-third as large as the Isle of Wight, and extremely fruitful. It is governed by the head of a certain tribe, who are all magicians. The eldest in succession is prince or governor. He has a noble palace, and a park of about three thousand acres, surrounded by a wall of hewn stone twenty feet high. In this park are several small enclosures for cattle, corn, and gardening.

The Governor and his family are served and attended by domestics of a kind somewhat unusual. By his skill in necromancy he has a power of calling whom he pleases from the dead and commanding their service for twenty-four hours, but no longer. Nor can he call the same persons up again in less than three months, except upon very extraordinary occasions.

When we arrived at the island, which was about eleven in the morning, one of the gentlemen who accompanied me went to the Governor and desired admittance for a stranger, who came on purpose to have the honor of attending on his Highness. This was immediately granted, and we all three entered the gate of the palace between two rows of guards, armed and dressed after a very antique manner, and something in their countenances made my flesh creep with a horror I cannot express. We passed through several apartments, between servants of the same sort, ranked on each side as before, till we came to the chamber of presence, where, after three profound obeisances and a few general questions, we were permitted to sit on three stools near the lowest step of his Highness's throne. He understood the language of Balnibarbi, although it was different from that of his island. He desired me to give him some account of my travels; and to let me see that I should be treated without ceremony he dismissed all his attendants with a turn of his finger, at which to my great astonishment they vanished in an instant, like visions in a dream when we awake on a sudden. I could not recover myself in some time, till the Governor assured me that I should receive no hurt.

Observing my two companions to be under no concern, who had been often entertained in the same manner, I began to take courage and related to his Highness a short history of my several adventures, yet not without some hesitation, and frequently looking behind me to the place where I had seen those domestic specters. I had the honor to dine with the Governor, where a new set of ghosts served up the meat and waited at table. I now observed myself to be less terrified than I had been in the morning. I stayed till sunset, but humbly desired his Highness to excuse me for not accepting his invitation of lodging in the palace. My two friends and I lay at a private house in the town adjoining, which is the capital of this little island; and the next morning we returned to pay our duty to the Governor, as he was pleased to command us.

After this manner we continued in the island for ten days, most part of every day with the Governor and at night in our lodging. I soon grew so familiarized to the sight of spirits that the third or fourth time they

gave me no emotion at all, or, if I had any apprehensions left, my curiosity prevailed over them. For his
Highness the Governor ordered me to call up whatever persons I would choose to name, and in whatever
numbers among all the dead from the beginning of the
world to the present time, and command them to answer any questions I should think fit to ask; with this
condition, that my questions must be confined within
the compass of the times they lived in. And one thing
I might depend upon, they would certainly tell me
truth, for lying was a talent of no use in the lower
world.

I made my humble acknowledgments to his Highness for so great a favor. We were in a chamber from
whence there was a fair prospect into the park. And
because my first inclination was to be entertained

with scenes of pomp and magnificence, I desired to see
Alexander the Great, at the head of his army just after
the battle of Arbela. Upon a motion of the Governor's finger he immediately appeared in a large field
under the window where we stood. Alexander was
called up into the room. It was with great difficulty
that I understood his Greek, and had but little of my
own. He assured me upon his honor that he was not
poisoned, but died of a fever by excessive drinking.

Next I saw Hannibal passing the Alps, who told me
he had not a drop of vinegar in his camp.

I saw Caesar and Pompey at the head of their troops,
just ready to engage. I saw the former in his last great
triumph. I desired that the senate of Rome might appear before me in one large chamber, and an assembly
of somewhat a later age in counterview in another.
The first seemed to be an assembly of heroes and demi-
gods; the other a knot of peddlers, pickpockets, high-
waymen, and bullies.

The Governor at my request gave the sign for
Caesar and Brutus to advance toward us. I was struck
with a profound veneration at the sight of Brutus, and
could easily discover the most consummate virtue, the
greatest intrepidity and firmness of mind, the truest
love of his country, and general benevolence for mankind in every lineament of his countenance. I observed with much pleasure that these two persons
were in good intelligence with each other, and Caesar
freely confessed to me that the greatest actions of his
own life were not equal by many degrees to the glory
of taking it away. I had the honor to have much conversation with Brutus; and was told that his ancestor
Junius, Socrates, Epaminondas, Cato the younger, Sir

Thomas More, and himself were perpetually together: a sextumvirate to which all the ages of the world cannot add a seventh.

I had a deep desire to see the world in every period of antiquity. I chiefly fed my eyes with beholding the destroyers of tyrants and usurpers, and the restorers of liberty to oppressed and injured nations. But I particularly wanted to see those ancients who were most renowned for wit and learning. I set apart one day for that purpose. I proposed that Homer and Aristotle might appear at the head of all their commentators. But these were so numerous that some hundreds were forced to attend in the court and outward rooms of the palace. I knew and could distinguish those two heroes at first sight, not only from the crowd but from each other. Homer was the taller and comelier person of the two, walked very erect for one of his age, and his eyes were the most quick and piercing I ever beheld. Aristotle stooped much, and made use of a staff. His visage was meager, his hair lank and thin, and his voice hollow.

The two gentlemen who conducted me to the island were pressed by their private affairs to return in three days, which I employed in seeing some of the modern dead, who had made the greatest figure for two or three hundred years past in our own and other countries of Europe. Having been always a great admirer of old illustrious families, I desired the Governor would call up a dozen or two of kings with their ancestors in order for eight or nine generations. But my disappointment was grievous and unexpected. For instead of a long train with royal diadems, I saw in one family two fiddlers, three spruce courtiers, and an

Italian prelate; in another, a barber, an abbot, and two cardinals. I have too great a veneration for crowned heads to dwell any longer on so nice a subject. But as to counts, marquesses, dukes, earls, and the like, I was not so scrupulous. And I confess it was not without some pleasure that I found myself able to trace the particular features, by which certain families are distinguished, up to their originals. I could plainly discover from whence one family derives a long chin, why a second has abounded with knaves for two generations, and fools for two more; why a third happened to be crackbrained, and a fourth to be sharpers. How cruelty, falsehood, and cowardice grew to be characteristics by which certain families are distinguished as much as by their coat of arms.

I was chiefly disgusted with modern history. For having strictly examined all the persons of greatest name in the courts of princes for a hundred years past, I found how the world had been misled by writers, to ascribe the greatest exploits in war to cowards, the wisest counsel to fools, Roman virtue to betrayers of their country, piety to atheists, truth to informers; how many innocent and excellent persons had been condemned to death or banishment; how many villains had been exalted to high places.

I took leave of his Highness the Governor of Glubbdubdrib, and returned with my two companions to Maldonada, where after a fortnight's waiting, a ship was ready to sail for Luggnagg. I was a month in this voyage. We had one violent storm, and were under a necessity of steering westward to get into the trade wind. On the 21st of April, 1709, we sailed into the river of Clumegnig, which is a seaport town, at the southeast point of Luggnagg. We cast anchor within a league of the town, and made a signal for a pilot. Two of them came on board in less than half an hour, by whom we were guided between certain shoals and rocks, which are very dangerous in the passage, to a large basin, where a fleet may ride in safety within a cable's length of the town wall.

Some of our sailors, whether out of treachery or inadvertence, had informed the pilots that I was a stranger and a great traveler, whereof these gave notice to a customhouse officer, by whom I was examined very strictly upon my landing. This officer spoke to me in the language of Balnibarbi, which by the force of much commerce is generally understood in that town, especially by seamen and those employed in the customs. I gave him a short account of some particulars, and made my story as plausible and consistent as I could. But I thought it necessary to disguise my country, and call myself an Hollander, because my intentions were for Japan and I knew the Dutch were the only Europeans permitted to enter into that kingdom.

I therefore told the officer that, having been shipwrecked on the coast of Balnibarbi, and cast on a rock, I was received up into Laputa, or the Flying Island (of which he had often heard), and was now endeavoring to get to Japan, from whence I might find a convenience of returning to my own country. The officer said I must be confined till he could receive orders from court, for which he would write immediately, and hoped to receive an answer in a fortnight.

I was carried to a convenient lodging, with a sentry placed at the door. However I had the liberty of a large garden, and was treated with humanity enough, being maintained all the time at the King's charge. I was visited by several persons, chiefly out of curiosity, because it was reported that I came from countries very remote of which they had never heard.

I hired a young man who came in the same ship to be an interpreter. He was a native of Luggnagg, but had lived some years at Maldonada, and was a perfect master of both languages. By his assistance I was able to hold a conversation with those who came to visit me; but this consisted only of their questions and my answers.

The dispatch came from court about the time we expected. It contained a warrant for conducting me and my retinue to Traldragdubb by a party of ten horse. All my retinue was that poor lad for an interpreter, whom I persuaded into my service, and at my humble request we had each of us a mule to ride on. A messenger was dispatched half a day's journey before us, to give the King notice of my approach, and to desire that his Majesty would please appoint a day and hour when it would be his gracious pleasure that I might have the honor to *lick the dust before his footstool.*

This is the court style, and I found it to be more than matter of form. For upon my admittance two days after my arrival, I was commanded to crawl on my belly and lick the floor as I advanced. But on account of my being a stranger, care was taken to have it made so clean that the dust was not offensive. However, this was a peculiar grace, not allowed to any but persons of the highest rank, when they desire an admittance. Nay, sometimes the floor is strewn with dust on purpose, when the person to be admitted happens to have powerful enemies at court. And I have seen a great lord with his mouth so crammed that when he had crept to the proper distance from the throne he was not able to speak a word. Neither is there any remedy, because it is capital for those who receive an audience to spit or wipe their mouths in his Majesty's presence.

There is indeed another custom, which I cannot altogether approve of. When the King has a mind to put any of his nobles to death in a gentle indulgent manner, he commands to have the floor strewn with a certain brown powder, of a deadly composition, which being licked up kills him in twenty-four hours. But in justice to this prince's great clemency, and the care he has of his subjects' lives, it must be mentioned for his honor that strict orders are given to have the infected parts of the floor well washed after every such execution; which if his domestics neglect, they are in danger of incurring his royal displeasure.

When I had crept within four yards of the throne I raised myself gently upon my knees, and then striking my forehead seven times on the ground I pronounced the following words, as they had been taught me the night before, *Ickpling gloffthrobb squutserumm blhiop mlashnalt zwin tnodbalkguffh slhiophad gurdlubh asht.* This is the compliment established by the laws of the land for all persons admitted to the King's presence. It may be rendered into English thus: "May your Celestial Majesty outlive the sun, eleven moons and a half."

To this the King returned some answer, which I could not understand, yet I replied as I had been directed: *Fluft drin yalerick dwuldom prastrad mir-push*, which properly signifies, "My tongue is in the mouth of my friend," and by this expression was meant that I desired leave to bring my interpreter; whereupon the young man already mentioned was accordingly introduced, by whose intervention I answered as many questions as his Majesty could put in over an hour. I spoke in the Balnibarbian tongue, and my interpreter delivered my meaning in that of Luggnagg.

The King was much delighted with my company and ordered his High Chamberlain to appoint a lodging in the court for me and my interpreter, with a daily allowance for my table and a large purse of gold for my common expenses.

I stayed three months in this country out of perfect obedience to his Majesty, who was pleased highly to favor me and made me very honorable offers. But I thought it more consistent with prudence and justice to pass the remainder of my days with my wife and family.

His Majesty having often pressed me to accept some employment in his court, and finding me absolutely determined to return to my native country, was pleased to give me his license to depart, and honored me with a letter of recommendation under his own hand to the Emperor of Japan.

On the 6th of May, 1709, I took a solemn leave of his Majesty and all my friends. In six days I found a vessel ready to carry me to Japan, and spent fifteen days in the voyage.

We landed at a small port town called Xamoschi, situated on the southeast part of Japan. The town lies on the western point, where there is a narrow strait, leading northward into a long arm of the sea, upon the northwest part of which Yedo the metropolis stands. At landing, I showed the customhouse officers my letter from the King of Luggnagg to his Imperial Majesty.

The magistrates of the town, hearing of my letter, received me as a public minister. They provided me with carriages and servants, and bore my charges to Yedo. Here I was admitted to an audience, and delivered my letter, which was opened with great ceremony, and explained to the Emperor by an interpreter, who then gave me notice by his Majesty's order. This interpreter was a person employed to transact affairs with the Hollanders. He soon conjectured by my countenance that I was a European, and therefore repeated his Majesty's commands in Low Dutch, which he spoke perfectly well. I answered (as I had before determined) that I was a Dutch merchant, shipwrecked in a very remote country, from whence I traveled by sea and land to Luggnagg, and then took shipping for Japan, where I knew my countrymen often traded, and with some of these I hoped to get an opportunity of returning into Europe. I therefore most humbly entreated his royal favor, to give order that I should be conducted in safety to Nangasac.

I arrived at Nangasac, after a very long and troublesome journey. I soon fell into the company of some Dutch sailors belonging to the *Amboyna*, of Amsterdam. I had lived long in Holland, pursuing my studies at Leyden, and I spoke Dutch well. The seamen soon knew from whence I came last. They were curious to inquire into my voyages and course of life.

I made up a story as short and probable as I could, but concealed the greatest part. I knew many persons in Holland. I was able to invent names for my parents, whom I pretended to be obscure people in the province of Gelderland. I would have given the captain (one Theodorus Vangrult) what he pleased to ask for my voyage to Holland; but understanding I was a surgeon, he was contented to take half the usual rate, on condition that I would serve him in the way of my calling.

Nothing happened worth mentioning in this voyage. We sailed with a fair wind to the Cape of Good Hope, where we stayed only to take in fresh water. On the 10th of April we arrived safe at Amsterdam, having lost only three men by sickness in the voyage, and a fourth who fell from the foremast into the sea, not far from the coast of Guinea. From Amsterdam I soon after set sail for England in a small vessel belonging to that city.

On the 16th of April, 1710, we put in at the Downs. I landed the next morning, and saw once more my native country after an absence of five years and six months complete. I went straight to Redriff, where I arrived the same day at two in the afternoon, and found my wife and family in good health.

CHAPTER 19

The Houyhnhnms' Country

I CONTINUED AT home with my wife and children about five months in a very happy condition, if I could have learned the lesson of knowing when I was well off. I left my poor wife and children, and accepted an advantageous offer made me to be captain of the *Adventure*, a stout merchantman. We set sail from Portsmouth upon the 7th of August, 1710.

I had several men die in my ship of tropical fever, so that I was forced to get recruits out of Barbadoes, and the Leeward Islands, where I touched by the direction of the merchants who employed me. This I had soon too much cause to repent, for I found afterward that most of them had been buccaneers. I had fifty hands on board, and my orders were that I should trade with the Indians in the South Sea, and make what discoveries I could. Those rogues whom I had picked up formed a conspiracy to seize the ship and secure me. This they did one morning, rushing into my cabin, and binding me hand and foot, threatening to throw me overboard if I offered to stir.

I told them I was their prisoner and would submit. This they made me swear to do, and then they unbound me, only fastening one of my legs with a chain near my bed, and placed a sentry at my door with his piece charged, who was commanded to shoot me dead if I attempted my liberty. They sent me down victuals and drink, and took the government of the ship to themselves.

Their design was to turn pirates, and plunder the Spaniards, which they could not do till they got more men. But first they resolved to sell the goods in the ship, and then go to Madagascar for recruits, several among them having died since my confinement. They sailed many weeks, and traded with the Indians, but I knew not what course they took, being kept a close prisoner in my cabin, and expecting nothing less than to be murdered, as they often threatened me.

One day James Welch came down to my cabin and said he had orders from the captain to set me ashore. They forced me into the longboat, letting me put on my best suit of clothes, which were as good as new, and a small bundle of linen, but no arms except my sword. And they were so civil as not to search my pockets, into which I conveyed what money I had, with some other little necessaries. They rowed about a league, and then set me down on a strand. I desired them to tell me what country it was. They all swore they knew no more than myself, but said that the captain was resolved, after they had sold the lading, to get rid of me in the first place where they could discover land. They pushed off immediately, advising me to make haste for fear of being overtaken by the tide, and so bade me farewell.

In this desolate condition I advanced forward, and soon got upon firm ground, where I sat down on a bank to rest myself and consider what I had best do. When I was a little refreshed I went up into the country, resolving to deliver myself to the first savages I should meet, and purchase my life from them by some bracelets, glass rings, and other toys which sailors usually provide themselves with in those voyages.

The land was divided by long rows of trees, not regularly planted, but naturally growing. There was plenty of grass, and several fields of oats. I walked very circumspectly for fear of being surprised, or suddenly shot with an arrow from behind or on either side. I fell into a beaten road, where I saw many tracks of human feet, and some of cows, but most of horses.

At last I beheld several animals in a field, and one or two of the same kind sitting in trees. Their shape was very singular and deformed, which a little discomposed me, so that I lay down behind a thicket to observe them better. Some of them coming forward near the place where I lay gave me an opportunity of distinctly marking their form. Their heads and breasts were covered with a thick hair, some frizzled and others lank. They had beards like goats, and a long ridge of hair down their backs and the foreparts of their legs and feet, but the rest of their bodies were bare, so that I might see their skins, which were of a brown buff color. Upon the whole, I never beheld in all my travels so disagreeable an animal, nor one against which I naturally conceived so strong an antipathy.

Thinking I had seen enough, full of contempt and aversion, I got up and pursued the beaten road, hoping it might direct me to the cabin of some Indian. I had not got far when I met one of these creatures full in my way, and coming up directly to me. The ugly monster, when he saw me, distorted several ways every feature of his visage, and stared as at an object he had never seen before; then approaching nearer, lifted up his forepaw, whether out of curiosity or mischief, I could not tell. But I drew my sword, and gave him a good blow with the flat side of it, for I dare not strike him with the edge, fearing the inhabitants might be provoked against me, if they should come to know that I had killed or maimed any of their cattle.

When the beast felt the smart, he drew back, and roared so loud that a herd of at least forty came flocking about me from the next field, howling and making odious faces. But I ran to the body of a tree, and leaning my back against it, kept them off by waving my sword.

In the midst of this distress, I observed them all to run away of a sudden as fast as they could, at which I ventured to leave the tree, and pursue the road, wondering what it was that could put them into this fright. But looking on my left hand, I saw a horse walking softly in the field; which my persecutors having sooner discovered, was the cause of their flight.

The horse started a little when he came near me, but soon recovering himself, looked full in my face with manifest tokens of wonder. He viewed my hands and feet, walking round me several times. I would have pursued my journey, but he placed himself directly in the way, yet looking with a very mild aspect, never offering the least violence. We stood gazing at each other for some time. At last I took the boldness to reach my hand toward his neck, with a design to stroke it, using the common style and whistle of jockeys when they are going to handle a strange horse. But this animal, seeming to receive my civilities with disdain, shook his head and bent his brows, softly raising up his right forefoot to remove my hand. Then he neighed three or four times, but in so different a cadence that I almost began to think he was speaking to himself in some language of his own.

While he and I were thus employed, another horse came up; who applying himself to the first in a very formal manner, they gently struck each other's right hoof before, neighing several times by turns, and varying the sound, which seemed to be almost articulate. They went some paces off, as if it were to confer together, walking side by side, backward and forward, like persons deliberating upon some affair of weight, but often turning their eyes toward me, as it were to watch that I might not escape.

I was amazed to see such actions and behavior in brute beasts, and concluded with myself that if the inhabitants of this country were endowed with a proportionable degree of reason they must needs be the wisest people upon earth. This thought gave me so much comfort that I resolved to go forward until I could discover some house or village, or meet with any of the natives, leaving the two horses to discourse together as they pleased. But the first, who was a dapple gray, observing me to steal off, neighed after me in so expressive a tone that I fancied myself to understand what he meant. Whereupon I turned back and came near him, to expect his further commands, but concealing my fear as much as I could, for I began to be in some pain, how this adventure might terminate.

The two horses came up close to me, looking with great earnestness upon my face and hands. The gray steed rubbed my hat all round with his right forehoof, and discomposed it so much that I was forced to adjust it better, by taking it off, and settling it again; whereat both he and his companion (who was a brown bay) appeared to be much surprised. The latter felt the lappet of my coat, and finding it to hang loose about me, they both looked with new signs of wonder. He stroked my right hand, seeming to admire the softness and color. But he squeezed it so hard between his hoof and his pastern that I was forced to roar; after which they both touched me with all possible tenderness. They were under great perplexity about my shoes and stockings, which they felt very often, neighing to each other, and using various gestures, not unlike those of a philosopher when he would attempt to solve some new and difficult phenomenon.

Upon the whole, the behavior of these animals was so orderly and rational, so acute and judicious, that I at last concluded they must needs be magicians, who had thus metamorphosed themselves upon some design and, seeing a stranger in the way, were resolved to divert themselves with him. Perhaps they were really amazed at the sight of a man so very different in habit, feature, and complexion from those who might probably live in so remote a climate. Upon the strength of this reasoning, I ventured to address them in the following manner:

"Gentlemen, if you be conjurers, as I have good cause to believe, you can understand any language.

Therefore I make bold to let your worships know that I am a poor distressed Englishman, driven by his misfortunes upon your coast, and I entreat one of you to let me ride upon his back, as if he were a real horse, to some house or village where I can be relieved. In return of which favor I will make you a present of this knife and bracelet" (taking them out of my pocket).

The two creatures stood silent while I spoke, seeming to listen with great attention. And when I had ended, they neighed frequently toward each other, as if they were engaged in serious conversation. I plainly observed that their language expressed the passions very well, and the words might with little pains be resolved into an alphabet more easily than the Chinese.

I could frequently distinguish the word *Yahoo*, which was repeated by each of them several times. And although it was impossible for me to conjecture what it meant, yet while the two horses were busy in conversation I endeavored to practice this word upon my tongue. And as soon as they were silent, I boldly pronounced Yahoo in a loud voice, imitating, at the same time, as near as I could, the neighing of a horse. At this they were both visibly surprised, and the gray repeated the same word twice, as if he meant to teach me the right accent, wherein I spoke after him as well as I could, and found myself perceivably to improve every time, though very far from any degree of perfection. Then the bay tried me with a second word, much harder to be pronounced; but reducing it to the English orthography, may be spelt thus: *Houyhnhnm*. I did not succeed in this so well as the former, but after two or three further trials, I had better fortune. And they both appeared amazed at my capacity.

After some further discourse, which I then con-jectured might relate to me, the two friends took their leave, with the same compliment of striking each other's hoofs. And the gray made me signs that I should walk before him, wherein I thought it prudent to comply, till I could find a better director. When I offered to slacken my pace, he would cry *hhuun*, *hhuun*. I guessed his meaning, and gave him to under-stand as well as I could that I was weary, and not able to walk faster; upon which he would stand awhile to let me rest.

Having traveled about three miles, we came to a long kind of building, made of timber stuck in the ground, and wattled across. The roof was low, and covered with straw. I now began to be a little com-forted, and took out some toys, which travelers usu-ally carry for presents to the savage Indians of Amer-ica and other parts, in hopes the people of the house would be thereby encouraged to receive me kindly. The horse made me a sign to go in first.

It was a large room with a smooth clay floor, and a rack and manger extending the whole length on one side. There were three nags, and two mares, not eat-ing, but some of them sitting down upon their hams, which I very much wondered at; but wondered more to see the rest employed in domestic business. These seemed but ordinary cattle; however, this confirmed my first opinion, that a people who could so far civi-lize brute animals must needs excel in wisdom all the nations of the world. The gray came in just after, and thereby prevented any ill treatment which the others might have given me. He neighed to them several times in a style of authority, and received answers.

Beyond this room there were three others, reaching the length of the house, to which you passed through three doors, opposite to each other, in the manner of a vista. We went through the second room toward the third. Here the gray walked in first, beckoning me to attend. I waited in the second room, and got ready my presents for the master and mistress of the house. They were two knives, three bracelets of false pearl, a small looking glass, and a bead necklace. The horse neighed three or four times, and I waited to hear some answers in a human voice, but I heard no other returns than in the same dialect, only one or two a little shriller than his.

I began to think that this house must belong to some person of great note among them, because there appeared so much ceremony before I could gain admittance. But that a man of quality should be served all by horses was beyond my comprehension. I feared my brain was disturbed by my sufferings and misfortunes.

I roused myself, and looked about me in the room where I was left alone. This was furnished like the first, only after a more elegant manner. I rubbed my eyes often, but the same objects still occurred. I pinched my arms and sides to awake myself, hoping I might be in a dream. I then absolutely concluded that all these appearances could be nothing else but necromancy and magic. But I had no time to pursue these reflections, for the gray horse came to the door and made me a sign to follow him into the third room, where I saw a very comely mare, together with a colt and foal, sitting on their haunches upon mats of straw, not unartfully made, and perfectly neat and clean.

The mare, soon after my entrance, rose from her mat, and coming up close, after having nicely observed my hands and face, gave me a most contemptuous look. Then turning to the horse, I heard the word *Yaho*o often repeated betwixt them; the meaning of which word I could not then comprehend, although it was the first I had learned to pronounce. But I was soon better informed, to my everlasting mortification. For the horse, beckoning to me with his head, and repeating the word *hhuun*, *hhuun*, as he did upon the road, which I understood was to attend him, led me out into a kind of court, where was another building at some distance from the house.

Here we entered, and I saw three of these detestable creatures, whom I first met after my landing, feeding upon roots, and the flesh of some animals, which I afterward found to be that of asses and dogs, and now and then a cow dead by accident or disease. They were all tied by the neck with strong withes, fastened to a beam. They held their food between the claws of their forefeet, and tore it with their teeth.

The master horse ordered a sorrel nag, one of his servants, to untie the largest of these animals, and take him into the yard. The beast and I were brought close together, and our countenances diligently compared, both by master and servant, who thereupon repeated several times the word *Yahoo*. My horror and astonishment are not to be described, when I observed in this abominable animal a perfect human figure. The face of it indeed was flat and broad, the nose depressed, the lips large, and the mouth wide.

The forefeet of the Yahoo differed from my hands in nothing else but the length of the nails, the coarse-

The beast and I were brought close together

ness and brownness of the palms, and the hairiness on the backs. There was the same resemblance between our feet, with the same differences, which I knew very well, though the horses did not, because of my shoes and stockings; the same in every part of our bodies, except as to hairiness and color, which I have already described.

The great difficulty that seemed to stick with the two horses was to see the rest of my body so very different from that of a Yahoo, for which I was obliged to my clothes, whereof they had no conception. The sorrel nag offered me a root, which he held between his hoof and pastern. I took it in my hand, and having smelt it, returned it to him again as civilly as I could. He brought out of the Yahoo's kennel a piece of ass's flesh, but it smelt so offensively that I turned from it with loathing. He then threw it to the Yahoo, by whom it was greedily devoured. He afterward showed me a wisp of hay, and a fetlock full of oats. But I shook my head, to signify that neither of these were food for me.

And indeed, I now apprehended that I must absolutely starve if I did not get to some of my own species. As to those filthy Yahoos, although there were few greater lovers of mankind, at that time, than myself, yet I confess I never saw any sensitive being so detestable on all accounts; and the more I came near them the more hateful they grew, while I stayed in that country. This the master horse observed by my behavior, and therefore sent the Yahoo back to his kennel.

He then put his forehoof to his mouth, at which I was much surprised, although he did it with ease, and with a motion that appeared perfectly natural, and made other signs to know what I would eat. But I could not return him such an answer as he was able to apprehend. And if he had understood me, I did not see how it was possible to contrive any way for finding myself nourishment. While we were thus engaged, I observed a cow passing by, whereupon I pointed to her, and expressed a desire to let me go and milk her. This had its effect. He led me back into the house, and ordered a mare-servant to open a room, where a good store of milk lay in earthen and wooden vessels, after a very orderly and cleanly manner. She gave me a large bowlful, of which I drank very heartily and found myself well refreshed.

About noon I saw coming toward the house a kind of vehicle, drawn like a sledge by four Yahoos. There was in it an old steed, who seemed to be of quality. He alighted with his hind feet forward, having by accident got a hurt in his left forefoot. He came to dine with our horse, who received him with great civility. They dined in the best room, and had oats boiled in milk for the second course, which the old horse ate warm, but the rest cold.

Their mangers were placed circular in the middle of the room, and divided into several partitions, round which they sat on their haunches upon bosses of straw. In the middle was a large rack with angles answering to every partition of the manger; so that each horse and mare ate their own hay, and their own mash of oats and milk, with much decency and regularity. The behavior of the young colt and foal appeared very modest, and that of the master and mistress extremely cheerful and complaisant to their guest. The gray ordered me to stand by him, and much discourse passed between him and his friend concerning me, as I found by the stranger's often looking on me, and the frequent repetition of the word *Yahoo*.

I happened to wear my gloves, which the master gray, observing, seemed perplexed, showing signs of wonder what I had done to my forefeet. He put his hoof three or four times to them, as if he would signify that I should reduce them to their former shape, which I presently did, pulling off both my gloves, and putting them into my pocket. This occasioned further talk, and I saw the company was pleased with my behavior, whereof I soon found the good effects. I was ordered to speak the few words I understood, and while they were at dinner the master taught me the names for oats, milk, fire, water, and some others; which I could readily pronounce after him, having from my youth a great facility in learning languages.

When dinner was done the master horse took me aside, and by signs and words made me understand the concern that he was in because I had nothing to eat. Oats in their tongue are called *hlunnh*. This word I pronounced two or three times. For although I had refused them at first, yet upon second thoughts I considered that I could contrive to make of them a kind of bread, which might be sufficient with milk to keep me alive till I could make my escape to some other country and to creatures of my own species.

The horse immediately ordered a white mare-servant of his family to bring me a good quantity of oats in a sort of wooden tray. These I heated before the fire as well as I could, and rubbed them till the husks came off, which I made a shift to winnow from the grain.

I ground and beat them between two stones, then took water, and made them into a paste or cake, which I toasted at the fire, and ate warm with milk. It was at first a very insipid diet, though common enough in many parts of Europe, but grew tolerable by time. And having been often reduced to hard fare in my life, this was not the first experiment I had made how easily nature is satisfied. And I cannot but observe that I never had one hour's sickness while I stayed in this island.

I sometimes made a shift to catch a rabbit or bird by snares made of Yahoos' hairs, and I often gathered wholesome herbs, which I boiled, or ate as salads with my bread, and now and then, for a rarity, I made a little butter, and drank the whey. I was at first at a great loss for salt, but custom soon reconciled the want of it; and I am confident that the frequent use of salt among us is an effect of luxury.

When it grew toward evening, the master horse ordered a place for me to lodge in. It was but six yards from the house, and separated from the stable of the Yahoos. Here I got some straw and, covering myself with my own clothes, slept very sound.

CHAPTER 20

Gulliver Understands the Speech of the Master Horse

———

MY PRINCIPAL endeavor was to learn the language, which my master (for so I shall henceforth call him) and his children and every servant of his house were desirous to teach me. For they looked upon it as a prodigy that a brute animal should discover such marks of a rational creature. I pointed to everything and inquired the name of it, which I wrote down in my journal book when I was alone, and corrected my bad accent by desiring those of the family to pronounce it often. In this employment, a sorrel nag, one of the underservants, was ready to assist me.

The curiosity and impatience of my master were so great that he spent many hours of his leisure to instruct me. He was convinced (as he afterward told me) that I must be a Yahoo, but my teachableness, civility, and cleanliness astonished him; which were qualities altogether so opposite to those animals. He was most perplexed about my clothes, reasoning sometimes with himself whether they were a part of my body, for I never pulled them off till the family were asleep and got them on before they waked in the morning. My master was eager to learn from where I came, how I acquired those appearances of reason which I showed in all my actions, and to know my story from my own mouth, which he hoped he should soon do by the great proficiency I made in learning and pronouncing their words and sentences.

In about ten weeks' time I was able to understand most of his questions, and in three months could give him some tolerable answers. He was extremely curious to know from what part of the country I came, and how I was taught to imitate a rational creature; because the Yahoos (whom he saw I exactly resembled in my head, hands, and face), with some appearance of cunning, and the strongest disposition to mischief, were observed to be the most unteachable of all brutes. I answered that I came over the sea from a far place, with many others of my own kind, in a great hollow vessel made of the bodies of trees; that my companions forced me to land on this coast, and then left me to shift for myself. It was with some difficulty, and by the help of many signs, that I brought him to understand me.

He replied, that I must needs be mistaken, or that I *said the thing which was not*. (For they have no word in their language to express lying or falsehood.) He knew it was impossible that there could be a country beyond the sea, or that a parcel of brutes could move a wooden vessel whither they pleased upon water. He was sure no Houyhnhnm alive could make such a vessel, nor would trust Yahoos to manage it.

I told my master that I was at a loss for expression, but would improve as fast as I could; and hoped in a short time I should be able to tell him wonders. He was pleased to direct his own mare, his colt and foal, and the servants of the family, to take all opportunities of instructing me, and every day for two or three hours he was at the same pains himself. Several horses and mares of quality in the neighborhood came often to our house upon the report spread of a wonderful Yahoo that could speak like a Houyhnhnm and seemed in his words and actions to show some glimmerings of reason. These delighted to converse with me. They put many questions, and received such answers as I was able to return. By all these advantages I made so great a progress that in five months from my arrival I understood whatever was spoke and could express myself tolerably well.

The Houyhnhnms who came to visit my master with the design of seeing and talking with me, could hardly believe me to be a right Yahoo, because my body had a different covering from others of my kind. They were astonished to observe me without the usual hair or skin, except on my head, face, and hands; but I discovered that secret to my master, upon an accident which happened about a fortnight before.

I have already told the reader, that every night when the family were gone to bed it was my custom to strip and cover myself with my clothes. It happened one morning early that my master sent for me by the sorrel nag, who was his valet; when he came I was fast asleep, my clothes fallen off on one side, and my shirt above my waist. I awakened at the noise he made, and observed him to deliver his message in some disorder; after which he went to my master, and in a great fright gave him a very confused account of what he had seen. This I presently discovered; for going as soon as I was dressed to pay my attendance upon his Honor, he asked me the meaning of what his servant had reported, that I was not the same thing when I slept as I appeared to be at other times; that his valet assured him, some part of me was white, some yellow, at least not so white, and some brown.

I had hitherto concealed the secret of my dress, in order to distinguish myself as much as possible from that cursed race of Yahoos; but now I found it in vain to do so any longer. Besides, I considered that my clothes and shoes would soon wear out, which already were in a declining condition, and must be supplied by some contrivance from the hides of Yahoos or other brutes; whereby the whole secret would be known. I therefore told my master that in the country from which I came those of my kind always covered their bodies with the hairs of certain animals prepared by art, as well for decency as to avoid the inclemencies of air, both hot and cold; of which, as to my own person, I would give him immediate conviction, if he pleased to command me; only desiring his excuse, if I did not expose those parts that nature taught us to conceal. He said my discourse was all very strange, but especially the last part; for he could not understand why nature should teach us to conceal what nature had given. That neither himself nor family were ashamed of any parts of their bodies; but however I might do as I pleased. Whereupon I first unbuttoned my coat and pulled it off. I did the same with my waistcoat; I drew off my shoes, stockings, and breeches. I let my shirt down to my waist, and drew up the bottom, fastening it like a girdle about my middle.

My master observed the whole performance with great signs of curiosity and admiration. He took up all my clothes in his pastern, one piece after another, and examined them diligently; he then stroked my body very gently and looked round me several times, after which he said it was plain I must be a perfect Yahoo; but that I differed very much from the rest of my species, in the softness and whiteness and smoothness of my skin, my want of hair in several parts of my body, the shape and shortness of my claws behind and before, and my affectation of walking continually on my two hind feet. He desired to see no more, and gave me leave to put on my clothes again, for I was shuddering with cold.

I expressed my uneasiness at his giving me so often the appellation of Yahoo, an odious animal for which I had so utter a hatred and contempt. I begged he would forbear applying that word to me, and take the same order in his family, and among his friends whom he suffered to see me. I requested likewise that the secret of my having a false covering to my body might be known to none but himself, at least as long as my present clothing should last; for as to what the sorrel nag his valet had observed, his Honor might command him to conceal it.

All this my master very graciously consented to, and thus the secret was kept till my clothes began to wear out, which I was forced to supply by several contrivances that shall hereafter be mentioned. In the meantime he desired I would go on with my utmost diligence to learn their language, because he was more astonished at my capacity for speech and reason than at the figure of my body, whether it were covered or not; adding that he waited with some impatience to hear the wonders which I promised to tell him.

From thenceforward he doubled the pains he had been at to instruct me; he brought me into all company, and made them treat me with civility, because, as he told them privately, this would put me into good humor and make me more diverting.

Every day when I waited on him, besides the trouble he was at in teaching, he would ask me several questions concerning myself, which I answered as well as I could.

I explained that I came from a very far country with about fifty more of my own species; that we traveled upon the seas, in a great hollow vessel made of wood, and larger than his Honor's house. I described the ship to him in the best terms I could, and explained by the help of my handkerchief displayed, how it was driven forward by the wind. I said that after a quarrel among us I was set on shore on this coast, where I walked forward without knowing whither, till he delivered me from the persecution of those execrable Yahoos.

He asked me who made the ship, and how it was possible that the Houyhnhnms of my country would leave it to the management of brutes. My answer was that I dare proceed no further in my relation unless he would give me his word and honor that he would not be offended, and then I would tell him the wonders I had so often promised.

He agreed; and I went on by assuring him that the ship was made by creatures like myself, who in all the countries I had traveled, as well as in my own, were the only governing, rational animals; and that upon my arrival here I was as much astonished to see the Houyhnhnms act like rational beings as he or his friends could be in finding some marks of reason in a creature he was pleased to call a Yahoo, to which I owned my resemblance in every part but could not account for their degenerate and brutal nature.

I said further that if good fortune ever restored me to my native country, to relate my travels here, everybody would believe that I *said the thing which was not;* that I invented the story out of my own head. And with all possible respect to himself, his family and friends, and under his promise of not being offended, our countrymen would hardly think it probable that a Houyhnhnm should be the presiding creature of a nation and a Yahoo the brute.

When I asserted that the Yahoos were the only governing animals in my country, which my master said was altogether past his conception, he desired to know whether we had Houyhnhnms among us, and what was their employment. I told him we had great numbers, that in summer they grazed in the fields, and in winter were kept in houses, with hay and oats, where Yahoo servants were employed to rub their skins smooth, comb their manes, serve them with food, and make their beds.

"I understand you well," said my master, "it is now very plain, from all you have spoken, that whatever share of reason the Yahoos pretend to, the Houyhnhnms are your masters. I heartily wish our Yahoos would be so tractable."

I begged his Honor would please to excuse me from

proceeding any further, because I was very certain that the account he expected from me would be highly displeasing. But he insisted in commanding me to let him know the best and the worst. I told him he should be obeyed. I owned that the Houyhnhnms among us, whom we called horses, were the most generous and comely animals we had, that they excelled in strength and swiftness. And when they belonged to persons of quality, employed in traveling, racing, or drawing chariots, they were treated with much kindness and care, till they fell into diseases or became foundered in the feet. Then they were sold, and used to all kind of drudgery till they died; after which their skins were stripped and sold for what they were worth, and their bodies left to be devoured by dogs and birds of prey.

But the common race of horses had not so good fortune, being kept by farmers and carriers, and other mean people, who put them to great labor, and fed them worse. I described, as well as I could, our way of riding, the shape and use of a bridle, a saddle, a spur, and a whip, of harness and wheels. I added that we fastened plates of a certain hard substance called iron at the bottom of their feet, to preserve their hoofs from being broken by the stony ways on which we often traveled.

My master, after some expressions of great indignation, wondered how we dared to venture upon a Houyhnhnm's back, for he was sure that the weakest servant in his house would be able to shake off the strongest Yahoo, or by lying down and rolling on his back squeeze the brute to death. I answered that our horses were trained up from three or four years old

to the several uses we intended them for; that if any
of them proved intolerably vicious, they were employed for carriages; that they were severely beaten
while they were young, for any mischievous tricks;
that they were indeed sensible of rewards and punish-
ments. But his Honor would please to consider that
they had not the least tincture of reason any more
than the Yahoos in this country.

It put me to the pains of many circumlocutions to
give my master a right idea of what I spoke, for their
language does not abound in variety of words because
their wants and passions are fewer than among us.
But it is impossible to represent his noble resentment
at our savage treatment of the Houyhnhnm race.

He said if it were possible there could be any country where Yahoos alone were endowed with reason,
they certainly must be the governing animal, because
reason will in time always prevail against brutal
strength. But considering the frame of our bodies, and
especially of mine, he thought no creature of equal
bulk was so ill contrived for employing that reason in
the common offices of life. Whereupon he desired to
know whether those among whom I lived resembled
me or the Yahoos of his country. I assured him that I
was as well shaped as most of my age; but the younger
and the females were much more soft and tender, and
the skins of the latter generally as white as milk.

He said I differed indeed from other Yahoos, being
much more cleanly, and not altogether so deformed,
but in point of real advantage he thought I differed for
the worse: that my nails were of no use either to my
fore or hind feet. As to my forefeet, he could not
properly call them by that name, for he never ob-

served me to walk upon them; that they were too soft to bear the ground; that I generally went with them uncovered, neither was the covering I sometimes wore on them of the same shape or so strong as that on my feet behind.

He then began to find fault with other parts of my body: the flatness of my face, the prominence of my nose, my eyes placed directly in front, so that I could not look on either side without turning my head; that I was not able to feed myself without lifting one of my forefeet to my mouth; and therefore nature had placed these joints to answer that necessity. He knew not what could be the use of those several clefts and divisions in my feet behind; that these were too soft to bear the hardness and sharpness of stones without a covering made from the skin of some other brute; that my whole body wanted a fence against heat and cold, which I was forced to put on and off every day with tediousness and trouble. However, he said he would debate the matter no further, because he was more desirous to know my own story, the country where I was born, and the several actions and events of my life before I came here.

I said my birth was of honest parents in an island called England, governed by a female whom we called a queen. I was bred a surgeon, whose trade it is to cure wounds and hurts in the body, got by accident or violence. I left home to get riches, whereby I might maintain myself and family when I should return. In my last voyage I was commander of the ship and had about fifty Yahoos under me, many of whom died at sea, and I was forced to replace them by others picked out from several nations. Our ship was twice in danger of being sunk: the first time by a great storm, and the second by striking against a rock.

Here my master interposed, asking me how I could persuade strangers out of different countries to venture with me, after the losses I had sustained and the hazards I had run. I said they were fellows of desperate fortunes, forced to fly from the places of their birth on account of their poverty or their crimes; none of whom dared return to their native countries for fear of being hanged or of starving in a jail, and therefore were under the necessity of seeking a livelihood in other places.

During this discourse my master was pleased to interrupt me several times. I had made use of roundabout language in describing to him the nature of the several crimes for which most of our crew had been forced to fly their country. This labor took up several days' conversation before he was able to comprehend me. He was wholly at a loss to know what could be the use or necessity of practicing those vices. I endeavored to give some ideas of the desire of power and riches, of the terrible effects of intemperance, malice, and envy. All this I was forced to define and describe by the putting of cases. After which, like one whose imagination was struck with something never seen or heard of before, he would lift up his eyes with amazement and indignation. Power, government, war, law, punishment, and a thousand other things had no terms wherein his language could express them, which made it difficult to give my master any conception of what I meant.

CHAPTER 21

Gulliver Discusses England and Makes Observations on the Houyhnhnms

─────────

THE FOLLOWING extract of many conversations I had with my master contains the most material points which were discoursed at several times for above two years; his Honor often desiring fuller satisfaction as I further improved in the Houyhnhnm tongue. I laid before him, as well as I could, the whole state of Europe; I discoursed of trade and manufactures, of arts and sciences; and the answers I gave to all the questions he made, as they arose upon several subjects, were a fund of conversation not to be exhausted.

I told him about the revolution under the Prince of Orange and about the long war with France wherein the greatest powers of Christendom were engaged. I computed that about a million Yahoos might have been killed in the whole progress of it, and perhaps a hundred or more cities taken, and thrice as many ships burnt or sunk.

He asked me what were the usual causes or motives that made one country go to war with another. I answered they were innumerable, but I should only mention a few of the chief. Sometimes the ambition of princes, who never think they have land or people enough to govern; sometimes the corruption of ministers, who engage their master in a war in order to stifle or divert the clamor of the subjects against their evil administration. Difference in opinions has cost many millions of lives.

Sometimes the quarrel between two princes is to decide which of them shall dispossess a third of his dominions, where neither of them pretends to any right. Sometimes one prince quarrels with another, for fear the other should quarrel with him. Sometimes a war is entered upon because the enemy is too strong, and sometimes because he is too weak. Sometimes our neighbors want the things which we have, or have the things which we want; and we both fight, till they take ours or give us theirs.

"What you have told me," said my master, "upon the subject of war does indeed show most admirably the effects of that reason you pretend to. However, it is happy that the shame is greater than the danger; and that nature has left you utterly uncapable of doing much mischief.

"For your mouths lying flat with your faces, you can hardly bite each other to any purpose, unless by consent. Then as to the claws upon your feet before and behind, they are so short and tender that one of our Yahoos would drive a dozen of yours before him.

And therefore in recounting the numbers of those who have been killed in battle, I cannot but think that you have *said the thing which is not*."

I could not forbear shaking my head and smiling a little at his ignorance. And being no stranger to the art of war, I gave him a description of cannons, muskets, pistols, bullets, powder, swords, bayonets, battles, sieges, retreats, attacks, undermines, countermines, bombardments, sea fights; ships sunk with a thousand men, twenty thousand killed on each side; dying groans, trampling to death under horses' feet; flight, pursuit, victory; plundering, stripping, burning, and destroying. And to set forth the valor of my own dear countrymen, I assured him that I had seen them blow up a hundred enemies at once in a siege, and as many in a ship.

I was going on to more particulars, when my master commanded me silence. He said whoever understood the nature of Yahoos might easily believe it possible for so vile an animal to be capable of every action I had named, if their strength and cunning equaled their malice.

He added that he had heard too much upon the subject of war, both in this and some former discourses. There was another point which a little perplexed him at present. I had informed him that some of our crew left their country on account of being ruined by law; that I had already explained the meaning of the word; but he was at a loss how it should come to pass that the law, which was intended for every man's preservation, should be any man's ruin.

I said there was a society of men among us, bred up from their youth in the art of proving that white is black, and black is white, according as they are paid. To this society all the rest of the people are slaves. "For example, if my neighbor has a mind to my cow, he hires a lawyer to prove that he ought to have my cow from me. I must then hire another to defend my right, it being against all rules of law that any man should be allowed to speak for himself.

"In pleading they studiously avoid entering into the merits of the cause, but are loud, violent, and tedious in dwelling upon all circumstances which are not to the purpose. For instance, in the case already mentioned, they never desire to know what claim or title my adversary has to my cow; but whether the said cow were red or black, her horns long or short, whether the field I graze her in be round or square, whether she was milked at home or abroad, what diseases she is subject to, and the like. After this they adjourn the cause from time to time, and perhaps in ten, twenty, or thirty years come to an issue."

My master was yet wholly at a loss to understand what motives could incite this race of lawyers to perplex and weary themselves, and engage in a confederacy of injustice, merely for the sake of injuring their fellow animals; neither could he comprehend what I meant in saying they did it for hire. Whereupon I was at much pains to describe to him the use of money, the materials it was made of, and the value of the metals; that when a Yahoo had got a great store of this precious substance, he was able to purchase whatever he had a mind to: the finest clothing, the noblest houses, great tracts of land, the most costly meats and drinks. Therefore since money alone was able to perform all these feats, our Yahoos thought they could never have enough of it to spend or save. The rich man enjoyed the fruit of the poor man's labor, and the latter were a thousand to one in proportion to the former. That the bulk of our people were forced to live miserably, by laboring every day for small wages to make a few live plentifully.

His Honor was still perplexed, for he believed that all animals had a title to their share in the productions of the earth, and especially those who presided over the rest. Therefore he desired to know what these costly meats were, and how any of us happened to want them. Whereupon I enumerated as many sorts as came into my head, with the various methods of dressing them, which could not be done without sending vessels by sea to every part of the world, as well for liquors to drink as for sauces and innumerable other conveniences.

I assured him that this whole globe of earth must be at least three times gone round before one of our better female Yahoos could get her breakfast or a cup to put it in. He said that must needs be a miserable country which cannot furnish food for its own inhabitants. But what he chiefly wondered at was how such vast tracts of ground as I described should be wholly without fresh water, and the people put to the necessity of sending over the sea for drink.

I replied that England (the dear place of my nativity) was computed to produce three times the quantity of food that its inhabitants are able to consume, as well as liquors extracted from grain or pressed out of the fruit of certain trees, which made excellent drink, and the same proportion in every other convenience of life. But, in order to feed the luxury and intemperance of the males, and the vanity of the females, we sent away the greatest part of our necessary things to other countries, from whence in return we brought the materials of diseases, folly, and vice, to spend among ourselves.

I explained that wine was not imported among us from foreign countries, to supply the want of water or other drinks, but because it was a sort of liquid which made us merry by putting us out of our senses, diverted all melancholy thoughts, raised our hopes, and banished our fears, suspended every office of reason for a time, and deprived us of the use of our limbs, till we fell into a profound sleep; although it must be confessed, that we always awoke sick and dispirited and that the use of this liquor filled us with diseases, which made our lives uncomfortable and short.

But besides all this, the bulk of our people supported themselves by furnishing the necessities or conveniences of life to the rich, and to each other. "For instance," I said, "when I am at home and dressed as I ought to be, I carry on my body the workmanship of a hundred tradesmen. The building and furniture of my house employ as many more, and five times the number to adorn my wife."

I was going on to tell him of another sort of people, who get their livelihood by attending the sick, having upon some occasions informed his Honor that many of my crew had died of diseases. But here it was with the utmost difficulty that I brought him to apprehend what I meant. He could easily conceive that a Houyhnhnm grew weak and heavy a few days before his death, or by some accident might hurt a limb. But that nature, who works all things to perfection, should suffer any pains to breed in our bodies, he thought impossible, and desired to know the reason of so unaccountable an evil. I told him we fed on a thousand things which operated contrary to each other; that we ate when we were not hungry, and drank without the provocation of thirst; that we sat whole nights drinking strong liquors without eating a bit, which disposed us to sloth, inflamed our bodies, and precipitated or prevented digestion. To remedy which there was a sort of people bred up among us, in the profession or pretense of curing the sick.

I must freely confess that the many virtues of those excellent quadrupeds placed in opposite view to human corruptions had so far opened my eyes and enlarged my understanding that I began to view the actions and passions of man in a very different light, and to think the honor of my own kind not worth managing. Besides, it was impossible for me to do so before a person of so acute a judgment as my master, who daily convinced me of a thousand faults in myself, whereof I had not the least perception before, and which among us would never be numbered even among human infirmities. I had likewise learned from his example an utter detestation of all falsehood or disguise, and truth appeared so amiable to me, that I determined upon sacrificing everything to it.

I had not been a year in this country before I contracted such a love and veneration for the inhabitants that I entered on a firm resolution never to return to human kind, but to pass the rest of my life among these admirable Houyhnhnms in the contemplation and practice of every virtue; where I could have no example or incitement to vice. But it was decreed by fortune, my perpetual enemy, that so great a felicity should not fall to my share.

My master made many comparisons between me and the Yahoos, often to my disadvantage. And our reasons for waging war seemed no more valid to him than the causes of quarrels among the Yahoos: they fought over food and shining stones found in the fields, which they hoarded as Europeans hoarded wealth.

As I ought to have understood human nature much better than I supposed it possible for my master to do, so it was easy to apply the character he gave of the Yahoos to myself and my countrymen. And I believed I could yet make further discoveries from my own observation. I therefore often begged him to let me go among the herds of Yahoos in the neighborhood, to which he always very graciously consented. He ordered one of his servants, a strong sorrel nag, very honest and good-natured, to be my guard, without whose protection I dare not undertake such adventures.

By what I could discover, the Yahoos appear to be the most unteachable of all animals, their capacities never reaching higher than to draw or carry burdens. Yet I am of opinion this defect arises chiefly from a perverse disposition. For they are cunning, malicious, treacherous, and revengeful. They are strong and hardy, but of a cowardly spirit, and by consequence, insolent, abject, and cruel. It is observed that the red-haired of both sexes much exceed the rest in strength and activity.

The Houyhnhnms keep the Yahoos for present use in huts not far from the house. But the rest are sent abroad to certain fields, where they dig up roots, eat several kinds of herbs, and sometimes catch weasels and wild rats which they greedily devour. Nature has taught them to dig deep holes with their nails on the side of a rising ground, wherein they lie by themselves. The kennels of the females are larger, sufficient to hold two or three cubs. They swim from their infancy like frogs, and are able to continue long underwater, where they often take fish, which the females carry home to their young.

Having lived three years in this country, the reader I suppose will expect that I should, like other travelers, give him some account of the manners and customs of its inhabitants, which it was indeed my principal study to learn.

Friendship and benevolence are the two principal virtues among the Houyhnhnms, and these not confined to particular objects, but universal to the whole race. For a stranger from the remotest part is equally treated with the nearest neighbor, and wherever he goes looks upon himself as at home. They preserve decency and civility in the highest degrees, but are altogether ignorant of ceremony. They have no fondness for their colts or foals, but the care they take in educating them proceeds entirely from the dictates of reason. And I observed my master to show the same affection to his neighbor's issue that he had for his own. They will have it that nature teaches them to love the whole species, and it is reason only that makes a distinction of persons, where there is a superior degree of virtue.

In educating the youth of both sexes, their method is admirable, and highly deserves our imitation. These are not suffered to taste a grain of oats, except upon certain days, till eighteen years old; nor milk, but very rarely; and in summer they graze two hours in the morning, and as long in the evening. But the servants are not allowed above half that time, and a great part of their grass is brought home, which they eat at the most convenient hours, when they can be best spared from work.

Temperance, industry, exercise, and cleanliness are the lessons equally enjoined to the young ones of both sexes. My master thought it monstrous in us to give the females a different kind of education from the males, except in some articles of domestic management.

The Houyhnhnms train up their youth to strength, speed, and hardiness, by exercising them in running races up and down steep hills, and over hard stony grounds. When they are all in a sweat, they are ordered to leap over head and ears into a pond or river. Four times a year the youth of a certain district meet to show their proficiency in running and leaping, and other feats of strength and agility; where the victor is rewarded with a song made in his or her praise.

Every fourth year, in the spring, there is a representative council of the whole nation, which meets in a plain about twenty miles from our house, and continues about five or six days. Here they inquire into the state and condition of the several districts; whether they abound or be deficient in hay or oats, or cows or Yahoos. And wherever there is any want (which is seldom) it is immediately supplied by unanimous consent and contribution.

The Houyhnhnms have no letters, and consequently

their knowledge is all traditional. But there being few events of any moment among a people so well united, naturally disposed to every virtue, wholly governed by reason, and cut off from all commerce with other nations, the historical part is easily preserved without burdening their memories. I have already observed that they are subject to no diseases, and therefore can have no need of physicians. However, they have excellent medicines composed of herbs, to cure accidental bruises and cuts.

They calculate the year by the revolution of the sun and the moon, but use no subdivisions into weeks. They are well enough acquainted with the motions of those two heavenly bodies, and understand the nature of eclipses; and this is the utmost progress of their astronomy.

In poetry they must be allowed to excel all other mortals. Their verses usually contain either some exalted notions of friendship and benevolence or the praises of those who were victors in races and other bodily exercises.

Their buildings, although very rude and simple, are not inconvenient, but well contrived to defend them from all injuries of cold and heat. They have a kind of tree, which at forty years old loosens in the root, and falls with the first storm. These trees grow very straight, and being pointed like stakes with a sharp stone (for the Houyhnhnms know not the use of iron), they stick them erect in the ground about ten inches apart, and then weave in oat straw, or sometimes wattles betwixt them. The roof is made after the same manner, and so are the doors.

The Houyhnhnms use the hollow part between the

pastern and the hoof of their forefeet as we do our hands, and this with greater dexterity than I could at first imagine. I have seen a white mare of our family thread a needle (which I lent her on purpose) with that joint. They milk their cows, reap their oats, and do all the work which requires hands, in the same manner. They have a kind of hard flints, which by grinding against other stones they form into instruments, that serve instead of wedges, axes, and hammers. With tools made of these flints they likewise cut their hay and reap their oats. The Yahoos draw home the sheaves in carriages, and the servants tread them in certain covered huts, to get out the grain, which is kept in stores. They make a rude kind of earthen and wooden vessels, and bake the former in the sun.

If they can avoid casualties, they die only of old age, and are buried in the most obscure places that can be found, their friends and relations expressing neither joy nor grief at their departure. Nor does the dying person discover the least regret that he is leaving the world, any more than if he were upon returning home from a visit to one of his neighbors. I remember my master having once made an appointment with a friend and his family to come to his house upon some affair of importance. On the day fixed the mistress and her two children came very late. She made two excuses, first for her husband, who, as she said, happened that very morning to *shnuwnh*. The word is strongly expressive in their language, but not easily rendered into English; it signifies "to retire to his first mother." Her excuse for not coming sooner was that, her husband dying late in the morning, she was a good while consulting her servants about a convenient place where his body should be laid. I observed she behaved herself at our house as cheerfully as the rest, and died about three months after.

They live generally to seventy or seventy-five years, very seldom to fourscore. Some weeks before their death they feel a gradual decay, but without pain. During this time they are much visited by their friends, because they cannot go abroad with their usual ease and satisfaction. However, about ten days before their death, which they seldom fail in computing, they return the visits that have been made them by those who are nearest in the neighborhood, being carried in a convenient sledge drawn by Yahoos. This vehicle they use, not only upon this occasion, but when they grow old, upon long journeys, or when they are lamed by any accident. And therefore when the dying Houyhnhnms return those visits, they take a solemn leave of their friends, as if they were going to some remote part of the country, where they designed to pass the rest of their lives.

I could with great pleasure enlarge further upon the manners and virtues of this excellent people, but must close upon that subject and proceed to relate my own sad catastrophe.

CHAPTER 22

Gulliver Is Forced
to Return Home

I HAD SETTLED my little economy to my own heart's
content. My master had ordered a room to be
made for me after their manner, about six yards from
the house; the sides and floors of which I plastered
with clay, and covered with rush-mats of my own
contriving. I had beaten hemp, which there grows
wild, and made of it a sort of ticking. This I filled
with the feathers of several birds I had taken with
snares, and were excellent food. I had fashioned two
chairs with my knife, the sorrel nag helping me in the
more laborious part.

When my clothes were worn to rags, I made myself
others with the skins of rabbits and of a certain beautiful animal about the same size, the skin of which is
covered with a fine down. Of these I likewise made
very tolerable stockings. I soled my shoes with wood
which I cut from a tree and fitted to the upper leather;
when this was worn out, I supplied it with skins dried
in the sun. I often got honey out of hollow trees,

which I mingled with water, or ate with my bread. No man could more verify the truth of these two maxims: "Nature is very easily satisfied" and "Necessity is the mother of invention."

I enjoyed perfect health of body and tranquillity of mind. I did not feel the treachery or inconstancy of a friend, nor the injuries of a secret or open enemy.

I had the favor of being admitted to several Houyhnhnms, who came to visit or dine with my master; where his Honor graciously suffered me to wait in the room, and listen to their discourse. Both he and his company would often descend to ask me questions, and receive my answers. I had also sometimes the honor of attending my master in his visits to others. I never presumed to speak, except in answer to a question. No person spoke without being pleased himself, and pleasing his companions; there was no interruption, heat, or difference of sentiments.

I freely confess that all the little knowledge I have of any value was acquired by the lectures I received from my master, and from hearing the discourses of him and his friends. I admired the strength, comeliness, and speed of the inhabitants; and such a constellation of virtues in such amiable persons produced in me the highest veneration.

When I thought of my family, my friends, my countrymen, or human race in general, I considered them as they really were: Yahoos in shape and disposition, perhaps a little more civilized, and qualified with the gift of speech, but making no other use of reason than to improve and multiply their vices. When I happened to behold the reflection of my own form in a lake or fountain, I turned away my face in horror

and detestation of myself and could better endure the
sight of a common Yahoo than of my own person.

By conversing with the Houyhnhnms, and looking
upon them with delight, I fell to imitate their gait and
gesture, which is now grown into a habit, and my
friends often tell me in a blunt way that I trot like a
horse; which, however, I take for a great compliment.
In speaking I am apt to fall into the voice and manner
of the Houyhnhnms, and hear myself ridiculed on that
account without the least mortification.

In the midst of all this happiness, and when I looked
upon myself to be fully settled for life, my master sent
for me one morning a little earlier than his usual hour.
I observed by his countenance that he was in some
perplexity, and at a loss how to begin what he had to
speak. After a short silence he told me he did not
know how I would take what he was going to say: in
the last general assembly, when the affair of the Yahoos was entered upon, the representatives had taken
offense at his keeping a Yahoo (meaning myself) in
his family more like a Houyhnhnm than a brute animal. He was known frequently to converse with me,
as if he could receive some advantage or pleasure in
my company. Such a practice was not agreeable to
reason or nature, nor a thing ever heard of before
among them.

The assembly did therefore exhort him either to
employ me like the rest of my species or command me
to swim back to the place from where I came. The
first of these expedients was utterly rejected by all the
Houyhnhnms who had ever seen me at his house or
their own. For they alleged that because I had some
rudiments of reason, it was to be feared I might be able

to seduce them into the woody and mountainous parts of the country and foment a revolt.

My master added that he was daily pressed by the Houyhnhnms of the neighborhood to have the assembly's edict executed, which he could not put off much longer. He doubted it would be impossible for me to swim to another country, and therefore wished I would contrive some sort of vehicle resembling those I had described to him, that might carry me on the sea; in which work I should have the assistance of his own servants, as well as those of his neighbors. He concluded that for his own part he could have been content to keep me in his service as long as I lived.

I was struck with the utmost grief and despair at my master's discourse, and being unable to support the agonies I was under, I fell into a swoon at his feet. When I came to myself he told me that he concluded I had been dead (for these people are subject to no such weakness). I answered in a faint voice that death would have been too great a happiness; that although I could not blame the assembly's edict, or the urgency of his friends, yet, in my weak and corrupt judgment, I thought it might consist with reason to have been less rigorous.

I could not swim a league, and probably the nearest land to theirs might be distant above a hundred. Many materials necessary for making a small vessel to carry me off were wholly wanting in this country, which, however, I would attempt in obedience and gratitude to his Honor, although I concluded the thing to be impossible, and therefore looked on myself as already devoted to destruction. That the certain prospect of an unnatural death was the least of my evils; for supposing I should escape with life by some strange adventure, how could I think with temper of passing my days among Yahoos?

After presenting him with my humble thanks for the offer of his servants' assistance in making a vessel, and desiring a reasonable time for so difficult a work, I told him I would endeavor to obey him.

My master in a few words made me a very gracious reply, allowed me the space of two months to finish my boat; and ordered the sorrel nag, my fellow servant (for so at this distance I may presume to call him), to follow my instructions, because I told my master that his help would be sufficient, and I knew he had a tenderness for me.

In his company my first business was to go to that part of the coast where my rebellious crew had ordered me to be set on shore. I got upon a height, and looking on every side into the sea, fancied I saw a small island toward the northeast. I took out my pocket glass, and could then clearly distinguish it about five leagues off, as I computed. But it appeared to the sorrel nag to be only a blue cloud; for as he had no conception of any country besides his own, so he could not be as expert in distinguishing remote objects at sea.

After I had discovered this island, I considered no further; but resolved it should, if possible, be the first place of my banishment, leaving the consequence to fortune.

I returned home, and consulting with the sorrel nag, we went into a copse at some distance, where I with my knife, and he with a sharp flint fastened very artificially after their manner to a wooden handle, cut down several oak wattles about the thickness of a walking staff, and some larger pieces.

In six weeks' time, with the help of the sorrel nag, who performed the parts that required most labor, I finished a sort of Indian canoe, but much larger, covering it with skins well stitched together with hempen threads of my own making. My sail was likewise composed of skins; and I likewise provided myself with four paddles. I laid in a stock of boiled flesh, of rabbits and fowls, and took with me two vessels, one filled with milk and the other with water.

I tried my canoe in a large pond near my master's house, and then corrected in it what was amiss; stopping all the chinks with tallow, till I found it stanch and able to bear me and my freight. And when it was as complete as I could possible make it, I had it drawn on a carriage very gently by Yahoos to the seaside, under the conduct of the sorrel nag and another servant.

When all was ready, and the day came for my departure, I took leave of my master and lady and the whole family, my eyes flowing with tears, and my heart quite sunk with grief. But his Honor, out of curiosity, and perhaps (if I may speak it without vanity) partly out of kindness, was determined to see me in my canoe, and got several of his neighboring friends to accompany him.

I was forced to wait above an hour for the tide, and then observing the wind very fortunately bearing toward the island to which I intended to steer my course, I took a second leave of my master; but as I was going to prostrate myself to kiss his hoof, he did me the honor to raise it gently to my mouth.

I paid my respects to the rest of the Houyhnhnms in his Honor's company; then getting into my canoe, I pushed off.

I began this desperate voyage on February 15, 1714–15, at nine o'clock in the morning. The wind was very favorable; however, I made use at first only of my paddles. Then considering that I should soon be weary, and that the wind might chop about, I ventured to set up my little sail. Thus with the help of the tide I went at the rate of a league and a half an hour, as near as I could guess. My master and his friends continued on the shore till I was almost out of sight; and I often heard the sorrel nag (who always loved me) crying out, *Hnuy illa nyha majah Yahoo:* "Take care of thyself, gentle Yahoo."

My design was, if possible, to discover some small island uninhabited, yet sufficient by my labor to furnish me with the necessaries of life, so horrible was the idea I conceived of returning to live in the society and under the government of Yahoos. For in such a solitude as I desired I could at least enjoy my own thoughts, and reflect with delight on the virtues of the Houyhnhnms.

I resolved to steer my course eastward, hoping to reach the southwest coast of New Holland, and perhaps some such island as I desired, lying westward of it. By six in the evening I computed I had gone at least eighteen leagues, when I spied a very small island about half a league off, which I soon reached. It was nothing but a rock, with one creek, naturally arched by the force of tempests. Here I put in my canoe, and climbing up a part of the rock, I could plainly discover land to the east, extending from south to north.

I lay all night in my canoe, and repeating my voyage early in the morning, I arrived in seven hours to the southeast point of New Holland. This confirmed me in the opinion I have long entertained, that the maps and charts place this country at least three degrees more to the east than it really is.

I saw no inhabitants in the place where I landed, and being unarmed, I was afraid of venturing far into the country. I found some shellfish on the shore, and ate them raw, not daring to kindle a fire for fear of being discovered by the natives. I continued three days feeding on oysters and limpets, to save my own provisions; and I fortunately found a brook of excellent water, which gave me great relief.

On the fourth day, venturing out early a little too far, I saw twenty or thirty natives upon a height, not above five hundred yards from me. They were men, women, and children round a fire, as I could discover by the smoke. One of them spied me, and giving notice to the rest, five of them advanced toward me, leaving the women and children at the fire. I made what haste I could to the shore, and getting into my canoe, shoved off. The savages ran after me, and before I could get far enough into the sea, discharged an arrow, which wounded me deeply on the inside of my left knee (I shall carry the mark to my grave). I feared the arrow might be poisoned, and paddling out of the reach of their darts (being a calm day) I made a shift to suck the wound and dress it as well as I could.

I was at a loss what to do, for I durst not return to the same landing place, but stood to the north, and was forced to paddle; for the wind, though very gen-

tle, was against me, blowing northwest. As I was looking about for a secure landing place, I saw a sail to the
north-northeast, which appearing every minute more
visible, I was in some doubt whether I should wait for
them or no. But at last my detestation of the Yahoo
race prevailed, and turning my canoe, I sailed and
paddled together to the south, and got into the same
creek from whence I set out in the morning, choosing
rather to trust myself among these barbarians than
live with European Yahoos. I drew up my canoe as
close as I could to the shore and hid myself behind a
stone by the little brook, which, as I have already said,
was excellent water.

The ship came within half a league of this creek and
sent her longboat with barrels to take in fresh water
(for the place it seems was very well known), but I
did not observe it till the boat was almost on shore, and
it was too late to seek another hiding place. The seamen at their landing observed my canoe and, rum-
maging it all over, easily conjectured that the owner
could not be far off. Four of them well armed
searched every cranny and lurking hole, till at last
they found me flat on my face behind the stone.

They gazed awhile in admiration at my strange uncouth dress, my coat made of skins, my wooden-
soled shoes, and my furred stockings; from whence,
however, they concluded I was not a native of the
place, who all go naked. One of the seamen in Portuguese bid me rise, and asked who I was. I understood
that language very well, and getting upon my feet,
said I was a poor Yahoo, banished from the Houyhnhnms, and desired they would please to let me depart.
They admired to hear me answer them in their own

tongue, and saw by my complexion I must be a European, but were at a loss to know what I meant by Yahoos and Houyhnhnms, and at the same time fell a-laughing at my strange tone in speaking, which resembled the neighing of a horse.

I trembled all the while between fear and hatred. I again desired leave to depart, and was gently moving to my canoe; but they laid hold of me, desiring to know what country I was of, whence I came, with many other questions. I told them I was born in England, from whence I came about five years ago, and then their country and ours were at peace. I therefore hoped they would not treat me as an enemy, since I meant them no harm, but was a poor Yahoo, seeking some place where to pass the remainder of his life.

When they began to talk, I thought I never heard or saw anything so unnatural; for it appeared to me as monstrous as if a dog or a cow should speak in England, or a Yahoo in Houyhnhnm-land. The honest Portuguese were equally amazed at my strange dress, and the odd manner of delivering my words, which however they understood very well. They spoke to me with great humanity, and said they were sure the captain would carry me gratis to Lisbon, from whence I might return to my own country. Two of the seamen would go back to the ship, inform the captain of what they had seen, and receive his order. In the meantime, unless I would give my solemn oath not to fly, they would secure me by force. I thought it best to comply with their proposal. They were very curious to know my story, but I gave them very little satisfaction; and they all conjectured that my misfortunes had impaired my reason.

In two hours the boat, which went laden with barrels of water, returned with the captain's command to fetch me on board. I fell on my knees to preserve my liberty; but all was in vain, and the men having tied me with cords, heaved me into the boat, from whence I was taken into the ship, and from thence into the captain's cabin.

His name was Pedro de Mendez and he was a very courteous and generous person. He entreated me to give some account of myself, and desired to know what I would eat or drink. He said I should be used as well as himself, and spoke so many obliging things that I wondered to find such civilities from a Yahoo. However, I remained silent and sullen. I was ready to faint at the very smell of him and his men. At last I desired something to eat out of my own canoe; but he ordered me a chicken and some wine, and then directed I should be put to bed in a very clean cabin.

After dinner Don Pedro came to me and assured me he only meant to do me all the service he was able, and spoke so very movingly that at last I condescended to treat him like an animal which had some little portion of reason. I gave him a very short relation of my voyage, of the conspiracy against me by my own men, of the country where they set me on shore, and of my three years' residence there—all which he looked upon as if it were a dream or a vision. Whereat I took great offense, for I had quite forgotten the faculty of lying, so peculiar to Yahoos in all countries where they preside, and, consequently, the disposition of suspecting truth in others of their own species. I asked him whether it were the custom in his country to *say the thing that was not*. I assured him I had almost forgotten what he meant by falsehood, and if I had lived a thousand years in Houyhnhnm-land, I should never have heard a lie from the meanest servant.

The captain, a wise man, after many endeavors to catch me tripping in some part of my story, at last began to have a better opinion of my veracity, and the rather because he confessed he met with a Dutch skipper who pretended to have landed with five others of his crew upon a certain island or continent south of New Holland, where they went for fresh water, and observed a horse driving before him several animals exactly resembling those I described under the name of Yahoos. But he added that since I professed so inviolable an attachment to truth, I must give him my word of honor to bear him company in this voyage, without attempting anything against my life, or else he would continue me a prisoner till we arrived at Lisbon. I gave him the promise he required, but at the same time protested that I would suffer the greatest hardships rather than return to live among Yahoos.

Our voyage passed without any considerable accident. In gratitude to the captain I sometimes sat with him at his earnest request, and strove to conceal my antipathy to humankind, although it often broke out, which he suffered to pass without observation. But the greatest part of the day I confined myself to my cabin, to avoid seeing any of the crew.

We arrived at Lisbon, November 5, 1715. At our landing the captain forced me to cover myself with his cloak, to prevent the rabble from crowding about me. I was conveyed to his own house, and at my earnest request he led me up to the highest room backwards. I begged him to conceal from all persons what

I had told him of the Houyhnhnms, because the least hint of such a story would not only draw numbers of people to see me, but probably put me in danger of being imprisoned. The captain persuaded me to accept a suit of clothes newly made. I would not suffer the tailor to take my measure, but, since Don Pedro was almost of my size, they fitted me well enough. He outfitted me with other necessaries all new.

The captain had no wife, nor above three servants, none of which were suffered to attend at meals, and his whole deportment was so obliging, added to very good *human* understanding, that I really began to tolerate his company. He gained so far upon me that I ventured to look out of the back window. By degrees I was brought into another room, from whence I peeped into the street, but drew my head back in a fright. In a week's time he got me down to the door. I found my terror gradually lessened, but my hatred and contempt seemed to increase. I was at last bold enough to walk the street in his company.

In ten days Don Pedro, to whom I had given some account of my domestic affairs, put it upon me as a matter of honor and conscience that I ought to return to my native country and live at home with my wife and children. He told me there was an English ship in the port just ready to sail, and he would furnish me with all things necessary.

I complied at last, finding I could not do better. I left Lisbon the 24th day of November, in an English merchantman, but who was the master I never inquired. Don Pedro accompanied me to the ship, and lent me twenty pounds. During this last voyage I had no commerce with the master or any of his men; but pretending I was sick, kept close in my cabin. On the 5th of December, 1715, we cast anchor in the Downs about nine in the morning, and at three in the afternoon I got safe to my house at Redriff.

My wife and family received me with great surprise and joy, because they had concluded me certainly dead. But I must freely confess the sight of them filled me only with hatred, disgust, and contempt, and the more by reflecting on the near alliance I had to them. For although since my unfortunate exile from the Houyhnhnm country I had compelled myself to tolerate the sight of Yahoos, and to converse with Don Pedro de Mendez, yet my memory and imagination were perpetually filled with the virtues and ideas of those exalted Houyhnhnms.

At the time I am writing it is five years since my last return to England: during the first year I could not endure my wife or children in my presence, much less could I suffer them to eat in the same room. To this hour they dare not presume to touch my bread, or drink out of the same cup, neither was I ever able to let one of them take me by the hand. The first money I laid out was to buy two young stallions, which I keep in a good stable, and next to them the groom is my greatest favorite. My horses understand me tolerably well. I converse with them at least four hours every day. They are strangers to bridle or saddle; they live in great amity with me, and friendship to each other.

Thus, gentle reader, I have given thee a faithful history of my travels for sixteen years and above seven months; wherein I have not been so studious of ornament as truth.

It is easy for us who travel into remote countries, which are seldom visited by Englishmen or other Europeans, to form descriptions of wonderful animals both at sea and land. Whereas a traveler's chief aim should be to make men wiser and better, and to improve their minds by the bad as well as good example of what they deliver concerning foreign places.

Having thus answered the only objection that can ever be raised against me as a traveler, I here take a final leave of all my courteous readers, and return to enjoy my own speculations in my little garden at Redriff; to apply those excellent lessons of virtue which I learned among the Houyhnhnms; to instruct the Yahoos of my own family as far as I shall find them docile animals; to behold my figure often in a glass, and thus if possible habituate myself by time to tolerate the sight of a human creature; to lament the brutality of Houyhnhnms in my own country, but always treat their persons with respect, for the sake of my noble master, his family, his friends, and the whole Houyhnhnm race, whom these of ours have the honor to resemble.

I began last week to permit my wife to sit at dinner with me, at the farthest end of a long table, and to answer (but with the utmost brevity) the few questions I ask her. And although it be hard for a man late in life to remove old habits, I am not altogether out of hopes in some time to suffer a neighbor Yahoo in my company, without the apprehensions I am yet under of his teeth or his claws.

☆ Treasure Island ☆

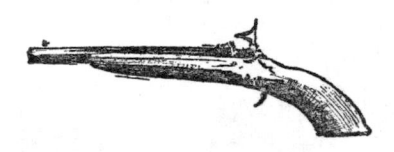

BURIED GOLD, a treasure map, mutiny on the high seas—
these are the elements Robert Louis Stevenson weaves
into a tale which has stirred the blood and imagination of
generations of readers.

From the beginning, when the mysterious old "Captain" roars his pirate songs at the *Admiral Benbow* and
Old Pew, a soft-spoken but horrifying creature, comes
tapping with his stick, young Jim Hawkins knows something odd, dangerous, *secret* is stirring.

Squire Trelawney and Dr. Livesey determine to see the
business to its end, equipping a ship for the voyage and
taking Jim along as cabin boy. But once at sea, Long John
Silver and all Captain Flint's old pirate crew dispute the
rights of honest men—and carve themselves permanent
niches in the hall of infamy!

Treasure Island

By Robert Louis Stevenson

Illustrated by Gerald McCann

COMPANION LIBRARY

Grosset & Dunlap
PUBLISHERS
NEW YORK

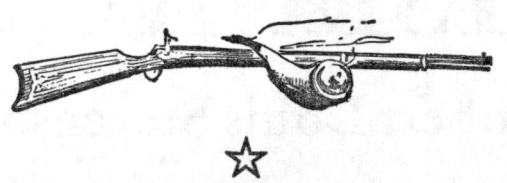

☆

TO S.L.O.

AN AMERICAN GENTLEMAN,
IN ACCORDANCE WITH
WHOSE CLASSIC TASTE
THE FOLLOWING NARRATIVE
HAS BEEN DESIGNED,
IT IS NOW IN RETURN
FOR NUMEROUS
DELIGHTFUL HOURS,
AND WITH THE KINDEST WISHES

DEDICATED

BY HIS AFFECTIONATE FRIEND

THE AUTHOR

Contents

PART IV: THE STOCKADE

PART V: MY SEA ADVENTURE

PART VI: CAPTAIN SILVER

☆ Treasure Island ☆

TO THE HESITATING PURCHASER

IF *sailor tales to sailor tunes,*
Storm and adventure, heat and cold,
If schooners, islands, and maroons,
And Buccaneers and buried Gold,
And all the old romance, retold
Exactly in the ancient way,
Can please, as me they pleased of old,
The wiser youngsters of today:

SO *be it, and fall on! If not,*
If studious youth no longer crave,
His ancient appetites forgot,
Kingston, or Ballantyne the brave,
Or Cooper of the wood and wave:
So be it, also! And may I
And all my pirates share the grave
Where these and their creations lie!

PART I

The Old Buccaneer

☆ I ☆

The Old Sea Dog at the "Admiral Benbow"

SQUIRE TRELAWNEY, Dr. Livesey, and the rest of these gentlemen having asked me to write down the whole particulars about Treasure Island, from the beginning to the end, keeping nothing back but the bearings of the island, and that only because there is still treasure not yet lifted, I take up my pen in the year of grace 17—, and go back to the time when my father kept the "Admiral Benbow" inn, and the brown old seaman with the saber cut first took up his lodging under our roof.

I remember him as if it were yesterday, as he came plodding to the inn door, his sea chest following behind him in a handbarrow; a tall, strong, heavy, nut-brown man; his tarry pigtail falling over the shoulders of his soiled blue coat; his hands ragged and scarred, with black, broken nails; and the saber cut across one cheek, a dirty, livid white. I remember him looking round the cove and whistling to himself as he did so,

and then breaking out in that old sea song that he sang
so often afterward:

> *"Fifteen men on the dead man's chest—*
> *Yo-ho-ho, and a bottle of rum!"*

in the high, old, tottering voice that seemed to have
been tuned and broken at the capstan bars. Then he
rapped on the door with a bit of stick like a handspike
that he carried, and when my father appeared, called
roughly for a glass of rum. This, when it was brought
to him, he drank slowly, like a connoisseur, lingering
on the taste, and still looking about him at the cliffs and
up at our signboard.

"This is a handy cove," says he at length, "and a
pleasant sittyated grogshop. Much company, mate?"

My father told him no, very little company, the
more was the pity.

"Well, then," said he, "this is the berth for me. Here
you, matey," he cried to the man who trundled the
barrow, "bring up alongside and help up my chest. I'll
stay here a bit," he continued. "I'm a plain man; rum
and bacon and eggs is what I want, and that head up
there for to watch ships off. What you mought call
me? You mought call me captain. Oh, I see what
you're at—there," and he threw down three or four
gold pieces on the threshold. "You can tell me when
I've worked through that," says he, looking as fierce as
a commander.

And, indeed, bad as his clothes were and coarsely as
he spoke, he had none of the appearance of a man who
sailed before the mast; but seemed like a mate or
skipper, accustomed to be obeyed or to strike. The
man who came with the barrow told us the mail had
set him down the morning before at the "Royal

George"; that he had inquired what inns there were along the coast, and hearing ours well spoken of, I suppose, and described as lonely, had chosen it from the others for his place of residence. And that was all we could learn of our guest.

He was a very silent man by custom. All day he hung round the cove or upon the cliffs, with a brass telescope; all evening he sat in a corner of the parlor next the fire, and drank rum and water very strong. Mostly he would not speak when spoken to; only look up sudden and fierce, and blow through his nose like a foghorn; and we and the people who came about our house soon learned to let him be. Every day, when he came back from his stroll, he would ask if any seafaring men had gone by along the road. At first we thought it was the want of company of his own kind that made him ask this question, but at last we began to see he was desirous to avoid them. When a seaman put up at the "Admiral Benbow" (as now and then some did, making by the coast road from Bristol), he would look in at him through the curtained door before he entered the parlor; and he was always sure to be as silent as a mouse when any such was present. For me, at least, there was no secret about the matter, for I was, in a way, a sharer in his alarms. He had taken me aside one day and promised me a silver fourpenny on the first of every month if I would only keep my "weather eye open for a seafaring man with one leg," and let him know the moment he appeared. Often enough, when the first of the month came round, and I applied to him for my wage, he would only blow through his nose at me and stare me down; but before the week was out he was sure to think better of it, bring me my fourpenny piece, and repeat his former

orders to look out for "the seafaring man with one leg."

How that personage haunted my dreams I need scarcely tell you. On stormy nights, when the wind shook the four corners of the house and the surf roared along the cove and up the cliffs, I would see him in a thousand forms and with a thousand diabolical expressions. Now the leg would be cut off at the knee, now at the hip; now he was a monstrous kind of creature who had never had but the one leg, and that in the middle of his body. To see him leap and run and pursue me over hedge and ditch was the worst of nightmares. And altogether I paid pretty dear for my monthly fourpenny piece, in the shape of these abominable fancies.

But though I was so terrified by the idea of the seafaring man with one leg, I was far less afraid of the captain himself than anybody else who knew him. There were nights when he took a deal more rum and water than his head would carry; and then he would sometimes sit and sing his wicked, old, wild sea songs, minding nobody; but sometimes he would call for glasses round and force all the trembling company to listen to his stories or bear a chorus to his singing. Often I have heard the house shaking with "Yo-ho-ho, and a bottle of rum," all the neighbors joining in for dear life, with the fear of death upon them, and each singing louder than the other to avoid remark. For in these fits he was the most overriding companion ever known; he would slap his hand on the table for silence all round; he would fly up in a passion of anger at a question, or sometimes because none was put, and so he judged the company was not following his story.

Nor would he allow anyone to leave the inn till he had drunk himself sleepy and reeled off to bed.

His stories were what frightened people worst of all. Dreadful stories they were: about hanging, and walking the plank, and storms at sea, and the Dry Tortugas, and wild deeds and places on the Spanish Main. By his own account he must have lived his life among some of the wickedest men that God ever allowed upon the sea; and the language in which he told these stories shocked our plain country people almost as much as the crimes that he described. My father was always saying the inn would be ruined, for people would soon cease coming there to be tyrannized over and put down, and sent shivering to their beds; but I really believe his presence did us good. People were frightened at the time, but on looking back they rather liked it; it was a fine excitement in a quiet country life; and there was even a party of the younger men who pretended to admire him, calling him a "true sea dog," and a "real old salt," and suchlike names, and saying there was the sort of man that made England terrible at sea.

In one way, indeed, he bade fair to ruin us, for he kept on staying week after week, and at last month after month, so that all the money had been long exhausted, and still my father never plucked up the heart to insist on having more. If ever he mentioned it, the captain blew through his nose so loudly that you might say he roared, and stared my poor father out of the room. I have seen him wringing his hands after such a rebuff, and I am sure the annoyance and the terror he lived in must have greatly hastened his early and unhappy death.

All the time he lived with us the captain made no change whatever in his dress but to buy some stockings from a hawker. One of the cocks of his hat having fallen down, he let it hang from that day forth, though it was a great annoyance when it blew. I remember the appearance of his coat, which he patched himself upstairs in his room, and which, before the end, was nothing but patches. He never wrote or received a letter, and he never spoke with any but the neighbors, and with these, for the most part, only when drunk on rum. The great sea chest none of us had ever seen open.

He was only once crossed, and that was toward the end, when my poor father was far gone in a decline that took him off. Dr. Livesey came late one afternoon to see the patient, took a bit of dinner from my mother, and went into the parlor to smoke a pipe until his horse should come down from the hamlet, for we had no stabling at the old "Benbow." I followed him in, and I remember observing the contrast the neat, bright doctor, with his powder as white as snow, and his bright, black eyes and pleasant manners, made with the coltish countryfolk, and above all, with that filthy, heavy, bleared scarecrow of a pirate of ours, sitting far gone in rum with his arms on the table. Suddenly he—the captain, that is—began to pipe up his eternal song:

> "*Fifteen men on the dead man's chest—*
> *Yo-ho-ho, and a bottle of rum!*
> *Drink and the devil had done for the rest—*
> *Yo-ho-ho, and a bottle of rum!*"

At first I had supposed "the dead man's chest" to be that identical big box of his upstairs in the front room,

and the thought had been mingled in my nightmares with that of the one-legged seafaring man. But by this time we had all long ceased to pay any particular notice to the song; it was new, that night, to nobody but Dr. Livesey, and on him I observed it did not produce an agreeable effect, for he looked up for a moment quite angrily before he went on with his talk to old Taylor, the gardener, on a new cure for the rheumatics. In the meantime, the captain gradually brightened up at his own music and at last flapped his hand upon the table before him in a way we all knew to mean—silence. The voices stopped at once, all but Dr. Livesey's; he went on as before, speaking clear and kind and drawing briskly at his pipe between every word or two. The captain glared at him for a while, flapped his hand again, glared still harder, and at last broke out with a villainous, low oath: "Silence, there, between decks!"

"Were you addressing me, sir?" says the doctor; and when the ruffian had told him, with another oath, that this was so, "I have only one thing to say to you, sir," replies the doctor, "that if you keep on drinking rum, the world will soon be quit of a very dirty scoundrel!"

The old fellow's fury was awful. He sprang to his feet, drew and opened a sailor's clasp knife, and, balancing it open on the palm of his hand, threatened to pin the doctor to the wall.

The doctor never so much as moved. He spoke to him, as before, over his shoulder, and in the same tone of voice; rather high, so that all the room might hear, but perfectly calm and steady:

"If you do not put that knife this instant in your pocket, I promise, upon my honor, you shall hang at the next assizes."

Then followed a battle of looks between them; but the captain soon knuckled under, put up his weapon, and resumed his seat, grumbling like a beaten dog.

"And now, sir," continued the doctor, "since I now know there's such a fellow in my district, you may count I'll have an eye upon you day and night. I'm not a doctor only, I'm a magistrate; and if I catch a breath of complaint against you, if it's only for a piece of incivility like tonight's, I'll take effectual means to have you hunted down and routed out of this. Let that suffice."

Soon after, Dr. Livesey's horse came to the door and he rode away; but the captain held his peace that evening, and for many evenings to come.

☆ II ☆

———————

Black Dog Appears and Disappears

IT WAS not very long after this that there occurred the first of the mysterious events that rid us at last of the captain, though not, as you will see, of his affairs. It was a bitter cold winter, with long, hard frosts and heavy gales; and it was plain from the first that my poor father was little likely to see the spring. He sank daily, and my mother and I had all the inn upon our hands; and were kept busy enough, without paying much regard to our unpleasant guest.

It was one January morning, very early—a pinching, frosty morning—the cove all gray with hoarfrost, the ripple lapping softly on the stones, the sun still low and only touching the hilltops and shining far to seaward. The captain had risen earlier than usual, and set out down the beach, his cutlass swinging under the broad skirts of the old blue coat, his brass telescope under his arm, his hat tilted back upon his head. I remember his breath hanging like smoke in his wake as he strode off, and the last sound I heard of him, as he

turned the big rock, was a loud snort of indignation, as though his mind was still running upon Dr. Livesey.

Well, mother was upstairs with father; and I was laying the breakfast table against the captain's return, when the parlor door opened and a man stepped in on whom I had never set my eyes before. He was a pale, tallowy creature, wanting two fingers of the left hand; and, though he wore a cutlass, he did not look much like a fighter. I had always my eye open for sea-faring men, with one leg or two, and I remember this one puzzled me. He was not sailorly, and yet he had a smack of the sea about him too.

I asked him what was for his service, and he said he would take rum; but as I was going out of the room to fetch it, he sat down upon a table and motioned me to draw near. I paused where I was with my napkin in my hand.

"Come here, sonny," says he. "Come nearer here."

I took a step nearer.

"Is this here table for my mate Bill?" he asked, with a kind of leer.

I told him I did not know his mate Bill, and this was for a person who stayed in our house, whom we called the captain.

"Well," said he, "my mate Bill would be called the captain, as like as not. He has a cut on one cheek, and a mighty pleasant way with him, particularly in drink, has my mate Bill. We'll put it, for argument like, that your captain has a cut on one cheek—and we'll put it, if you like, that that cheek's the right one. Ah, well! I told you. Now, is my mate Bill in this here house?"

I told him he was out walking.

"Which way, sonny? Which way is he gone?"

And when I had pointed out the rock and told him

how the captain was likely to return, and how soon, and answered a few other questions, "Ah," said he, "this'll be as good as drink to my mate Bill."

The expression of his face as he said these words was not at all pleasant, and I had my own reasons for thinking that the stranger was mistaken, even supposing he meant what he said. But it was no affair of mine, I thought; and, besides, it was difficult to know what to do. The stranger kept hanging about just inside the inn door, peering round the corner like a cat waiting for a mouse. Once I stepped out myself into the road, but he immediately called me back, and, as I did not obey quick enough for his fancy, a most horrible change came over his tallowy face, and he ordered me in, with an oath that made me jump. As soon as I was back again he returned to his former manner, half fawning, half sneering, patted me on the shoulder, told me I was a good boy, and he had taken quite a fancy to me. "I have a son of my own," said he, "as like you as two blocks, and he's all the pride of my 'art. But the great thing for boys is discipline, sonny—discipline. Now, if you had sailed along of Bill, you wouldn't have stood there to be spoke to twice—not you. That was never Bill's way, nor the way of sich as sailed with him. And here, sure enough, is my mate Bill, with a spyglass under his arm, bless his old 'art, to be sure. You and me'll just go back into the parlor, sonny, and get behind the door, and we'll give Bill a little surprise —bless his 'art, I say again."

So saying, the stranger backed along with me into the parlor, and put me behind him in the corner, so that we were both hidden by the open door. I was very uneasy and alarmed, as you may fancy, and it rather added to my fears to observe that the stranger

was certainly frightened himself. He cleared the hilt of his cutlass and loosened the blade in the sheath; and all the time we were waiting there he kept swallowing as if he felt what we used to call a lump in the throat.

At last in strode the captain, slammed the door behind him, without looking to the right or left, and marched straight across the room to where his breakfast awaited him.

"Bill," said the stranger, in a voice that I thought he had tried to make bold and big.

The captain spun round on his heel and fronted us; all the brown had gone out of his face, and even his nose was blue; he had the look of a man who sees a ghost, or the evil one, or something worse, if anything can be; and, upon my word, I felt sorry to see him, all in a moment, turn so old and sick.

"Come, Bill, you know me; you know an old shipmate, Bill, surely," said the stranger.

The captain made a sort of gasp.

"Black Dog!" said he.

"And who else?" returned the other, getting more at his ease. "Black Dog as ever was, come for to see his old shipmate Billy, at the 'Admiral Benbow' inn. Ah, Bill, Bill, we have seen a sight of times, us two, since I lost them two talons," holding up his mutilated hand.

"Now, look here," said the captain, "you've run me down; here I am; well, then, speak up: what is it?"

"That's you, Bill," returned Black Dog, "you're in the right of it, Billy. I'll have a glass of rum from this dear child here, as I've took such a liking to, and we'll sit down, if you please, and talk square, like old shipmates."

When I returned with the rum they were already seated on either side of the captain's breakfast table—

Black Dog next to the door, and sitting sideways, so as to have one eye on his old shipmate and one, as I thought, on his retreat.

He bade me go, and leave the door wide open. "None of your keyholes for me, sonny," he said; and I left them together, and retired into the bar.

For a long time, though I certainly did my best to listen, I could hear nothing but a low gabbling; but at last the voices began to grow higher, and I could pick up a word or two, mostly oaths, from the captain.

"No, no, no, no; and an end of it!" he cried once. And again ,"If it comes to swinging, swing all, say I."

Then all of a sudden there was a tremendous explosion of oaths and other noises—the chair and table went over in a lump, a clash of steel followed, and then a cry of pain, and the next instant I saw Black Dog in full flight, and the captain hotly pursuing, both with drawn cutlasses, and the former streaming blood from the left shoulder. Just at the door, the captain aimed at the fugitive one last tremendous cut, which would certainly have split him to the chin had it not been intercepted by our big signboard of Admiral Benbow. You may see the notch on the lower side of the frame to this day.

That blow was the last of the battle. Once out upon the road, Black Dog, in spite of his wound, showed a wonderful clean pair of heels, and disappeared over the edge of the hill in half a minute. The captain, for his part, stood staring at the signboard like a bewildered man. Then he passed his hand over his eyes several times, and at last turned back into the house.

"Jim," says he, "rum"; and as he spoke, he reeled a little, and caught himself with one hand against the wall.

The chair and table went over, a clash of steel followed

"Are you hurt?" cried I.

"Rum," he repeated. "I must get away from here. Rum! rum!"

I ran to fetch it; but I was quite unsteadied by all that had fallen out, and I broke one glass and fouled the tap, and while I was still getting in my own way I heard a loud fall in the parlor and, running in, beheld the captain lying full length upon the floor. At the same instant my mother, alarmed by the cries and fighting, came running downstairs to help me. Between us we raised his head. He was breathing very loud, and hard; but his eyes were closed, and his face a horrible color.

"Dear, deary me," cried my mother, "what a disgrace upon the house! And your poor father sick!"

In the meantime, we had no idea what to do to help the captain, nor any other thought but that he had got his death-hurt in the scuffle with the stranger. I got the rum, to be sure, and tried to put it down his throat, but his teeth were tightly shut and his jaws as strong as iron. It was a happy relief for us when the door opened and Dr. Livesey came in, on his visit to my father.

"Oh, doctor," we cried, "what shall we do? Where is he wounded?"

"Wounded? A fiddlestick's end!" said the doctor. "No more wounded than you or I. The man has had a stroke, as I warned him. Now, Mrs. Hawkins, just you run upstairs to your husband, and tell him, if possible, nothing about it. For my part, I must do my best to save this fellow's trebly worthless life; and, Jim, you get me a basin."

When I got back with the basin, the doctor had already ripped up the captain's sleeve, and exposed his

great sinewy arm. It was tattooed in several places. "Here's luck," "A fair wind," and "Billy Bones his fancy" were very neatly and clearly executed on the forearm; and up near the shoulder there was a sketch of a gallows and a man hanging from it—done, as I thought, with great spirit.

"Prophetic," said the doctor, touching this picture with his finger. "And now, Master Billy Bones, if that be your name, we'll have a look at the color of your blood. Jim," he said, "are you afraid of blood?"

"No, sir," said I.

"Well, then," said he, "you hold the basin," and with that he took his lancet from his case and opened a vein.

A great deal of blood was taken before the captain opened his eyes and looked mistily about him. First he recognized the doctor, with an unmistakable frown; then his glance fell upon me, and he looked relieved. But suddenly his color changed, and he tried to raise himself, crying:

"Where's Black Dog?"

"There is no Black Dog here," said the doctor, "except what you have on your own back. You have been drinking rum; you have had a stroke, precisely as I told you; and I have just, very much against my own will, dragged you head foremost out of the grave. Now, Mr. Bones—"

"That's not my name," he interrupted.

"Much I care," returned the doctor. "It's the name of a buccaneer of my acquaintance, and I call you by it for the sake of shortness; and what I have to say to you is this: one glass of rum won't kill you, but if you take one you'll take another and another, and I stake my wig if you don't break off short you'll die—do you understand that?—die, and go to your own place, like

the man in the Bible. Come, now, make an effort. I'll help you to your bed for once."

Between us, with much trouble, we managed to hoist him upstairs, and laid him on his bed, where his head fell back on the pillow as if he were almost fainting.

"Now, mind you," said the doctor, "I clear my conscience—the name of rum for you is death."

And with that he went off to see my father, taking me with him by the arm.

"This is nothing," he said, as soon as he had closed the door. "I have drawn blood enough to keep him quiet awhile; he should lie for a week where he is—that is the best thing for him and you; but another stroke would settle him."

☆ III ☆

The Black Spot

ABOUT NOON I stopped at the captain's door with some cooling drinks and medicines. He was lying very much as we had left him, only a little higher, and he seemed both weak and excited.

"Jim," he said, "you're the only one here that's worth anything; and you know I've been always good to you. Never a month but I've given you a silver fourpenny for yourself. And now you see, mate, I'm pretty low, and deserted by all; and, Jim, you'll bring me one noggin of rum, now, won't you, matey?"

"The doctor—" I began.

But he broke in cursing the doctor, in a feeble voice but heartily. "Doctors is all swabs," he said; "and that doctor there, why, what do he know about seafaring men? I been in places hot as pitch, and mates dropping round with yellow jack, and the blessed land a-heaving like the sea with earthquakes—what do the doctor know of lands like that?—and I lived on rum, I tell you. It's been meat and drink, and man and wife, to me; and if I'm not to have my rum now I'm a poor

old hulk on a lee shore, my blood'll be on you, Jim, and that doctor swab," and he ran on again for a while with curses. "Look, Jim, how my fingers fidges," he continued in the pleading tone. "I can't keep 'em still, not I. I haven't had a drop this blessed day. That doctor's a fool, I tell you. If I don't have a drain o' rum, Jim, I'll have the horrors; I seen some on 'em already. I seen old Flint in the corner there, behind you; as plain as print, I seen him; and if I get the horrors, I'm a man that has lived rough, and I'll raise Cain. Your doctor hisself said one glass wouldn't hurt me. I'll give you a golden guinea for a noggin, Jim."

He was growing more and more excited, and this alarmed me for my father, who was very low that day and needed quiet; besides, I was reassured by the doctor's words, now quoted to me, and rather offended by the offer of a bribe.

"I want none of your money," said I, "but what you owe my father. I'll get you one glass, and no more."

When I brought it to him he seized it greedily, and drank it out. "Aye, aye," said he, "that's some better, sure enough. And now, matey, did that doctor say how long I was to lie here in this berth?"

"A week at least," said I.

"Thunder!" he cried. "A week! I can't do that; they'd have the black spot on me by then. The lubbers is going about to get the wind of me this blessed moment; lubbers as couldn't keep what they got, and want to nail what is another's. Is that seamanly behavior, now, I want to know? But I'm a saving soul. I never wasted good money of mine, nor lost it neither; and I'll trick 'em again. I'm not afraid on 'em. I'll shake out another reef, matey, and daddle 'em again."

As he was thus speaking he had risen from bed with

great difficulty, holding to my shoulder with a grip that almost made me cry out, and moving his legs like so much dead weight. His words, spirited as they were in meaning, contrasted sadly with the weakness of the voice in which they were uttered. He paused when he had got into a sitting position on the edge.

"That doctor's done me," he murmured. "My ears is singing. Lay me back."

Before I could do much to help him he had fallen back again to his former place, where he lay for a while silent. "Jim," he said, at length, "you saw that seafaring man today!"

"Black Dog?" I asked.

"Ah! Black Dog," says he. "*He's* a bad 'un; but there's worse that put him on. Now, if I can't get away nohow, and they tip me the black spot, mind you, it's my old sea chest they're after; you get on a horse—you can, can't you? Well, then, you get on a horse, and go to—well, yes, I will!—to that eternal doctor swab, and tell him to pipe all hands—magistrates and sich—and he'll lay 'em aboard at the 'Admiral Benbow'—all old Flint's crew, man and boy, all on 'em that's left. I was first mate, I was, old Flint's first mate, and I'm the on'y one as knows the place. He gave it me at Savannah, when he lay a-dying, like as if I was to now, you see. But you won't peach unless they get the black spot on me, or unless you see that Black Dog again, or a seafaring man with one leg, Jim—him above all."

"But what is the black spot, captain?" I asked.

"That's a summons, mate. I'll tell you if they get that. But you keep your weather eye open, Jim, and I'll share with you equals, upon my honor."

He wandered a little longer, his voice growing

weaker; but soon after I had given him his medicine, which he took like a child, with the remark, "If ever a seaman wanted drugs, it's me," he fell at last into a heavy, swoonlike sleep, in which I left him. What I should have done had all gone well I do not know. Probably I should have told the whole story to the doctor; for I was in mortal fear lest the captain should repent of his confessions and make an end of me. But as things fell out, my poor father died quite suddenly that evening, which put all other matters on one side. Our natural distress, the visits of the neighbors, the arranging of the funeral, and all the work of the inn to be carried on in the meanwhile, kept me so busy that I had scarcely time to think of the captain, far less to be afraid of him.

He got downstairs next morning, to be sure, and had his meals as usual, though he ate little, and had more, I am afraid, than his usual supply of rum, for he helped himself out of the bar, scowling and blowing through his nose, and no one dared to cross him. On the night before the funeral he was as drunk as ever; and it was shocking, in that house of mourning, to hear him singing away at his ugly old sea song; but, weak as he was, we were all in the fear of death for him, and the doctor was suddenly taken up with a case many miles away and was never near the house after my father's death. I have said the captain was weak; and indeed he seemed rather to grow weaker than regain his strength. He clambered up and down stairs, and went from the parlor to the bar and back again, and sometimes put his nose out of doors to smell the sea, holding onto the walls as he went for support, and breathing hard and fast like a man on a steep mountain. He never particularly addressed me, and it is my belief he

had as good as forgotten his confidences; but his temper was more flighty and, allowing for his bodily weakness, more violent than ever. He had an alarming way now, when he was drunk, of drawing his cutlass and laying it bare before him on the table. But, with all that, he minded people less, and seemed shut up in his own thoughts and rather wandering. Once, for instance, to our extreme wonder, he piped up to a different air, a kind of country love song, that he must have learned in his youth before he had begun to follow the sea.

So things passed until, the day after the funeral, and about three o'clock of a bitter, foggy, frosty afternoon, I was standing at the door for a moment, full of sad thoughts about my father, when I saw someone drawing slowly near along the road. He was plainly blind, for he tapped before him with a stick, and wore a great green shade over his eyes and nose; and he was hunched, as if with age or weakness, and wore a huge old tattered sea cloak with a hood, that made him appear positively deformed. I never saw in my life a more dreadful-looking figure. He stopped a little distance from the inn, and, raising his voice in an odd singsong, addressed the air in front of him:

"Will any kind friend inform a poor blind man, who has lost the precious sight of his eyes in the gracious defense of his native country, England, and God bless King George!—where or in what part of this country he may now be?"

"You are at the 'Admiral Benbow,' Black Hill Cove, my good man," said I.

"I hear a voice," said he, "a young voice. Will you give me your hand, my kind, young friend, and lead me in?"

I held out my hand, and the horrible, soft-spoken, eyeless creature gripped it in a moment like a vise. I was so much startled that I struggled to withdraw; but the blind man pulled me close up to him with a single action of his arm.

"Now, boy," he said, "take me in to the captain."

"Sir," said I, "upon my word I dare not."

"Oh," he sneered, "that's it! Take me in straight, or I'll break your arm."

And he gave it, as he spoke, a wrench that made me cry out.

"Sir," said I, "it is for yourself I mean. The captain is not what he used to be. He sits with a drawn cutlass. Another gentleman—"

"Come, now, march," interrupted he; and I never heard a voice so cruel, and cold, and ugly as that blind man's. It cowed me more than the pain; and I began to obey him at once, walking straight in at the door and toward the parlor, where our sick old buccaneer was sitting, dazed with rum. The blind man clung close to me, holding me in one iron fist, and leaning almost more of his weight on me than I could carry. "Lead me straight up to him, and when I'm in view, cry out, 'Here's a friend for you, Bill.' If you don't, I'll do this"; and with that he gave me a twitch that I thought would have made me faint. Between this and that, I was so utterly terrified of the blind beggar that I forgot my terror of the captain, and as I opened the parlor door, cried out the words he had ordered, in a trembling voice.

The poor captain raised his eyes, and at one look the rum went out of him, and left him staring sober. The expression of his face was not so much of terror as of mortal sickness. He made a movement to rise, but I do

not believe he had enough force left in his body.

"Now, Bill, sit where you are," said the beggar. "If I can't see, I can hear a finger stirring. Business is business. Hold out your left hand. Boy, take his left hand by the wrist, and bring it near to my right."

We both obeyed him to the letter, and I saw him pass something from the hollow of the hand that held his stick into the palm of the captain's, which closed upon it instantly.

"And now that's done," said the blind man; and at the words he suddenly left hold of me, and, with incredible accuracy and nimbleness, skipped out of the parlor and into the road, where, as I still stood motionless, I could hear his stick go tap-tap-tapping into the distance.

It was some time before either I or the captain seemed to gather our senses; but at length, and about at the same moment, I released his wrist, which I was still holding, and he drew in his hand and looked sharply into the palm.

"Ten o'clock!" he cried. "Six hours. We'll do them yet." And he sprang to his feet.

Even as he did so, he reeled, put his hand to his throat, stood swaying for a moment, and then, with a peculiar sound, fell from his whole height face foremost to the floor.

I ran to him at once, calling to my mother. But haste was all in vain. The captain had been struck dead by thundering apoplexy. It is a curious thing to understand, for I had certainly never liked the man, though of late I had begun to pity him, but as soon as I saw that he was dead I burst into a flood of tears. It was the second death I had known, and the sorrow of the first was still fresh in my heart.

☆ IV ☆

The Sea Chest

I LOST no time, of course, in telling my mother all that I knew, and perhaps should have told her long before, and we saw ourselves at once in a difficult and dangerous position. Some of the man's money—if he had any—was certainly due to us; but it was not likely that our captain's shipmates, above all the two specimens seen by me, Black Dog and the blind beggar, would be inclined to give up their booty in payment of the dead man's debts. The captain's order to mount at once and ride for Dr. Livesey would have left my mother alone and unprotected, which was not to be thought of. Indeed, it seemed impossible for either of us to remain much longer in the house: the fall of coals in the kitchen grate, the very ticking of the clock, filled us with alarms. The neighborhood, to our ears, seemed haunted by approaching footsteps; and what between the dead body of the captain on the parlor floor and the thought of that detestable blind beggar hovering near at hand, and ready to return, there were

moments when, as the saying goes, I jumped in my skin for terror. Something must speedily be resolved upon; and it occurred to us at last to go forth together and seek help in the neighboring hamlet. No sooner said than done. Bareheaded as we were, we ran out at once in the gathering evening and the frosty fog.

The hamlet lay not many hundred yards away though out of view, on the other side of the next cove; and what greatly encouraged me, it was in an opposite direction from that whence the blind man had made his appearance, and whither he had presumably returned. We were not many minutes on the road, though we sometimes stopped to lay hold of each other and hearken. But there was no unusual sound— nothing but the low wash of the ripple and the croaking of the inmates of the wood.

It was already candlelight when we reached the hamlet, and I shall never forget how much I was cheered to see the yellow shine in doors and windows; but that, as it proved, was the best of the help we were likely to get in that quarter. For—you would have thought men would have been ashamed of themselves —no soul would consent to return with us to the "Admiral Benbow." The more we told of our troubles, the more—man, woman, and child—they clung to the shelter of their houses. The name of Captain Flint, though it was strange to me, was well enough known to some there and carried a great weight of terror. Some of the men who had been to field work on the far side of the "Admiral Benbow" remembered, besides, to have seen several strangers on the road, and, taking them to be smugglers, to have bolted away; and one at least had seen a little lugger in what we called Kitt's Hole. For that matter, anyone who was a com-

rade of the captain's was enough to frighten them to death. And the short and the long of the matter was that, while we could get several who were willing enough to ride to Dr. Livesey's, which lay in another direction, not one would help us to defend the inn.

They say cowardice is infectious, but then argument is, on the other hand, a great emboldener; and so when each had said his say, my mother made them a speech. She would not, she declared, lose money that belonged to her fatherless boy; "if none of the rest of you dare," she said, "Jim and I dare. Back we will go, the way we came, and small thanks to you big, hulking, chicken-hearted men. We'll have that chest open, if we die for it. And I'll thank you for that bag, Mrs. Crossley, to bring back our lawful money in."

Of course, I said I would go with my mother, and of course they all cried out at our foolhardiness; but even then not a man would go along with us. All they would do was to give me a loaded pistol lest we were attacked, and to promise to have horses ready saddled, in case we were pursued on our return; while one lad was to ride forward to the doctor's in search of armed assistance.

My heart was beating finely when we two set forth in the cold night upon this dangerous venture. A full moon was beginning to rise and peered redly through the upper edges of the fog, and this increased our haste, for it was plain that, before we came forth again, all would be as bright as day, and our departure exposed to the eyes of any watchers. We slipped along the hedges, noiseless and swift, nor did we see or hear anything to increase our terrors, till, to our relief, the door of the "Admiral Benbow" had closed behind us.

I slipped the bolt at once, and we stood and panted

for a moment in the dark, alone in the house with the dead captain's body. Then my mother got a candle in the bar, and, holding each other's hands, we advanced into the parlor. He lay as we had left him, on his back, with his eyes open, and one arm stretched out.

"Draw down the blind, Jim," whispered my mother; "they might come and watch outside. And now," said she, when I had done so, "we have to get the key off *that;* and who's to touch it, I should like to know!" and she gave a kind of sob as she said the words.

I went down on my knees at once. On the floor close to his hand there was a little round of paper, blackened on the one side. I could not doubt that this was the *black spot;* and taking it up, I found written on the other side, in a very good clear hand, this short message: "You have till ten tonight."

"He had till ten, mother," said I; and just as I said it, our old clock began striking. This sudden noise startled us shockingly; but the news was good, for it was only six.

"Now, Jim," she said, "that key."

I felt in his pockets, one after another. A few small coins, a thimble, and some thread and big needles, a piece of pigtail tobacco bitten away at the end, his gully with the cracked handle, a pocket compass, and a tinderbox, were all that they contained, and I began to despair.

"Perhaps it's round his neck," suggested my mother.

Overcoming a strong repugnance, I tore open his shirt at the neck, and there, sure enough, hanging to a bit of tarry string, which I cut with his own gully, we found the key. At this triumph we were filled with hope and hurried upstairs, without delay, to the little

room where he had slept so long and where his box had stood since the day of his arrival.

It was like any other seaman's chest on the outside, the initial "B" burned on the top of it with a hot iron, and the corners somewhat smashed and broken as by long, rough usage.

"Give me the key," said my mother; and though the lock was very stiff, she had turned it and thrown back the lid in a twinkling.

A strong smell of tobacco and tar rose from the interior, but nothing was to be seen on the top except a suit of very good clothes, carelessly brushed and folded. They had never been worn, my mother said. Under that, the miscellany began—a quadrant, a tin cannikin, several sticks of tobacco, two brace of very handsome pistols, a piece of bar silver, an old Spanish watch and some other trinkets of little value and mostly of foreign make, a pair of compasses mounted with brass, and five or six curious West Indian shells. I have often wondered since why he should have carried about these shells with him in his wandering, guilty, and hunted life.

In the meantime, we had found nothing of any value but the silver and the trinkets, and neither of these were in our way. Underneath there was an old boat cloak, whitened with sea salt on many a harbor bar. My mother pulled it up with impatience, and there lay before us, the last things in the chest, a bundle tied up in oilcloth, and looking like papers, and a canvas bag, that gave forth, at a touch, the jingle of gold.

"I'll show these rogues that I'm an honest woman," said my mother. "I'll have my dues, and not a farthing over. Hold Mrs. Crossley's bag." And she began to count over the amount of the captain's score

from the sailor's bag into the one that I was holding.

It was a long, difficult business, for the coins were of all countries and sizes—doubloons, and louis d'ors, and guineas, and pieces of eight, and I know not what besides, all shaken together at random. The guineas, too, were about the scarcest, and it was with these only that my mother knew how to make her count.

When we were about halfway through, I suddenly put my hand upon her arm; for I had heard in the silent, frosty air a sound that brought my heart into my mouth—the tap-tapping of the blind man's stick upon the frozen road. It drew nearer and nearer, while we sat holding our breath. Then it struck sharp on the inn door, and then we could hear the handle being turned, and the bolt rattling as the wretched being tried to enter; and then there was a long time of silence both within and without. At last the tapping recommenced and, to our indescribable joy and gratitude, died slowly away again until it ceased to be heard.

"Mother," said I, "take the whole and let's be going." For I was sure the bolted door must have seemed suspicious and would bring the whole hornet's nest about our ears; though how thankful I was that I had bolted it, none could tell who had never met that terrible blind man.

But my mother, frightened as she was, would not consent to take a fraction more than was due to her, and was obstinately unwilling to be content with less. It was not yet seven, she said, by a long way; she knew her rights and she would have them; and she was still arguing with me when a little low whistle sounded a good way off upon the hill. That was enough, and more than enough, for both of us.

"I'll take what I have," she said, jumping to her feet.

"And I'll take this to square the count," said I, picking up the oilskin packet.

Next moment we were both groping downstairs, leaving the candle by the empty chest; and the next we had opened the door and were in full retreat. We had not started a moment too soon. The fog was rapidly dispersing; already the moon shone quite clear on the high ground on either side; and it was only in the exact bottom of the dell and round the tavern door that a thin veil still hung unbroken to conceal the first steps of our escape. Far less than halfway to the hamlet, very little beyond the bottom of the hill, we must come forth into the moonlight. Nor was this all; for the sound of several footsteps running came already to our ears, and as we looked back in their direction, a light tossing to and fro and still rapidly advancing showed that one of the newcomers carried a lantern.

"My dear," said my mother suddenly, "take the money and run on. I am going to faint."

This was certainly the end for both of us, I thought. How I cursed the cowardice of the neighbors; how I blamed my poor mother for her honesty and her greed, for her past foolhardiness and present weakness! We were just at the little bridge, by good fortune; and I helped her, tottering as she was, to the edge of the bank, where, sure enough, she gave a sigh and fell on my shoulder. I do not know how I found the strength to do it at all, and I am afraid it was roughly done; but I managed to drag her down the bank and a little way under the arch. Farther I could not move her, for the bridge was too low to let me do more than crawl below it. So there we had to stay— my mother almost entirely exposed and both of us within earshot of the inn.

☆ V ☆

The Last of the Blind Man

MY CURIOSITY, in a sense, was stronger than my fear; for I could not remain where I was, but crept back to the bank again, whence, sheltering my head behind a bush of broom, I might command the road before our door. I was scarcely in position ere my enemies began to arrive, seven or eight of them, running hard, their feet beating out of time along the road, and the man with the lantern some paces in front. Three men ran together, hand in hand; and I made out, even through the mist, that the middle man of this trio was the blind beggar. The next moment his voice showed me that I was right.

"Down with the door!" he cried.

"Aye, aye, sir!" answered two or three; and a rush was made upon the "Admiral Benbow," the lantern-bearer following. And then I could see them pause, and hear speeches passed in a lower key, as if they were surprised to find the door open. But the pause

was brief, for the blind man again issued his commands. His voice sounded louder and higher, as if he were afire with eagerness and rage.

"In, in, in!" he shouted, and cursed them for their delay.

Four or five of them obeyed at once, two remaining on the road with the formidable beggar. There was a pause, then a cry of surprise, and then a voice shouting from the house:

"Bill's dead!"

But the blind man swore at them again for their delay.

"Search him, some of you shirking lubbers, and the rest of you aloft and get the chest," he cried.

I could hear their feet rattling up our old stairs, so that the house must have shook with it. Promptly afterwards fresh sounds of astonishment arose; the window of the captain's room was thrown open with a slam and a jingle of broken glass; and a man leaned out into the moonlight, head and shoulders, and addressed the blind beggar on the road below him.

"Pew," he cried, "they've been before us. Someone's turned the chest out alow and aloft."

"Is it there?" roared Pew.

"The money's there."

The blind man cursed the money.

"Flint's fist, I mean," he cried.

"We don't see it here nohow," returned the man.

"Here, you below there, is it on Bill?" cried the blind man again.

At that, another fellow, probably the one who had remained below to search the captain's body, came to the door of the inn. "Bill's been overhauled a'ready," said he, "nothin' left."

"It's these people of the inn—it's that boy. I wish I had put his eyes out!" cried the blind man, Pew. "They were here no time ago—they had the door bolted when I tried it. Scatter, lads, and find 'em."

"Sure enough, they left their glim here," said the fellow from the window.

"Scatter and find 'em! Rout the house out!" reiterated Pew, striking with his stick upon the road.

Then there followed a great to-do through all our old inn, heavy feet pounding to and fro, furniture thrown over, doors kicked in, until the very rocks reechoed, and the men came out again, one after another, on the road, and declared that we were nowhere to be found. And just then the same whistle that had alarmed my mother and myself over the dead captain's money was once more clearly audible through the night, but this time twice repeated. I had thought it to be the blind man's trumpet, so to speak, summoning his crew to the assault; but I now found that it was a signal from the hillside toward the hamlet, and, from its effect upon the buccaneers, a signal to warn them of approaching danger.

"There's Dirk again," said one. "Twice! We'll have to budge, mates."

"Budge, you skulk!" cried Pew. "Dirk was a fool and a coward from the first—you wouldn't mind him. They must be close by; they can't be far; you have your hands on it. Scatter and look for them, dogs! Oh, shiver my soul," he cried, "if I had eyes!"

This appeal seemed to produce some effect, for two of the fellows began to look here and there among the lumber, but halfheartedly, I thought, and with half an eye to their own danger all the time, while the rest stood irresolute on the road.

"You have your hands on thousands, you fools, and you hang a leg! You'd be as rich as kings if you could find it, and you know it's here, and you stand there skulking. There wasn't one of you dared face Bill, and I did it—a blind man! And I'm to lose my chance for you! I'm to be a poor, crawling beggar, sponging for rum, when I might be rolling in a coach! If you had the pluck of a weevil in a biscuit you would catch them still."

"Hang it, Pew, we've got the doubloons!" grumbled one.

"They might have hid the blessed thing," said another. "Take the Georges, Pew, and don't stand here squalling."

Squalling was the word for it, Pew's anger rose so high at these objections; till at last, his passion completely taking the upper hand, he struck at them right and left in his blindness, and his stick sounded heavily on more than one.

These, in their turn, cursed back at the blind miscreant, threatened him in horrid terms, and tried in vain to catch the stick and wrest it from his grasp.

This quarrel was the saving of us, for while it was still raging, another sound came from the top of the hill on the side of the hamlet—the tramp of horses galloping. Almost at the same time a pistol shot, flash and report, came from the hedge side. And that was plainly the last signal of danger, for the buccaneers turned at once and ran, separating in every direction, one seaward along the cove, one slant across the hill, and so on, so that in half a minute not a sign of them remained but Pew. Him they had deserted, whether in sheer panic or out of revenge for his ill words and blows, I know not; but there he remained behind, tap-

ping up and down the road in a frenzy, and groping and calling for his comrades. Finally he took the wrong turn, and ran a few steps past me, toward the hamlet, crying:

"Johnny, Black Dog, Dirk," and other names, "you won't leave old Pew, mates—not old Pew!"

Just then the noise of horses topped the rise and four or five riders came in sight in the moonlight and swept at full gallop down the slope.

At this Pew saw his error, turned with a scream, and ran straight for the ditch, into which he rolled. But he was on his feet again in a second and made another dash, now utterly bewildered, right under the nearest of the coming horses.

The rider tried to save him, but in vain. Down went Pew with a cry that rang high into the night; and the four hoofs trampled and spurned him and passed by. He fell on his side, then gently collapsed upon his face, and moved no more.

I leaped to my feet and hailed the riders. They were pulling up, at any rate, horrified at the accident; and I soon saw what they were. One, tailing out behind the rest, was a lad that had gone from the hamlet to Dr. Livesey's; the rest were revenue officers, whom he

had met by the way and with whom he had had the intelligence to return at once. Some news of the lugger in Kitt's Hole had found its way to Supervisor Dance and set him forth that night in our direction,

and to that circumstance my mother and I owed our preservation from death.

Pew was dead, stone dead. As for my mother, when we had carried her up to the hamlet, a little cold water and salts very soon brought her back again, and she was none the worse for her terror though she still continued to deplore the balance of the money. In the meantime the supervisor rode on, as fast as he could, to Kitt's Hole; but his men had to dismount and grope down the dingle, leading, and sometimes supporting, their horses, and in continual fear of ambushes; so it was no great matter for surprise that when they got down to the Hole the lugger was already underway, though still close in. He hailed her. A voice replied, telling him to keep out of the moonlight or he would get some lead in him, and at the same time a bullet whistled close by his arm. Soon after, the lugger doubled the point and disappeared. Mr. Dance stood there, as he said, "like a fish out of water," and all he could do was to dispatch a man to B—— to warn the cutter. "And that," said he, "is just about as good as nothing. They've got off clean, and there's an end. Only," he added, "I'm glad I trod on Master Pew's corns," for by this time he had heard my story.

I went back with him to the "Admiral Benbow," and you cannot imagine a house in such a state of smash; the very clock had been thrown down by these fellows in their furious hunt after my mother and myself; and though nothing had actually been taken away except the captain's moneybag and a little silver from the till, I could see at once that we were ruined. Mr. Dance could make nothing of the scene.

"They got the money, you say? Well, then, Hawkins, what in fortune were they after? More money?"

"No, sir; not money, I think," replied I. "In fact, sir, I believe I have the thing in my breast pocket; and, to tell you the truth, I should like to get it put in safety."

"To be sure, boy; quite right," said he. "I'll take it, if you like."

"I thought, perhaps, Dr. Livesey—" I began.

"Perfectly right," he interrupted very cheerily, "perfectly right—a gentleman and a magistrate. And, now I come to think of it, I might as well ride round there myself and report to him or squire. Master Pew's dead, when all's done; not that I regret it, but he's dead, you see, and people will make it out against an officer of his majesty's revenue, if make it out they can. Now, I'll tell you, Hawkins: if you like, I'll take you along."

I thanked him heartily for the offer, and we walked back to the hamlet where the horses were. By the time I had told mother of my purpose they were all in the saddle.

"Dogger," said Mr. Dance, "you have a good horse; take up this lad behind you."

As soon as I was mounted, holding onto Dogger's belt, the supervisor gave the word and the party struck out at a bouncing trot on the road to Dr. Livesey's house.

The Captain's Papers

———

WE RODE hard all the way, till we drew up before Dr. Livesey's door. The house was all dark to the front.

Mr. Dance told me to jump down and knock, and Dogger gave me a stirrup to descend by. The door was opened almost at once by the maid.

"Is Dr. Livesey in?" I asked.

No, she said, he had come home in the afternoon but had gone up to the Hall to dine and pass the evening with the squire.

"So there we go, boys," said Mr. Dance.

This time, as the distance was short, I did not mount, but ran with Dogger's stirrup leather to the lodge gates and up the long, leafless, moonlit avenue to where the white line of the Hall buildings looked on either hand on great old gardens. Here Mr. Dance dismounted and, taking me along with him, was admitted at a word into the house.

The servant led us down a matted passage, and showed us at the end into a great library, all lined with bookcases and busts upon the top of them, where the squire and Dr. Livesey sat, pipe in hand, on either side of a bright fire.

I had never seen the squire so near at hand. He was a tall man, over six feet high, and broad in proportion and he had a bluff, rough-and-ready face, all roughened and reddened and lined in his long travels. His eyebrows were very black and moved readily, and this gave him a look of some temper, not bad, you would say, but quick and high.

"Come in, Mr. Dance," says he, very stately and condescending.

"Good evening, Dance," says the doctor, with a nod. "And good evening to you, friend Jim. What good wind brings you here?"

The supervisor stood up straight and stiff and told his story like a lesson; and you should have seen how the two gentlemen leaned forward and looked at each other, and forgot to smoke in their surprise and interest. When they heard how my mother went back to the inn, Dr. Livesey fairly slapped his thigh and the squire cried "Bravo!" and broke his long pipe against the grate. Long before it was done, Mr. Trelawney (that, you will remember, was the squire's name) had got up from his seat and was striding about the room, and the doctor, as if to hear the better, had taken off his powdered wig and sat there, looking very strange indeed with his own close-cropped, black poll.

At last Mr. Dance finished the story.

"Mr. Dance," said the squire, "you are a very noble fellow. And as for riding down that black, atrocious miscreant, I regard it as an act of virtue, sir, like stamping on a cockroach. This lad Hawkins is a trump, I perceive. Hawkins, will you ring that bell? Mr. Dance must have some ale."

"And so, Jim," said the doctor, "you have the thing that they were after, have you?"

"Here it is, sir," said I, and gave him the oilskin packet.

The doctor looked it all over, as if his fingers were itching to open it; but, instead of doing that, he put it quietly in the pocket of his coat.

"Squire," said he, "when Dance has had his ale he must, of course, be off on his majesty's service; but I mean to keep Jim Hawkins here to sleep at my house, and, with your permission, I propose we should have up the cold pie, and let him sup."

"As you will, Livesey," said the squire; "Hawkins has earned better than cold pie."

So a big pigeon pie was brought in and put on a side table, and I made a hearty supper, for I was as hungry as a hawk, while Mr. Dance was further complimented, and at last dismissed.

"And now, squire," said the doctor.

"And now, Livesey," said the squire, in the same breath.

"One at a time, one at a time," said Dr. Livesey, with a laugh. "You have heard of this Flint, I suppose?"

"Heard of him!" cried the squire. "Heard of him, you say! He was the bloodthirstiest buccaneer that sailed. Blackbeard was a child to Flint. The Spaniards were so prodigiously afraid of him that I tell you, sir, I was sometimes proud he was an Englishman. I've seen his topsails with these eyes, off Trinidad, and the cowardly son of a rum puncheon that I sailed with put back—put back, sir, into Port-of-Spain."

"Well, I've heard of him myself, in England," said the doctor. "But the point is, had he money?"

"Money!" cried the squire. "Have you heard the story? What were these villains after but money?

What do they care for but money? For what would they risk their rascally carcasses but money?"

"That we shall soon know," replied the doctor. "But you are so confoundedly hotheaded and exclamatory that I cannot get a word in. What I want to know is this: supposing that I have here in my pocket some clue to where Flint buried his treasure, will that treasure amount to much?"

"Amount, sir!" cried the squire. "It will amount to this: if we have the clue you talk about, I fit out a ship in Bristol dock and take you and Hawkins here along with me, and I'll have that treasure if I search a year."

"Very well," said the doctor. "Now, then, if Jim is agreeable, we'll open the packet." And he laid it before him on the table.

The bundle was sewed together, and the doctor had to get out his instrument case and cut the stitches with his medical scissors. It contained two things—a book and a sealed paper.

"First of all we'll try the book," observed the doctor.

The squire and I were both peering over his shoulder as he opened it, for Dr. Livesey had kindly motioned me to come round from the side table, where I had been eating, to enjoy the sport of the search. On the first page there were only some scraps of writing, such as a man with a pen in his hand might make for idleness or practice. One was the same as the tattoo mark, "Billy Bones his fancy"; then there was "Mr. W. Bones, mate," "No more rum," "Off Palm Key he got itt," and some other snatches, mostly single words and unintelligible. I could not help wondering who it was that had "got itt," and what "itt" was that he got. A knife in his back, as like as not.

"Not much instruction there," said Dr. Livesey, as he passed on.

The next ten or twelve pages were filled with a curious series of entries. There was a date at one end of the line and at the other a sum of money, as in common account books; but instead of explanatory writing, only a varying number of crosses between the two. On the 12th of June, 1745, for instance, a sum of seventy pounds had plainly become due to someone, and there was nothing but six crosses to explain the cause. In a few cases, to be sure, the name of a place would be added, as "Offe Caraccas"; or a mere entry of latitude and longitude, as "sixty-two degrees seventeen minutes twenty seconds, nineteen degrees two minutes forty seconds."

The record lasted over nearly twenty years, the amount of the separate entries growing larger as time went on, and at the end a grand total had been made out after five or six wrong additions, and these words appended, "Bones, his pile."

"I can't make head or tail of this," said Dr. Livesey.

"The thing is as clear as noonday," cried the squire. "This is the blackhearted hound's account book. These crosses stand for the names of ships or towns that they sank or plundered. The sums are the scoundrel's share, and where he feared an ambiguity, you see he added something clearer. 'Offe Caraccas,' now; you see, here was some unhappy vessel boarded off that coast. God help the poor souls that manned her —coral long ago."

"Right!" said the doctor. "See what it is to be a traveler. Right! And the amounts increase, you see, as he rose in rank."

There was little else in the volume but a few bear-

ings of places noted in the blank leaves toward the end, and a table for reducing French, English, and Spanish moneys to a common value.

"Thrifty man!" cried the doctor. "He wasn't the one to be cheated."

"And now," said the squire, "for the other."

The paper had been sealed in several places with a thimble by way of seal; the very thimble, perhaps, that I had found in the captain's pocket. The doctor opened the seals with great care, and there fell out the map of an island, with latitude and longitude, soundings, names of hills, and bays, and inlets, and every particular that would be needed to bring a ship to a safe anchorage upon its shores. It was about nine miles long and five across, shaped, you might say, like a fat dragon standing up, and had two fine landlocked harbors, and a hill in the center part marked "The Spyglass." There were several additions of a later date; but, above all, three crosses of red ink—two on the north part of the island, one in the southwest, and, besides this last, in the same red ink and in a small, neat hand, very different from the captain's tottery characters, these words: "Bulk of treasure here."

Over on the back the same hand had written this further information:

Tall tree, Spyglass shoulder, bearing a point to the N. of N.N.E.

Skeleton Island E.S.E. and by E.

Ten feet.

The bar silver is in the north cache; you can find it by the trend of the east hummock, ten fathoms south of the black crag with the face on it.

The arms are easy found, in the sand hill, N. point of north inlet cape, bearing E. and a quarter N.   J.F.

That was all; but brief as it was, and to me incomprehensible, it filled the squire and Dr. Livesey with delight.

"Livesey," said the squire, "you will give up this wretched practice at once. Tomorrow I start for Bristol. In three weeks' time—three weeks!—two weeks—ten days—we'll have the best ship, sir, and the choicest crew in England. Hawkins shall come as cabin boy. You'll make a famous cabin boy, Hawkins. You, Livesey, are ship's doctor; I am admiral. We'll take Redruth, Joyce, and Hunter. We'll have favorable winds, a quick passage, and not the least difficulty in finding the spot, and money to eat—to roll in—to play duck and drake with ever after."

"Trelawney," said the doctor, "I'll go with you; and, I'll go bail for it, so will Jim, and be a credit to the undertaking. There's only one man I'm afraid of."

"And who's that?" cried the squire. "Name the dog, sir!"

"You," replied the doctor; "for you cannot hold your tongue. We are not the only men who know of this paper. These fellows who attacked the inn tonight—bold, desperate blades, for sure—and the rest who stayed aboard that lugger, and more, I dare say, not far off, are, one and all, through thick and thin, bound that they'll get that money. We must none of us go alone till we get to sea. Jim and I shall stick together in the meanwhile; you'll take Joyce and Hunter when you ride to Bristol; and, from first to last, not one of us must breathe a word of what we've found."

"Livesey," returned the squire, "you are always in the right of it. I'll be as silent as the grave."

PART II

The Sea Cook

☆ VII ☆

I Go to Bristol

———

IT WAS longer than the squire imagined ere we were ready for the sea, and none of our first plans—not even Dr. Livesey's of keeping me beside him—could be carried out as we intended. The doctor had to go to London for a physician to take charge of his practice; the squire was hard at work at Bristol; and I lived on at the Hall under the charge of old Redruth, the gamekeeper, almost a prisoner, but full of sea dreams and the most charming anticipations of strange islands and adventures. I brooded by the hour together over the map, all the details of which I well remembered. Sitting by the fire in the housekeeper's room, I approached that island, in my fancy, from every possible direction; I explored every acre of its surface; I climbed a thousand times to that tall hill they call the Spyglass, and from the top enjoyed the most wonderful and changing prospects. Sometimes the isle was thick with savages, with whom we fought;

sometimes full of dangerous animals that hunted us; but in all my fancies nothing occurred to me so strange and tragic as our actual adventures.

So the weeks passed on, till one fine day there came a letter addressed to Dr. Livesey, with this addition, "To be opened, in case of his absence, by Tom Redruth, or young Hawkins." Obeying this order, we found, or rather, I found—for the gamekeeper was a poor hand at reading anything but print—the following important news:

OLD ANCHOR INN, BRISTOL, March 1, 17—.
DEAR LIVESEY: As I do not know whether you are at the Hall or still in London, I send this in double to both places.

The ship is bought and fitted. She lies at anchor, ready for sea. You never imagined a sweeter schooner—a child might sail her—two hundred tons; name, *Hispaniola*.

I got her through my old friend, Blandly, who has proved himself throughout the most surprising trump. The admirable fellow literally slaved in my interest, and so, I may say, did everyone in Bristol, as soon as they got wind of the port we sailed for—treasure, I mean.

"Redruth," said I, interrupting the letter, "Dr. Livesey will not like that. The squire has been talking, after all."

"Well, who's a better right?" growled the gamekeeper. "A pretty rum go if squire ain't to talk for Dr. Livesey, I should think."

At that I gave up all attempt at commentary, and read straight on:

Blandly himself found the *Hispaniola*, and by the most admirable management got her for the merest trifle. There is a class of men in Bristol monstrously prejudiced against Blandly. They go the length of declaring that

this honest creature would do anything for money, that the *Hispaniola* belonged to him, and that he sold it me absurdly high—the most transparent calumnies. None of them dare, however, to deny the merits of the ship.

So far there was not a hitch. The workpeople, to be sure—riggers and what not—were most annoyingly slow; but time cured that. It was the crew that troubled me.

I wished a round score of men—in case of natives, buccaneers, or the odious French—and I had the worry of the deuce itself to find so much as half a dozen, till the most remarkable stroke of fortune brought me the very man that I required.

I was standing on the dock, when, by the merest accident, I fell in talk with him. I found he was an old sailor, kept a public house, knew all the seafaring men in Bristol, had lost his health ashore, and wanted a good berth as cook to get to sea again. He had hobbled down there that morning, he said, to get a smell of the salt.

I was monstrously touched—so would you have been —and, out of pure pity, I engaged him on the spot to be ship's cook. Long John Silver, he is called, and has lost a leg; but that I regarded as a recommendation, since he lost it in his country's service, under the immortal Hawke. He has no pension, Livesey. Imagine the abominable age we live in!

Well, sir, I thought I had found only a cook, but it was a crew I had discovered. Between Silver and myself we got together in a few days a company of the toughest old salts imaginable—not pretty to look at, but fellows, by their faces, of the most indomitable spirit. I declare we could fight a frigate.

Long John even got rid of two out of six or seven I had already engaged. He showed me in a moment that they were just the sort of fresh-water swabs we had to fear in an adventure of importance.

I am in the most magnificent health and spirits, eating like a bull, sleeping like a tree, yet I shall not enjoy a moment till I hear my old tarpaulins tramping round the capstan. Seaward ho! Hang the treasure! It's the glory

of the sea that has turned my head. So now, Livesey, come post; do not lose an hour, if you respect me.

Let young Hawkins go at once to see his mother, with Redruth for a guard; and then both come full speed to Bristol.

JOHN TRELAWNEY.

POSTSCRIPT.—I did not tell you that Blandly, who, by the way, is to send a consort after us if we don't turn up by the end of August, had found an admirable fellow for sailing master—a stiff man, which I regret, but, in all other respects, a treasure. Long John Silver unearthed a very competent man for a mate, a man named Arrow. I have a boatswain who pipes, Livesey; so things shall go man-o'-war fashion on board the good ship *Hispaniola*.

I forgot to tell you that Silver is a man of substance; I know of my own knowledge that he has a banker's account, which has never been overdrawn. He leaves his wife to manage the inn; and as she is a woman of color, a pair of old bachelors like you and me may be excused for guessing that it is the wife quite as much as the health, that sends him back to roving.   J.T.

P. P. S.—Hawkins may stay one night with his mother.
J.T.

You can fancy the excitement into which that letter put me. I was half beside myself with glee; and if ever I despised a man, it was old Tom Redruth, who could do nothing but grumble and lament. Any of the under-gamekeepers would gladly have changed places with him; but such was not the squire's pleasure, and the squire's pleasure was like law among them all. Nobody but old Redruth would have dared so much as even to grumble.

The next morning he and I set out on foot for the "Admiral Benbow," and there I found my mother in good health and spirits. The captain, who had so long been a cause of so much discomfort, was gone where the wicked cease from troubling. The squire had had

everything repaired, and the public rooms and the sign repainted, and had added some furniture—above all, a beautiful armchair for mother in the bar. He had found her a boy as an apprentice also, so that she should not want help while I was gone.

It was on seeing that boy that I understood, for the first time, my situation. I had thought up to that moment of the adventures before me, not at all of the home that I was leaving; and now, at sight of this clumsy stranger, who was to stay here in my place beside my mother, I had my first attack of tears. I am afraid I led that boy a dog's life; for as he was new to the work, I had a hundred opportunities of setting him right and putting him down, and I was not slow to profit by them.

The night passed, and the next day, after dinner, Redruth and I were afoot again, and on the road. I said good-by to mother and the cove where I had lived since I was born, and the dear old "Admiral Benbow" —since he was repainted, no longer quite so dear. One of my last thoughts was of the captain, who had so often strode along the beach with his cocked hat, his saber-cut cheek, and his old brass telescope. Next moment we had turned the corner, and my home was out of sight.

The mail picked us up about dusk at the "Royal George" on the heath. I was wedged in between Redruth and a stout old gentleman, and in spite of the swift motion and the cold night air I must have dozed a great deal from the very first, and then slept like a log uphill and downdale through stage after stage; for when I was awakened, at last, it was by a punch in the ribs, and I opened my eyes, to find that we were standing still before a large building in a city

street, and that the day had already broken a long time.

"Where are we?" I asked.

"Bristol," said Tom. "Get down."

Mr. Trelawney had taken up his residence at an inn far down the docks, to superintend the work upon the schooner. Thither we had now to walk, and our way, to my great delight, lay along the quays and beside the great multitude of ships of all sizes and rigs and nations. In one, sailors were singing at their work; in another, there were men aloft, high over my head, hanging to threads that seemed no thicker than a spider's. Though I had lived by the shore all my life, I seemed never to have been near the sea till then. The smell of tar and salt was something new. I saw the most wonderful figureheads, that had all been far over the ocean. I saw, besides, many old sailors, with rings in their ears, and whiskers curled in ringlets, and tarry pigtails, and their swaggering, clumsy sea walk; and if I had seen as many kings or archbishops I could not have been more delighted.

And I was going to sea myself; to sea in a schooner, with a piping boatswain, and pig-tailed singing seamen; to sea, bound for an unknown island, and to seek for buried treasures!

While I was still in this delightful dream, we came suddenly in front of a large inn, and met Squire Trelawney, all dressed out like a sea officer, in stout blue cloth, coming out of the door with a smile on his face, and a capital imitation of a sailor's walk.

"Here you are," he cried, "and the doctor came last night from London. Bravo! the ship's company complete!"

"Oh, sir," cried I, "when do we sail?"

"Sail!" says he. "We sail tomorrow!"

☆ VIII ☆

At the Sign of the "Spyglass"

———————

WHEN I HAD DONE breakfasting, the squire gave me a note addressed to John Silver, at the sign of the "Spyglass," and told me I should easily find the place by following the line of the docks, and keeping a bright lookout for a little tavern with a large brass telescope for sign. I set off, overjoyed at this opportunity to see some more of the ships and seamen, and picked my way among a great crowd of people and carts and bales, for the dock was now at its busiest, until I found the tavern in question.

It was a bright enough little place of entertainment. The sign was newly painted; the windows had neat red curtains; the floor was cleanly sanded. There was a street on each side, and an open door on both, which made the large, low room pretty clear to see in, in spite of clouds of tobacco smoke. The customers were mostly seafaring men; and they talked so loudly that I hung at the door, almost afraid to enter.

As I was waiting, a man came out of a side room, and, at a glance, I was sure he must be Long John. His left leg was cut off close by the hip, and under the left

shoulder he carried a crutch, which he managed with wonderful dexterity, hopping about upon it like a bird. He was very tall and strong, with a face as big as a ham—plain and pale, but intelligent and smiling. Indeed, he seemed in the most cheerful spirits, whistling as he moved about among the tables, with a merry word or a slap on the shoulder for the more favored of his guests.

Now, to tell you the truth, from the very first mention of Long John in Squire Trelawney's letter I had taken a fear in my mind that he might prove to be the very one-legged sailor whom I had watched for so long at the old "Benbow." But one look at the man before me was enough. I had seen the captain, and Black Dog, and the blind man Pew, and I thought I knew what a buccaneer was like—a very different creature, according to me, from this clean and pleasant-tempered landlord.

I plucked up courage at once, crossed the threshold, and walked right up to the man where he stood, propped on his crutch, talking to a customer.

"Mr. Silver, sir?" I asked, holding out the note.

"Yes, my lad," said he; "such is my name, to be sure. And who may you be?" And then as he saw the squire's letter he seemed to me to give something almost like a start.

"Oh!" said he, quite loud, and offering his hand. "I see. You are our new cabin boy; pleased I am to see you." He took my hand in his large firm grasp.

Just then one of the customers at the far side rose suddenly and made for the door. It was close by him, and he was out in the street in a moment. But his hurry had attracted my notice, and I recognized him at a glance. It was the tallow-faced man, wanting two

fingers, who had come first to the "Admiral Benbow."

"Oh," I cried, "stop him! It's Black Dog!"

"I don't care two coppers who he is," cried Silver. "But he hasn't paid his score. Harry, run and catch him." One of the others who was nearest the door leaped up, and started in pursuit.

"If he were Admiral Hawke he shall pay his score," cried Silver; and then, relinquishing my hand, "Who did you say he was?'" he asked. "Black what?'"

"Dog, sir," said I. "Has Mr. Trelawney not told you of the buccaneers? He was one of them."

"So?" cried Silver. "In my house! Ben, run and help Harry. One of those swabs, was he? Was that you drinking with him, Morgan? Step up here and tell us."

The man whom he called Morgan—an old, gray-haired, mahogany-faced sailor—came forward pretty sheepishly, rolling his quid.

"Now, Morgan," said Long John very sternly, "you never clapped your eyes on that Black—Black Dog before, did you, now?"

"Not I, sir," said Morgan, with a salute.

"You didn't know his name, did you?"

"No, sir."

"By the powers, Tom Morgan, it's as good for you!" exclaimed the landlord. "If you had been mixed up with the like of that you would never have put another foot in my house, you may lay to that. And what was he saying to you?"

"I don't rightly know, sir," answered Morgan.

"Do you call that a head on your shoulders, or a blessed deadeye?" cried Long John. "Don't rightly know, don't you! Perhaps you don't happen to rightly know who you was speaking to, perhaps?

Come, now, what was he jawing—v'yages, cap'ns, ships? Pipe up! What was it?"

"We was a-talkin' of keelhauling," said Morgan.

"Keelhauling, was you? And a mighty suitable

thing, too, and you may lay to that. Get back to your place for a lubber, Tom."

And then, as Morgan rolled back to his seat, Silver added to me in a confidential whisper, that was very flattering, as I thought:

"He's quite an honest man, Tom Morgan, on'y stupid. And now," he ran on again, aloud, "let's see —Black Dog? No, I don't know the name, not I. Yet I kind of think I've—yes, I've seen the swab. He used to come here with a blind beggar, he used."

"That he did, you may be sure," said I. "I knew that blind man, too. His name was Pew."

"It was!" cried Silver, now quite excited. "Pew! That were his name for certain. Ah, he looked a shark, he did! If we run down this Black Dog, now, there'll be news for Cap'n Trelawney! Ben's a good runner; few seamen run better than Ben. He should run him down, hand over hand, by the powers! He talked o' keelhauling, did he? *I'll* keelhaul him!"

All the time he was jerking out these phrases he was stumping up and down the tavern on his crutch, slapping tables with his hand, and giving such a show of excitement as would have convinced an Old Bailey judge or a Bow Street runner. My suspicions had been thoroughly reawakened on finding Black Dog at the "Spyglass," and I watched the cook narrowly. But he was too deep, and too ready, and too clever for me, and by the time the two men had come back out of breath, and confessed that they had lost the track in a crowd, and been scolded like thieves, I would have gone bail for the innocence of Long John Silver.

"See here, now, Hawkins," said he, "here's a blessed hard thing on a man like me, now, ain't it? There's Cap'n Trelawney—what's he to think? Here I have

this confounded son of a Dutchman sitting in my own house drinking of my own rum! Here you comes and tells me of it plain; and here I let him give us all the slip before my blessed deadlights! Now, Hawkins, you do me justice with the cap'n. You're a lad, you are, but you're as smart as paint. I see that when you first came in. Now, here it is: What could I do, with this old timber I hobble on? When I was an a.b. master mariner I'd have come up alongside of him, hand over hand, and broached him to in a brace of old shakes, I would; but now—"

And then, all of a sudden, he stopped, and his jaw dropped as though he had remembered something.

"The score!" he burst out. "Three goes o' rum! Why, shiver my timbers, if I hadn't forgotten my score!"

And, falling on a bench, he laughed until the tears ran down his cheeks. I could not help joining; and we laughed together, peal after peal, until the tavern rang.

"Why, what a precious old sea calf I am!" he said at last, wiping his cheeks. "You and me should get on well, Hawkins, for I'll take my davy I should be rated ship's boy. But come, now, stand by to go about. This won't do. Dooty is dooty, messmates. I'll put on my old cocked hat, and step along of you to Cap'n Trelawney, and report this here affair. For, mind you, it's serious, young Hawkins; and neither you nor me's come out of it with what I should make so bold as to call credit. Nor you neither, says you; not smart—none of the pair of us smart. But dash my buttons! that was a good 'un about my score."

And he began to laugh again, and that so heartily that, though I did not see the joke as he did, I was again obliged to join him in his mirth.

On our little walk along the quays he made himself the most interesting companion, telling me about the different ships that we passed by, their rig, tonnage, and nationality, explaining the work that was going forward—how one was discharging, another taking in cargo, and a third making ready for sea; and every now and then telling me some little anecdote of ships or seamen, or repeating a nautical phrase till I had learned it perfectly. I began to see that here was one of the best of possible shipmates.

When we got to the inn, the squire and Dr. Livesey were seated together, finishing a quart of ale with a toast in it, before they should go aboard the schooner on a visit of inspection.

Long John told the story from first to last, with a great deal of spirit and the most perfect truth. "That was how it were, now, weren't it, Hawkins?" he would say, now and again, and I could always bear him entirely out.

The two gentlemen regretted that Black Dog had got away; but we all agreed there was nothing to be done, and after he had been complimented, Long John took up his crutch and departed.

"All hands aboard by four this afternoon," shouted the squire, after him.

"Aye, aye, sir," cried the cook, in the passage.

"Well, squire," said Dr. Livesey, "I don't put much faith in your discoveries, as a general thing; but I will say this, John Silver suits me."

"The man's a perfect trump," declared the squire.

"And now," added the doctor, "Jim may come on board with us, may he not?"

"To be sure, he may," says squire. "Take your hat, Hawkins, and we'll see the ship."

☆ IX ☆

Powder and Arms

―――――――――

THE *Hispaniola* lay some way out, and we went under the figureheads and round the sterns of many other ships, and their cables sometimes grated underneath our keel and sometimes swung above us. At last, however, we got alongside, and were met and saluted as we stepped aboard, by the mate, Mr. Arrow, a brown old sailor with earrings in his ears and a squint. He and the squire were very thick and friendly, but I soon observed that things were not the same between Mr. Trelawney and the captain.

This last was a sharp-looking man, who seemed angry with everything on board, and was soon to tell us why, for we had hardly got down into the cabin when a sailor followed us.

"Captain Smollett, sir, axing to speak with you," said he.

"I am always at the captain's orders. Show him in," said the squire.

The captain, who was close behind his messenger,

entered at once, and shut the door behind him.

"Well, Captain Smollett, what have you to say? All well, I hope; all shipshape and seaworthy?"

"Well, sir," said the captain, "better speak plain, I believe, even at the risk of offense. I don't like this cruise; I don't like the men; and I don't like my officer. That's short and sweet."

"Perhaps, sir, you don't like the ship?" inquired the squire, very angry, as I could see.

"I can't speak as to that, sir, not having seen her tried," said the captain. "She seems a clever craft; more I can't say."

"Possibly, sir, you may not like your employer either?" says the squire.

But here Dr. Livesey cut in.

"Stay a bit," said he, "stay a bit. No use of such questions as that but to produce ill-feeling. The captain has said too much or he has said too little, and I'm bound to say that I require an explanation of his words. You don't, you say, like this cruise. Now, why?"

"I was engaged, sir, on what we called sealed orders, to sail this ship for that gentleman where he should bid me," said the captain. "So far so good. But now I find that every man before the mast knows more than I do. I don't call that fair, now, do you?"

"No," said Dr. Livesey, "I don't."

"Next," said the captain, "I learn we are going after treasure—hear it from my own hands, mind you. Now, treasure is ticklish work; I don't like treasure voyages on any account; and I don't like them, above all, when they are secret, and when (begging your pardon, Mr. Trelawney) the secret has been told to the parrot."

"Silver's parrot?" asked the squire.

"It's a way of speaking," said the captain. "Blabbed, I mean. It's my belief neither of you gentlemen know what you are about; but I'll tell you my way of it—life or death, and a close run."

"That is all clear, and, I dare say, true enough," replied Dr. Livesey. "We take the risk; but we are not so ignorant as you believe us. Next, you say you don't like the crew. Are they not good seamen?"

"I don't like them, sir," returned Captain Smollett. "And I think I should have had the choosing of my own hands, if you go to that."

"Perhaps you should," replied the doctor. "My friend should, perhaps, have taken you along with him; but the slight, if there be one, was unintentional. And you don't like Mr. Arrow?"

"I don't, sir. I believe he's a good seaman; but he's too free with the crew to be a good officer. A mate should keep himself to himself—shouldn't drink with the men before the mast!"

"Do you mean he drinks?" cried the squire.

"No, sir," replied the captain; "only that he's too familiar."

"Well, now, and the short and long of it, captain?" asked the doctor. "Tell us what you want."

"Well, gentlemen, are you determined to go on this cruise?"

"Like iron," answered the squire.

"Very good," said the captain. "Then, as you've heard me very patiently, saying things that I could not prove, hear me a few words more. They are putting the powder and the arms in the forehold. Now, you have a good place under the cabin; why not put them there?—first point. Then you are bringing four of

your own people with you, and they tell me some of them are to be berthed forward. Why not give them the berths here beside the cabin?—second point."

"Any more?" asked Mr. Trelawney.

"One more," said the captain. "There's been too much blabbing already."

"Far too much," agreed the doctor.

"I'll tell you what I've heard myself," continued Captain Smollett: "That you have a map of an island; that there's crosses on the map to show where treasure is; and that the island lies—" And then he named the latitude and longitude exactly.

"I never told that," cried the squire, "to a soul!"

"The hands know it, sir," returned the captain.

"Livesey, that must have been you or Hawkins," cried the squire.

"It doesn't much matter who it was," replied the doctor. And I could see that neither he nor the captain paid much regard to Mr. Trelawney's protestations. Neither did I, to be sure, he was so loose a talker; yet in this case I believe he was really right, and that nobody had told the situation of the island.

"Well, gentlemen," continued the captain, "I don't know who has the map; but I make it a point, it shall be kept secret even from me and Mr. Arrow. Otherwise I would ask you to let me resign."

"I see," said the doctor. "You wish us to keep this matter dark, and to make a garrison of the stern part of the ship, manned with my friend's own people, and provided with all the arms and powder on board. In other words, you fear a mutiny."

"Sir," said Captain Smollett, "with no intention to take offense, I deny your right to put words into my

mouth. No captain, sir, would be justified in going to sea at all if he had ground enough to say that. As for Mr. Arrow, I believe him thoroughly honest; some of the men are the same; all may be for what I know. But I am responsible for the ship's safety and the life of every man Jack aboard of her. I see things going, as I think, not quite right. And I ask you to take certain precautions or let me resign my berth. And that's all."

"Captain Smollett," began the doctor, with a smile, "did you ever hear the fable of the mountain and the mouse? You'll excuse me, I dare say, but you remind me of that fable. When you came in here I'll stake my wig you meant more than this."

"Doctor," said the captain, "you are smart. When I came in here I meant to get discharged. I had no thought that Mr. Trelawney would hear a word."

"No more I would," cried the squire. "Had Livesey not been here I should have seen you to the deuce. As it is, I have heard you. I will do as you desire; but I think the worse of you."

"That's as you please, sir," said the captain. "You'll find I do my duty."

And with that he took his leave.

"Trelawney," said the doctor, "contrary to all my notions, I believe you have managed to get two honest men on board with you—that man and John Silver."

"Silver, if you like," cried the squire; "but as for that intolerable humbug, I declare I think his conduct unmanly, unsailorly, and downright un-English."

"Well," says the doctor, "we shall see."

When we came on deck, the men had begun already to take out the arms and powder, yo-ho-ing at their

work, while the captain and Mr. Arrow stood by superintending.

The new arrangement was quite to my liking. The whole schooner had been overhauled; six berths had been made astern, out of what had been the afterpart of the main hold; and this set of cabins was only joined to the galley and forecastle by a sparred passage on the port side. It had been originally meant that the captain, Mr. Arrow, Hunter, Joyce, the doctor, and the squire were to occupy these six berths. Now Redruth and I were to get two of them, and Mr. Arrow and the captain were to sleep on deck in the companion, which had been enlarged on each side till you might almost have called it a roundhouse. Very low it was still, of course; but there was room to swing two hammocks, and even the mate seemed pleased with the arrangement. Even he, perhaps, had been doubtful as to the crew, but that is only guess; for, as you shall hear, we had not long the benefit of his opinoin.

We were all hard at work, changing the powder and the berths, when the last man or two, and Long John along with them, came off in a shore boat.

The cook came up the side like a monkey for cleverness and, as soon as he saw what was doing, "So ho, mates!" says he, "what's this?"

"We're a-changing of the powder, Jack," answers one.

"Why, by the powers," cried Long John, "if we do, we'll miss the morning tide!"

"My orders!" said the captain shortly. "You may go below, my man. Hands will want supper."

"Aye, aye, sir," answered the cook; and, touching his forelock, he disappeared at once in the direction of his galley.

"That's a good man, captain," said the doctor.

"Very likely," replied Captain Smollett. "Easy with that, men—easy," he ran on, to the fellows who were shifting the powder; and then suddenly observing me examining the swivel we carried amidships, a long brass nine—"Here, you ship's boy," he cried, "out o' that! Off with you to the cook and get some work."

And then as I was hurrying off I heard him say, quite loudly, to the doctor:

"I'll have no favorites on my ship."

I assure you I was quite of the squire's way of thinking, and hated the captain deeply.

☆ X ☆

The Voyage

———

ALL THAT NIGHT we were in a great bustle getting things stowed in their place, and boatfuls of the squire's friends, Mr. Blandly and the like, coming off to wish him a good voyage and a safe return. We never had a night at the "Admiral Benbow" when I had half the work; and I was dog-tired when, a little before dawn, the boatswain sounded his pipe, and the crew began to man the capstan bars. I might have been twice as weary, yet I would not have left the deck; all was so new and interesting to me—the brief commands, the shrill note of the whistle, the men bustling to their places in the glimmer of the ship's lanterns.

"Now, Barbecue, tip us a stave," cried one voice.

"The old one," cried another.

"Aye, aye, mates," said Long John, who was standing by, with his crutch under his arm, and at once broke out in the air and words I knew so well:

"Fifteen men on the dead man's chest—"

And then the whole crew bore chorus:

"Yo-ho-ho, and a bottle of rum!"

And at the third "ho!" drove the bars before them with a will.

Even at that exciting moment it carried me back to the old "Admiral Benbow" in a second; and I seemed to hear the voice of the captain piping in the chorus. But soon the anchor was short up; soon it was hanging dripping at the bows; soon the sails began to draw, and the land and shipping to flit by on either side; and before I could lie down to snatch an hour of slumber the *Hispaniola* had begun her voyage to the Isle of Treasure.

I am not going to relate that voyage in detail. It was fairly prosperous. The ship proved to be a good ship, the crew were capable seamen, and the captain thoroughly understood his business. But before we came the length of Treasure Island, two or three things had happened which require to be known.

Mr. Arrow, first of all, turned out even worse than the captain had feared. He had no command among the men, and people did what they pleased with him. But that was by no means the worst of it; for after a day or two at sea he began to appear on deck with hazy eyes, red cheeks, stuttering tongue, and other marks of drunkenness. Time after time he was ordered below in disgrace. Sometimes he fell and cut himself; sometimes he lay all day long in his little bunk at one side of the companion; sometimes for a day or two he would be almost sober and attend to his work at least passably.

In the meantime, we could never make out where he got the drink. That was the ship's mystery. Watch

him as we pleased, we could do nothing to solve it; and when we asked him to his face, he would only laugh, if he were drunk, and if he were sober, deny solemnly that he ever tasted anything but water.

He was not only useless as an officer, and a bad influence among the men, but it was plain that at this rate he must soon kill himself outright; so nobody was much surprised, nor very sorry, when one dark night, with a head sea, he disappeared entirely and was seen no more.

"Overboard!" said captain. "Well, gentlemen, that saves the trouble of putting him in irons."

But there we were, without a mate; and it was necessary, of course, to advance one of the men. The boatswain, Job Anderson, was the likeliest man aboard, and, though he kept his old title, he served in a way as mate. Mr. Trelawney had followed the sea, and his knowledge made him very useful, for he often took a watch himself in easy weather. And the cockswain, Israel Hands, was a careful, wily, old, experienced seaman, who could be trusted at a pinch with almost anything.

He was a great confidant of Long John Silver, and so the mention of his name leads me on to speak of our ship's cook, Barbecue, as the men called him.

Aboard ship he carried his crutch by a lanyard round his neck, to have both hands as free as possible. It was something to see him wedge the foot of the crutch against a bulkhead, and, propped against it, yielding to every movement of the ship, get on with his cooking like someone safe ashore. Still more strange was it to see him in the heaviest of weather cross the deck. He had a line or two rigged up to help him across the widest spaces—Long John's earrings,

they were called; and he would hand himself from one place to another, now using the crutch, now trailing it alongside by the lanyard, as quickly as another man could walk. Yet some of the men who had sailed with him before expressed their pity to see him so reduced.

"He's no common man, Barbecue," said the cockswain to me. "He had good schooling in his young days, and can speak like a book when so minded; and brave—a lion's nothing alongside of Long John! I seen him grapple four, and knock their heads together —him unarmed."

All the crew respected and even obeyed him. He had a way of talking to each, and doing everybody some particular service. To me he was unweariedly kind; and always glad to see me in the galley, which he kept as clean as a new pin; the dishes hanging up burnished, and his parrot in a cage in one corner.

"Come away, Hawkins," he would say; "come and have a yarn with John. Nobody more welcome than yourself, my son. Sit you down and hear the news. Here's Cap'n Flint—I calls my parrot Cap'n Flint after the famous buccaneer—here's Cap'n Flint predicting success to our v'yage. Wasn't you, cap'n?"

And the parrot would say, with great rapidity: "Pieces of eight! pieces of eight! pieces of eight!" till you wondered that it was not out of breath, or till John threw his handkerchief over the cage.

"Now, that bird," he would say, "is, maybe, two hundred years old, Hawkins—they lives forever mostly; and if anybody's seen more wickedness, it must be the devil himself. She's sailed with England, the great Cap'n England, the pirate. She's been at Madagascar, and at Malabar, and Surinam, and Providence, and Portobello. She was at the fishing up of

the wrecked plate ships. It's there she learned 'Pieces of eight,' and little wonder; three hundred and fifty thousand of 'em, Hawkins! She was at the boarding of the Viceroy of the Indies out of Goa, she was; and to look at her you would think she was a babby. But you smelt powder—didn't you, cap'n?"

"Stand by to go about," the parrot would scream.

"Ah, she's a handsome craft, she is," the cook would say, and give her sugar from his pocket, and then the bird would peck at the bars and swear straight on, passing belief for wickedness. "There," John would add, "you can't touch pitch and not be mucked, lad. Here's this poor old innocent bird o' mine swearing blue fire, and none the wiser, you may lay to that. She would swear the same, in a manner of speaking, before chaplain." And John would touch his forelock with a solemn way he had, that made me think he was the best of men.

In the meantime, the squire and Captain Smollett were still on pretty distant terms with each other. The squire made no bones about the matter; he despised the captain. The captain, on his part, never spoke but when he was spoken to, and then sharp and short and dry, and not a word wasted. He owned, when driven into a corner, that he seemed to have been wrong about the crew, that some of them were as brisk as he wanted to see, and all had behaved fairly well. As for the ship, he had taken a downright fancy to her. "She'll lie a point nearer the wind than a man has a right to expect of his own married wife, sir. But," he would add, "all I say is we're not home again, and I don't like the cruise."

The squire, at this, would turn away and march up and down the deck, chin in air.

"A trifle more of that man," he would say, "and I shall explode."

We had some heavy weather, which only proved the qualities of the *Hispaniola*. Every man on board seemed well content, and they must have been hard to please if they had been otherwise; for it is my belief there was never a ship's company so spoiled since Noah put to sea. Double grog was going on the least excuse; there was duff on odd days, as, for instance, if the squire heard it was any man's birthday; and always a barrel of apples standing broached in the waist, for anyone to help himself that had a fancy.

"Never knew good come of it yet," the captain said to Dr. Livesey. "Spoil foc's'le hands, make devils. That's my belief."

But good did come of the apple barrel, as you shall hear; for if it had not been for that, we should have had no note of warning and might all have perished by the hand of treachery.

This was how it came about.

We had run up the trades to get the wind of the island we were after—I am not allowed to be more plain—and now we were running down for it with a bright lookout day and night. It was about the last day of our outward voyage, by the largest computation; sometime that night, or, at latest, before noon of the morrow, we should sight the Treasure Island. We were heading S.S.W., and had a steady breeze abeam and a quiet sea. The *Hispaniola* rolled steadily, dipping her bowsprit now and then with a whiff of spray. All was drawing alow and aloft; everyone was in the bravest spirits, because we were now so near an end of the first part of our adventure.

Now, just after sundown, when all my work was

over, and I was on my way to my berth, it occurred to me that I should like an apple. I ran on deck. The watch was all forward looking out for the island. The man at the helm was watching the luff of the sail and whistling away gently to himself, and that was the only sound excepting the swish of the sea against the bows and around the sides of the ship.

In I got bodily into the apple barrel, and found there was scarce an apple left; but, sitting down there in the dark, what with the sound of the waters and the rocking movement of the ship, I had either fallen asleep or was on the point of doing so when a heavy man sat down with rather a clash close by. The barrel shook as he leaned his shoulders against it, and I was just about to jump up when the man began to speak. It was Silver's voice, and, before I had heard a dozen words, I would not have shown myself for all the world, but lay there, trembling and listening, in the extreme of fear and curiosity; for from these dozen words I understood that the lives of all the honest men aboard depended upon me alone.

What I Heard in the Apple Barrel

————

NO, NOT I," said Silver. "Flint was cap'n; I was quartermaster, along of my timber leg. The same broadside I lost my leg, old Pew lost his deadlights. It was a master surgeon, him that ampytated me—out of college and all—Latin by the bucket, and what not; but he was hanged like a dog, and sun-dried like the rest, at Corso Castle. That was Roberts' men, that was, and comed of changing names to their ships— *Royal Fortune* and so on. Now, what a ship was christened, so let her stay, I says. So it was with the *Cassandra*, as brought us all safe home from Malabar, after England took the Viceroy of the Indies; so it was with the old *Walrus*, Flint's old ship, as I've seen a-muck with the red blood and fit to sink with gold."

"Ah!" cried another voice, that of the youngest hand on board, and evidently full of admiration, "he was the flower of the flock, was Flint!"

"Davis was a man, too, by all accounts," said Silver. "I never sailed along of him; first with England, then with Flint, that's my story; and now here on my own account, in a manner of speaking. I laid by nine hun-

dred safe, from England, and two thousand after Flint. That ain't bad for a man before the mast—all safe in bank. 'Tain't earning now, it's saving does it, you may lay to that. Where's all England's men now? I dunno. Where's Flint's? Why, most on 'em aboard here, and glad to get the duff—been begging before that, some on 'em. Old Pew, as had lost his sight, and might have thought shame, spends twelve hundred pound in a year, like a lord in Parliament. Where is he now? Well, he's dead now and under hatches; but for two year before that, shiver my timbers! the man was starving. He begged, and he stole, and he cut throats, and starved at that, by the powers!"

"Well, it ain't much use, after all," said the young seaman.

" 'Tain't much use for fools, you may lay to it—that, nor nothing," cried Silver. "But now, you look here: you're young, you are, but you're as smart as paint. I see that when I set my eyes on you, and I'll talk to you like a man."

You may imagine how I felt when I heard this abominable old rogue addressing another in the very same words of flattery as he had used to myself. I think, if I had been able, that I would have killed him through the barrel. Meantime, he ran on, little supposing he was overheard.

"Here it is about gentlemen of fortune. They lives rough, and they risk swinging, but they eat and drink like fighting cocks, and when a cruise is done, why, it's hundreds of pounds instead of hundreds of farthings in their pockets. Now, the most goes for rum and a good fling, and to sea again in their shirts. But that's not the course I lay. I puts it all away, some here, some there, and none too much anywheres, by

"Gentlemen of fortune usually trusts little among themselves"

reason of suspicion. I'm fifty, mark you; once back from this cruise, I set up gentleman in earnest. Time enough, too, says you. Ah, but I've lived easy in the meantime; never denied myself o' nothing heart desires, and slep' soft and ate dainty all my days, but when at sea. And how did I begin? Before the mast, like you!"

"Well," said the other, "but all the other money's gone now, ain't it? You daren't show face in Bristol after this."

"Why, where might you suppose it was?" asked Silver derisively.

"At Bristol, in banks and places," answered his companion.

"It were," said the cook; "it were when we weighed anchor. But my old missis has it all by now. And the 'Spyglass' is sold, lease and goodwill and rigging; and the old girl's off to meet me. I would tell you where, for I trust you; but it 'ud make jealousy among the mates."

"And can you trust your missis?" asked the other.

"Gentlemen of fortune," returned the cook, "usually trusts little among themselves, and right they are, you may lay to it. But I have a way with me, I have. When a mate brings a slip on his cable—one as knows me, I mean—it won't be in the same world with old John. There was some that was feared of Pew, and some that was feared of Flint; but Flint his own self was feared of me. Feared he was, and proud. They was the roughest crew afloat, was Flint's; the devil himself would have been afeared to go to sea with them. Well, now, I tell you, I'm not a boasting man, and you seen yourself how easy I keep company; but when I was quartermaster, *lambs* wasn't the word for

Flint's old buccaneers. Ah, you may be sure of yourself in old John's ship."

"Well, I tell you now," replied the lad, "I didn't half a quarter like the job till I had this talk with you, John; but there's my hand on it now."

"And a brave lad you were, and smart, too," answered Silver, shaking hands so heartily that all the barrel shook, "and a finer figurehead for a gentleman of fortune I never clapped my eyes on."

By this time I had begun to understand the meaning of their terms. By a "gentleman of fortune" they plainly meant neither more nor less than a common pirate, and the little scene that I had overheard was the last act in the corruption of one of the honest hands—perhaps of the last one left aboard. But on this point I was soon to be relieved, for, Silver giving a little whistle, a third man strolled up and sat down by the party.

"Dick's square," said Silver.

"Oh, I know'd Dick was square," returned the voice of the cockswain, Israel Hands. "He's no fool, is Dick." And he turned his quid and spat. "But, look here," he went on, "here's what I want to know, Barbecue: how long are we a-going to stand off and on like a blessed bumboat? I've had a'most enough of Cap'n Smollett; he's hazed me long enough, by thunder! I want to go into that cabin, I do. I want their pickles and wines, and that."

"Israel," said Silver, "your head ain't much account, nor ever was. But you're able to hear, I reckon; leastways, your ears is big enough. Now, here's what I say: you'll berth forward, and you'll live hard, and you'll speak soft, and you'll keep sober, till I give the word, and you may lay to that, my son."

"Well, I don't say no, do I?" growled the cockswain. "What I say is, when? That's what I say."

"When! by the powers!" cried Silver. "Well, now, if you want to know, I'll tell you when. The last moment I can manage; and that's when. Here's a first-rate seaman, Cap'n Smollett, sails the blessed ship for us. Here's this squire and doctor with a map and such —I don't know where it is, do I? No more do you, says you. Well, then, I mean this squire and doctor shall find the stuff, and help us to get it aboard, by the powers. Then we'll see. If I was sure of you all, sons of double Dutchmen, I'd have Cap'n Smollett navigate us halfway back again before I struck."

"Why, we're all seamen aboard here, I should think," said the lad Dick.

"We're all foc's'le hands, you mean," snapped Silver. "We can steer a course, but who's to set one? That's what all you gentlemen split on, first and last. If I had my way, I'd have Cap'n Smollett work us back into the trades at least; then we'd have no blessed miscalculations and a spoonful of water a day. But I know the sort you are. I'll finish with 'em at the island, as soon's the blunt's on board, and a pity it is. But you're never happy till you're drunk. Split my sides, I've a sick heart to sail with the likes of you!"

"Easy all, Long John!" cried Israel. "Who's a-crossin' of you?"

"Why, how many tall ships, think ye, now, have I seen laid aboard? And how many brisk lads drying in the sun at Execution Dock?" cried Silver. "And all for this same hurry and hurry and hurry. You hear me? I seen a thing or two at sea, I have. If you would on'y lay your course, and a p'int to windward, you would ride in carriages, you would. But not you! I

know you. You'll have your mouthful of rum tomorrow, and go hang."

"Everybody know'd you was a kind of a chapling, John; but there's others as could hand and steer as well as you," said Israel. "They liked a bit o' fun, they did. They wasn't so high and dry nohow, but took their fling, like jolly companions every one."

"So?" says Silver. "Well, and where are they now? Pew was that sort, and he died a beggarman. Flint was, and he died of rum at Savannah. Ah, they was a sweet crew, they was! On'y, tell me where are they?"

"But," asked Dick, "when we do lay 'em athwart, what are we to do with 'em, anyhow?"

"There's the man for me!" cried the cook admiringly. "That's what I call business. Well, what would you think? Put 'em ashore like maroons? That would have been England's way. Or cut 'em down like that much pork? That would have been Flint's or Billy Bones'."

"Billy was the man for that," said Israel. " 'Dead men don't bite,' says he. Well, he's dead now hisself; he knows the long and short on it now; and if ever a rough hand come to port, it was Billy."

"Right you are," said Silver, "rough and ready. But mark you here: I'm an easy man—I'm quite the gentleman, says you; but this time it's serious. Dooty is dooty, mates. I give my vote—death. When I'm in Parlyment, and riding in my coach, I don't want none of these sealawyers in the cabin a-coming home, unlooked for, like the devil at prayers. Wait is what I say; but when the time comes, why, let her rip!"

"John," cries the cockswain, "you're a man!"

"You'll say so, Israel, when you see," said Silver. "Only one thing I claim—I claim Trelawney. I'll

wring his calf's head off his body with these hands. Dick!" he added, breaking off, "you just jump up, like a sweet lad, and get me an apple, to wet my pipe like."

You may fancy the terror I was in! I should have leaped out and run for it, if I had found the strength; but my limbs and heart alike misgave me. I heard Dick begin to rise, and then someone seemingly stopped him, and the voice of Hands exclaimed:

"Oh, stow that! Don't you get sucking of that bilge, John. Let's have a go of the rum."

"Dick," said Silver, "I trust you. I've a gauge on the keg, mind. There's the key; you fill a pannikin and bring it up."

Terrified as I was, I could not help thinking to myself that this must have been how Mr. Arrow got the strong waters that destroyed him.

Dick was gone but a little while, and during his absence Israel spoke straight in the cook's ear. It was but a word or two that I could catch, and yet I gathered some important news; for, besides other scraps that tended to the same purpose, this whole clause was audible: "Not another man of them'll jine." Hence there were still faithful men on board.

When Dick returned, one after another of the trio took a pannikin and drank—one "To luck"; another with a "Here's to old Flint"; and Silver himself saying, in a kind of song, "Here's to ourselves, and hold your luff, plenty of prizes and plenty of duff."

Just then a sort of brightness fell upon me in the barrel, and, looking up, I found the moon had risen, and was silvering the mizzentop and shining white on the luff of the foresail; and almost at the same time the voice of the lookout shouted, "Land ho!"

☆ XII ☆

Council of War

THERE WAS a great rush of feet across the deck.
I could hear people tumbling up from the cabin and
the foc's'le; and, slipping in an instant outside my
barrel, I dived behind the foresail, made a double toward the stern, and came out upon the open deck in
time to join Hunter and Dr. Livesey in the rush for
the weather bow.

There all hands were already congregated. A belt
of fog had lifted almost simultaneously with the appearance of the moon. Away to the southwest of us
we saw two low hills, about a couple of miles apart,
and rising behind one of them a third and higher hill,
whose peak was still buried in the fog. All three
seemed sharp and conical in figure.

So much I saw, almost in a dream, for I had not yet
recovered from my horrid fear of a minute or two before. And then I heard the voice of Captain Smollett

issuing orders. The *Hispaniola* was laid a couple of points nearer the wind and now sailed a course that would just clear the island on the east.

"And now, men," said the captain, when all was sheeted home, "has any one of you ever seen that land ahead?"

"I have, sir," said Silver. "I've watered there with a trader I was cook in."

"The anchorage is on the south, behind an islet, I fancy?" asked the captain.

"Yes, sir; Skeleton Island they calls it. It were a main place for pirates once, and a hand we had on board knowed all their names for it. That hill to the nor'ard they calls the Foremast Hill; there are three hills in a row running south'ard—fore, main, and mizzen, sir. But the main—that's the big 'un, with the cloud on it—they usually calls the Spyglass, by reason of a lookout they kept when they was in the anchorage cleaning; for it's there they cleaned their ships, sir, asking your pardon."

"I have a chart here," says Captain Smollett. "See if that's the place."

Long John's eyes burned in his head as he took the chart; but, by the fresh look of the paper, I knew he was doomed to disappointment. This was not the map we found in Billy Bones' chest, but an accurate copy, complete in all things—names and heights and soundings—with the single exception of the red crosses and the written notes. Sharp as must have been his annoyance, Silver had the strength of mind to hide it.

"Yes, sir," said he, "this is the spot, to be sure; and very prettily drawn out. Who might have done that, I wonder? The pirates were too ignorant, I reckon. Aye, here it is: 'Capt. Kidd's Anchorage'—just the

name my shipmate called it. There's a strong current runs along the south, and then away nor'ard up the west coast. Right you was, sir," says he, "to haul your wind and keep the weather of the island. Leastways, if such was your intention as to enter and career, and there ain't no better place for that in these waters."

"Thank you, my man," says Captain Smollett. "I'll ask you, later on, to give us a help. You may go."

I was surprised at the coolness with which John avowed his knowledge of the island; and I own I was half frightened when I saw him drawing nearer to myself. He did not know, to be sure, that I had overheard his counsel from the apple barrel, and yet I had, by this time, taken such a horror of his cruelty, duplicity, and power that I could scarce conceal a shudder when he laid his hand upon my arm.

"Ah," says he, "this here is a sweet spot, this island —a sweet spot for a lad to get ashore on. You'll bathe, and you'll climb trees, and you'll hunt goats, you will; and you'll get aloft on them hills like a goat yourself. Why, it makes me young again. I was going to forget my timber leg, I was. It's a pleasant thing to be young, and have ten toes, and you may lay to that. When you want to go a bit of exploring, you just ask old John, and he'll put up a snack for you to take along."

And clapping me in the friendliest way upon the shoulder, he hobbled off forward, and went below.

Captain Smollett, the squire, and Dr. Livesey were talking together on the quarter-deck, and, anxious as I was to tell them my story, I durst not interrupt them openly. While I was still casting about in my thoughts to find some probable excuse, Dr. Livesey called me to his side. He had left his pipe below, and being a slave to tobacco, had meant that I should fetch it; but

as soon as I was near enough to speak and not to be overheard, I broke out immediately: "Doctor, let me speak. Get the captain and squire down to the cabin, and then make some pretense to send for me. I have terrible news."

The doctor changed countenance a little, but next moment he was master of himself.

"Thank you, Jim," said he quite loudly, "that was all I wanted to know," as if he had asked me a question.

And with that he turned on his heel and rejoined the other two. They spoke together for a little, and though none of them started, or raised his voice, or so much as whistled, it was plain enough that Dr. Livesey had communicated my request; for the next thing that I heard was the captain giving an order to Job Anderson, and all hands were piped on deck.

"My lads," said Captain Smollett, "I've a word to say to you. This land that we have sighted is the place we have been sailing for. Mr. Trelawney, being a very openhanded gentleman, as we all know, has just asked me a word or two, and as I was able to tell him that every man on board had done his duty, alow and aloft, as I never ask to see it done better, why, he and I and the doctor are going below to the cabin to drink *your* health and luck, and you'll have grog served out for you to drink *our* health and luck. I'll tell you what I think of this: I think it handsome. And if you think as I do, you'll give a good sea cheer for the gentleman that does it."

The cheer followed—that was a matter of course; but it rang out so full and hearty that I confess I could hardly believe these same men were plotting for our blood.

"One more cheer for Cap'n Smollett," cried Long John, when the first had subsided.

And this also was given with a will.

On the top of that the three gentlemen went below, and not long after, word was sent forward that Jim Hawkins was wanted in the cabin.

I found them all three seated round the table, a bottle of Spanish wine and some raisins before them, and the doctor smoking away, with his wig on his lap, and that, I knew, was a sign that he was agitated. The stern window was open, for it was a warm night, and you could see the moon shining behind on the ship's wake.

"Now, Hawkins," said the squire, "you have something to say. Speak up."

I did as I was bid, and as short as I could make it told the whole details of Silver's conversation. Nobody interrupted me till I was done, nor did any one of the three of them make so much as a movement, but they kept their eyes upon my face from first to last.

"Jim," said Dr. Livesey, "take a seat."

And they made me sit down at table beside them, poured me out a glass of wine, filled my hands with raisins, and all three, one after the other, and each with a bow, drank my good health, and their service to me, for my luck and courage.

"Now, captain," said the squire, "you were right, and I was wrong. I own myself an ass, and I await your orders."

"No more an ass than I, sir," returned the captain. "I never heard of a crew that meant to mutiny but what showed signs before, for any man that had an eye in his head to see the mischief and take steps according. But this crew," he added, "beats me."

"Captain," said the doctor, "with your permission, that Silver's a very remarkable man."

"He'd look remarkably well from a yardarm, sir," returned the captain. "But this is talk; this don't lead to anything. I see three or four points, and with Mr. Trelawney's permission I'll name them."

"You, sir, are the captain. It is for you to speak," says Mr. Trelawney grandly.

"First point," began Mr. Smollett. "We must go on, because we can't turn back. If I gave the word to go about, they would rise at once. Second point, we have time before us—at least until this treasure's found. Third point, there are faithful hands. Now, sir, it's got to come to blows sooner or later; and what I propose is to take time by the forelock, as the saying is, and come to blows some fine day when they least expect it. We can count, I take it, on your own home servants, Mr. Trelawney?"

"As upon myself," declared the squire.

"Three," reckoned the captain, "ourselves make seven, counting Hawkins, here. Now, about the honest hands?"

"Most likely Trelawney's own men," said the doctor; "those he had picked up for himself before he lit on Silver."

"Nay," replied the squire. "Hands was one of mine."

"I did think I could have trusted Hands," added the captain.

"And to think that they're all Englishmen!" broke out the squire. "Sir, I could find it in my heart to blow the ship up."

"Well, gentlemen," said the captain, "the best that I can say is not much. We must lay to, if you please,

and keep a bright lookout. It's trying on a man, I know. It would be pleasanter to come to blows. But there's no help for it till we know our men. Lay to, and whistle for a wind, that's my view."

"Jim here," said the doctor, "can help us more than anyone. The men are not shy with him, and Jim is a noticing lad."

"Hawkins, I put prodigious faith in you," added the squire.

I began to feel pretty desperate at this, for I felt altogether helpless; and yet, by an odd train of circumstances, it was indeed through me that safety came. In the meantime, talk as we pleased, there were only seven out of the twenty-six on whom we knew we could rely; and out of these seven, one was a boy, so that the grown men on our side were six to their nineteen.

PART III

My Shore Adventure

☆ XIII ☆

How My Shore Adventure Began

THE APPEARANCE of the island when I came on deck next morning was altogether changed. Although the breeze had now utterly ceased, we had made a great deal of way during the night and were now lying becalmed about half a mile to the southeast of the low eastern coast. Gray-colored woods covered a large part of the surface. This even tint was indeed broken up by streaks of yellow sand break in the lower lands, and by many tall trees of the pine family, outtopping the others—some singly, some in clumps; but the general coloring was uniform and sad. The hills ran up clear above the vegetation in spires of naked rock. All were strangely shaped, and the Spyglass, which was by three or four hundred feet the tallest on the island, was likewise the strangest in configuration, running up sheer from almost every side and then suddenly cut off at the top like a pedestal to put a statue on.

The *Hispaniola* was rolling scuppers under in the ocean swell. The booms were tearing at the blocks, the rudder was banging to and fro, and the whole ship

creaking, groaning, and jumping like a manufactory. I had to cling tight to the backstay, and the world turned giddily before my eyes; for though I was a good enough sailor when there was way on, this standing still and being rolled about like a bottle was a thing I never learned to stand without a qualm or so, above all in the morning on an empty stomach.

Perhaps it was this—perhaps it was the look of the island, with its gray, melancholy woods, and wild stone spires, and the surf that we could both see and hear foaming and thundering on the steep beach—at least, although the sun shone bright and hot, and the shore birds were fishing and crying all around us, and you would have thought anyone would have been glad to get to land after being so long at sea, my heart sank, as the saying is, into my boots; and from that first look onward, I hated the very thought of Treasure Island.

We had a dreary morning's work before us, for there was no sign of any wind, and the boats had to be got out and manned, and the ship warped three or four miles round the corner of the island, and up the narrow passage to the haven behind Skeleton Island. I volunteered for one of the boats, where I had, of course, no business. The heat was sweltering, and the men grumbled fiercely over their work. Anderson was in command of my boat, and instead of keeping the crew in order, he grumbled as loud as the worst.

"Well," he said, with an oath, "it's not forever."

I thought this was a very bad sign; for, up to that day, the men had gone briskly and willingly about their business; but the very sight of the island had relaxed the cords of discipline.

All the way in, Long John stood by the steersman

and conned the ship. He knew the passage like the palm of his hand; and though the man in the chains got everywhere more water than was down on the chart, John never hesitated once.

"There's a strong scour with the ebb," he said, "and this here passage has been dug out, in a manner of speaking, with a spade."

We brought up just where the anchor was in the chart, about a third of a mile from each shore, the mainland on one side and Skeleton Island on the other. The bottom was clean sand. The plunge of our anchor sent up clouds of birds wheeling and crying over the woods; but in less than a minute they were down again, and all was once more silent.

The place was entirely landlocked, buried in woods, the trees coming right down to high-water mark, the shores mostly flat, and the hilltops standing round at a distance in a sort of amphitheater, one here, one there. Two little rivers, or, rather, two swamps, emptied out into this pond, as you might call it; and the foliage round that part of the shore had a kind of poisonous brightness. From the ship we could see nothing of the house or stockade, for they were quite buried among trees; and if it had not been for the chart on the companion, we might have been the first that had ever anchored there since the island arose out of the seas.

There was not a breath of air moving, nor a sound but that of the surf booming half a mile away along the beaches and against the rocks outside. A peculiar stagnant smell hung over the anchorage—a smell of sodden leaves and rotting tree trunks. I observed the doctor sniffing and sniffing, like someone tasting a bad egg.

"I don't know about treasure," he said, "but I'll stake my wig there's fever here."

If the conduct of the men had been alarming in the boat, it became truly threatening when they had come aboard. They lay about the deck growling together in talk. The slightest order was received with a black look, and grudgingly and carelessly obeyed. Even the honest hands must have caught the infection, for there was not one man aboard to mend another. Mutiny, it was plain, hung over us like a thundercloud.

And it was only we of the cabin party who perceived the danger. Long John was hard at work going from group to group, spending himself in good advice, and as for example no man could have shown a better. He fairly outstripped himself in willingness and civility; he was all smiles to everyone. If an order were given, John would be on his crutch in an instant, with the cheeriest "aye-aye, sir!" in the world; and when there was nothing else to do, he kept up one song after another, as if to conceal the others' discontent.

Of all the gloomy features of that gloomy afternoon, this obvious anxiety on the part of Long John appeared the worst. We held a council in the cabin.

"Sir," said the captain, "if I risk another order, the whole ship'll come about our ears by the run. You see, sir, here it is. I get a rough answer, do I not? Well, if I speak back, pikes will be going in two shakes; if I don't, Silver will see there's something under that, and the game's up. Now we've only one man to rely on."

"And who is that?" asked the squire.

"Silver, sir," returned the captain; "he's as anxious as you and I to smother things up. This is a tiff; he'd soon talk 'em out of it if he had the chance, and what I propose to do is to give him the chance. Let's allow

the men an afternoon ashore. If they all go, why, we'll fight the ship. If they none of them go, well, then, we hold the cabin, and God defend the right. If some go, you mark my word, sir, Silver'll bring 'em aboard again as mild as lambs."

It was so decided; loaded pistols were served out to all the sure men; Hunter, Joyce, and Redruth were taken into our confidence, and received the news with less surprise and a better spirit than we had looked for, and then the captain went on deck and addressed the crew.

"My lads," said he, "we've had a hot day, and are all tired and out of sorts. A turn ashore'll hurt nobody —the boats are still in the water; you can take the gigs, and as many as please may go ashore for the afternoon. I'll fire a gun half an hour before sundown."

I believe the silly fellows must have thought they would break their shins over treasure as soon as they were landed; for they all came out of their sulks in a moment and gave a cheer that started the echo in a faraway hill, and sent the birds once more flying and squalling round the anchorage.

The captain was too bright to be in the way. He whipped out of sight in a moment, leaving Silver to arrange the party; and I fancy it was as well he did so. Had he been on deck, he could no longer so much as have pretended not to understand the situation. It was as plain as day. Silver was the captain, and a mighty rebellious crew he had of it. The honest hands —and I was soon to see it proved that there were such on board—must have been very stupid fellows. Or, rather, I suppose the truth was this, that all hands were disaffected by the example of the ringleaders—only some more, some less; and a few, being good fellows in

the main, could neither be led nor driven any further. It is one thing to be idle and skulk, and quite another to take a ship and murder a number of innocent men.

At last, however, the party was made up. Six fellows were to stay on board, and the remaining thirteen, including Silver, began to embark.

Then it was that there came into my head the first of the mad notions that contributed so much to save our lives. If six men were left by Silver, it was plain our party could not take and fight the ship; and since only six were left, it was equally plain that the cabin party had no present need of my assistance. It occurred to me at once to go ashore. In a jiffy I had slipped over the side, and curled up in the foresheets of the nearest boat, and almost at the same moment she shoved off.

No one took notice of me, only the bow oar saying, "Is that you, Jim? Keep your head down." But Silver, from the other boat, looked sharply over and called out to know if that were me; and from that moment I began to regret what I had done.

The crews raced for the beach; but the boat I was in, having some start, and being at once the lighter and the better manned, shot far ahead of her consort, and the bow had struck among the shoreside trees, and I had caught a branch and swung myself out, and plunged into the nearest thicket, while Silver and the rest were still a hundred yards behind.

"Jim, Jim!" I heard him shouting.

But you may suppose I paid no heed; jumping, ducking, and breaking through, I ran straight before my nose, till I could run no longer.

The First Blow

———————

I WAS SO PLEASED at having given the slip to Long John that I began to enjoy myself and look around me with some interest on the strange land that I was in.

I had crossed a marshy tract full of willows, bulrushes, and odd, outlandish, swampy trees; and I had now come out upon the skirts of an open piece of undulating, sandy country, about a mile long, dotted with a few pines, and a great number of contorted trees, not unlike the oak in growth, but pale in the foliage like willows. On the far side of the open stood one of the hills, with two quaint, craggy peaks, shining vividly in the sun.

I now felt for the first time the joy of exploration. The isle was uninhabited; my shipmates I had left behind, and nothing lived in front of me but dumb brutes and fowls. I turned hither and thither among the trees. Here and there were flowering plants, unknown to me; here and there I saw snakes, and one raised his head from a ledge of rock and hissed at me

with a noise not unlike the spinning of a top. Little did I suppose that he was a deadly enemy and that the noise was the famous rattle.

Then I came to a long thicket of these oaklike trees —live, or evergreen, oaks, I heard afterward they should be called—which grew low along the sand like brambles, the boughs curiously twisted, the foliage compact, like thatch. The thicket stretched down from the top of one of the sandy knolls, spreading and growing taller as it went, until it reached the margin of the broad, reedy fen, through which the nearest of the little rivers soaked its way into the anchorage. The marsh was steaming in the strong sun, and the outline of the Spyglass trembled through the haze.

All at once there began to go a sort of bustle among the bulrushes: a wild duck flew up with a quack, another followed, and soon over the whole surface of the marsh a great cloud of birds hung screaming and circling in the air. I judged at once that some of my shipmates must be drawing near along the borders of the fen. Nor was I deceived; for soon I heard the very distant and low tones of a human voice, which, as I continued to give ear, grew steadily louder and nearer.

This put me in a great fear, and I crawled under cover of the nearest live oak, and squatted there, hearkening, as silent as a mouse.

Another voice answered; and then the first voice, which I now recognized to be Silver's, once more took up the story, and ran on for a long while in a stream, only now and again interrupted by the other. By the sound they must have been talking earnestly, and almost fiercely; but no distinct word came to my hearing.

At last the speakers seemed to have paused, and perhaps to have sat down; for not only did they cease to draw any nearer, but the birds themselves began to grow more quiet, and to settle again to their places in the swamp.

And now I began to feel that I was neglecting my business; that since I had been so foolhardy as to come ashore with these desperadoes, the least I could do was to overhear them at their councils; and that my plain and obvious duty was to draw as close as I could manage, under the favorable ambush of the crouching trees.

I could tell the direction of the speakers pretty exactly, not only by the sound of their voices, but by the behavior of the few birds that still hung in alarm above the heads of the intruders.

Crawling on all fours I made steadily but slowly toward them, till at last, raising my head to an aperture among the leaves, I could see clear down into a little green dell beside the marsh, and closely set about with trees, where Long John Silver and another of the crew stood face to face in conversation.

The sun beat full upon them. Silver had thrown his hat beside him on the ground, and his great, smooth, blond face, all shining with heat, was lifted to the other man's in a kind of appeal.

"Mate," he was saying, "it's because I thinks gold dust of you—gold dust, and you may lay to that! If I hadn't took to you like pitch, do you think I'd have been here a-warning of you? All's up—you can't make nor mend; it's to save your neck that I am speaking, and if one of the wild 'uns knew it, where 'ud I be, Tom—now, tell me, where 'ud I be?"

"Silver," said the other man—and I observed he was

not only red in the face, but spoke as hoarse as a crow, and his voice shook, too, like a taut rope—"Silver," says he, "you're old, and you're honest, or has the name for it; and you've money, too, which lots of poor sailors hasn't; and you're brave, or I'm mistook. And will you tell me you'll let yourself be led away with that kind of a mess of swabs? Not you! As sure as God sees me, I'd sooner lose my hand. If I turn ag'in my dooty—"

And then all of a sudden he was interrupted by a noise. I had found one of the honest hands—well, here, at that same moment, came news of another. Far away out in the marsh there arose, all of a sudden, a sound like a cry of anger, then another on the back of it, and then one horrid, long-drawn scream. The rocks of the Spyglass re-echoed it a score of times; the whole troop of marsh birds rose again, darkening heaven, with a simultaneous whir; and long after that death yell was still ringing in my brain, silence had re-established its empire, and only the rustle of the redescending birds and the boom of the distant surges disturbed the languor of the afternoon.

Tom had leaped at the sound, like a horse at the spur, but Silver had not winked an eye. He stood where he was, resting lightly on his crutch, watching his companion like a snake about to spring.

"John!" said the sailor, stretching out his hand.

"Hands off!" cried Silver, leaping back a yard, as it seemed to me, with the speed and security of a trained gymnast.

"Hands off, if you like, John Silver," said the other. "It's a black conscience that can make you feared of me. But, in heaven's name, tell me what was that?"

"That?" returned Silver, smiling away but warier

than ever, his eye a mere pin point in his big face, but gleaming like a crumb of glass. "That? Oh, I reckon that'll be Alan."

And at this, poor Tom flashed out like a hero.

"Alan!" he cried. "Then rest his soul for a true seaman! And as for you, John Silver, long you've been a mate of mine, but you're mate of mine no more. If I die like a dog, I'll die in my dooty. You've killed Alan, have you? Kill me, too, if you can. But I defies you."

And with that, this brave fellow turned his back directly on the cook and set off walking for the beach. But he was not destined to go far. With a cry, John seized the branch of a tree, whipped the crutch out of his armpit, and sent that uncouth missile hurtling through the air. It struck poor Tom, point foremost and with stunning violence, right between the shoulders in the middle of his back. His hands flew up, he gave a sort of gasp, and fell.

Whether he were injured much or little, none could ever tell. Like enough, to judge from the sound, his back was broken on the spot. But he had no time given him to recover. Silver, agile as a monkey, even without leg or crutch, was on top of him next moment, and had twice buried his knife up to the hilt in that defenseless body. From my place of ambush, I could hear him pant aloud as he struck the blows.

I do not know what it rightly is to faint, but I do know that for the next little while the whole world swam away from before me in a whirling mist: Silver and the birds, and the tall Spyglass hilltop, going round and round and topsy-turvy before my eyes, and all manner of bells ringing and distant voices shouting in my ear.

When I came again to myself, the monster had pulled himself together, his crutch under his arm, his hat upon his head. Just before him Tom lay motionless upon the sward; but the murderer minded him not a whit, cleansing his bloodstained knife the while upon a wisp of grass. Everything else was unchanged, the sun still shining mercilessly on the steaming marsh and the tall pinnacle of the mountain, and I could scarce persuade myself that murder had been actually done and a human life cruelly cut short a moment since, before my eyes.

But now John put his hand into his pocket, brought out a whistle, and blew upon it several modulated blasts that rang far across the heated air. I could not tell, of course, the meaning of the signal, but it instantly awoke my fears. More men would be coming. I might be discovered. They had already slain two of the honest people; after Tom and Alan, might not I come next?

Instantly I began to extricate myself and crawl back again, with what speed and silence I could manage, to the more open portion of the wood. As I did so, I could hear hails coming and going between the old buccaneer and his comrades, and this sound of danger lent me wings. As soon as I was clear of the thicket I ran as I never ran before, scarce minding the direction of my flight, so long as it led me from the murderers; and as I ran, fear grew and grew upon me, until it turned into a kind of frenzy.

Indeed, could anyone be more entirely lost than I? When the gun fired, how should I dare to go down to the boats among those fiends, still smoking from their crime? Would not the first of them who saw me wring my neck like a snipe's? Would not my absence itself

be an evidence to them of my alarm, and therefore of my fatal knowledge? It was all over, I thought. Good-by to the *Hispaniola;* good-by to the squire, the doctor, and the captain! There was nothing left for me but death by starvation or death by the hands of the mutineers.

All this while, as I say, I was still running, and without taking any notice I had drawn near to the foot of the little hill with the two peaks and had got into a part of the island where the live oaks grew more widely apart and seemed more like forest trees in their bearing and dimensions. Mingled with these were a few scattered pines, some fifty, some nearer seventy feet high. The air, too, smelled more fresh than down beside the marsh.

And here a fresh alarm brought me to a standstill with a thumping heart.

The Man of the Island

FROM THE SIDE of the hill, which was here steep and stony, a spout of gravel was dislodged and fell rattling and bounding through the trees. My eyes turned instinctively in that direction and I saw a figure leap with great rapidity behind the trunk of a pine. What it was, whether bear or man or monkey, I could in nowise tell. It seemed dark and shaggy; more I knew not. But the terror of this new apparition brought me to a stand.

I was now, it seemed, cut off upon both sides; behind me the murderers, before me this lurking nondescript. And immediately I began to prefer the dangers that I knew to those I knew not. Silver himself appeared less terrible in contrast with this creature of the woods, and I turned on my heel and, looking sharply behind me over my shoulder, began to retrace my steps in the direction of the boats.

Instantly the figure reappeared, and, making a wide

circuit, began to head me off. I was tired, at any rate; but had I been as fresh as when I rose, I could see it was in vain for me to contend in speed with such an adversary. From trunk to trunk the creature flitted like a deer, running manlike on two legs, but unlike any man that I had ever seen, stooping almost double as it ran. Yet a man it was, I could no longer be in doubt about that.

I began to recall what I had heard of cannibals. I was within an ace of calling for help. But the mere fact that he was a man, however wild, had somewhat reassured me, and my fear of Silver began to revive in proportion. I stood still, therefore, and cast about for some method of escape; and as I was so thinking, the recollection of my pistol flashed into my mind. As soon as I remembered I was not defenseless, courage glowed again in my heart, and I set my face resolutely for this man of the island, and walked briskly toward him.

He was concealed by this time behind another tree trunk, but he must have been watching me closely, for as soon as I began to move in his direction he reappeared and took a step to meet me. Then he hesitated, drew back, came forward again, and at last, to my wonder and confusion, threw himself on his knees and held out his clasped hands in supplication.

At that I once more stopped.

"Who are you?" I asked.

"Ben Gunn," he answered, and his voice sounded hoarse and awkward, like a rusty lock. "I'm poor Ben Gunn, I am; and I haven't spoke with a Christian these three years."

I could now see that he was a white man like myself, and that his features were even pleasing. His skin,

wherever it was exposed, was burned by the sun; even his lips were black, and his fair eyes looked quite startling in so dark a face. Of all the beggarmen that I had seen or fancied, he was the chief for raggedness. He was clothed with tatters of old ship's canvas and old sea cloth; and this extraordinary patchwork was all held together by a system of the most various and incongruous fastenings, brass buttons, bits of stick, and loops of tarry gaskin. About his waist he wore an old brass-buckled leather belt, which was the one thing solid in his whole accouterment.

"Three years!" I cried. "Were you shipwrecked?"

"Nay, mate," said he—"marooned."

I had heard the word, and I knew it stood for a horrible kind of punishment common enough among the buccaneers, in which the offender is put ashore with a little powder and shot, and left behind on some desolate and distant island.

"Marooned three years agone," he continued, "and lived on goats since then, and berries, and oysters. Wherever a man is, says I, a man can do for himself. But, mate, my heart is sore for Christian diet. You mightn't happen to have a piece of cheese about you, now? No? Well, many's the long night I've dreamed of cheese—toasted, mostly—and woke up again, and here I were."

"If ever I can get aboard again," said I, "you shall have cheese by the stone."

All this time he had been feeling the stuff of my jacket, smoothing my hands, looking at my boots, and generally, in the intervals of his speech, showing a childish pleasure in the presence of a fellow creature. But at my last words he perked up into a kind of startled slyness.

"If ever you can get aboard again, says you?" he repeated. "Why, now, who's to hinder you?"

"Not you, I know," was my reply.

"And right you was," he cried. "Now you—what do you call yourself, mate?"

"Jim," I told him.

"Jim, Jim," says he, quite pleased apparently. "Well, now, Jim, I've lived that rough as you'd be ashamed to hear of. Now, for instance, you wouldn't think I had had a pious mother—to look at me?" he asked.

"Why, no, not in particular," I answered.

"Ah, well," said he, "but I had—remarkable pious. And I was a civil, pious boy, and could rattle off my catechism that fast, as you couldn't tell one word from another. And here's what it come to, Jim, and it begun with chuck-farthen on the blessed gravestones! That's what it begun with, but it went further'n that; and so my mother told me, and predicked the whole, she did, the pious woman! But it were Providence that put me here. I've thought it all out in this here lonely island, and I'm back on piety. You don't catch me tasting rum so much; but just a thimbleful for luck, of course, the first chance I have. I'm bound I'll be good, and I see the way to. And, Jim"—looking all round him, and lowering his voice to a whisper—"I'm rich."

I now felt sure that the poor fellow had gone crazy in his solitude; and I suppose I must have shown the feeling in my face, for he repeated the statement hotly:

"Rich! rich! I says. And I'll tell you what: I'll make a man of you, Jim. Ah, Jim, you'll bless your stars, you will, you was the first that found me!"

And at this there came suddenly a lowering shadow

over his face, and he tightened his grasp upon my hand, and raised a forefinger threateningly before my eyes.

"Now, Jim, you tell me true: that ain't Flint's ship?" he asked.

At this I had a happy inspiration. I began to believe that I had found an ally, and I answered him at once.

"It's not Flint's ship, and Flint is dead; but I'll tell you true, as you ask me—there are some of Flint's hands aboard; worse luck for the rest of us."

"Not a man—with one—leg?" he gasped.

"Silver?" I asked.

"Ah, Silver!" says he; "that were his name."

"He's the cook, and the ringleader too."

He was still holding me by the wrist, and at that he gave it quite a wring.

"If you was sent by Long John," he said, "I'm as good as pork, and I know it. But where was you, do you suppose?"

I had made my mind up in a moment, and by way of answer told him the whole story of our voyage and the predicament in which we found ourselves. He heard me with the keenest interest, and when I had done he patted me on the head.

"You're a good lad, Jim," he said; "and you're all in a clove hitch, ain't you? Well, you just put your trust in Ben Gunn—Ben Gunn's the man to do it. Would you think it likely, now, that your squire would prove a liberal-minded one in case of help—him being in a clove hitch, as you remark?"

I told him the squire was the most liberal of men.

"Aye, but you see," returned Ben Gunn, "I didn't mean giving me a gate to keep, and a suit of livery clothes, and such; that's not my mark, Jim. What I

mean is, would he be likely to come down to the toon of, say, one thousand pounds out of money that's as good as a man's own already?"

"I am sure he would," said I. "As it was, all hands were to share."

"*And* a passage home?" he added, with a look of great shrewdness.

"Why," I cried, "the squire's a gentleman. And, besides, if we got rid of the others, we should want you to help work the vessel home."

"Ah," said he, "so you would." And he seemed very much relieved.

"Now, I'll tell you what," he went on. "So much I'll tell you, and no more. I were in Flint's ship when he buried the treasure; he and six along—six strong seamen. They was ashore nigh on a week, and us standing off and on in the old *Walrus*. One fine day up went the signal, and here come Flint by himself in a little boat, and his head done up in a blue scarf. The sun was getting up, and mortal white he looked about the cutwater. But there he was, you mind, and the six all dead—dead and buried. How he done it, not a man aboard us could make out. It was battle, murder, and sudden death, leastways—him against six. Billy Bones was the mate; Long John, he was quartermaster; and they asked him where the treasure was. 'Ah,' says he, 'you can go ashore, if you like, and stay,' he says; 'but as for the ship, she'll beat up for more, by thunder!' That's what he said.

"Well, I was in another ship three years back, and we sighted this island. 'Boys,' said I, 'here's Flint's treasure; let's land and find it.' The cap'n was displeased at that; but my messmates were all of a mind, and landed. Twelve days they looked for it, and

every day they had the worse word for me, until one fine morning all hands went aboard. 'As for you, Benjamin Gunn,' says they, 'here's a musket,' they says, 'and a spade and pickax. You can stay here, and find Flint's money for yourself,' they says.

"Well, Jim, three years have I been here, and not a bite of Christian diet from that day to this. But now, you look here; look at me. Do I look like a man before the mast? No, says you. Nor I weren't, neither, I says."

And with that he winked and pinched me hard.

"Just you mention them words to your squire, Jim" —he went on: "Nor he weren't, neither—that's the words. Three years he were the man of this island, light and dark, fair and rain; and sometimes he would, maybe, think upon a prayer (says you), and sometimes he would, maybe, think of his old mother, so be as she's alive (you'll say); but the most part of Gunn's time (this is what you'll say)—the most part of his time was took up with another matter. And then you'll give him a nip, like I do."

And he pinched me again in the most confidential manner.

"Then," he continued—"then you'll up, and you'll say this: Gunn is a good man (you'll say), and he puts a precious sight more confidence—a precious sight, mind that—in a gen'leman born than in these gen'lemen of fortune, having been one hisself."

"Well," I said, "I don't understand one word that you've been saying. But that's neither here nor there, for how am I to get on board?"

"Ah," said he, "that's the hitch for sure. Well, there's my boat, that I made with my two hands. I keep her under the white rock. If the worst come to

the worst, we might try that after dark. Hi!" he broke out, "what's that?"

For just then, although the sun had still an hour or two to run, all the echoes of the island awoke and bellowed to the thunder of a cannon.

"They have begun to fight!" I cried. "Follow me."

And I began to run toward the anchorage, my terrors all forgotten; while, close at my side, the marooned man in his goatskins trotted easily and lightly.

"Left, left," says he; "keep to your left hand, mate Jim! Under the trees with you! There's where I killed my first goat. They don't come down here now; they're all mastheaded on them mountains for the fear of Benjamin Gunn. Ah! and there's the cetemery"—cemetery, he must have meant. "You see the mounds? I come here and prayed, nows and thens, when I thought maybe a Sunday would be about doo. It weren't quite a chapel, but it seemed more solemn like; and then, says you, Ben Gunn was shorthanded— no chapling, nor so much as a Bible and a flag, you says."

So he kept talking as I ran, neither expecting nor receiving any answer.

The cannon shot was followed, after a considerable interval, by a volley of small arms.

Another pause, and then, not a quarter of a mile in front of me, I beheld the Union Jack flutter in the air above a wood.

PART IV

The Stockade

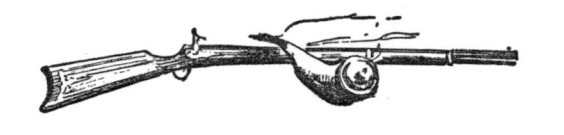

Narrative Continued by the Doctor:
How the Ship Was Abandoned

———————

IT WAS about half past one—three bells in the sea phrase—that the two boats went ashore from the *Hispaniola*. The captain, the squire, and I were talking matters over in the cabin. Had there been a breath of wind, we should have fallen on the six mutineers who were left aboard with us, slipped our cable, and away to sea. But the wind was wanting; and, to complete our helplessness, down came Hunter with the news that Jim Hawkins had slipped into a boat and was gone ashore with the rest.

It never occurred to us to doubt Jim Hawkins, but we were alarmed for his safety. With the men in the temper they were in, it seemed an even chance if we should see the lad again. We ran on deck. The pitch was bubbling in the seams; the nasty stench of the place turned me sick; if ever a man smelled fever and dysentery, it was in that abominable anchorage. The six scoundrels were sitting grumbling under a sail in the forecastle; ashore we could see the gigs made fast,

and a man sitting in each, hard by where the river runs in. One of them was whistling "Lillibullero."

Waiting was a strain; and it was decided that Hunter and I should go ashore with the jolly boat in quest of information.

The gigs had leaned to their right; but Hunter and I pulled straight in, in the direction of the stockade upon the chart. The two who were left guarding their boats seemed in a bustle at our appearance; "Lillibullero" stopped off, and I could see the pair discussing what they ought to do. Had they gone and told Silver, all might have turned out differently; but they had their orders, I suppose, and decided to sit quietly where they were and hark back again to "Lillibullero."

There was a slight bend in the coast, and I steered so as to put it between us; even before we landed we had thus lost sight of the gigs. I jumped out, and came as near running as I durst, with a big silk handkerchief under my hat for coolness' sake, and a brace of pistols ready primed for safety.

I had not gone a hundred yards when I reached the stockade.

This was how it was: A spring of clear water rose almost at the top of a knoll. Well, on the knoll, and enclosing the spring, they had clapped a stout log house, fit to hold twoscore of people on a pinch, and loopholed for musketry on every side. All round this they had cleared a wide space, and then the thing was completed by a paling six feet high, without door or opening, too strong to pull down without time and labor, and too open to shelter the besiegers. The people in the log house had them in every way; they stood quiet in shelter and shot the others like partridges. All they wanted was a good watch and food;

for, short of a complete surprise, they might have held the place against a regiment.

What particularly took my fancy was the spring. For, though we had a good enough place of it in the cabin of the *Hispaniola*, with plenty of arms and ammunition, and things to eat, and excellent wines, there had been one thing overlooked—we had no water. I was thinking this over when there came ringing over the island the cry of a man at the point of death. I was not new to violent death—I have served his Royal Highness the Duke of Cumberland, and got a wound myself at Fontenoy—but I know my pulse went dot and carry one. "Jim Hawkins is gone," was my first thought.

It is something to have been an old soldier, but more still to have been a doctor. There is no time to dilly-dally in our work. And so now I made up my mind instantly, and with no time lost returned to the shore and jumped on board the jolly boat.

By good fortune Hunter pulled a good oar. We made the water fly, and the boat was soon alongside and I aboard the schooner.

I found them all shaken, as was natural. The squire was sitting down, as white as a sheet, thinking of the harm he had led us to, the good soul! and one of the six forecastle hands was little better.

"There's a man," says Captain Smollett, nodding toward him, "new to this work. He came nigh-hand fainting, doctor, when he heard the cry. Another touch of the rudder and that man would join us."

I told my plan to the captain, and between us we settled on the details of its accomplishment.

We put old Redruth in the gallery between the cabin and the forecastle, with three or four loaded

muskets and a mattress for protection. Hunter brought the boat round under the stern port, and Joyce and I set to work loading her with powder tins, muskets, bags of biscuit, kegs of pork, a cask of cognac, and my invaluable medicine chest.

In the meantime, the squire and the captain stayed on deck, and the latter hailed the cockswain, who was the principal man aboard.

"Mr. Hands," he said, "here are two of us with a brace of pistols each. If any one of you six makes a signal of any description, that man's dead."

They were a good deal taken aback and, after a little consultation, one and all tumbled down the fore companion, thinking, no doubt, to take us on the rear. But when they saw Redruth waiting for them in the sparred gallery they went about ship at once, and a head popped out again on deck.

"Down, dog!" cries the captain.

And the head popped back again; and we heard no more, for the time, of these six very fainthearted seamen.

By this time, tumbling things in as they came, we had the jolly boat loaded as much as we dared. Joyce and I got out through the stern port, and we made for shore again, as fast as oars could take us.

This second trip fairly aroused the watchers along shore. "Lillibullero" was dropped again; and just before we lost sight of them behind the little point, one of them whipped ashore and disappeared. I had half a mind to change my plan and destroy their boats, but I feared that Silver and the others might be close at hand, and all might very well be lost by trying for too much.

We had soon touched land in the same place as be-

fore, and set to provision the blockhouse. All three made the first journey, heavily laden, and tossed our stores over the palisade. Then, leaving Joyce to guard them—one man, to be sure, but with half a dozen muskets—Hunter and I returned to the jolly boat and loaded ourselves once more. So we proceeded, without pausing to take breath, till the whole cargo was bestowed, when the two servants took up their position in the blockhouse, and I, with all my power, sculled back to the *Hispaniola*.

That we should have risked a second boatload seems more daring than it really was. They had the advantage of numbers, of course, but we had the advantage of arms. Not one of the men ashore had a musket, and before they could get within range for pistol shooting, we flattered ourselves we should be able to give a good account of a half dozen at least.

The squire was waiting for me at the stern window, all his faintness gone from him. He caught the painter and made it fast, and we fell to loading the boat for our very lives. Pork, powder, and biscuit was the cargo, with only a musket and a cutlass apiece for the squire and me and Redruth and the captain. The rest of the arms and powder we dropped overboard in two fathoms and a half of water, so that we could see the bright steel shining far below us in the sun, on the clean, sandy bottom.

By this time the tide was beginning to ebb, and the ship was swinging round to her anchor. Voices were heard faintly hallooing in the direction of the two gigs; and though this reassured us for Joyce and Hunter, who were well to the eastward, it warned our party to be off.

Redruth retreated from his place in the gallery, and

dropped into the boat, which we then brought round to the ship's counter, to be handier for Captain Smollett.

"Now, men," said he, "do you hear me?"

There was no answer from the forecastle.

"It's to you, Abraham Gray—it's to you I am speaking."

Still no reply.

"Gray," resumed Mr. Smollett, a little louder, "I am leaving this ship, and I order you to follow your captain. I know you are a good man at bottom, and I dare say not one of the lot of you's as bad as he makes out. I have my watch here in my hand; I give you thirty seconds to join me in."

There was a pause.

"Come, my fine fellow," continued the captain, "don't hang so long in stays. I'm risking my life, and the lives of these good gentlemen here every second."

There was a sudden scuffle, a sound of blows, and out burst Abraham Gray with a knife cut on the side of the cheek, and came running to the captain, like a dog to the whistle.

"I'm with you, sir," said he.

And the next moment he and the captain had dropped aboard of us, and we had shoved off and given way.

We were clear out of the ship, but not yet ashore in our stockade.

☆ XVII ☆

Narrative Continued by the Doctor:
The Jolly Boat's Last Trip

THIS FIFTH TRIP WAS quite different from any
of the others. In the first place, the little gallipot of a
boat that we were in was gravely overloaded. Five
grown men, and three of them—Trelawney, Redruth,
and the captain—over six feet high, was already more
than she was meant to carry. Add to that the powder,
pork, and bread bags. The gunwale was lipping
a-stern. Several times we shipped a little water, and
my breeches and the tails of my coat were all soaking
wet before we had gone a hundred yards.

The captain made us trim the boat, and we got her to
lie a little more evenly. All the same we were afraid to
breathe.

In the second place, the ebb was now making—a
strong rippling current running westward through the
basin, and then south'ard and seaward down the
straits by which we had entered in the morning. Even
the ripples were a danger to our overloaded craft; but
the worst of it was that we were swept out of our true

course and away from our proper landing place behind the point. If we let the current have its way, we
should come ashore beside the gigs, where the pirates
might appear at any moment.

"I cannot keep her head for the stockade, sir," said I
to the captain. I was steering, while he and Redruth,
two fresh men, were at the oars. "The tide keeps
washing her down. Could you pull a little stronger?"

"Not without swamping the boat," said he. "You
must bear up, sir, if you please—bear up until you see
you're gaining."

I tried, and found by experiment that the tide kept
sweeping us westward until I had laid her head due
east, or just about right angles to the way we ought
to go.

"We'll never get ashore at this rate," said I.

"If it's the only course that we can lie, sir, we must
even lie it," returned the captain. "We must keep up-
stream. You see, sir," he went on, "if once we dropped
to leeward of the landing place, it's hard to say where
we should get ashore, besides the chance of being
boarded by the gigs; whereas the way we go the current must slacken, and then we can dodge back along
the shore."

"The current's less a'ready, sir," said the man Gray,
who was sitting in the foresheets; "you can ease her off
a bit."

"Thank you, my man," said I, quite as if nothing had
happened; for we had all quietly made up our minds
to treat him like one of ourselves.

Suddenly the captain spoke up again, and I thought
his voice was a little changed.

"The gun!" said he.

"I have thought of that," said I, for I made sure he

was thinking of a bombardment of the fort. "They could never get the gun ashore, and if they did, they could never haul it through the woods."

"Look astern, doctor," replied the captain.

We had entirely forgotten the long nine; and there, to our horror, were the five rogues busy about her, getting off her jacket, as they called the stout tarpaulin cover under which she sailed. Not only that, but it flashed into my mind at the same moment that the round shot and the powder for the gun had been left behind, and a stroke with an ax would put it all into the possession of the evil ones aboard.

"Israel was Flint's gunner," said Gray hoarsely.

At any risk we put the boat's head direct for the landing place. By this time we had got so far out of the run of the current that we kept steerageway even at our necessarily gentle rate of rowing, and I could keep her steady for the goal. But the worst of it was that, with the course I now held, we turned our broadside instead of our stern to the *Hispaniola* and offered a target like a barn door.

I could hear, as well as see, that brandy-faced rascal, Israel Hands, plumping down a round shot on the deck.

"Who's the best shot?" asked the captain.

"Mr. Trelawney, out and away," said I.

"Mr. Trelawney, will you please pick me off one of these men, sir? Hands, if possible," said the captain.

Trelawney was as cool as steel. He looked to the priming of his gun.

"Now," cried the captain, "easy with that gun, sir, or you'll swamp the boat. All hands stand by to trim her when he aims."

The squire raised his gun, the rowing ceased, and we

leaned over to the other side to keep the balance, and all was so nicely contrived that we did not ship a drop.

They had the gun, by this time, slewed round upon the swivel, and Hands, who was at the muzzle with the rammer, was, in consequence, the most exposed. However, we had no luck; for just as Trelawney fired, down he stooped, the ball whistled over him, and it was one of the other four who fell.

The cry he gave was echoed, not only by his companions on board, but by a great number of voices from the shore, and looking in that direction I saw the other pirates trooping out from among the trees and tumbling into their places in the boats.

"Here come the gigs, sir," said I.

"Give way then," cried the captain. "We mustn't mind if we swamp her now. If we can't get ashore all's up."

"Only one of the gigs is being manned, sir," I added, "the crew of the other is most likely going round by shore to cut us off."

"They'll have a hot run, sir," returned the captain. "Jack ashore, you know. It's not them I mind; it's the round shot. Carpet bowls! My lady's maid couldn't miss. Tell us, squire, when you see the match, and we'll hold water."

In the meanwhile we had been making headway at a good pace for a boat so overloaded, and we had shipped but little water in the process. We were now close in, thirty or forty strokes and we should beach her; for the ebb had already disclosed a narrow belt of sand below the clustering trees. The gig was no longer to be feared; the little point had already concealed it from our eyes. The ebb tide, which had so cruelly delayed us, was now making reparation and

delaying our assailants. The one source of danger was the gun.

"If I durst," said the captain, "I'd stop and pick off another man."

But it was plain that they meant nothing should delay their shot. They had never so much as looked at their fallen comrade, though he was not dead, and I could see him trying to crawl away.

"Ready!" cried the squire.

"Hold!" cried the captain, quick as an echo.

And he and Redruth backed with a great heave that sent her stern bodily under water. The report fell in at the same instant of time. This was the first that Jim heard, the sound of the squire's shot not having reached him. Where the ball passed, not one of us precisely knew; but I fancy it must have been over our heads, and that the wind of it may have contributed to our disaster.

At any rate, the boat sank by the stern, quite gently, in three feet of water, leaving the captain and myself, facing each other, on our feet. The other three took complete headers and came up again, drenched and bubbling.

So far there was no great harm. No lives were lost, and we could wade ashore in safety. But there were all our stores at the bottom, and, to make things worse, only two guns out of five remained in a state for service. Mine I had snatched from my knees and held over my head, by a sort of instinct. As for the captain, he had carried his over his shoulder by a bandoleer, and, like a wise man, lock uppermost. The other three had gone down with the boat.

To add to our concern, we heard voices already drawing near us in the woods alongshore; and we had

not only the danger of being cut off from the stockade in our half-crippled state, but the fear before us
whether, if Hunter and Joyce were attacked by half
a dozen, they would have the sense and conduct to
stand firm. Hunter was steady, that we knew; Joyce
was a doubtful case—a pleasant, polite man for a valet,
and to brush one's clothes, but not entirely fitted for a
man of war.

With all this in our minds, we waded ashore as fast
as we could, leaving behind us the poor jolly boat,
and a good half of all our powder and provisions.

Narrative Continued by the Doctor: End of the First Day's Fighting

———

WE MADE our best speed across the strip of wood that now divided us from the stockade, and at every step we took the voices of the buccaneers rang nearer. Soon we could hear their footfalls as they ran, and the cracking of the branches as they breasted across a bit of thicket.

I began to see we should have a brush for it in earnest, and looked to my priming.

"Captain," said I, "Trelawney is the dead shot. Give him your gun; his own is useless."

They exchanged guns, and Trelawney, silent and cool as he had been since the beginning of the bustle, hung a moment on his heel to see that all was fit for service. At the same time, observing Gray to be unarmed, I handed him my cutlass. It did all our hearts good to see him spit in his hand, knit his brows, and make the blade sing through the air. It was plain from every line of his body that our new hand was worth his salt.

Forty paces farther we came to the edge of the wood and saw the stockade in front of us. We struck the enclosure about the middle of the south side, and

almost at the same time seven mutineers—Job Anderson, the boatswain, at their head—appeared in full cry at the southwestern corner.

They paused, as if taken aback; and before they recovered, not only the squire and I, but Hunter and Joyce from the blockhouse, had time to fire. The four shots came in rather a scattering volley; but they did the business: one of the enemy actually fell, and the rest, without hesitation, turned and plunged into the trees.

After reloading, we walked down the outside of the palisade to see to the fallen enemy. He was stone dead —shot through the heart.

We began to rejoice over our good success, when just at that moment a pistol cracked in the bush, a ball whistled close past my ear, and poor Tom Redruth

stumbled and fell his length on the ground. Both the squire and I returned the shot; but as we had nothing to aim at, it is probable we only wasted powder. Then we reloaded, and turned our attention to poor Tom.

The captain and Gray were already examining him; and I saw with half an eye that all was over.

I believe the readiness of our return volley had scattered the mutineers once more, for we were suffered without further molestation to get the poor old gamekeeper hoisted over the stockade, and carried, groaning and bleeding, into the log house.

Poor old fellow, he had not uttered one word of surprise, complaint, fear, or even acquiescence, from the very beginning of our troubles till now, when we had laid him down in the log house to die. He had lain like a Trojan behind his mattress in the gallery; he had followed every order silently, doggedly, and well; he was the oldest of our party by a score of years; and now, sullen, old, serviceable servant, it was he that was to die.

The squire dropped down beside him on his knees and kissed his hand, crying like a child.

"Be I going, doctor?" he asked.

"Tom, my man," said I, "you're going home."

"I wish I had had a lick at them with the gun first," he replied.

"Tom," said the squire, "say you forgive me, won't you?"

"Would that be respectful like, from me to you, squire?" was the answer. "Howsoever, so be it, amen!"

After a little while of silence, he said he thought somebody might read a prayer. "It's the custom, sir,"

he added apologetically. And not long after, without another word, he passed away.

In the meantime, the captain, whom I had observed to be wonderfully swollen about the chest and pockets, had turned out a great many various stores—the British colors, a Bible, a coil of stoutish rope, pen, ink, the logbook, and pounds of tobacco. He had found a longish fir tree lying felled and trimmed in the enclosure and, with the help of Hunter, had set it up at the corner of the log house where the trunks crossed and made an angle. Then, climbing on the roof, he had with his own hand bent and run up the colors.

This seemed mightily to relieve him. He re-entered the log house and set about counting up the stores, as if nothing else existed. But he had an eye on Tom's passage, for all that; and as soon as all was over, came forward with another flag, and reverently spread it on the body.

"Don't you take on, sir," he said, shaking the squire's hand. "All's well with him; no fear for a hand that's been shot down in his duty to captain and owner. It mayn't be good divinity, but it's a fact."

Then he pulled me aside.

"Dr. Livesey," he said, "in how many weeks do you and squire expect the consort?"

I told him it was a question, not of weeks, but of months; that if we were not back by the end of August, Blandly was to send to find us, but neither sooner nor later. "You can calculate for yourself," I said.

"Why, yes," returned the captain, scratching his head, "and making a large allowance, sir, for all the gifts of Providence, I should say we were pretty close hauled."

"How do you mean?" I asked.

"It's a pity, sir, we lost that second load. That's what I mean," replied the captain. "As for powder and shot, we'll do. But the rations are short, very short—so short, Dr. Livesey, that we're, perhaps, as well without that extra mouth."

And he pointed to the dead body under the flag.

Just then, with a roar and a whistle, a round shot passed high above the roof of the log house and plumped far beyond us in the wood.

"Oho!" said the captain. "Blaze away! You've little enough powder already, my lads."

At the second trial the aim was better, and the ball descended inside the stockade, scattering a cloud of sand, but doing no further damage.

"Captain," said the squire, "the house is quite invisible from the ship. It must be the flag they are aiming at. Would it not be wiser to take it in?"

"Strike my colors!" cried the captain. "No, sir, not I." And, as soon as he had said the words, I think we all agreed with him. For it was not only a piece of stout, seamanly good feeling, it was good policy besides, and showed our enemies that we despised their cannonade.

All through the evening they kept thundering away. Ball after ball flew over or fell short, or kicked up the sand in the enclosure, but they had to fire so high that the shot fell dead and buried itself in the soft sand. We had no ricochet to fear; and though one popped in through the roof of the log house and out again through the floor, we soon got used to that sort of horseplay and minded it no more than cricket.

"There is one thing good about all this," observed the captain, "the wood in front of us is likely clear. The ebb has made a good while; our stores should be

uncovered. Volunteers to go and bring in pork."

Gray and Hunter were the first to come forward. Well armed, they stole out of the stockade, but it proved a useless mission. The mutineers were bolder than we fancied, or they put more trust in Israel's gunnery. For four or five of them were busy carrying off our stores, and wading out with them to one of the gigs that lay close by, pulling an oar or so to hold her steady against the current. Silver was in the stern sheets in command; and every man of them was now provided with a musket from some secret magazine of their own.

The captain sat down to his log, and here is the beginning of the entry:

"Alexander Smollett, master; David Livesey, ship's doctor; Abraham Gray, carpenter's mate; John Trelawney, owner; John Hunter and Richard Joyce, owner's servants, landsmen—being all that is left faithful of the ship's company—with stores for ten days at short rations, came ashore this day, and flew British colors on the log house in Treasure Island. Thomas Redruth, owner's servant, landsman, shot by the mutineers; James Hawkins, cabin boy—"

And at the same time I was wondering over poor Jim Hawkins' fate.

A hail on the land side.

"Somebody hailing us," said Hunter, who was on guard.

"Doctor! squire! captain! Hullo, Hunter, is that you?" came the cries.

And I ran to the door in time to see Jim Hawkins, safe and sound, come climbing over the stockade.

☆ XIX ☆

Narrative Resumed by Jim Hawkins:
The Garrison in the Stockade

AS SOON as Ben Gunn saw the colors he came to a halt, stopped me by the arm, and sat down.

"Now," said he, "there's your friends, sure enough."

"Far more likely it's the mutineers," I answered.

"That!" he cried. "Why, in a place like this, where nobody puts in but gen'lemen of fortune, Silver would fly the Jolly Roger, you don't make no doubt of that. No; that's your friends. There's been blows, too, and I reckon your friends has had the best of it; and here they are ashore in the old stockade, as was made years and years ago by Flint. Ah! he was the man to have a headpiece, was Flint! Barring rum, his match were never seen. He were afraid of none, not he; on'y Silver—Silver was that genteel."

"Well," said I, "that may be so, and so be it; all the more reason that I should hurry on and join my friends."

"Nay, mate," returned Ben, "not you. You're a good boy, or I'm mistook; but you're on'y a boy, all

told. Now, Ben Gunn is fly. Rum wouldn't bring me there, where you're going—not rum wouldn't, till I see your born gen'lemen, and gets it on his word of honor. And you won't forget my words: 'A precious sight (that's what you'll say), a precious sight more confidence'—and then nips him."

And he pinched me the third time with the same air of cleverness.

"And when Ben Gunn is wanted, you know where to find him, Jim. Just where you found him today. And him that comes is to have a white thing in his hand: and he's to come alone. Oh! and you'll say this: 'Ben Gunn,' says you, 'has reasons of his own.'"

"Well," said I, "I believe I understand. You have something to propose, and you wish to see the squire or the doctor; and you're to be found where I found you. Is that all?"

"And when? says you," he added. "Why, from about noon observation to about six bells."

"Good," said I, "and now may I go?"

"You won't forget?" he inquired anxiously. "Precious sight, and reasons of his own, says you. Reasons of his own; that's the mainstay, as between man and man. Well, then"—still holding me—"I reckon you can go, Jim. And, Jim, if you was to see Silver, you wouldn't go for to sell Ben Gunn? Wild horses wouldn't draw it from you? No, says you. And if them pirates camp ashore, Jim, what would you say but there'd be widders in the morning?"

Here he was interrupted by a loud report, and a cannon ball came tearing through the trees and pitched in the sand, not a hundred yards from where we two were talking together. The next moment each of us had taken to his heels in a different direction.

For a good hour to come, frequent reports shook the island, and balls kept crashing through the woods. I moved from hiding place to hiding place, always pursued, or so it seemed to me, by these terrifying missiles. But toward the end of the bombardment, though still I durst not venture in the direction of the stockade, where the balls fell oftenest, I had begun, in a manner, to pluck up my heart again; and after a long detour to the east, crept down among the shore-side trees.

The sun had just set, the sea breeze was rustling and tumbling in the woods, and ruffling the gray surface of the anchorage; the tide, too, was far out, and great tracts of sand lay uncovered; the air, after the heat of the day, chilled me through my jacket.

The *Hispaniola* still lay where she had anchored; but, sure enough, there was the Jolly Roger—the black flag of piracy—flying from her peak. Even as I looked, there came another red flash and another report that sent the echoes clattering, and one more round shot whistled through the air. It was the last of the cannonade.

I lay for some time watching the bustle which succeeded the attack. Men were demolishing something with axes on the beach near the stockade; the poor jolly boat, I afterward discovered. Away, near the mouth of the river, a great fire was glowing among the trees, and between that point and the ship one of the gigs kept coming and going, the men, whom I had seen so gloomy, shouting at the oars like children. But there was a sound in their voices which suggested rum.

At length I thought I might return toward the stockade. I was pretty far down on the low, sandy

spit that incloses the anchorage to the east, and is joined at half-water to Skeleton Island; and now, as I rose to my feet, I saw, some distance farther down the spit, and rising from among low bushes, an isolated rock, pretty high, and peculiarly white in color. It occurred to me that this might be the white rock of which Ben Gunn had spoken, and that someday or other a boat might be wanted, and I should know where to look for one.

Then I skirted among the woods until I had regained the rear, or shoreward side, of the stockade, and was soon warmly welcomed by the faithful party.

I had soon told my story, and began to look about me. The log house was made of unsquared trunks of pine—roof, walls, and floor. The latter stood in several places as much as a foot or a foot and a half above the surface of the sand. There was a porch at the door, and under this porch the little spring welled up into an artificial basin of a rather odd kind—no other than a great ship's kettle of iron, with the bottom knocked out and sunk to "her bearings," as the captain said, among the sand.

Little had been left beside the framework of the house; but in one corner there was a stone slab laid down by way of hearth, and an old rusty iron basket to contain the fire.

The slopes of the knoll and all the inside of the stockade had been cleared of timber to build the house, and we could see by the stumps what a fine and lofty grove had been destroyed. Most of the soil had been washed away or buried in drift after the removal of the trees; only where the streamlet ran down from the kettle a thick bed of moss and some ferns and little creeping bushes were still green among the sand.

Very close around the stockade—too close for defense, they said—the wood still flourished high and dense, all of fir on the land side, but toward the sea with a large admixture of live oaks.

The cold evening breeze, of which I have spoken, whistled through every chink of the rude building and sprinkled the floor with a continual rain of fine sand. There was sand in our eyes, sand in our teeth, sand in our suppers, sand dancing in the spring at the bottom of the kettle, for all the world like porridge beginning to boil. Our chimney was a square hole in the roof; it was but a little part of the smoke that found its way out, and the rest eddied about the house and kept us coughing and wiping the eye.

Add to this that Gray, the new man, had his face tied up in a bandage for a cut he had got in breaking away from the mutineers; and that poor old Tom Redruth, still unburied, lay along the wall, stiff and stark, under the Union Jack.

If we had been allowed to sit idle we should all have fallen in the blues, but Captain Smollett was never the man for that. All hands were called up before him, and he divided us into watches. The doctor, and Gray, and I, for one; the squire, Hunter, and Joyce, upon the other. Tired though we all were, two were sent out for firewood; two more were set to dig a grave for Redruth; the doctor was named cook; I was put sentry at the door; and the captain himself went from one to another, keeping up our spirits and lending a hand wherever it was wanted.

From time to time the doctor came to the door for a little air and to rest his eyes, which were almost smoked out of his head; and whenever he did so, he had a word for me.

"That man Smollett," he said once, "is a better man than I am. And when I say that it means a deal, Jim."

Another time he came and was silent for a while. Then he put his head on one side, and looked at me.

"Is this Ben Gunn a man?" he asked.

"I do not know, sir," said I. "I am not very sure whether he's sane."

"If there's any doubt about the matter, he is," returned the doctor. "A man who has been three years biting his nails on a desert island, Jim, can't expect to appear as sane as you or me. It doesn't lie in human nature. Was it cheese you said he had a fancy for?"

"Yes, sir, cheese," I answered.

"Well, Jim," says he, "just see the good that comes of being dainty in your food. You've seen my snuff-box, haven't you? But you never saw me take snuff, did you? The reason being that in my snuffbox I carry a piece of Parmesan cheese—a cheese which is made in Italy, very nutritious. Well, that's for Ben Gunn!"

Before supper was eaten we buried old Tom in the sand, and stood round him for a while bareheaded in the breeze. A good deal of firewood had been got in, but not enough for the captain's fancy; and he shook his head over it, and told us we "must get back to this tomorrow rather livelier." Then, when we had eaten our pork and each had a good stiff glass of brandy grog, the three chiefs got together in a corner to discuss our prospects.

It appears they were at their wits' end what to do, the stores being so low that we must have been starved into surrender long before help came. But our best hope, it was decided, was to kill off the buccaneers until they either hauled down their flag or ran away

with the *Hispaniola*. From nineteen they were already reduced to fifteen, two others were wounded, and one, at least—the man shot beside the gun—severely wounded, if he were not dead. Every time we had a crack at them, we were to take it, saving our own lives, with the extremest care. And, besides that, we had two able allies—rum and the climate.

As for the first, though we were about half a mile away we could hear them roaring and singing late into the night; and as for the second, the doctor staked his wig that, camped where they were in the marsh, and unprovided with remedies, the half of them would be on their backs before a week.

"So," he added, "if we are not all shot down first, they'll be glad to be packing in the schooner. It's always a ship, and they can get to buccaneering again, I suppose."

"First ship that ever I lost," said Captain Smollett.

I was dead tired, as you may fancy; and when I got to sleep, which was not till after a great deal of tossing, I slept like a log of wood.

The rest had long been up, and had already breakfasted and increased the pile of firewood by about half as much again, when I was awakened by a bustle and the sound of voices.

"Flag of truce!" I heard someone say; and then, immediately after, with a cry of surprise, "Silver himself!"

And, at that, up I jumped and, rubbing my eyes, ran to a loophole in the wall.

☆ XX ☆

Silver's Embassy

———————

SURE ENOUGH, there were two men just outside
the stockade, one of them waving a white cloth; the
other, no less a person than Silver himself, standing
placidly by.

It was still quite early, and the coldest morning that
I think I ever was abroad in; a chill that pierced into
the marrow. The sky was bright and cloudless overhead, and the tops of the trees shone rosily in the sun.
But where Silver stood with his lieutenant all was still
in shadow, and they waded knee-deep in a low white
vapor, that had crawled during the night out of the
morass. The chill and the vapor taken together told a
poor tale of the island. It was plainly a damp, feverish,
unhealthy spot.

"Keep indoors, men," said the captain. "Ten to one,
this is a trick."

Then he hailed the buccaneer.

"Who goes? Stand, or we fire."

"Flag of truce," cried Silver.

The captain was in the porch, keeping himself care-

fully out of the way of a treacherous shot should any be intended. He turned and spoke to us:

"Doctor's watch on the lookout. Dr. Livesey, take the north side, if you please; Jim, the east; Gray, west. The watch below, all hands to load muskets. Lively, men, and careful."

And then he turned again to the mutineers.

"And what do you want with your flag of truce?" he cried.

This time it was the other man who replied.

"Cap'n Silver, sir, to come on board and make terms," he shouted.

"Cap'n Silver! Don't know him. Who's he?" cried the captain. And we could hear him adding to himself: "Cap'n, is it? My heart, and here's promotion!"

Long John answered for himself.

"Me, sir. These poor lads have chosen me cap'n, after your desertion, sir"—laying a particular emphasis upon the word "desertion." "We're willing to submit, if we can come to terms, and no bones about it. All I ask is your word, Cap'n Smollett, to let me safe and sound out of this here stockade, and one minute to get out o' shot before a gun is fired."

"My man," said Captain Smollett, "I have not the slightest desire to talk to you. If you wish to talk to me, you can come, that's all. If there's any treachery it'll be on your side, and the Lord help you."

"That's enough, cap'n," shouted Long John cheerily. "A word from you's enough. I know a gentleman, and you may lay to that."

We could see the man who carried the flag of truce attempting to hold Silver back. Nor was that wonderful, seeing how cavalier had been the captain's answer. But Silver laughed at him aloud and slapped

him on the back, as if the idea of alarm had been absurd. Then he advanced to the stockade, threw over his crutch, got a leg up, and with great vigor and skill succeeded in surmounting the fence and dropping safely to the other side.

I will confess that I was far too much taken up with what was going on to be of the slightest use as sentry; indeed, I had already deserted my eastern loophole and crept up behind the captain, who had now seated himself on the threshold, with his elbows on his knees, his head in his hands, and his eyes fixed on the water, as it bubbled out of the old iron kettle in the sand. He was whistling to himself, "Come, Lasses and Lads."

Silver had terrible hard work getting up the knoll. What with the steepness of the incline, the thick tree stumps, and the soft sand, he and his crutch were as helpless as a ship in stays. But he stuck to it like a man in silence, and at last arrived before the captain, whom he saluted in the handsomest style. He was tricked out in his best; an immense blue coat, thick with brass buttons, hung as low as to his knees, and a fine laced hat was set on the back of his head.

"Here you are, my man," said the captain, raising his head. "You had better sit down."

"You ain't a-going to let me inside, cap'n?" complained Long John. "It's a main cold morning to be sure, sir, to sit outside upon the sand."

"Why, Silver," said the captain, "if you had pleased to be an honest man, you might have been sitting in your galley. It's your own doing. You're either my ship's cook—and then you were treated handsome—or Cap'n Silver, a common mutineer and pirate, and then you can go hang!"

"Well, well, cap'n," returned the sea cook, sitting

down as he was bidden on the sand, "you'll have to give me a hand up again, that's all. A sweet pretty place you have of it here. Ah, there's Jim! The top of the morning to you, Jim. Doctor, here's my service. Why, there you all are together like a happy family, in a manner of speaking."

"If you have anything to say, my man, better say it," said the captain.

"Right you were, Cap'n Smollett," replied Silver. "Dooty is dooty, to be sure. Well, now, you look here, that was a good lay of yours last night. I don't deny it was a good lay. Some of you pretty handy with a handspike end. And I'll not deny neither but what some of my people was shook—maybe all was shook; maybe I was shook myself; maybe that's why I'm here for terms. But you mark me, cap'n, it won't do twice, by thunder! We'll have to do sentry-go, and ease off a point or so on the rum. Maybe you think we were all a sheet in the wind's eye. But I'll tell you I was sober; I was on'y dog tired; and if I'd awoke a second sooner I'd a' caught you at the act, I would. He wasn't dead when I got round to him, not he."

"Well?" says Captain Smollett, as cool as can be.

All that Silver said was a riddle to him, but you would never have guessed it from his tone. As for me, I began to have an inkling. Ben Gunn's last words came back to my mind. I began to suppose that he had paid the buccaneers a visit while they all lay drunk together round their fire, and I reckoned up with glee that we had only fourteen enemies to deal with.

"Well, here it is," said Silver. "We want that treasure, and we'll have it—that's our point! You would just as soon save your lives, I reckon; and that's yours. You have a chart, haven't you?"

"That's as may be," replied the captain.

"Oh, well, you have, I know that," returned Long John. "You needn't be so husky with a man; there ain't a particle of service in that, and you may lay to it. What I mean is, we want your chart. Now, I never meant you no harm, myself."

"That won't do with me, my man," interrupted the captain. "We know exactly what you meant to do, and we don't care; for now, you see, you can't do it."

And the captain looked at him calmly and proceeded to fill a pipe.

"If Abe Gray—" Silver broke out.

"Avast there!" cried Mr. Smollett. "Gray told me nothing, and I asked him nothing; and what's more I would see you and him and this whole island blown clean out of the water into blazes first. So there's my mind for you, my man, on that."

This little whiff of temper seemed to cool Silver down. He had been growing nettled before, but now he pulled himself together.

"Like enough," said he. "I would set no limits to what gentlemen might consider shipshape, or might not, as the case were. And, seein' as how you are about to take a pipe, cap'n, I'll make so free as to do likewise."

And he filled a pipe and lighted it; and the two men sat silently smoking for quite a while, now looking each other in the face, now stopping their tobacco, now leaning forward to spit. It was as good as the play to see them.

"Now," resumed Silver, "here it is. You give us the chart to get the treasure by, and drop shooting poor seamen, and stoving of their heads in while asleep. You do that, and we'll offer you a choice. Either you

come aboard along of us, once the treasure shipped, and then I'll give you my affydavy, upon my word of honor, to clap you somewhere safe ashore. Or, if that ain't to your fancy, some of my hands being rough, and having old scores, on account of hazing, then you can stay here, you can. We'll divide stores with you, man for man; and I'll give my affydavy, as before, to speak the first ship I sight, and send 'em here to pick you up. Now you'll own that's talking. Handsomer you couldn't look to get, not you. And I hope"—raising his voice—"that all hands in this here blockhouse will overhaul my words, for what is spoke to one is spoke to all."

Captain Smollett rose from his seat and knocked out the ashes of his pipe in the palm of his left hand.

"Is that all?" he asked.

"Every last word, by thunder!" answered John. "Refuse that, and you've seen the last of me but musket balls."

"Very good," said the captain. "Now you'll hear me. If you'll come up one by one, unarmed, I'll engage to clap you all in irons, and take you home to a fair trial in England. If you won't, my name is Alexander Smollett, I've flown my sovereign's colors, and I'll see you all to Davy Jones. You can't find the treasure. You can't sail the ship—there's not a man among you fit to sail the ship. You can't fight us—Gray, there, got away from five of you. Your ship's in irons, Master Silver; you're on a lee shore, and so you'll find. I stand here and tell you so; and they're the last good words you'll get from me, for, in the name of heaven, I'll put a bullet in your back when next I meet you. Tramp, my lad. Bundle out of this, please, hand over hand, and double quick."

Silver's face was a picture; his eyes started in his head with wrath. He angrily shook the fire out of his pipe.

"Give me a hand up!" he cried.

"Not I," returned the captain.

"Who'll give me a hand up?" he roared.

Not a man among us moved. Growling the foulest imprecations, he crawled along the sand till he got hold of the porch and could hoist himself again upon his crutch. Then he spat into the spring.

"There!" he cried, "that's what I think of ye. B-fore an hour's out, I'll stove in your old blockhouse like a rum puncheon. Laugh, by thunder, laugh! Before an hour's out ye'll laugh upon the other side. Them that die'll be the lucky ones."

And with a dreadful oath he stumbled off, plowed down the sand, was helped across the stockade, after four or five failures, by the man with the flag of truce, and disappeared in an instant afterward among the trees.

☆ XXI ☆

The Attack

_____

AS SOON as Silver disappeared, the captain, who had been closely watching him, turned toward the interior of the house, and found not a man of us at his post but Gray. It was the first time we had ever seen him angry.

"Quarters!" he roared. And then, as we all slunk back to our places, "Gray," he said, "I'll put your name in the log; you've stood by your duty like a seaman. Mr. Trelawney, I'm surprised at you, sir. Doctor, I thought you had worn the king's coat! If that was how you served at Fontenoy, sir, you'd have been better in your berth."

The doctor's watch were all back at their loopholes, the rest were busy loading the spare muskets, and everyone with a red face, you may be certain, and a flea in his ear, as the saying is.

The captain looked on for a while in silence. Then he spoke.

"My lads," said he, "I've given Silver a broadside. I pitched it in red-hot on purpose; and before the hour's

out, as he said, we shall be boarded. We're outnumbered, I needn't tell you that, but we fight in shelter; and, a minute ago, I should have said we fought with discipline. I've no manner of doubt that we can drub them, if you choose." Then he went the rounds, and saw, as he said, that all was clear.

On the two short sides of the house, east and west, there were only two loopholes; on the south side where the porch was, two again; and on the north side, five. There was a round score of muskets for the seven of us; the firewood had been built into four piles—tables, you might say—one about the middle of each side, and on each of these tables some ammunition and four loaded muskets were laid ready to the hand of the defenders. In the middle, lay the cutlasses.

"Toss out the fire," said the captain; "the chill is past, and we mustn't have smoke in our eyes."

The iron fire basket was carried bodily out by Mr. Trelawney, and the embers smothered among sand.

"Hawkins hasn't had his breakfast. Hawkins, help yourself, and back to your post to eat it," continued Captain Smollett. "Lively, now, my lad; you'll want it before you've done. Hunter, serve out a round of brandy to all hands."

And while this was going on, the captain completed, in his own mind, the plan of the defense.

"Doctor, you will take the door," he resumed.

"See, and don't expose yourself; keep within, and fire through the porch. Hunter, take the east side, there. Joyce, you stand by the west, my man. Mr. Trelawney, you are the best shot—you and Gray will take this long north side, with the five loopholes; it's there the danger is. If they can get up to it, and fire in upon us through our own ports, things would begin to

look dirty. Hawkins, neither you nor I are much account at the shooting; we'll stand by to load and bear a hand."

As the captain had said, the chill was past. As soon as the sun had climbed above our girdle of trees, it fell with all its force upon the clearing, and drank up the vapors at a draught. Soon the sand was baking, and the resin melting in the logs of the blockhouse. Jackets and coats were flung aside; shirts thrown open at the neck, and rolled up to the shoulders; and we stood there, each at his post, in a fever of heat and anxiety.

An hour passed away.

"Hang them!" said the captain. "This is as dull as the doldrums. Gray, whistle for a wind."

And just at that moment came the first news of the attack.

"If you please, sir," said Joyce, "if I see anyone am I to fire?"

"I told you so!" cried the captain.

"Thank you, sir," returned Joyce, with the same quiet civility.

Nothing followed for a time; but the remark had set us all on the alert, straining ears and eyes—the musketeers with their pieces balanced in their hands, the captain out in the middle of the blockhouse, with his mouth very tight and a frown on his face.

So some seconds passed, till suddenly Joyce whipped up his musket and fired. The report had scarcely died away ere it was repeated and repeated from without in a scattering volley, shot behind shot, like a string of geese, from every side of the enclosure. Several bullets struck the log house, but not one entered; and, as the smoke cleared away and vanished, the stockade and the woods around it looked as quiet

and empty as before. Not a bough waved, not the gleam of a musket barrel betrayed the presence of our foes.

"Did you hit your man?" asked the captain.

"No, sir," replied Joyce. "I believe not, sir."

"Next best thing to tell the truth," muttered Captain Smollett. "Load his gun, Hawkins. How many should you say there were on your side, doctor?"

"I know precisely," said Dr. Livesey. "Three shots were fired on this side. I saw the three flashes—two close together—one farther to the west."

"Three!" repeated the captain. "And how many on yours, Mr. Trelawney?"

But this was not so easily answered. There had come many from the north—seven, by the squire's computation; eight or nine, according to Gray. From the east and west only a single shot had been fired. It was plain, therefore, that the attack would be developed from the north, and that on the other three sides we were only to be annoyed by a show of hostilities. But Captain Smollett made no change in his arrangements. If the mutineers succeeded in crossing the stockade, he argued, they would take possession of any unprotected loophole, and shoot us down like rats in our own stronghold.

Nor had we much time left to us for thought. Suddenly, with a loud huzza, a little cloud of pirates leaped from the woods on the north side, and ran straight on the stockade. At the same moment, the fire was once more opened from the woods, and a rifle ball sang through the doorway, and knocked the doctor's musket into bits.

The boarders swarmed over the fence like monkeys. Squire and Gray fired again and yet again; three men

He appeared suddenly in the doorway and fell upon the doctor

fell, one forward into the enclosure, two back on the outside. But of these, one was evidently more frightened than hurt, for he was on his feet again in a crack and instantly disappeared among the trees.

Two had bit the dust, one had fled, four had made good their footing inside our defenses; while from the shelter of the woods seven or eight men, each evidently supplied with several muskets, kept up a hot though useless fire on the log house.

The four who had boarded made straight before them for the building, shouting as they ran, and the men among the trees shouted back to encourage them. Several shots were fired; but such was the hurry of the marksmen that not one appears to have taken effect. In a moment the four pirates had swarmed up the mound and were upon us.

The head of Job Anderson, the boatswain, appeared at the middle loophole. "At 'em, all hands—all hands!" he roared, in a voice of thunder.

At the same moment another pirate grasped Hunter's musket by the muzzle, wrenched it from his hands, plucked it through the loophole, and, with one stunning blow, laid the poor fellow senseless on the floor. Meanwhile, a third, running unharmed all round the house, appeared suddenly in the doorway and fell with his cutlass on the doctor.

Our position was utterly reversed. A moment since we were firing under cover at an exposed enemy; now it was we who lay uncovered and could not return a blow.

The log house was full of smoke, to which we owed our comparative safety. Cries and confusion, the flashes and reports of pistol shots and one loud groan rang in my ears.

"Out, lads, out, and fight 'em in the open! Cutlasses!" cried the captain.

I snatched a cutlass from the pile and someone, at the same time snatching another, gave me a cut across the knuckles which I hardly felt. I dashed out of the door into the clear sunlight. Someone was close behind, I knew not who. Right in front the doctor was pursuing his assailant down the hill, and just as my eyes fell upon him, beat down his guard and sent him sprawling on his back, with a great slash across the face.

"Round the house, lads! round the house!" cried the captain; and even in the hurly-burly I perceived a change in his voice.

Mechanically I obeyed, turned eastward, and with my cutlass raised, ran round the corner of the house. Next moment I was face to face with Anderson. He roared aloud, and his hanger went up above his head, flashing in the sunlight. I had not time to be afraid, but as the blow still hung impending, leaped in a trice upon one side, and, missing my foot in the soft sand, stumbled, and rolled headlong down the slope.

When I had first sallied from the door, the other mutineers had been already swarming up the palisade to make an end of us. One man in a red nightcap, with his cutlass in his mouth, had even got upon the top and thrown a leg across. Well, so short had been the interval that when I found my feet again all was in the same posture, the fellow with the red nightcap still halfway over, another still just showing his head above the top of the stockade. And yet, in this breath of time, the fight was over, and the victory was ours.

Gray, following close behind me, had cut down the big boatswain ere he had time to recover from his lost

blow. Another had been shot at a loophole in the very act of firing into the house, and now lay in agony, the pistol still smoking in his hand. A third, as I had seen, the doctor had disposed of at a blow. Of the four who had scaled the palisade, one only remained unaccounted for, and he, having left his cutlass on the field, was now clambering out again with the fear of death upon him.

"Fire—fire from the house!" cried the doctor. "And you, lads, back into cover."

But his words were unheeded, no shot was fired, and the last boarder made good his escape and disappeared

with the rest into the wood. In three seconds nothing remained of the attacking party but the five who had fallen, four on the inside and one on the outside of the palisade.

The doctor and Gray and I ran full speed for shelter. The survivors would soon be back where they had left their muskets, and at any moment the fire might recommence.

The house was by this time somewhat cleared of smoke, and we saw at a glance the price we had paid for victory. Hunter lay beside his loophole, stunned; Joyce, by his, shot through the head, never to move again; while right in the center, the squire was supporting the captain, one as pale as the other.

"The captain's wounded," said Mr. Trelawney.

"Have they run?" asked Mr. Smollett.

"All that could, you may be bound," returned the doctor; "but there's five of them will never run again."

"Five!" cried the captain. "Come, that's better.

Five against three leaves us four to nine. That's better odds than we had at starting. We were seven to nineteen then, or thought we were, and that's as bad to bear." [1]

---

[1] The mutineers were soon only eight in number, for the man shot by Mr. Trelawney on board the schooner died that same evening of his wound. But this was, of course, not known till after by the faithful party.

PART V

My Sea Adventure

☆ XXII ☆

How My Sea Adventure Began

THERE WAS no return of the mutineers—not so much as another shot out of the woods. They had "got their rations for that day," as the captain put it, and we had the place to ourselves and a quiet time to overhaul the wounded and get dinner. Squire and I cooked outside in spite of the danger, and even outside we could hardly tell what we were at, for horror of the loud groans that reached us from the doctor's patients.

Out of the eight men who had fallen in the action, only three still breathed—that one of the pirates who had been shot at the loophole, Hunter, and Captain Smollett; and of these the first two were as good as dead; the mutineer, indeed, died under the doctor's knife, and Hunter, do what we could, never recovered consciousness in this world. He lingered all day, breathing loudly like the old buccaneer at home in his apoplectic fit; but the bones of his chest had been crushed by the blow and his skull fractured in falling,

and some time in the following night, without sign or sound, he went to his Maker.

As for the captain, his wounds were grievous indeed, but not dangerous. No organ was fatally injured. Anderson's ball—for it was Job that shot him first—had broken his shoulder blade and touched the lung, not badly; the second had only torn and displaced some muscles in the calf. He was sure to recover, the doctor said, but in the meantime, and for weeks to come, he must not walk nor move his arm, nor so much as speak when he could help it.

My own accidental cut across the knuckles was a fleabite. Dr. Livesey patched it up with plaster and pulled my ears for me into the bargain.

After dinner the squire and the doctor sat by the captain's side awhile in consultation; and when they had talked to their hearts' content, it being then a little past noon, the doctor took up his hat and pistols, girt on a cutlass, put the chart in his pocket, and with a musket over his shoulder crossed the palisade on the north side and set off briskly through the trees.

Gray and I were sitting together at the far end of the blockhouse, to be out of earshot of our officers consulting; and Gray took his pipe out of his mouth and fairly forgot to put it back again, so thunderstruck he was at this occurrence.

"Why, in the name of Davy Jones," said he, "is Dr. Livesey mad?"

"Why, no," says I. "He's about the last of this crew for that, I take it."

"Well, shipmate," said Gray, "mad he may not be; but if *he's* not, you mark my words, I am."

"I take it," replied I, "the doctor has his idea; and if I am right, he's going now to see Ben Gunn."

I was right, as appeared later; but, in the meantime, the house being stifling hot and the little patch of sand inside the palisade ablaze with midday sun, I began to get another thought into my head, which was not by any means so right. What I began to do was to envy the doctor, walking in the cool shadow of the woods, with the birds about him, and the pleasant smell of the pines, while I sat grilling, with my clothes stuck to the hot resin, and so much blood about me, and so many poor dead bodies lying all around, that I took a disgust of the place that was almost as strong as fear.

All the time I was washing out the blockhouse, and then washing up the things from dinner, this disgust and envy kept growing stronger and stronger, till at last, being near a bread bag, and no one then observing me, I took the first step toward my escapade, and filled both pockets of my coat with biscuit.

I was a fool, if you like, and certainly I was going to do a foolish, overbold act; but I was determined to do it with all the precautions in my power. These biscuits, should anything befall me, would keep me, at least, from starving till far on in the next day.

The next thing I laid hold of was a brace of pistols, and as I already had a powder horn and bullets, I felt myself well supplied with arms.

As for the scheme I had in my head, it was not a bad one in itself. I was to go down the sandy spit that divides the anchorage on the east from the open sea, find the white rock I had observed last evening, and ascertain whether it was there or not that Ben Gunn had hidden his boat; a thing quite worth doing, as I still believe. But as I was certain I should not be allowed to leave the enclosure, my only plan was to take French leave, and slip out when nobody was watch-

ing; and that was so bad a way of doing it as made the thing itself wrong. But I was only a boy, and I had made up my mind.

Well, as things at last fell out, I found an admirable opportunity. The squire and Gray were busy helping the captain with his bandages; the coast was clear; I made a bolt for it over the stockade and into the thickest of the trees, and before my absence was observed I was out of cry of my companions.

This was my second folly, far worse than the first, as I left but two sound men to guard the house; but like the first, it was a help toward saving all of us.

I took my way straight for the east coast of the island, for I was determined to go down the seaside of the spit to avoid all chance of observation from the anchorage. It was already late in the afternoon, although still warm and sunny. As I continued to thread the tall woods I could hear from far before me not only the continuous thunder of the surf, but a certain tossing of foliage and grinding of boughs which showed me the sea breeze had set in higher than usual. Soon cool draughts of air began to reach me, and a few steps farther I came forth into the open borders of the grove, and saw the sea lying blue and sunny to the horizon, and the surf tumbling and tossing its foam along the beach.

I have never seen the sea quiet round Treasure Island. The sun might blaze overhead, the air be without a breath, the surface smooth and blue, but still these great rollers would be running along all the external coast, thundering and thundering by day and night; and I scarce believe there is one spot in the island where a man would be out of earshot of their noise.

I walked along beside the surf with great enjoy-

ment, till, thinking I was now got far enough to the south, I took the cover of some thick bushes and crept warily up to the ridge of the spit.

Behind me was the sea, in front the anchorage. The sea breeze, as though it had the sooner blown itself out by its unusual violence, was already at an end; it had been succeeded by light, variable airs from the south and southeast, carrying great banks of fog; and the anchorage, under lee of Skeleton Island, lay still and leaden as when first we entered it. The *Hispaniola*, in that unbroken mirror, was exactly portrayed from the truck to the waterline, the Jolly Roger hanging from her peak.

Alongside lay one of the gigs, Silver in the stern sheets—him I could always recognize—while a couple of men were leaning over the stern bulwarks, one of them with a red cap—the very rogue that I had seen some hours before, stride-legs upon the palisade. Apparently they were talking and laughing, though at that distance—upward of a mile—I could, of course, hear no word of what was said. All at once there began the most horrid, unearthly screaming, which at first startled me badly, though I had soon remembered the voice of Captain Flint, and even thought I could make out the bird by her bright plumage as she sat perched upon her master's wrist.

Soon after, the jolly boat shoved off and pulled for shore, and the man with the red cap and his comrade went below by the cabin companion.

Just about the same time the sun had gone down behind the Spyglass, and as the fog was collecting rapidly, it began to grow dark in earnest. I saw I must lose no time if I were to find the boat that evening.

The white rock, visible enough above the brush, was

still some eighth of a mile farther down the spit, and it took me a goodish while to get up with it, crawling, often on all fours, among the scrub. Night had almost come when I laid my hand on its rough sides. Right below it there was an exceedingly small hollow of green turf, hidden by banks and a thick underwood about knee-deep, that grew there very plentifully; and in the center of the dell, sure enough, a little tent of goatskins, like what the gypsies carry about with them in England.

I dropped into the hollow, lifted the side of the tent, and there was Ben Gunn's boat—homemade if ever anything was homemade: a rude, lopsided framework of tough wood and stretched upon that a covering of goatskin, with the hair inside. The thing was extremely small, even for me, and I can hardly imagine that it could have floated with a full-sized man. There was one thwart set as low as possible, a kind of stretcher in the bows, and a double paddle for propulsion.

I had not then seen a coracle, such as the ancient Britons made, but I have seen one since, and I can give you no fairer idea of Ben Gunn's boat than by saying it was like the first and the worst coracle ever made by man. But the great advantage of the coracle it certainly possessed, for it was exceedingly light and portable.

Well, now that I had found the boat, you would have thought I had had enough of truantry for once; but, in the meantime, I had taken another notion, and become so obstinately fond of it that I would have carried it out, I believe, in the teeth of Captain Smollett himself. This was to slip out under cover of the night, cut the *Hispaniola* adrift and let her go ashore

where she fancied. I had quite made up my mind that the mutineers, after their repulse of the morning, had nothing nearer their hearts than to up-anchor and away to sea; this, I thought, it would be a fine thing to prevent, and now that I had seen how they left their watchman unprovided with a boat I thought it might be done with little risk.

Down I sat to wait for darkness, and made a hearty meal of biscuit. It was a night out of ten thousand for my purpose. The fog had now buried all heaven. As the last rays of daylight dwindled and disappeared, absolute blackness settled down on Treasure Island. And when at last I shouldered the coracle and groped my way stumblingly out of the hollow where I had supped, there were but two points visible on the whole anchorage.

One was the great fire on shore, by which the defeated pirates lay carousing in the swamp. The other, a mere blur of light upon the darkness, indicated the position of the anchored ship. She had swung round to the ebb—her bow was now toward me—the only lights on board were in the cabin; and what I saw was merely a reflection on the fog of the strong rays that flowed from the stern window.

The ebb had already run some time, and I had to wade through a long belt of swampy sand, where I sank several times above the ankle, before I came to the edge of the retreating water, and wading a little way in, with some strength and dexterity, set my coracle keel downward on the surface.

☆ XXIII ☆

The Ebb Tide Runs

———

THE CORACLE—as I had ample reason to know before I was done with her—was a very safe boat for a person of my height and weight, both buoyant and clever in a seaway; but she was the most cross-grained, lopsided craft to manage. Do as you pleased, she always made more leeway than anything else, and turning round and round was the maneuver she was best at. Even Ben Gunn himself has admitted that she was "queer to handle till you knew her way."

Certainly I did not know her way. She turned in every direction but the one I was bound to go; the most part of the time we were broadside on, and I am very sure I never should have made the ship at all but for the tide. By good fortune, paddle as I pleased, the tide was still sweeping me down; and there lay the *Hispaniola* right in the fairway, hardly to be missed.

First she loomed before me like a blot of something yet blacker than darkness, then her spars and hull began to take shape, and the next moment, as it seemed (for, the farther I went, the brisker grew the current

of the ebb), I was alongside of her hawser, and had laid hold.

The hawser was as taut as a bowstring, and the current so strong she pulled upon her anchor. All round the hull, in the blackness, the rippling current bubbled and chattered like a little mountain stream. One cut with my sea gully, and the *Hispaniola* would go humming down the tide.

So far so good; but it next occurred to my recollection that a taut hawser, suddenly cut, is a thing as dangerous as a kicking horse. Ten to one, if I were so foolhardy as to cut the *Hispaniola* from her anchor, I and the coracle would be knocked clean out of the water.

This brought me to a full stop, and if fortune had not again particularly favored me I should have had to abandon my design. But the light airs which had begun blowing from the southeast and south had hauled round after nightfall into the southwest. Just while I was meditating, a puff came, caught the *Hispaniola*, and forced her up into the current; and, to my great joy, I felt the hawser slacken in my grasp and the hand by which I held it dip for a second under water.

With that I made my mind up, took out my gully, opened it with my teeth, and cut one strand after another till the vessel swung only by two. Then I lay quiet, waiting to sever these last when the strain should be once more lightened by a breath of wind.

All this time I had heard the sound of loud voices from the cabin; but, to say truth, my mind had been so entirely taken up with other thoughts that I had scarcely given ear. Now, however, when I had nothing else to do, I began to pay more heed.

One I recognized for the cockswain's, Israel Hands,

that had been Flint's gunner in former days. The other was, of course, my friend of the red nightcap. Both men were plainly the worse of drink, and they were still drinking; for, even while I was listening, one of them, with a drunken cry, opened the stern window and threw out something, which I divined to be an empty bottle. But they were not only tipsy; it was plain that they were furiously angry. Oaths flew like hailstones, and every now and then there came forth such an explosion as I thought was sure to end in blows. But each time the quarrel passed off, and the voices grumbled lower for a while, until the next crisis came and, in its turn, passed away without result.

On shore I could see the glow of the great campfire burning warmly through the shoreside trees. Someone was singing a dull, old, droning sailor's song, with a droop and a quaver at the end of every verse, and seemingly no end to it at all but the patience of the singer. I had heard it on the voyage more than once, and remembered these words:

> "But one man of her crew alive,
>   What put to sea with seventy-five."

And I thought it was a ditty rather too dolefully appropriate for a company that had met such cruel losses in the morning. But, indeed, from what I saw, all these buccaneers were as callous as the sea they sailed on.

At last the breeze came; the schooner sidled and drew nearer in the dark; I felt the hawser slacken once more, and with a good, tough effort, cut the last fibers through.

The breeze had but little action on the coracle, and I was almost instantly swept against the bows of the *Hispaniola*. At the same time the schooner began to

turn upon her heel, spinning slowly, end for end, across the current.

I wrought like a fiend, for I expected every moment to be swamped; and since I found I could not push the coracle directly off, I now shoved straight astern. At length I was clear of my dangerous neighbor; and just as I gave the last impulsion, my hands came across a light cord that was trailing overboard across the stern bulwarks. Instantly I grasped it.

Why I should have done so I can hardly say. It was at first mere instinct; but once I had it in my hands and found it fast, curiosity began to get the upper hand, and I determined I should have one look through the cabin window.

I pulled in hand over hand on the cord, and, when I judged myself near enough, rose at infinite risk to about half my height, and thus commanded the roof and a slice of the interior of the cabin.

By this time the schooner and her little consort were gliding pretty swiftly through the water; indeed, we had already fetched up level with the campfire. The ship was talking, as sailors say, loudly, treading the innumerable ripples with an incessant weltering splash; and until I got my eye above the window sill I could not comprehend why the watchmen had taken no alarm. One glance, however, was sufficient; and it was only one glance that I durst take from that unsteady skiff. It showed me Hands and his companion locked together in deadly wrestle, each with a hand upon the other's throat.

I dropped upon the thwart again, none too soon, for I was near overboard. I could see nothing for the moment, but these two furious, encrimsoned faces, swaying together under the smoky lamp; and I shut my

eyes to let them grow once more familiar with the darkness.

The endless ballad had come to an end at last, and the whole diminished company about the campfire had broken into the chorus I had heard so often:

> *"Fifteen men on the dead man's chest—*
> *Yo-ho-ho, and a bottle of rum!*
> *Drink and the devil had done for the rest—*
> *Yo-ho-ho, and a bottle of rum!"*

I was just thinking how busy drink and the devil were at that very moment in the cabin of the *Hispaniola* when I was surprised by a sudden lurch of the coracle. At the same moment she yawed sharply and seemed to change her course. The speed in the meantime had strangely increased.

I opened my eyes at once. All round me were ripples, combing over with a sharp, bristling sound, and slightly phosphorescent. The *Hispaniola* herself, a few yards in whose wake I was still being whirled along, seemed to stagger in her course, and I saw her spars toss a little against the blackness of the night; nay, as I looked longer, I made sure she also was wheeling to the southward.

I glanced over my shoulder, and my heart jumped against my ribs. There, right behind me, was the glow of the campfire. The current had turned at right angles, sweeping round along with it the tall schooner and the little dancing coracle; ever quickening, ever bubbling higher, ever muttering louder, it went spinning through the narrows for the open sea.

Suddenly the schooner in front of me gave a violent yaw, turning, perhaps, through twenty degrees; and almost at the same moment one shout followed an-

other from on board; I could hear feet pounding on the companion ladder; and I knew that the two drunkards had at last been interrupted in their quarrel and awakened to a sense of their disaster.

I lay down flat in the bottom of that wretched skiff, and devoutly recommended my spirit to its Maker. At the end of the straits, I made sure we must fall into some bar of raging breakers, where all my troubles would be ended speedily; and though I could, perhaps, bear to die, I could not bear to look upon my fate as it approached.

So I must have lain for hours, continually beaten to and fro upon the billows, now and again wetted with flying sprays, and never ceasing to expect death at the next plunge. Gradually weariness grew upon me; a numbness, an occasional stupor, fell upon my mind even in the midst of my terrors; until sleep at last supervened, and in my sea-tossed coracle I lay and dreamed of home and the old "Admiral Benbow."

The Cruise of the Coracle

———————

IT WAS broad day when I awoke, and found myself tossing at the southwest end of Treasure Island. The sun was up, but was still hid from me behind the great bulk of the Spyglass, which on this side descended almost to the sea in formidable cliffs.

Haulbowline Head and Mizzenmast Hill were at my elbow, the hill bare and dark, the head bound with cliffs forty or fifty feet high, and fringed with great masses of fallen rock. I was scarce a quarter of a mile to seaward, and it was my first thought to paddle in and land.

That notion was soon given over. Among the fallen rocks the breakers spouted and bellowed; loud reverberations, heavy sprays flying and falling, succeeded one another from second to second; and I saw myself, if I ventured nearer, dashed to death upon the rough shore or spending my strength in vain to scale the beetling crags.

Nor was that all. For crawling together on flat ta-

bles of rock, or letting themselves drop into the sea with loud reports, I beheld huge slimy monsters—soft snails, as it were, of incredible bigness—two or three score of them together, making the rocks to echo with their barkings.

I have understood since that they were sea lions, and entirely harmless. But the look of them, added to the difficulty of the shore and the high running of the surf, was more than enough to disgust me of that landing place. I felt willing rather to starve at sea than to confront such perils.

In the meantime I had a better chance, as I supposed, before me. North of Haulbowline Head the land runs in a long way, leaving, at low tide, a long stretch of yellow sand. To the north of that, again, there comes another cape—Cape of the Woods, as it was marked upon the chart—buried in tall green pines, which descended to the margin of the sea.

I remembered what Silver had said about the current that sets northward along the whole west coast of Treasure Island. And, seeing from my position that I was already under its influence, I preferred to leave Haulbowline Head behind me, and reserve my strength for an attempt to land upon the kindlier-looking Cape of the Woods.

There was a great, smooth swell upon the sea. The wind blowing steady and gentle from the south, there was no contrariety between that and the current, and the billows rose and fell steadily in long, unbroken lines.

Had it been otherwise, I must long ago have perished; but as it was, it is surprising how easily and securely my little and light boat could ride. Often, as I still lay at the bottom, and kept no more than an eye

above the gunwale, I would see a big blue summit heaving close above me; yet the coracle would but bounce a little, dance as if on springs, and subside on the other side into the trough as lightly as a bird.

I began after a little to grow very bold, and sat up to try my skill at paddling. But even a small change in the disposition of the weight will produce violent changes in the behavior of a coracle. And I had hardly moved before the boat, giving up at once her gentle dancing movement, ran straight down a slope of water so steep that it made me giddy, and stuck her nose, with a spout of spray, deep into the side of the next wave.

I was drenched and terrified and fell instantly back into my old position, whereupon the coracle seemed to find her head again and led me as softly as before among the billows. It was plain she was not to be interfered with, and at that rate, since I could in no way influence her course, what hope had I left of reaching land?

I began to be horribly frightened, but I kept my head, for all that. First, moving with all care, I gradually baled out the coracle with my sea cap; then getting my eye once more above the gunwale, I set myself to study how it was she managed to slip so quietly through the rollers.

I found each wave, instead of the big, smooth, glossy mountain it looks from shore, or from a vessel's deck, was for all the world like any range of hills on the dry land, full of peaks and smooth places and valleys. The coracle, left to herself, turning from side to side, threaded, so to speak, her way through these lower parts, and avoided the steep slopes and higher, toppling summits of the waves.

"Well, now," thought I to myself, "it is plain I must lie where I am, and not disturb the balance; but it is plain, also, that I can put the paddle over the side and from time to time, in smooth places, give her a shove or two toward land." No sooner thought upon than done. There I lay on my elbows, in the most trying attitude, and every now and again gave a weak stroke or two to turn her head to shore.

It was very tiring, and slow work, yet I did visibly gain ground; and, as I drew near the Cape of the Woods, though I saw I must infallibly miss that point, I had still made some hundred yards of easting. I was, indeed, close in. I could see the cool, green treetops swaying together in the breeze, and I felt sure I should make the next promontory without fail.

It was high time, for I now began to be tortured with thirst. The glow of the sun from above, its thousandfold reflection from the waves, the sea water that fell and dried upon me, caking my very lips with salt, combined to make my throat burn and my brain ache. The sight of the trees so near at hand had almost made me sick with longing, but the current had soon carried me past the point; and, as the next reach of sea opened out, I beheld a sight that changed the nature of my thoughts.

Right in front of me, not half a mile away, I beheld the *Hispaniola* under sail. I made sure, of course, that I should be taken; but I was so distressed for want of water that I scarce knew whether to be glad or sorry at the thought. And, long before I had come to a conclusion, surprise had taken entire possession of my mind, and I could do nothing but stare and wonder.

The *Hispaniola* was under her mainsail and two jibs, and the beautiful white canvas shone in the sun like

snow or silver. When I first sighted her, all her sails
were drawing; she was lying a course about northwest; and I presumed the men on board were going
round the island on their way back to the anchorage.
Presently she began to fetch more and more to the
westward, so that I thought they had sighted me and
were going about in chase. At last, however, she fell
right into the wind's eye, was taken dead aback, and
stood there awhile helpless, with her sails shivering.

"Clumsy fellows," said I; "they must still be drunk
as owls." And I thought how Captain Smollett
would have set them skipping.

Meanwhile, the schooner gradually fell off, and
filled again upon another tack, sailed swiftly for a
minute or so, and brought up once more dead in the
wind's eye. Again and again was this repeated. To
and fro, up and down, north, south, east, and west, the
Hispaniola sailed by swoops and dashes, and at each
repetition ended as she had begun, with idly flapping
canvas. It became plain to me that nobody was steering. And, if so, where were the men? Either they
were dead drunk or had deserted her, I thought, and
perhaps if I could get on board, I might return the vessel to her captain.

The current was bearing coracle and schooner
southward at an equal rate. As for the latter's sailing,
it was so wild and intermittent, and she hung each
time so long in irons, that she certainly gained nothing, if she did not even lose. If only I dared to sit up
and paddle, I made sure that I could overhaul her. The
scheme had an air of adventure that inspired me, and
the thought of the water breaker beside the fore companion doubled my growing courage.

Up I got, was welcomed almost instantly by another

cloud of spray, but this time stuck to my purpose; and set myself, with all my strength and caution, to paddle after the unsteered *Hispaniola*. Once I shipped a sea so heavy that I had to stop and bail, with my heart fluttering like a bird; but gradually I got into the way of the thing and guided my coracle among the waves, with only now and then a blow upon her bows and a dash of foam in my face.

I was now gaining rapidly on the schooner. I could see the brass glisten on the tiller as it banged about; and still no soul appeared upon her decks. I could not choose but suppose she was deserted. If not, the men were lying drunk below, where I might batten them down, perhaps, and do what I chose with the ship.

For some time she had been doing the worst thing possible for me—standing still. She headed nearly due south, yawing, of course, all the time. Each time she fell off, her sails partly filled, and these brought her in a moment right to the wind again. I have said this was the worst thing possible for me; for helpless as she looked in this situation, with the canvas cracking like cannon and the blocks trundling and banging on the deck, she still continued to run away from me, not only with the speed of the current, but by the whole amount of her leeway, which was naturally great.

But now at last I had my chance. The breeze fell for some seconds very low, and the current gradually turning her, the *Hispaniola* revolved slowly round her center, and at last presented me her stern, with the cabin window still gaping open, and the lamp over the table still burning on into the day. The mainsail hung drooped like a banner. She was stock-still, but for the current.

For the last little while I had even lost; but now, re-

doubling my efforts, I began once more to overhaul the chase.

I was not a hundred yards from her when the wind came again in a clap; she filled on the port tack and was off again, stooping and skimming like a swallow.

My first impulse was one of despair, but my second was toward joy. Round she came till she was broadside on to me—round still till she had covered a half, and then two-thirds, and then three-quarters of the distance that separated us. I could see the waves boiling white under her forefoot. Immensely tall she looked to me from my low station in the coracle.

And then, of a sudden, I began to comprehend. I had scarce time to think—scarce time to act and save myself. I was on the summit of one swell when the schooner came stooping over the next. The bowsprit was over my head. I sprang to my feet and leaped, stamping the coracle under water. With one hand I caught the jibboom, while my foot was lodged between the stay and the brace; and as I still clung there panting, a dull blow told me that the schooner had charged down upon and struck the coracle, and that I was left without retreat on the *Hispaniola*.

☆ XXV ☆

I Strike the Jolly Roger

I HAD SCARCE GAINED a position on the bow-sprit when the flying jib flapped and filled upon the other tack, with a report like a gun. The schooner trembled to her keel under the reverse; but next moment, the other sails still drawing, the jib flapped back again and hung idle.

This had nearly tossed me off into the sea; and now I lost no time, crawled back along the bowsprit, and tumbled head foremost on the deck.

I was on the lee side of the forecastle, and the main-sail, which was still drawing, concealed from me a certain portion of the afterdeck. Not a soul was to be seen. The planks, which had not been swabbed since the mutiny, bore the print of many feet; and an empty bottle, broken by the neck, tumbled to and fro like a live thing in the scuppers.

Suddenly the *Hispaniola* came right into the wind. The jibs behind me cracked aloud; the rudder slammed to; the whole ship gave a sickening heave and shudder,

and at the same moment the main boom swung inboard, the sheet groaning in the blocks, and showed me the lee afterdeck.

There were the two watchmen, sure enough: red-cap on his back, as stiff as a handspike, with his arms stretched out like those of a crucifix, and his teeth showing through his open lips; Israel Hands propped against the bulwarks, his chin on his chest, his hands lying open before him on the deck, his face as white, under its tan, as a tallow candle.

For a while the ship kept bucking and sidling like a vicious horse, the sails filling, now on one tack, now on another, and the boom swinging to and fro till the mast groaned aloud under the strain. Now and again, too, there would come a cloud of light sprays over the bulwark, and a heavy blow of the ship's bows against the swell: so much heavier weather was made of it by this great rigged ship than by my homemade, lopsided coracle, now gone to the bottom of the sea.

At every jump of the schooner, red-cap slipped to and fro; but—what was ghastly to behold—neither his attitude nor his fixed teeth-disclosing grin was in any way disturbed by this rough usage. At every jump, too, Hands appeared still more to sink into himself and settle down upon the deck, his feet sliding ever the farther out, and the whole body canting toward the stern, so that his face became, little by little, hid from me; and at last I could see nothing beyond his ear and the frayed ringlet of one whisker.

At the same time, I observed, around both of them, splashes of dark blood upon the planks, and began to feel sure that they had killed each other in their drunken wrath.

While I was thus looking and wondering, in a calm

moment, when the ship was still, Israel Hands turned partly round, and, with a low moan, writhed himself back to the position in which I had seen him first. The moan, which told of pain and deadly weakness, and the way in which his jaw hung open, went right to my heart. But when I remembered the talk I had over-heard from the apple barrel, all pity left me.

I walked aft until I reached the mainmast.

"Come aboard, Mr. Hands," I said ironically.

He rolled his eyes round heavily; but he was too far gone to express surprise. All he could do was to utter one word: "Brandy."

It occurred to me there was no time to lose; and, dodging the boom as it once more lurched across the deck, I sliped aft, and down the companion stairs into the cabin.

It was such a scene of confusion as you can hardly fancy. All the lockfast places had been broken open in quest of the chart. The floor was thick with mud, where ruffians had sat down to drink or consult after wading in the marshes round their camp. The bulk-heads, all painted in clear white and beaded round with gilt, bore a pattern of dirty hands. Dozens of empty bottles clinked together in corners to the roll-ing of the ship. One of the doctor's medical books lay open on the table, half of the leaves gutted out, I sup-pose, for pipelights. In the midst of all this, the lamp still cast a smoky glow, obscure and brown as umber.

I went into the cellar; all the barrels were gone, and of the bottles a most surprising number had been drunk out and thrown away. Certainly, since the mu-tiny began, not a man of them could ever have been sober.

Foraging about, I found a bottle with some brandy

left, for Hands; and for myself I routed out some biscuit, some pickled fruits, a great bunch of raisins, and a piece of cheese. With these I came on deck, put down my own stock behind the rudderhead, and well out of the cockswain's reach, went forward to the water breaker, and had a good, deep drink of water, and then, and not till then, gave Hands the brandy.

He must have drunk a gill before he took the bottle from his mouth. "Aye," said he, "by thunder, but I wanted some o' that!"

I had sat down already in my corner and begun to eat.

"Much hurt?" I asked him.

He grunted, or, rather, I might say, he barked.

"If that doctor was aboard," he said, "I'd be right enough in a couple of turns; but I don't have no manner of luck, you see, and that's what's the matter with me. As for that swab, he's good and dead, he is," he added, indicating the man with the red cap. "He warn't no seaman, anyhow. And where mought you have come from?"

"Well," said I, "I've come aboard to take possession of this ship, Mr. Hands; and you'll please regard me as your captain until further notice."

He looked at me sourly enough, but said nothing. Some of the color had come back into his cheeks, though he still looked very sick, and still continued to slip out and settle down as the ship banged about.

"By the bye," I continued, "I can't have these colors, Mr. Hands; and, by your leave, I'll strike 'em. Better none than these."

And again dodging the boom, I ran to the color lines, handed down their cursed black flag, and chucked it overboard.

"God save the king!" said I, waving my cap; "and there's an end to Captain Silver!"

He watched me keenly and slyly, his chin all the while on his breast.

"I reckon," he said at last—"I reckon, Cap'n Hawkins, you'll kind of want to get ashore, now. S'pose we talks."

"Why, yes," says I, "with all my heart, Mr. Hands. Say on." And I went back to my meal with a good appetite.

"This man," he began, nodding feebly at the corpse —"O'Brien were his name—a rank Irelander—this man and me got the canvas on her, meaning for to sail her back. Well, *he's* dead now, he is—as dead as bilge; and who's to sail this ship, I don't see. Without I gives you a hint, you ain't that man, as far's I can tell. Now, look here, you gives me food and drink, and a old scarf or ankecher to tie my wound up, you do; and I'll tell you how to sail her; and that's about square all round, I take it."

"I'll tell you one thing," says I: "I'm not going back to Captain Kidd's anchorage. I mean to get into North Inlet, and beach her quietly there."

"To be sure you did," he cried. "Why, I ain't sich an infernal lubber, after all. I can see, can't I? I've tried my fling, I have, and I've lost, and it's you has the wind of me. North Inlet? Why, I haven't no ch'ice, not I! I'd help you sail her up to Execution Dock, by thunder! so I would."

Well, as it seemed to me, there was some sense in this. We struck our bargain on the spot. In three minutes I had the *Hispaniola* sailing easily before the wind along the coast of Treasure Island, with good hopes of turning the northern point ere noon, and beating

down again as far as North Inlet before high water, when we might beach her safely, and wait till the subsiding tide permitted us to land.

Then I lashed the tiller and went below to my own chest, where I got a soft silk handkerchief of my mother's. With this, and with my aid, Hands bound up the great bleeding stab he had received in the thigh, and after he had eaten a little and had a swallow or two more of the brandy, he began to pick up visibly, sat straighter up, spoke louder and clearer, and looked in every way another man.

The breeze served us admirably. We skimmed before it like a bird, the coast of the island flashing by, and the view changing every minute. Soon we were past the high lands and bowling beside low, sandy country, sparsely dotted with dwarf pines, and soon we were beyond that again, and had turned the corner of the rocky hill that ends the island on the north.

I was greatly elated with my new command, and pleased with the bright, sunshiny weather and these different prospects of the coast. I had now plenty of water and good things to eat, and my conscience, which had smitten me hard for my desertion, was quieted by the great conquest I had made. I should, I think, have had nothing left me to desire but for the eyes of the cockswain as they followed me derisively about the deck, and the odd smile that appeared continually on his face. It was a smile that had in it something of both pain and weakness—a haggard, old man's smile; but there was, besides that, a grain of derision, a shadow of treachery in his expression as he craftily watched, and watched, and watched me at my work.

☆ XXVI ☆

Israel Hands

THE WIND, serving us to a desire, now hauled into the west. We could run so much the easier from the northeast corner of the island to the mouth of the North Inlet. Only, as we had no power to anchor, and dared not beach her till the tide had flowed a good deal farther, time hung on our hands. The cockswain told me how to lay the ship to; and after a good many trials I succeeded, and we both sat in silence over another meal.

"Cap'n," said he, at length, with that same uncomfortable smile, "here's my old shipmate, O'Brien; s'pose you was to heave him overboard. I ain't partic'-lar as a rule, and I don't take no blame for settling his hash; but I don't reckon him ornamental, now, do you?"

"I'm not strong enough, and I don't like the job; and there he lies, for me," said I.

"This here's an unlucky ship—this *Hispaniola*, Jim," he went on, blinking. "There's a power of men been

killed in this *Hispaniola*—a sight o' poor seamen dead and gone since you and me took ship to Bristol. I never seen sich dirty luck, not I. There was this here O'Brien, now—he's dead, ain't he? Well, now, I'm no scholar, and you're a lad as can read and figure; and, to put it straight, do you take it as a dead man is dead for good, or do he come alive again?"

"You can kill the body, Mr. Hands, but not the spirit; you must know that already," I replied. "O'Brien there is in another world, and maybe watching us."

"Ah!" says he. "Well, that's unfort'nate—appears as if killing parties was a waste of time. Howsomever, sperrits don't reckon for much, by what I've seen. I'll chance it with the sperrits, Jim. And now, you've spoke up free, and I'll take it kind if you'd step down into that there cabin and get me a—well, a—shiver my timbers! I can't hit the name on't; well, you get me a bottle of wine, Jim—this here brandy's too strong for my head."

Now, the cockswain's hesitation seemed to be unnatural; and as for the notion of his preferring wine to brandy, I entirely disbelieved it. The whole story was a pretext. He wanted me to leave the deck—so much was plain; but with what purpose I could in no way imagine. His eyes never met mine; they kept wandering to and fro, up and down, now with a look to the sky, now with a flitting glance upon the dead O'Brien. All the time he kept smiling and putting his tongue out in the most guilty, embarrassed manner, so that a child could have told that he was bent on some deception. I was prompt with my answer, however, for I saw where my advantage lay; and that with a fellow

so densely stupid I could easily conceal my suspicions to the end.

"Some wine?" I said. "Far better. Will you have white or red?"

"Well, I reckon it's about the blessed same to me, shipmate," he replied; "so it's strong and plenty of it, what's the odds?"

"All right," I answered. "I'll bring you port, Mr. Hands. But I'll have to dig for it."

With that I scuttled down the companion with all the noise I could, slipped off my shoes, ran quietly along the sparred gallery, mounted the forecastle ladder and popped my head out of the fore companion. I knew he would not expect to see me there; yet I took every precaution possible to prevent discovery; and certainly the worst of my suspicions proved too true.

He had risen from his position to his hands and knees; and though his leg obviously hurt him pretty sharply when he moved—for I could hear him stifle a groan—yet it was at a good, rattling rate that he trailed himself across the deck. In half a minute he had reached the port scuppers, and picked, out of a coil of rope, a long knife, or rather a short dirk, discolored to the hilt with blood. He looked upon it for a moment, thrusting forth his underjaw, tried the point upon his hand, and then, hastily concealing it in the bosom of his jacket, trundled back again into his old place against the bulwark.

This was all that I required to know. Israel could move about; he was now armed; and if he had been at so much trouble to get rid of me, it was plain that I was meant to be the victim. What he would do afterward—whether he would try to crawl right across the

island from North Inlet to the camp among the swamps, or whether he would fire Long Tom, trusting that his own comrades might come first to help him, was, of course, more than I could say.

Yet I felt sure that I could trust him in one point, since in that our interests jumped together, and that was in the disposition of the schooner. We both desired to have her stranded safe enough, in a sheltered place, and so that, when the time came, she could be got off again with as little labor and danger as might be; and until that was done I considered that my life would certainly be spared.

While I was thus turning the business over in my mind, I had not been idle with my body. I had stolen back to the cabin, slipped once more into my shoes, and laid my hand at random on a bottle of wine, and now, with this for an excuse, I made my reappearance on the deck.

Hands lay as I had left him, all fallen together in a bundle, and with his eyelids lowered, as though he were too weak to bear the light. He looked up, however, at my coming, knocked the neck off the bottle, like a man who had done the same thing often, and took a good swig, with his favorite toast of "Here's luck!" Then he lay quiet for a little, and then, pulling out a stick of tobacco, begged me to cut him a quid.

"Cut me a junk o' that," says he, "for I haven't no knife, and hardly strength enough, so be as I had. Ah, Jim, Jim, I reckon I've missed stays! Cut me a quid, as'll likely be the last, lad; for I'm for my long home, and no mistake."

"Well," said I, "I'll cut you some tobacco; but if I was you and thought myself so bad, I would go to my prayers, like a Christian man."

"Why?" said he. "Now, you tell me why."

"Why?" I cried. "You were asking me just now about the dead. You've broken your trust; you've lived in sin and lies and blood; there's a man you killed lying at your feet this moment; and you ask me why! For God's mercy, Mr. Hands, that's why."

I spoke with a little heat, thinking of the bloody dirk he had hidden in his pocket, and designed, in his ill thoughts, to end me with. He, for his part, took a great draught of the wine, and spoke with the most unusual solemnity.

"For thirty years," he said, "I've sailed the seas, and seen good and bad, better and worse, fair weather and foul, provisions running out, knives going, and what not. Well, now I tell you, I never seen good come o' goodness yet. Him as strikes first is my fancy; dead men don't bite; them's my views—amen, so be it. And now, you look here," he added, suddenly changing his tone, "we've had about enough of this foolery. The tide's made good enough by now. You just take my orders, Cap'n Hawkins, and we'll sail slap in and be done with it."

All told, we had scarce two miles to run; but the navigation was delicate, the entrance to this northern anchorage was not only narrow and shoal, but lay east and west, so that the schooner must be nicely handled to be got in. I think I was a good, prompt subaltern, and I am very sure that Hands was an excellent pilot; for we went about and about, and dodged in, shaving the banks, with a certainty and a neatness that were a pleasure to behold.

Scarcely had we passed the heads before the land closed around us. The shores of North Inlet were as thickly wooded as those of the southern anchorage;

but the space was longer and narrower, and more like, what in truth it was, the estuary of a river. Right before us, at the southern end, we saw the wreck of a ship in the last stages of dilapidation. It had been a great vessel of three masts, but had laid so long exposed to the injuries of the weather that it was hung about with great webs of dripping seaweed, and on the deck of it shore bushes had taken root, and now flourished thick with flowers. It was a sad sight, but it showed us that the anchorage was calm.

"Now," said Hands, "look there; there's a pet bit for to beach a ship in. Fine flat sand, never a catspaw, trees all around of it, and flowers a-blowing like a garding on that old ship."

"And once beached," I inquired, "how shall we get her off again?"

"Why, so," he replied: "you take a line ashore there on the other side at low water; take a turn about one o' them big pines; bring it back, take a turn round the capstan, and lie to for the tide. Come high water, all hands take a pull upon the line, and off she comes as sweet as natur'. And now, boy, you stand by. We're near the bit now, and she's too much way on her. Starboard a little—so—steady—starboard—larboard a little—steady—steady!"

So he issued his commands, which I breathlessly obeyed; till, all of a sudden, he cried: "Now, my hearty, luff!" And I put the helm hard up, and the *Hispaniola* swung round rapidly and ran stem on for the low wooded shore.

The excitement of these last maneuvers had somewhat interfered with the watch I had kept hitherto, sharply enough, upon the cockswain. Even then I was still so much interested, waiting for the ship to touch,

that I had quite forgot the peril that hung over my head, and stood craning over the starboard bulwarks and watching the ripples spreading wide before the bows. I might have fallen without a struggle for my life had not a sudden disquietude seized upon me and made me turn my head. Perhaps I had heard a creak, or seen his shadow moving with the tail of my eye; perhaps it was an instinct like a cat's; but, sure enough, when I looked round, there was Hands, already half-way toward me, with the dirk in his right hand.

We must both have cried out aloud when our eyes met; but while mine was the shrill cry of terror, his was a roar of fury like a charging bull's. At the instant, he threw himself forward, and I leaped sideways toward the bows. As I did so I let go of the tiller, which sprang sharp to leeward; and I think this saved my life, for it struck Hands across the chest and stopped him, for the moment, dead.

Before he could recover, I was safe out of the corner where he had me trapped, with all the deck to dodge about. Just forward of the mainmast I stopped, drew a pistol from my pocket, took a cool aim, though he had already turned and was once more coming directly after me, and drew the trigger. The hammer fell, but there followed neither flash nor sound; the priming was useless with sea water. I cursed myself for my neglect. Why had not I, long before, reprimed and reloaded my only weapons? Then I should not have been as now, a mere fleeing sheep before this butcher.

Wounded as he was, it was wonderful how fast he could move, his grizzled hair tumbling over his face, and his face itself as red as a red ensign, with his haste and fury. I had no time to try my other pistol, nor,

indeed, much inclination, for I was sure it would be useless. One thing I saw plainly: I must not simply retreat before him, or he would speedily hold me boxed into the bows, as a moment since he had so nearly boxed me in the stern. Once so caught, and nine or ten inches of the bloodstained dirk would be my last experience on this side of eternity. I placed my palms against the mainmast, which was of a goodish bigness, and waited, every nerve upon the stretch.

Seeing that I meant to dodge, he also paused; and a moment or two passed in feints on his part and corresponding movements upon mine. It was such a game as I had often played at home about the rocks of Black Hill Cove; but never before, you may be sure, with such a wildly beating heart as now. Still, as I say, it was a boy's game, and I thought I could hold my own at it, against an elderly seaman with a wounded thigh. Indeed, my courage had begun to rise so high that I allowed myself a few darting thoughts on what would be the end of the affair; and while I saw certainly that I could spin it out for long, I saw no hope of any ultimate escape.

Well, while things stood thus, suddenly the *Hispaniola* struck, staggered, ground for an instant in the sand, and then, swift as a blow, canted over to the portside, till the deck stood at an angle of forty-five degrees, and about a puncheon of water splashed into the scupper holes, and lay in a pool between the deck and bulwark.

We were both of us capsized in a second, and both of us rolled, almost together, into the scuppers; the dead red-cap, with his arms still spread out, tumbling stiffly after us. So near were we, indeed, that my head came against the cockswain's foot with a crack that made

my teeth rattle. Blow and all, I was the first afoot again, for Hands had got involved with the dead body. The sudden canting of the ship had made the deck no place for running on; I had to find some new way of escape, and that upon the instant, for my foe was almost touching me. Quick as thought I sprang into the mizzen shrouds, rattled up hand over hand, and did not draw a breath till I was seated on the crosstrees.

I had been saved by being prompt; the dirk had struck not half a foot below me, as I pursued my upward flight; and there stood Israel Hands with his mouth open and his face upturned to mine, a perfect statue of surprise and disappointment.

Now that I had a moment to myself, I lost no time in changing the priming of my pistol, and then having one ready for service, and to make assurance doubly sure, I proceeded to draw the load of the other, and recharge it afresh from the beginning.

My new employment struck Hands all of a heap; he began to see the dice going against him; and after an obvious hesitation, he also hauled himself heavily into the shrouds, and, with the dirk in his teeth, began slowly and painfully to mount. It cost him no end of time and groans to haul his wounded leg behind him; and I had quietly finished my arrangements before he was much more than a third of the way up. Then, with a pistol in either hand, I addressed him. . .

"One more step, Mr. Hands," said I, "and I'll blow your brains out! Dead men don't bite, you know," I added, with a chuckle.

He stopped instantly. I could see by the working of his face that he was trying to think, and the process was so slow and laborious that, in my new-found security, I laughed aloud. Then, with a swallow or two,

"One more step, Mr. Hands," said I, "and I'll blow your brains out."

he spoke, his face still wearing the same expression of extreme perplexity. In order to speak he had to take the dagger from his mouth, but, in all else, he remained unmoved.

"Jim," says he, "I reckon we're fouled, you and me, and we'll have to sign articles. I'd have had you but for that there lurch: but I don't have no luck, not I; and I reckon I'll have to strike, which comes hard, you see, for a master mariner to a ship's younker like you, Jim."

I was drinking in his words and smiling away, as conceited as a cock upon a wall, when, all in a breath, back went his right hand over his shoulder. Something sang like an arrow through the air; I felt a blow and then a sharp pang, and there I was pinned by the shoulder to the mast. In the horrid pain and surprise of the moment—I scarce can say it was by my own volition, and I am sure it was without a conscious aim—both my pistols went off, and both escaped out of my hands. They did not fall alone; with a choked cry, the cockswain loosed his grasp upon the shrouds, and plunged head first into the water.

"Pieces of Eight"

———————

OWING TO THE CANT of the vessel, the masts hung far out over the water, and from my perch on the crosstrees I had nothing below me but the surface of the bay. Hands, who was not so far up, was, in consequence, nearer to the ship, and fell between me and the bulwarks. He rose once to the surface in a lather of foam and blood, and then sank again for good. As the water settled, I could see him lying huddled together on the clean, bright sand in the shadow of the vessel's sides. A fish or two whipped past his body. Sometimes, by the quivering of the water, he appeared to move a little, as if he were trying to rise. But he was dead enough, for all that, being both shot and drowned, and was food for fish in the very place where he had designed my slaughter.

I was no sooner certain of this than I began to feel sick, faint, and terrified. The hot blood was running over my back and chest. The dirk, where it had pinned my shoulder to the mast, seemed to burn like a hot iron; yet it was not so much these real sufferings that distressed me, for these, it seemed to me, I could bear without a murmur; it was the horror I had upon my mind of falling from the crosstrees into that still

green water, beside the body of the cockswain.

I clung with both hands till my nails ached, and I shut my eyes as if to cover up the peril. Gradually my mind came back again, my pulses quieted down to a more natural time, and I was once more in possession of myself.

It was my first thought to pluck forth the dirk; but either it struck too hard or my nerve failed me; and I desisted with a violent shudder. Oddly enough, that very shudder did the business. The knife, in fact, had come the nearest in the world to missing me altogether; it held me by a mere pinch of skin, and this the shudder tore away. The blood ran down the faster, to be sure; but I was my own master again, and only tacked to the mast by my coat and shirt.

These last I broke through with a sudden jerk, and then regained the deck by the starboard shrouds. For nothing in the world would I have again ventured, shaken as I was, upon the overhanging port shrouds, from which Israel had so lately fallen.

I went below, and did what I could for my wound; it pained me a good deal, and still bled freely; but it was neither deep nor dangerous, nor did it greatly gall me when I used my arm. Then I looked around me, and as the ship was now, in a sense, my own, I began to think of clearing it from its last passenger— the dead man, O'Brien.

He had pitched, as I have said, against the bulwarks, where he lay like some horrible, ungainly sort of puppet; life-size, indeed, but how different from life's color or life's comeliness! In that position I could easily have my way with him; and as the habit of tragical adventures had worn off almost all my terror for the dead, I took him by the waist as if he had been a

sack of bran, and, with one good heave, tumbled him overboard. He went in with a sounding plunge; the red cap came off, and remained floating on the surface; and as soon as the splash subsided, I could see him and Israel lying side by side, both wavering with the tremulous movement of the water. O'Brien, though still quite a young man, was very bald. There he lay, with that bald head across the knees of the man who had killed him, and the quick fishes steering to and fro.

I was now alone upon the ship; the tide had just turned. The sun was within so few degrees of setting that already the shadow of the pines upon the western shore began to reach right across the anchorage and fall in patterns on the deck. The evening breeze had sprung up, and though it was well warded off by the hill with the two peaks upon the east, the cordage had begun to sing a little softly to itself and the idle sails to rattle to and fro.

I began to see a danger to the ship. The jibs I speedily doused and brought tumbling to the deck; but the mainsail was a harder matter. Of course, when the schooner canted over, the boom had swung outboard, and the cap of it and a foot or two of sail hung even under water. I thought this made it still more dangerous; yet the strain was so heavy that I half feared to meddle. At last I got my knife and cut the halyards. The peak dropped instantly, a great belly of loose canvas floated broad upon the water; and since, pull as I liked, I could not budge the downhaul, that was the extent of what I could accomplish. For the rest, the *Hispaniola* must trust to luck, like myself.

By this time the whole anchorage had fallen into shadow—the last rays, I remember, falling through a glade of the wood and shining bright as jewels on the

flowery mantle of the wreck. It began to be chill; the
tide was rapidly fleeting seaward, the schooner settling more and more on her beam ends.

I scrambled forward and looked over. It seemed
shallow enough, and holding the cut hawser in both
hands for a last security, I let myself drop softly overboard. The water scarcely reached my waist; the sand
was firm and covered with ripple marks, and I waded
ashore in great spirits, leaving the *Hispaniola* on her
side, with her mainsail trailing wide upon the surface
of the bay. About the same time, the sun went fairly
down and the breeze whistled low in the dusk.

At least, and at last, I was off the sea, nor had I returned thence empty-handed. There lay the schooner,
clear at last from buccaneers and ready for our own
men to board and get to sea again. I had nothing
nearer my fancy than to get home to the stockade and
boast of my achievements. Possibly I might be blamed
a bit for my truantry, but the recapture of the *Hispaniola* was a clinching answer, and I hoped that even
Captain Smollett would confess I had not lost my time.

So thinking, and in famous spirits, I began to set my
face homeward for the blockhouse and my companions. I remembered that the most easterly of the rivers
which drain into Captain Kidd's Anchorage ran from
the two-peaked hill upon my left; and I bent my
course in that direction that I might pass the stream
while it was small. The wood was pretty open, and
keeping along the lower spurs I had soon turned the
corner of that hill, and not long after waded to the
mid-calf across the water course.

This brought me near to where I had encountered
Ben Gunn, the maroon; and I walked more circumspectly, keeping an eye on every side. The dusk had

come nigh-hand completely, and, as I opened out the cleft between the two peaks I became aware of a wavering glow against the sky, where, as I judged, the man of the island was cooking his supper before a roaring fire. And yet I wondered, in my heart, that he should show himself so careless. For if I could see this radiance, might it not reach the eyes of Silver himself where he camped upon the shore among the marshes?

Gradually the night fell blacker; it was all I could do to guide myself even roughly toward my destination: the double hill behind me and the Spyglass on my right hand loomed faint and fainter; the stars were few and pale; and in the low ground where I wandered I kept tripping among bushes and rolling into sandy pits.

Suddenly a kind of brightness fell about me. I looked up; a pale glimmer of moonbeams had alighted on the summit of the Spyglass, and soon after I saw something broad and silvery moving low down behind the trees, and knew the moon had risen.

With this to help me, I passed rapidly over what remained to me of my journey; and, sometimes walking, sometimes running, impatiently drew near to the stockade. Yet, as I began to thread the grove that lies before it, I was not so thoughtless but that I slacked my pace and went a trifle warily. It would have been a poor end of my adventures to get shot down by my own party in mistake.

The moon was climbing higher and higher; its light began to fall here and there in masses through the more open districts of the wood; and right in front of me a glow of a different color appeared among the trees. It was red and hot, and now and again it was a little darkened—as it were the embers of a bonfire.

For the life of me I could not think what it might be.

At last I came right down upon the borders of the clearing. The western end was already steeped in moonshine; the rest, and the blockhouse itself, still lay in a black shadow, checkered with long, silvery streaks of light. On the other side of the house an immense fire had burned itself into clear embers and shed a steady, red reverberation, contrasted strongly with the mellow paleness of the moon. There was not a soul stirring, nor a sound beside the noises of the breeze.

I stopped, with much wonder in my heart, and perhaps a little terror also. It had not been our way to build great fires; we were, indeed, by the captain's orders, somewhat niggardly of firewood; and I began to fear something had gone wrong while I was absent.

I stole round by the eastern end, keeping close in shadow, and at a convenient place, where the darkness was thickest, crossed the palisade.

To make assurance surer, I got upon my hands and knees and crawled, without a sound, toward the corner of the house. As I drew nearer, my heart was suddenly and greatly lightened. It is not a pleasant noise in itself, and I have often complained of it at other times, but just then it was like music to hear my friends snoring together so loud and peaceful in their sleep. The sea cry of the watch, that beautiful "All's well," never fell more reassuringly on my ear.

In the meantime, there was no doubt of one thing; they kept an infamous bad watch. If it had been Silver and his lads that were now creeping in on them, not a soul would have seen daybreak. That was what it was, thought I, to have the captain wounded; and again I blamed myself sharply for leaving them in

that danger with so few to mount guard.

By this time I had got to the door and stood up. All was dark within, so that I could distinguish nothing by the eye. As for sounds, there was the steady drone of the snorers, and a small occasional noise, a flickering or pecking that I could in no way account for.

With my arms before me I walked steadily in. I should lie down in my own place (I thought, with a silent chuckle) and enjoy their faces when they found me in the morning.

My foot struck something yielding—it was a sleeper's leg; and he turned and groaned, but without awakening.

And then, all of a sudden, a shrill voice broke forth out of the darkness:

"Pieces of eight! pieces of eight! pieces of eight! pieces of eight, pieces of eight!" and so forth, without pause or change, like the clacking of a tiny mill.

Silver's green parrot, Captain Flint! It was she whom I had heard pecking at a piece of bark; it was she, keeping better watch than any human being, who thus announced my arrival with her wearisome refrain.

I had no time left me to recover. At the sharp, clipping tone of the parrot, the sleepers awoke and sprang up; and with a mighty oath the voice of Silver cried: "Who goes?"

I turned to run, struck violently against one person, recoiled, and ran full into the arms of a second, who, for his part, closed upon and held me tight.

"Bring a torch, Dick," said Silver, when my capture was thus assured.

And one of the men left the log house, and presently returned with a lighted brand.

PART VI

Captain Silver

☆ XXVIII ☆

In the Enemy's Camp

———

THE RED GLARE of the torch, lighting up the interior of the blockhouse, showed me the worst of my apprehensions realized. The pirates were in possession of the house and stores: there was the cask of cognac, there were the pork and bread, as before; and, what tenfold increased my horror, not a sign of any prisoner. I could only judge that all had perished, and my heart smote me sorely that I had not been there to perish with them.

There were six of the buccaneers, all told; not another man was left alive. Five of them were on their feet, flushed and swollen, suddenly called out of the first sleep of drunkenness. The sixth had only risen upon his elbow: he was deadly pale, and the blood-stained bandage round his head told that he had recently been wounded, and still more recently dressed. I remembered the man who had been shot and had run back among the woods in the great attack, and doubted not that this was he.

The parrot sat, preening her plumage, on Long John's shoulder. He himself, I thought, looked some-

what paler and more stern than I was used to. He still wore the fine broadcloth suit in which he had fulfilled his mission, but it was bitterly the worse for wear, daubed with clay and torn with the sharp briers of the wood.

"So," said he, "here's Jim Hawkins, shiver my timbers! Dropped in like, eh? Well, come, I take that friendly."

And thereupon he sat down across the brandy cask, and began to fill a pipe.

"Give me a loan of the link, Dick," said he; and then, when he had a good light, "that'll do, lad," he added; "stick the glim in the wood heap; and you, gentlemen, bring yourselves to!—you needn't stand up

for Mr. Hawkins; *he'll* excuse you, you may lay to that. And so, Jim"—stopping the tobacco—"here you were, and quite a pleasant surprise for poor old John. I see you were smart when first I set my eyes on you; but this here gets away from me clean, it do."

To all this, as may be well supposed, I made no answer. They had set me with my back against the wall; and I stood there, looking Silver in the face, pluckily enough, I hope, to all outward appearance, but with black despair in my heart.

Silver took a whiff or two of his pipe with great composure, and then ran on again.

"Now, you see, Jim, so be as you *are* here," says he, "I'll give you a piece of my mind. I've always liked you, I have, for a lad of spirit, and the picter of my own self when I was young and handsome. I always wanted you to jine and take your share, and die a gentleman, and now, my cock, you've got to. Cap'n Smollett's a fine seaman, as I'll own up to any day, but stiff on discipline. 'Dooty is dooty,' says he, and right

he is. Just you keep clear of the cap'n. The doctor himself is gone dead again you—'ungrateful scamp,' was what he said; and the short and the long of the whole story is about here: you can't go back to your own lot, for they won't have you; and, without you start a third ship's company all by yourself, which might be lonely, you'll have to jine with Cap'n Silver."

So far so good. My friends, then, were still alive, and though I partly believed the truth of Silver's statement, that the cabin party were incensed at me for my desertion, I was more relieved than distressed by what I heard.

"I don't say nothing as to your being in our hands," continued Silver, "though there you are, and you may lay to it. I'm all for argyment; I never seen good come out o' threatening. If you like the service, well, you'll jine; and if you don't, Jim, why, you're free to answer no—free and welcome, shipmate; and if anything fairer can be said by mortal seaman, shiver my sides!"

"Am I to answer, then?" I asked, with a very tremulous voice. Through all this sneering talk I was made to feel the threat of death that overhung me, and my cheeks burned and my heart beat painfully.

"Lad," said Silver, "no one's a-pressing of you. Take your bearings. None of us won't hurry you, mate; time goes so pleasant in your company, you see."

"Well," says I, growing a bit bolder, "if I'm to choose, I declare I have a right to know what's what, and why you're here, and where my friends are."

"Wot's wot?" repeated one of the buccaneers, in a deep growl. "Ah, he'd be a lucky one as knowed that!"

"You'll, perhaps, batten down your hatches till you're spoke to, my friend," cried Silver truculently to this speaker. And then, in his first gracious tones, he replied to me: "Yesterday morning, Mr. Hawkins," said he, "in the dogwatch, down came Dr. Livesey with a flag of truce. Says he, 'Cap'n Silver, you're sold out. Ship's gone.' Well, maybe we'd been taking a glass, and a song to help it round. I won't say no. Leastways, none of us had looked out. We looked out, and, by thunder! the old ship was gone. I never seen a pack o' fools look fishier; and you may lay to that, if I tells you that looked the fishiest. 'Well,' says the doctor, 'let's bargain.' We bargained, him and I, and here we are: stores, brandy, blockhouse, the firewood you was thoughtful enough to cut, and, in a manner of speaking, the whole blessed boat, from crosstrees to kelson. As for them, they've tramped; I don't know where's they are." He drew again quietly at his pipe with a meditative air.

"And lest you should take it into that head of yours," he went on, "that you was included in the treaty, here's the last word that was said: 'How many are you,' says I, 'to leave?' 'Four,' says he—'four, and one of us wounded. As for that boy, I don't know where he is, confound him,' says he, 'nor I don't much care. We're about sick of him.' These was his words."

"Is that all?" I asked.

"Well, it's all that you're to hear, my son," returned Silver.

"And now I am to choose?"

"And now you are to choose, and you may lay to that," said Silver.

"Well," said I, "I am not such a fool but I know pretty well what I have to look for. Let the worst

come to the worst, it's little I care. I've seen too many die since I fell in with you. But there's a thing or two I have to tell you," I said, and by this time I was quite excited; "and the first is this: here you are, in a bad way: ship lost, treasure lost, men lost; your whole business gone to wreck; and if you want to know who did it—it was I! I was in the apple barrel the night we sighted land, and I heard you, John, and you, Johnson, and Hands, who is now at the bottom of the sea, and told every word you said before the hour was out. And as for the schooner, it was I who cut her cable, and it was I that killed the men you had aboard of her, and it was I who brought her where you'll never see her more, not one of you. The laugh's on my side; I've had the top of this business from the first; I no more fear you than I fear a fly. Kill me, if you please, or spare me. But one thing I'll say, and no more: if you spare me, bygones are bygones, and when you fellows are in court for piracy, I'll save you all I can. It is for you to choose. Kill another and do yourselves no good, or spare me and keep a witness to save you from the gallows."

I stopped, for, I tell you, I was out of breath, and, to my wonder, not a man of them moved, but all sat staring at me like as many sheep. And while they were still staring, I broke out again:

"And now, Mr. Silver," I said, "I believe you're the best man here, and if things go to the worst, I'll take it kind of you to let the doctor know the way I took it."

"I'll bear it in mind," said Silver, with an accent so curious that I could not, for the life of me, decide whether he were laughing at my request or had been favorably affected by my courage.

"I'll put one to that," cried the old mahogany-faced

seaman—Morgan by name—whom I had seen in Long John's public house upon the quays of Bristol. "It was him that knowed Black Dog."

"Well, and see here," added the sea cook. "I'll put another again to that, by thunder! for it was this same boy that faked the chart from Billy Bones. First and last, we've split upon Jim Hawkins!"

"Then here goes!" said Morgan, with an oath.

And he sprang up, drawing his knife as if he had been twenty.

"Avast, there!" cried Silver. "Who are you, Tom Morgan? Maybe you thought you was cap'n here, perhaps. By the powers, but I'll teach you better! Cross me, and you'll go where many a good man's gone before you, first and last, these thirty year back —some to the yardarm, shiver my timbers! and some by the board, and all to feed the fishes. There's never a man looked me between the eyes and seen a good day a'terwards, Tom Morgan, you may lay to that."

Morgan paused; but a hoarse murmur rose from the others. "Tom's right," said one. "I stood hazing long enough from one," added another. "I'll be hanged if I'll be hazed by you, John Silver."

"Did any of you gentlemen want to have it out with *me?*" roared Silver, bending far forward from his position on the keg, with his pipe still glowing in his right hand. "Put a name on what you're at; you ain't dumb, I reckon. Him that wants shall get it. Have I lived this many years, and a son of a rum puncheon cock his hat athwart my hawse at the latter end of it? You know the way; you're all gentlemen o' fortune, by your account. Well, I'm ready. Take a cutlass, him that dares, and I'll see the color of his inside, crutch and all, before that pipe's empty."

Not a man stirred; not a man answered.

"That's your sort, is it?" he added, returning his pipe to his mouth. "Well, you're a gay lot to look at, anyway. Not much worth to fight, you ain't. P'r'aps you can understand King George's English. I'm cap'n here by 'lection. I'm cap'n here because I'm the best man by a long sea mile. You won't fight, as gentlemen o' fortune should; then, by thunder, you'll obey, and you may lay to it! I like that boy, now; I never seen a better boy than that. He's more a man than any pair of rats of you in this here house, and what I say is this: let me see him that'll lay a hand on him—that's what I say, and you may lay to it."

There was a long pause after this. I stood straight up against the wall, my heart still going like a sledge hammer, but with a ray of hope now shining in my bosom. Silver leaned back against the wall, his arms crossed, his pipe in the corner of his mouth, as calm as though he had been in church; yet his eye kept wandering furtively, and he kept the tail of it on his unruly followers. They, on their part, drew gradually together toward the far end of the blockhouse, and the low hiss of their whispering sounded in my ear continuously, like a stream. One after another they would look up, and the red light of the torch would fall for a second on their nervous faces; but it was not toward me, it was toward Silver that they turned their eyes.

"You seem to have a lot to say," remarked Silver, spitting far into the air. "Pipe up and let me hear it."

"Ax your pardon, sir," returned one of the men, "you're pretty free with some of the rules; maybe you'll kindly keep an eye upon the rest. This crew's dissatisfied; this crew don't vally bullying a marlinspike; this crew has its rights like other crews, I'll make

so free as that; and by your own rules, I take it we can talk together. I ax your pardon, sir, acknowledging you for to be capting at this present; but I claim my right, and steps outside for a council."

And with an elaborate sea salute, this fellow, a long, ill-looking, yellow-eyed man of five and thirty, stepped coolly toward the door and disappeared out of the house. One after another the rest followed his example, each making a salute as he passed, each adding some apology. "According to rules," said one. "Foc's'le council," said Morgan. And so, with one remark or another, all marched out, and left Silver and me alone with the torch.

The sea cook instantly removed his pipe.

"Now, look you here, Jim Hawkins," he said, in a steady whisper, that was no more than audible, "you're within half a plank of death, and what's a long sight worse, of torture. They're going to throw me off. But, you mark, I stand by you through thick and thin. I didn't mean to; no, not till you spoke up. I was about desperate to lose that much blunt, and be hanged into the bargain. But I see you was the right sort. I says to myself: You stand by Hawkins, John, and Hawkins'll stand by you. You're his last card, and, by the living thunder, John, he's yours! Back to back, says I. You save your witness, and he'll save your neck!"

I began dimly to understand.

"You mean all's lost?" I asked.

"Aye, by gum, I do!" he answered. "Ship gone, neck gone—that's the size of it. Once I looked into that bay, Jim Hawkins, and seen no schooner—well, I'm tough, but I gave out. As for that lot and their council, mark me, they're outright fools and cowards.

I'll save your life—if so be as I can—from them. But, see here, Jim—tit for tat—you save Long John from swinging."

I was bewildered; it seemed a thing so hopeless he was asking—he, the old buccaneer, the ringleader throughout. "What I can do, that I'll do," I said.

"It's a bargain!" cried Long John. "You speak up plucky, and, by thunder! I've a chance."

He hobbled to the torch, where it stood propped among the firewood, and took a fresh light to his pipe.

"Understand me, Jim," he said, returning. "I've a head on my shoulders, I have. I'm on squire's side now. I know you've got that ship safe somewheres. How you done it, I don't know, but safe it is. I guess Hands and O'Brien turned soft. I never much believed in neither of *them*. Now you mark me. I ask no questions, nor I won't let others. I know when a game's up, I do; and I know a lad that's stanch. Ah, you that's young—you and me might have done a power of good together!"

He drew some cognac from the cask.

"Will you taste, messmate?" he asked; and when I had refused: "Well, I'll take a drain myself, Jim," said he. "I need a calker, for there's trouble on hand. And, talking o' trouble, why did that doctor give me the chart, Jim?"

My face expressed a wonder so unaffected that he saw the needlessness of further questions.

"Ah, well, he did, though," said he. "And there's something under that, no doubt—something, surely, under that, Jim—bad or good."

And he took another swallow of the brandy, shaking his great fair head like a man who looks forward to the worst.

☆ XXIX ☆

The Black Spot Again

————

THE COUNCIL of the buccaneers had lasted some time, when one of them re-entered the house, and with a repetition of the same salute, which had in my eyes an ironical air, begged for a moment's loan of the torch.

Silver briefly agreed; and the emissary retired again, leaving us together in the dark.

"There's a breeze coming, Jim," said Silver, who had, by this time, adopted quite a friendly and familiar tone.

I turned to the loophole nearest me and looked out. The embers of the great fire had so far burned themselves out and now glowed so low and duskily that I understood why these conspirators desired a torch. About halfway down the slope to the stockade, they were collected in a group; one held the light, another was on his knees in their midst, and I saw the blade of an open knife shine in his hand with varying colors, in the moon and torchlight. The rest were all somewhat stooping, as though watching the maneuvers of

this last. I could just make out that he had a book as well as a knife in his hand; and was still wondering how anything so incongruous had come in their possession, when the kneeling figure rose once more to his feet, and the whole party began to move together toward the house.

"Here they come," said I; and I returned to my former position, for it seemed beneath my dignity that they should find me watching them.

"Well, let 'em come, lad—let 'em come," said Silver cheerily. "I've still a shot in my locker."

The door opened, and the five men, standing huddled together just inside, pushed one of their number forward. In any other circumstances it would have been comical to see his slow advance, hesitating as he set down each foot, but holding his closed right hand in front of him.

"Step up, lad," cried Silver. "I won't eat you. Hand it over, lubber. I know the rules, I do; I won't hurt a depytation."

Thus encouraged, the buccaneer stepped forth more briskly, and having passed something to Silver, from hand to hand, slipped yet more smartly back again to his companions.

The sea cook looked at what had been given him.

"The black spot! I thought so," he observed. "Where might you have got the paper? Why, hillo! look here, now: this ain't lucky! You've gone and cut this out of a Bible. What fool's cut a Bible?"

"Ah, there!" said Morgan—"there! Wot did I say? No good'll come o' that, I said."

"Well, you've about fixed it now, among you," continued Silver. "You'll all swing now, I reckon. What softheaded lubber had a Bible?"

"It was Dick," said one.

"Dick, was it? Then Dick can get to prayers," said Silver. "He's seen his slice of luck, has Dick, and you may lay to that."

But here the long man with the yellow eyes struck in.

"Belay that talk, John Silver," he said. "This crew has tipped you the black spot in full council, as in dooty bound; just you turn it over, as in dooty bound, and see what's wrote there. Then you can talk."

"Thanky, George," replied the sea cook. "You always was brisk for business, and has the rules by heart, George, as I'm pleased to see. Well, what is it, anyway? Ah! 'Depposed'—that's it, is it? Very pretty wrote, to be sure; like print, I swear. Your hand o' write, George? Why, you was gettin' quite a leadin' man in this here crew. You'll be cap'n next, I shouldn't wonder. Just oblige me with that torch again, will you? This pipe don't draw."

"Come, now," said George, "you don't fool this crew no more. You're a funny man, by your account; but you're over now, and you'll maybe step down off that barrel, and help vote."

"I thought you said you knowed the rules," returned Silver contemptuously. "Leastways, if you don't, I do; and I wait here—and I'm still your cap'n, mind—till you outs with your grievances, and I reply; in the meantime, your black spot ain't worth a biscuit. After that, we'll see."

"Oh," replied George, "you don't be under no kind of apprehension; *we're* all square, we are. First, you've made a hash of this cruise—you'll be a bold man to say no to that. Second, you let the enemy out o' this here trap for nothing. Why did they want out? I dunno;

but it's pretty plain they wanted it. Third, you wouldn't let us go at them upon the march. Oh, we see through you, John Silver; you want to play booty, that's what's wrong with you. And then, fourth, there's this here boy."

"Is that all?" asked Silver quietly.

"Enough, too," retorted George. "We'll all swing and sun-dry for your bungling."

"Well, now, look here, I'll answer these four p'ints; one after another I'll answer 'em. I made a hash o' this cruise, did I? Well, now, you all know what I wanted; and you all know, if that had been done, that we'd 'a' been aboard the *Hispaniola* this night as ever was, every man of us alive, and fit, and full of good plum duff, and the treasure in the hold of her, by thunder! Well, who crossed me? Who forced my hand, as was the lawful cap'n? Who tipped me the black spot the day we landed, and began this dance? Ah, it's a fine dance—I'm with you there—and looks mighty like a hornpipe in a rope's end at Execution Dock by London town, it does. But who done it? Why, it was Anderson, and Hands, and you, George Merry! And you're the last aboveboard of that same meddling crew; and you have the Davy Jones' insolence to up and stand for cap'n over me—you, that sank the lot of us! By the powers! but this tops the stiffest yarn to nothing."

Silver paused, and I could see by the faces of George and his late comrades that these words had not been said in vain.

"That's for number one," cried the accused, wiping the sweat from his brow, for he had been talking with a vehemence that shook the house. "Why, I give you

my word, I'm sick to speak to you. You've neither sense nor memory, and I leave it to fancy where your mothers was that let you come to sea. Sea! Gentlemen o' fortune! I reckon tailors is your trade."

"Go on, John," said Morgan. "Speak up to the others."

"Ah, the others!" returned John. "They're a nice lot, ain't they? You say this cruise is bungled. Ah! by gum, if you could understand how bad it's bungled, you would see! We're that near the gibbet that my neck's stiff with thinking on it. You've seen 'em, maybe, hanged in chains, birds about 'em, seamen p'inting 'em out as they go down with the tide. 'Who's that?' says one. 'That! Why, that's John Silver. I knowed him well,' says another. And you can hear the chains ajangle as you go about and reach for the other buoy. Now, that's about where we are, every mother's son of us, thanks to him, and Hands, and Anderson, and other ruination fools of you. And if you want to know about number four, and that boy, why, shiver my timbers! isn't he a hostage? Are we a-going to waste a hostage? No, not us; he might be our last chance, and I shouldn't wonder. Kill that boy? Not me, mates! And number three? Ah, well, there's a deal to say to number three. Maybe you don't count it nothing to have a real college doctor come to see you every day—you, John, with your head broke—or you, George Merry, that had the ague shakes upon you not six hours agone, and has your eyes the color of lemon peel to this same moment on the clock? And maybe, perhaps, you didn't know there was a consort coming, either? But there is, and not so long till then; and we'll see who'll

be glad to have a hostage when it comes to that. And as for number two, and why I made a bargain—well, you came crawling on your knees to me to make it— on your knees you came, you was that downhearted— and you'd have starved, too, if I hadn't—but that's a trifle! You look there—that's why!"

And he cast down upon the floor a paper that I instantly recognized—none other than the chart on yellow paper, with the three red crosses, that I had found in the oilcloth at the bottom of the captain's chest. Why the doctor had given it to him was more than I could fancy.

But if it were inexplicable to me, the appearance of the chart was incredible to the surviving mutineers. They leaped upon it like cats upon a mouse. It went from hand to hand, one tearing it from another; and by the oaths and the cries and the childish laughter with which they accompanied their eager examination, you would have thought, not only they were fingering the very gold, but were at sea with it, besides, in safety.

"Yes," said one, "that's Flint, sure enough. J. F., and a score below, with a clove hitch to it; so he done ever."

"Mighty pretty," said George. "But how are we to get away with it, and us no ship?"

Silver suddenly sprang up, and supporting himself with a hand against the wall: "Now I give you warning, George," he cried. "One more word of your sauce, and I'll call you down and fight you. How? Why, how do I know? You had ought to tell me that —you and the rest, that lost me my schooner, with your interference, burn you! But not you, you can't; you hain't got the invention of a cockroach. But civil

you can speak, and shall, George Merry, you may lay to that."

"That's fair enow," said the old man Morgan.

"Fair! I reckon so," said the sea cook. "You lost the ship; I found the treasure. Who's the better man at that? And now I resign, by thunder! Elect whom you please to be your cap'n now; I'm done with it."

"Silver!" they cried. "Barbecue forever! Barbecue for cap'n!"

"So that's the toon, is it?" cried the cook. "George, I reckon you'll have to wait another turn, friend; and lucky for you as I'm not a revengeful man. But that was never my way. And now, shipmates, this black spot? 'Tain't much good now, is it? Dick's crossed his luck and spoiled his Bible, and that's about all."

"It'll do to kiss the book on still, won't it?" growled Dick, who was evidently uneasy at the curse he had brought upon himself.

"A Bible with a bit cut out!" returned Silver derisively. "Not it. It don't bind no more'n a ballad book."

"Don't it, though?" cried Dick, with a sort of joy. "Well, I reckon that's worth having, too."

"Here, Jim—here's a cur'osity for you," said Silver; and he tossed me the paper.

It was a round about the size of a crown piece. One side was blank, for it had been the last leaf; the other contained a verse or two of Revelation—these words among the rest, which struck sharply home upon my mind: "Without are dogs and murderers." The printed side had been blackened with wood ash, which already began to come off and soil my fingers; on the blank side had been written with the same material the one word "Depposed." I have that curiosity beside

me at this moment; but not a trace of writing now remains beyond a single scratch, such as a man might make with his thumbnail.

That was the end of the night's business. Soon after, with a drink all round, we lay down to sleep, and the outside of Silver's vengeance was to put George Merry up for sentinel, and threaten him with death if he should prove unfaithful.

It was long ere I could close an eye, and Heaven knows I had matter enough for thought in the man whom I had slain that afternoon, in my own most perilous position, and, above all, in the remarkable game that I saw Silver now engaged upon—keeping the mutineers together with one hand and grasping, with the other, after every means, possible and impossible, to make his peace and save his miserable life. He himself slept peacefully, and snored aloud; yet my heart was sore for him, wicked as he was, to think on the dark perils that environed, and the shameful gibbet that awaited him.

☆ XXX ☆

On Parole

I WAS wakened—indeed, we were all wakened, for I could see even the sentinel shake himself together from where he had fallen against the doorpost—by a clear, hearty voice hailing us from the margin of the wood:

"Blockhouse, ahoy!" it cried. "Here's the doctor."

And the doctor it was. Although I was glad to hear the sound, yet my gladness was not without admixture. I remembered with confusion my insubordinate and stealthy conduct; and when I saw where it had brought me—among what companions and surrounded by what dangers—I felt ashamed to look him in the face.

He must have risen in the dark, for the day had hardly come; and when I ran to a loophole and looked out, I saw him standing, like Silver once before, up to the mid-leg in creeping vapor.

"You, doctor! Top o' the morning to you, sir!"

cried Silver, broad awake and beaming with good nature in a moment. "Bright and early, to be sure; and it's the early bird, as the saying goes, that gets the rations. George, shake up your timbers, son, and help Dr. Livesey over the ship's side. All a-doin' well, your patients was—all well and merry."

So he pattered on, standing on the hilltop, with his crutch under his elbow, and one hand upon the side of the log house—quite the old John in voice, manner, and expression.

"We've quite a surprise for you, too, sir," he continued. "We've a little stranger here—he! he! A noo boarder and lodger, sir, and looking fit and taut as a fiddle; slep' like a supercargo, he did, right alongside of John—stem to stem we was, all night."

Dr. Livesey was by this time across the stockade and pretty near the cook; and I could hear the alteration in his voice as he said:

"Not Jim?"

"The very same Jim as ever was," says Silver.

The doctor stopped outright, although he did not speak, and it was some seconds before he seemed able to move on.

"Well, well," he said at last, "duty first and pleasure afterward, as you might have said yourself, Silver. Let us overhaul these patients of yours."

A moment afterward he had entered the blockhouse, and, with one grim nod to me, proceeded with his work among the sick. He seemed under no apprehension, though he must have known that his life, among these treacherous demons, depended on a hair; and he rattled on to his patients as if he were paying an ordinary professional visit in a quiet English family. His manner, I suppose, reacted on the men; for they

behaved to him as if nothing had occurred—as if he were still ship's doctor and they still faithful hands before the mast.

"You're doing well, my friend," he said to the fellow with the bandaged head, "and if ever any person had a close shave, it was you; your head must be as hard as iron. Well, George, how goes it? You're a pretty color, certainly; why, your liver, man, is upside down. Did you take that medicine? Did he take that medicine, men?"

"Aye, aye, sir, he took it, sure enough," returned Morgan.

"Because, you see, since I am mutineers' doctor, or prison doctor, as I prefer to call it," says Dr. Livesey, in his pleasantest way, "I make it a point of honor not to lose a man for King George (God bless him!) and the gallows."

The rogues looked at each other, but swallowed the home thrust in silence.

"Dick don't feel well, sir," said one.

"Don't he?" replied the doctor. "Well, step up here, Dick, and let me see your tongue. No, I should be surprised if he did! The man's tongue is fit to frighten the French. Another fever."

"Ah, there," said Morgan, "that comed of sp'iling Bibles."

"That comed—as you call it—of being arrant asses," retorted the doctor, "and not having sense enough to know honest air from poison and the dry land from a vile, pestiferous slough. I think it most probable—though, of course, it's only an opinion—that you'll all have the deuce to pay before you get that malaria out of your systems. Camp in a bog, would you? Silver, I'm surprised at you. You're less

of a fool than many, take you all round, but you don't appear to me to have a notion of the rules of health.

"Well," he added, after he had dosed them round, and they had taken his prescriptions with really laughable humility, more like charity school children than blood-guilty mutineers and pirates—"Well, that's done for today. And now I should wish to have a talk with that boy, please."

And he nodded his head in my direction carelessly.

George Merry was at the door, spitting and spluttering over some bad-tasted medicine; but at the first word of the doctor's proposal he swung round with a deep flush, and cried "No!" and swore.

Silver struck the barrel with his open hand.

"Si-lence!" he roared, and looked about him positively like a lion. "Doctor," he went on, in his usual tones, "I was a-thinking of that, knowing as how you had a fancy for the boy. We're all humbly grateful for your kindness, and, as you see, puts faith in you, and takes the drugs down like that much grog. And I take it I've found a way as'll suit all. Hawkins, will you give me your word of honor as a young gentleman—for a young gentleman you are, although poor born—your word of honor not to slip your cable?"

I readily gave the pledge required.

"Then, doctor," said Silver, "you just step outside o' that stockade, and once you're there, I'll bring the boy down on the inside, and I reckon you can yarn through the spars. Good day to you, sir, and all our dooties to the squire and Cap'n Smollett."

The explosion of disapproval, which nothing but Silver's black looks had restrained, broke out immediately the doctor had left the house. Silver was roundly accused of playing double—of trying to make

a separate peace for himself—of sacrificing the interests of his accomplices and victims; and, in one word, of the identical, exact thing that he was doing. It seemed to me so obvious, in this case, that I could not imagine how he was to turn their anger. But he was twice the man the rest were; and his last night's victory had given him a huge preponderance on their minds. He called them all the fools and dolts you can imagine, said it was necessary I should talk to the doctor, fluttered the chart in their faces, asked them if they could afford to break the treaty the very day they were bound a-treasure hunting.

"No, by thunder!" he cried, "it's us must break the treaty when the time comes; and till then I'll gammon that doctor, if I have to ile his boots with brandy."

And then he bade them get the fire lit, and stalked out upon his crutch, with his hand on my shoulder, leaving them in a disarray, and silenced by his volubility rather than convinced.

"Slow, lad, slow," he said. "They might round upon us in a twinkle of an eye, if we was seen to hurry."

Very deliberately, then, did we advance across the sand to where the doctor awaited us on the other side of the stockade, and as soon as we were within easy speaking distance, Silver stopped.

"You'll make a note of this here also, doctor," says he, "and the boy'll tell you how I saved his life, and were deposed for it, too, and you may lay to that. Doctor, when a man's steering as near the wind as me —playing chuck-farthing with the last breath in his body, like—you wouldn't think it too much, mayhap, to give him one good word? You'll please bear in mind it's not my life only now—it's that boy's into the bargain; and you'll speak me fair, doctor, and give me

a bit o' hope to go on, for the sake of mercy."

Silver was a changed man, once he was out there and had his back to his friends and the blockhouse; his cheeks seemed to have fallen in, his voice trembled; never was a soul more dead in earnest.

"Why, John, you're not afraid?" asked Dr. Livesey.

"Doctor, I'm no coward; no, not I—not *so* much!" and he snapped his fingers. "If I was I wouldn't say it. But I'll own up fairly, I've the shakes upon me for the gallows. You're a good man and a true; I never seen a better man! And you'll not forget what I done good, not any more than you'll forget the bad, I know. And I step aside—see here—and leave you and Jim alone. And you'll put that down for me, too, for it's a long stretch, is that!"

So saying, he stepped back a little way, till he was out of earshot, and there sat down upon a tree stump and began to whistle; spinning round now and again upon his seat so as to command a sight, sometimes of me and the doctor, and sometimes of his unruly ruffians as they went to and fro in the sand, between the fire—which they were busy rekindling—and the house, from which they brought forth pork and bread to make the breakfast.

"So, Jim," said the doctor sadly, "here you are. As you have brewed, so shall you drink, my boy. Heaven knows, I cannot find it in my heart to blame you; but this much I will say, be it kind or unkind: when Captain Smollett was well, you dared not have gone off; and when he was ill, and couldn't help it, by George, it was downright cowardly!"

I will own that I here began to weep. "Doctor," I said, "you might spare me. I have blamed myself enough; my life's forfeit anyway, and I should have

been dead by now, if Silver hadn't stood for me; and, doctor, believe this, I can die—and I dare say I deserve it—but what I fear is torture. If they torture me—"

"Jim," the doctor interrupted, and his voice was quite changed, "Jim, I can't have this. Whip over, and we'll run for it."

"Doctor," said I, "I passed my word."

"I know, I know," he cried. "We can't help that, Jim, now. I'll take it on my shoulders, holus bolus, blame and shame, my boy; but stay here I cannot let you. Jump! One jump, and you're out, and we'll run for it like antelopes."

"No," I replied, "you know right well you wouldn't do the thing yourself—neither you, nor squire, nor captain—and no more will I. Silver trusted me; I passed my word, and back I go. But, doctor, you did not let me finish. If they come to torture me, I might let slip a word of where the ship is; for I got the ship, part by luck and part by risking, and she lies in North Inlet, on the southern beach, and just below high water. At half tide she must be high and dry."

"The ship!" exclaimed the doctor.

Rapidly I described to him my adventures, and he heard me out in silence.

"There is a kind of fate in this," he observed, when I had done. "Every step, it's you that saves our lives; and do you suppose by any chance that we are going to let you lose yours? That would be a poor return, my boy. You found out the plot; you found Ben Gunn—the best deed that ever you did, or will do, though you live to ninety. Oh, by Jupiter, and talking of Ben Gunn! Why, this is the mischief in person. Silver!" he cried, "Silver!—I'll give you a piece of advice," he continued, as the cook drew near again;

"don't you be in any great hurry after that treasure."

"Why, sir, I do my possible, which that ain't," said Silver. "I can only, asking your pardon, save my life and the boy's by seeking for that treasure; and you may lay to that."

"Well, Silver," replied the doctor, "if that is so, I'll go one step further: look out for squalls when you find it."

"Sir," said Silver, "as between man and man, that's too much and too little. What you're after, why you left the blockhouse, why you've given me that there chart, I don't know, now, do I? And yet I done your bidding with my eyes shut and never a word of hope! But no, this here's too much. If you won't tell me what you mean plain out, just say so, and I'll leave the helm."

"No," said the doctor musingly, "I've no right to say more; it's not my secret, you see, Silver, or I give you my word I'd tell it you. But I'll go as far with you as I dare go, and a step beyond; for I'll have my wig sorted by the captain or I'm mistaken! And, first, I'll give you a bit of hope: Silver, if we both get alive out of this wolf trap, I'll do my best to save you, short of perjury."

Silver's face was radiant. "You couldn't say more, I'm sure, sir, not if you was my mother," he cried.

"Well, that's my first concession," added the doctor. "My second is a piece of advice: Keep the boy close beside you, and when you need help, halloo. I'm off to seek it for you, and that itself will show you if I speak at random. Good-by, Jim."

And Dr. Livesey shook hands with me through the stockade, nodded to Silver, and set off at a brisk pace into the wood.

The Treasure Hunt—Flint's Pointer

———

"JIM," said Silver, when we were alone, "if I saved your life, you saved mine; and I'll not forget it. I seen the doctor waving you to run for it—with the tail of my eye, I did; and I seen you say no, as plain as hearing. Jim, that's one to you. This is the first glint of hope I had since the attack failed, and I owe it you. And now, Jim, we're to go in for this here treasure hunting, with sealed orders too, and I don't like it; and you and me must stick close, back to back like, and we'll save our necks in spite o' fate and fortune."

Just then a man hailed us from the fire that break-fast was ready, and we were soon seated here and there about the sand over biscuit and fried junk. They had lit a fire fit to roast an ox; and it was now grown so hot that they could only approach it from the windward, and even there not without precaution. In the same wasteful spirit, they had cooked, I suppose, three times more than we could eat; and one of them,

with an empty laugh, threw what was left into the fire, which blazed and roared again over this unusual fuel. I never in my life saw men so careless of the morrow; hand to mouth is the only word that can describe their way of doing. And what with wasted food and sleeping sentries, though they were bold enough for a brush and be done with it, I could see their entire unfitness for anything like a prolonged campaign.

Even Silver, eating away, with Captain Flint upon his shoulder, had not a word of blame for their recklessness. And this the more surprised me, for I thought he had never shown himself so cunning as he did then.

"Aye, mates," said he, "it's lucky you have Barbecue to think for you with this here head. I got what I wanted, I did. Sure enough they have the ship. Where they have it, I don't know yet; but once we hit the treasure, we'll have to jump about and find out. And then, mates, us that has the boats, I reckon, has the upper hand."

Thus he kept running on, with his mouth full of the hot bacon: thus he restored their hope and confidence and, I suspect, repaired his own at the same time.

"As for hostage," he continued, "that's his last talk, I guess, with them he loves so dear. I've got my piece o' news, and thanky to him for that, but it's over and done. I'll take him in a line when we go treasure hunting, for we'll keep him like so much gold, in case of accidents, you mark, and in the meantime. Once we got the ship and treasure both, and off to sea like jolly companions, why, then, we'll talk Mr. Hawkins over, we will, and we'll give him his share, to be sure, for all his kindness."

It was no wonder the men were in a good humor now. For my part I was horribly cast down. Should the scheme he had now sketched prove feasible, Silver, already doubly a traitor, would not hesitate to adopt it. He had still a foot in either camp, and there was no doubt he would prefer wealth and freedom with the pirates to a bare escape from hanging, which was the best he had to hope on our side.

Nay, and even if things so fell out that he was forced to keep his faith with Dr. Livesey, even then what danger lay before us! What a moment that would be when the suspicions of his followers turned to certainty, and he and I should have to fight for dear life— he, a cripple, and I, a boy—against five strong and active seamen!

Add to this double apprehension the mystery that still hung over the behavior of my friends; their unexplained desertion of the stockade; their inexplicable cession of the chart; or, harder still to understand, the doctor's last warning to Silver, "Look out for squalls when you find it"; and you will readily believe how little taste I found in my breakfast, and with how uneasy a heart I set forth behind my captors on the quest for treasure.

We made a curious figure, had anyone been there to see us: all in soiled sailor clothes, and all but me armed to the teeth. Silver had two guns slung about him— one before and one behind—besides the great cutlass at his waist and a pistol in each pocket of his square-tailed coat. To complete his strange appearance, Captain Flint sat perched upon his shoulder and gabbling odds and ends of purposeless sea talk. I had a line about my waist, and followed obediently after

the sea cook, who held the loose end of the rope, now in his free hand, now between his powerful teeth. For all the world I was led like a dancing bear.

The other men were variously burdened: some carrying picks and shovels—for that had been the very first necessary they brought ashore from the *Hispaniola;* others laden with pork, bread, and brandy for the midday meal. All the stores, I observed, came from our stock; and I could see the truth of Silver's words the night before. Had he not struck a bargain with the doctor, he and his mutineers, deserted by the ship, must have been driven to subsist on clear water and the proceeds of their hunting. Water would have been little to their taste; a sailor is not usually a good shot; and besides all that, when they were so short of eatables, it was not likely they would be very flush of powder.

Well, thus equipped, we all set out—even the fellow with the broken head, who should certainly have kept in shadow—and straggled, one after another, to the beach, where the two gigs awaited us. Even these bore trace of the drunken folly of the pirates, one in a broken thwart, and both in their muddy and unbailed condition. Both were to be carried along with us, for the sake of safety; and so, with our numbers divided between them, we set forth upon the bosom of the anchorage.

As we pulled over, there was some discussion on the chart. The red cross was, of course, far too large to be a guide; and the terms of the note on the back, as you will hear, admitted of some ambiguity. They ran, the reader may remember, thus:

Tall tree, Spyglass shoulder, bearing a point to the N. of N.N.E.

Skeleton Island E.S.E. and by E.
Ten feet.

A tall tree was thus the principal mark. Now, right before us, the anchorage was bounded by a plateau from two to three hundred feet high, adjoining on the north the sloping southern shoulder of the Spyglass, and rising again toward the south into the rough, cliffy eminence called the Mizzenmast Hill. The top of the plateau was dotted thickly with pine trees of varying height. Every here and there, one of a different species rose forty or fifty feet clear above its neighbors, and which of these was the particular "tall tree" of Captain Flint could only be decided on the spot, and by the readings of the compass.

Yet, although that was the case, every man on board the boats had picked a favorite of his own ere we were halfway over, Long John alone shrugging his shoulders and bidding them wait till they were there.

We pulled easily, by Silver's directions, not to weary the hands prematurely; and, after quite a long passage, landed at the mouth of the second river—that which runs down a woody cleft of the Spyglass. Thence, bending to our left, we began to ascend the slope toward the plateau.

At the first outset, heavy, miry ground and a matted, marshy vegetation, greatly delayed our progress; but by little and little the hill began to steepen and become stony under foot, and the wood to change its character and to grow in a more open order. It was, indeed, a most pleasant portion of the island that we were now approaching. A heavy-scented broom and many flowering shrubs had almost taken the place of grass. Thickets of green nutmeg were dotted here

and there with the red columns and the broad shadow of the pines, and the first mingled their spice with the aroma of the others. The air, besides, was fresh and stirring, and this, under the sheer sunbeams, was a wonderful refreshment to our senses.

The party spread itself abroad, in a fan shape, shouting and leaping to and fro. About the center, and a good way behind the rest, Silver and I followed —I tethered by my rope, he plowing, with deep pants, among the sliding gravel. From time to time, indeed, I had to lend him a hand or he must have missed his footing and fallen backward down the hill.

We had thus proceeded for about half a mile, and were approaching the brow of the plateau, when the man upon the farthest left began to cry aloud, as if in terror. Shout after shout came from him, and the others began to run in his direction.

"He can't 'a' found the treasure," said old Morgan, hurrying past us from the right, "for that's clean a-top."

Indeed, as we found when we also reached the spot, it was something very different. At the foot of a pretty big pine, and involved in a green creeper, which had even partly lifted some of the smaller bones, a human skeleton lay, with a few shreds of clothing, on the ground. I believe a chill struck for a moment to every heart.

"He was a seaman," said George Merry, who, bolder than the rest, had gone up close and was examining the rags of clothing. "Leastways, this is good sea cloth."

"Aye, aye," said Silver, "like enough; you wouldn't look to find a bishop here, I reckon. But what sort of a way is that for bones to lie? 'Tain't in natur'."

Indeed, on a second glance, it seemed impossible to fancy that the body was in a natural position. But for some disarray (the work, perhaps, of the birds that had fed upon him or of the slow-growing creeper that had gradually enveloped his remains), the man lay perfectly straight—his feet pointing in one direction, his hands, raised above his head like a diver's, pointing directly in the opposite.

"I've taken a notion into my old numskull," observed Silver. "Here's the compass; there's the tiptop p'int o' Skeleton Island, stickin' out like a tooth. Just take a bearing, will you, along the line of them bones."

It was done. The body pointed straight in the direction of the island, and the compass read duly E.S.E. and by E.

"I thought so," cried the cook; "this here is a p'inter. Right up there is our line for the Pole Star and the jolly dollars. But, by thunder! if it don't make me cold inside to think of Flint. This is one of *his* jokes, and no mistake. Him and these six was alone here; he killed 'em, every man; and this one he hauled here and laid down by compass, shiver my timbers! They're long bones, and the hair's been yellow. Aye, that would be Allardyce. You mind Allardyce, Tom Morgan?"

"Aye, aye," returned Morgan, "I mind him; he owed me money, he did, and took my knife ashore with him."

"Speaking of knives," said another, "why don't we find his'n lying round? Flint warn't the man to pick a seaman's pocket; and the birds, I guess, would leave it be."

"By the powers, and that's true!" cried Silver.

"There ain't a thing left here," said Merry, still feel-

ing round among the bones, "not a copper doit nor a baccy box. It don't look nat'ral to me."

"No, by gum, it don't," agreed Silver; "not nat'ral nor not nice, says you. Great guns! messmates, but if Flint was living, this would be a hot spot for you and me. Six they were, and six are we; and bones is what they are now."

"I saw him dead with these here deadlights," said Morgan. "Billy took me in. There he laid, with penny pieces on his eyes."

"Dead—aye, sure enough he's dead and gone below," said the fellow with the bandage; "but if ever sperrit walked, it would be Flint's. Dear heart, but he died bad, did Flint!"

"Aye, that he did," observed another; "now he raged, and now he hollered for the rum, and now he sang. 'Fifteen Men' were his only song, mates, and I tell you true I never rightly liked to hear it since. It was main hot, and the windy was open, and I hear that old song comin' out as clear as clear—and the death-haul on the man already."

"Come, come," said Silver, "stow this talk. He's dead, and he don't walk, that I know; leastways, he won't walk by day, and you may lay to that. Care killed a cat. Fetch ahead for the doubloons."

We started, certainly, but in spite of the hot sun and the staring daylight, the pirates no longer ran separate and shouting through the wood, but kept side by side and spoke with bated breath. The terror of the dead buccaneer had fallen on their spirits.

The Treasure Hunt—The Voice Among the Trees

———————

PARTLY from the damping influence of this alarm, partly to rest Silver and the sick folk, the whole party sat down as soon as they had gained the brow of the ascent.

The plateau being somewhat tilted toward the west, this spot on which we had paused commanded a wide prospect on either hand. Before us, over the treetops, we beheld the Cape of the Woods fringed with surf; behind, we not only looked down upon the anchorage and Skeleton Island, but saw—clear across the spit and the eastern lowlands—a great field of open sea upon the east. Sheer above us rose the Spyglass, here dotted with single pines, there black with precipices. There was no sound but that of the distant breakers, mounting from all round, and the chirp of countless insects in the brush. Not a man, not a sail upon the sea; the very largeness of the view increased the sense of solitude.

Silver, as he sat, took certain bearings with his compass.

"There are three 'tall trees,'" said he, "about in the

right line from Skeleton Island. 'Spyglass shoulder,' I take it, means that lower p'int there. It's child's play to find the stuff now. I've half a mind to dine first."

"I don't feel sharp," growled Morgan. "Thinkin' o' Flint—I think it were—has done me."

"Ah, well, my son, you praise your stars he's dead," said Silver.

"He were an ugly devil," cried a third pirate, with a shudder; "that blue in the face, too!"

"That was how the rum took him," added Merry. "Blue! well, I reckon he was blue. That's a true word."

Ever since they had found the skeleton and got upon this train of thought they had spoken lower and lower, and they had almost got to whispering by now, so that the sound of their talk hardly interrupted the silence of the wood. All of a sudden, out of the middle of the trees in front of us, a thin, high, trembling voice struck up the well-known air and words:

> *"Fifteen men on the dead man's chest—*
> *Yo-ho-ho, and a bottle of rum!"*

I never have seen men more dreadfully affected than the pirates. The color went from their six faces like enchantment; some leaped to their feet, some clawed hold of others; Morgan groveled on the ground.

"It's Flint, by—!" cried Merry.

The song had stopped as suddenly as it began— broken off, you would have said, in the middle of a note, as though someone had laid his hand upon the singer's mouth. Coming so far through the clear, sunny atmosphere among the green treetops, I thought

it had sounded airily and sweetly; and the effect on my companions was the stranger.

"Come," said Silver, struggling with his ashen lips to get the word out, "this won't do. Stand by to go about. This is a rum start, and I can't name the voice: but it's someone skylarking—someone that's flesh and blood, and you may lay to that."

His courage had come back as he spoke, and some of the color to his face along with it. Already the others had begun to lend an ear to this encouragement, and were coming a little to themselves, when the same voice broke out again—not this time singing, but in a faint, distant hail, that echoed yet fainter among the clefts of the Spyglass.

"Darby M'Graw," it wailed—for that is the word that best describes the sound—"Darby M'Graw! Darby M'Graw!" again and again and again; and then rising a little higher, and with an oath that I leave out, "Fetch aft the rum, Darby!"

The buccaneers remained rooted to the ground, their eyes starting from their heads. Long after the voice had died away they still stared in silence, dreadfully, before them.

"That fixes it!" gasped one. "Let's go."

"They was his last words," moaned Morgan, "his last words aboveboard."

Dick had his Bible out and was praying volubly. He had been well brought up, had Dick, before he came to sea and fell among bad companions.

Still, Silver was unconquered. I could hear his teeth rattle in his head, but he had not yet surrendered.

"Nobody in this here island ever heard of Darby," he muttered; "not one but us that's here." And then, making a great effort, "Shipmates," he cried, "I'm here

to get that stuff, and I'll not be beat by man nor devil. I never was feared of Flint in his life and, by the powers, I'll face him dead. There's seven hundred thousand pound not a quarter of a mile from here. When did ever a gentleman o' fortune show his stern to that much dollars, for a boozy old seaman with a blue mug—and him dead, too?"

But there was no sign of reawakening courage in his followers; rather, indeed, of growing terror at the irreverence of his words. "Belay there, John!" said Merry. "Don't you cross a sperrit."

And the rest were all too terrified to reply. They would have run away severally had they dared, but fear kept them together, and kept them close by John, as if his daring helped them. He, on his part, had pretty well fought his weakness down.

"Sperrit? Well, maybe," he said. "But there's one thing not clear to me. There was an echo. Now, no man ever seen a sperrit with a shadow; well, then, what's he doing with an echo to him, I should like to know? That ain't in natur', surely?"

This argument seemed weak enough to me. But you can never tell what will affect the superstitious, and, to my wonder, George Merry was greatly relieved.

"Well, that's so," he said. "You've a head upon your shoulders, John, and no mistake. 'Bout ship, mates! This here crew is on a wrong tack, I do believe. And come to think on it, it was like Flint's voice, I grant you, but not just so clear-away like it, after all. It was liker somebody else's voice now—it was liker—"

"By the powers, Ben Gunn!" roared Silver.

"Aye, and so it were," cried Morgan, springing on his knees. "Ben Gunn it were!"

"It don't make much odds, do it, now?" asked Dick. "Ben Gunn's not here in the body, any more'n Flint."

But the older hands greeted this remark with scorn.

"Why, nobody minds Ben Gunn," cried Merry; "dead or alive, nobody minds him."

It was extraordinary how their spirits had returned and how the natural color had revived in their faces. Soon they were chatting together, with intervals of listening; and not long after, hearing no further sound, they shouldered the tools and set forth again, Merry walking first with Silver's compass to keep them on the right line with Skeleton Island. He had said the truth: dead or alive, nobody minded Ben Gunn.

Dick alone still held his Bible, and looked around him as he went, with fearful glances; but he found no sympathy, and Silver even joked him on his precautions.

"I told you," said he, "I told you you had sp'iled your Bible. If it ain't no good to swear by, what do you suppose a sperrit would give for it? Not that!" and he snapped his big fingers, halting a moment on his crutch.

But Dick was not to be comforted; indeed, it was soon plain to me that the lad was falling sick; hastened by heat, exhaustion, and the shock of his alarm, the fever predicted by Dr. Livesay was growing higher.

It was fine open walking here, upon the summit; our way lay a little downhill, for, as I have said, the plateau tilted toward the west. The pines, great and small, grew wide apart; and even between the clumps of nutmeg and azalea wide-open spaces baked in the hot sunshine. Striking, as we did, pretty near north-west across the island, we drew, on the one hand, ever nearer under the shoulders of the Spyglass and, on the

other, looked ever wider over that western bay where I had once tossed and trembled in the coracle.

The first of the tall trees was reached, and by the bearing proved the wrong one. So with the second. The third rose nearly two hundred feet into the air above a clump of underwood; a giant of a vegetable, with a red column as big as a cottage, and a wide shadow around in which a company could have maneuvered. It was conspicuous far to sea on both the east and west, and might have been entered as a sailing mark upon the chart.

But it was not its size that now impressed my companions; it was the knowledge that seven hundred thousand pounds in gold lay somewhere buried below its spreading shadow. The thought of the money, as they drew nearer, swallowed up their previous terrors. Their eyes burned in their heads; their feet grew speedier and lighter; their whole soul was bound up in that fortune, that whole lifetime of extravagance and pleasure, that lay waiting for each of them.

Silver hobbled, grunting, on his crutch; his nostrils stood out and quivered; he cursed like a madman when the flies settled on his hot and shiny countenance; he plucked furiously at the line that held me to him and, from time to time, turned his eyes upon me with a deadly look. Certainly he took no pains to hide his thoughts; and certainly I read them like print. In the immediate nearness of the gold, all else had been forgotten; his promise and the doctor's warning were both things of the past; and I could not doubt that he hoped to seize upon the treasure, find and board the *Hispaniola* under cover of night, cut every honest throat about that island, and sail away as he had at first intended, laden with crimes and riches.

Shaken as I was with these alarms, it was hard for me to keep up with the rapid pace of the treasure hunters. Now and again I stumbled, and it was then that Silver plucked so roughly at the rope and launched at me his murderous glances. Dick, who had dropped behind us and now brought up the rear, was babbling to himself both prayers and curses, as his fever kept rising. This also added to my wretchedness, and, to crown all, I was haunted by the thought of the tragedy that had once been acted on that plateau, when that ungodly buccaneer with the blue face—he who died at Savannah, singing and shouting for drink —had there, with his own hand, cut down his six accomplices. This grove, that was now so peaceful, must then have rung with cries, I thought; and even with the thought I could believe I heard it ringing still.

We were now at the margin of the thicket and more light shone through the trees.

"Huzza, mates, all together!" shouted Merry, and the foremost broke into a run.

And suddenly, not ten yards farther, we beheld them stop. A low cry arose. Silver doubled his pace, digging away with the foot of his crutch like one possessed; and next moment he and I had come also to a dead halt.

Before us was a great excavation, not very recent, for the sides had fallen in and grass had sprouted on the bottom. In this were the shaft of a pick broken in two and the boards of several packing cases strewn around. On one of these boards I saw, branded with a hot iron, the name *Walrus*—the name of Flint's ship.

All was clear to probation. The cache had been found and rifled: the seven hundred thousand pounds were gone!

☆ XXXIII ☆

The Fall of a Chieftain

———————

THERE never was such an overturn in this world. Each of these six men was as though he had been struck. But with Silver the blow passed almost instantly. Every thought of his soul had been set full-stretch, like a racer, on that money. Well, he was brought up in a single second, dead; and he kept his head, found his temper, and changed his plan before the others had had time to realize the disappointment.

"Jim," he whispered, "take that, and stand by for trouble."

And he passed me a double-barreled pistol.

At the same time he began quietly moving northward, and in a few steps had put the hollow between us two and the other five. Then he looked at me and nodded, as much as to say, "Here is a narrow corner," as, indeed, I thought it was. His looks were now quite friendly; and I was so revolted at these constant changes that I could not forbear whispering, "So you've changed sides again."

There was no time left for him to answer in. The

buccaneers, with oaths and cries, began to leap, one after another, into the pit, and to dig with their fingers, throwing the boards aside as they did so. Morgan found a piece of gold. He held it up with a perfect spout of oaths. It was a two-guinea piece, and it went from hand to hand among them for a quarter of a minute.

"Two guineas!" roared Merry, shaking it at Silver. "That's your seven hundred thousand pounds, is it? You're the man for bargains, ain't you? You're him that never bungled nothing, you woodenheaded lubber!"

"Dig away, boys," said Silver, with the coolest insolence, "you'll find some pignuts and I shouldn't wonder."

"Pignuts!" repeated Merry in a scream. "Mates, do you hear that? I tell you, now, that man there knew it all along. Look in the face of him, and you'll see it wrote there."

"Ah, Merry," remarked Silver, "standing for cap'n again? You're a pushing lad, to be sure."

But this time everyone was entirely in Merry's favor. They began to scramble out of the excavation, darting furious glances behind them. One thing I observed, which looked well for us: they all got out upon the opposite side from Silver.

Well, there we stood, two on one side, five on the other, the pit between us, and nobody screwed up high enough to offer the first blow. Silver never moved; he watched them, very upright on his crutch, and looked as cool as ever I saw him. He was brave, and no mistake.

At last Merry seemed to think a speech might help matters.

"Mates," says he, "there's two of them alone there: one's the old cripple that brought us all here and blundered us down to this; the other's that cub that I mean to have the heart of. Now, mates—"

He was raising his arm and his voice, and plainly meant to lead a charge. But just then—crack! crack! crack!—three musket shots flashed out of the thicket. Merry tumbled head foremost into the excavation; the man with the bandage spun round like a teetotum and fell all his length upon his side, where he lay dead, but still twitching; and the other three turned and ran for it with all their might.

Before you could wink, Long John had fired two barrels of a pistol into the struggling Merry; and as the man rolled up his eyes at him in the last agony, "George," said he, "I reckon I settled you."

At the same moment, the doctor, Gray, and Ben Gunn joined us, with smoking muskets, from among the nutmeg trees.

"Forward!" cried the doctor. "Double quick, my lads. We must head 'em off the boats."

And we set off at a great pace, sometimes plunging through the bushes to the chest.

I tell you, but Silver was anxious to keep up with us. The work that man went through, leaping on his crutch till the muscles of his chest were fit to burst, was work no sound man ever equaled; and so thinks the doctor. As it was, he was already thirty yards behind us, and on the verge of strangling, when we reached the brow of the slope.

"Doctor," he hailed, "see there! No hurry!"

Sure enough there was no hurry. In a more open part of the plateau we could see the three survivors still running in the same direction as they had started,

right for Mizzenmast Hill. We were already between them and the boats, and so we four sat down to breathe, while Long John, mopping his face, came slowly up with us.

"Thank ye kindly, doctor," says he. "You came in in about the nick, I guess, for me and Hawkins. And so it's you, Ben Gunn!" he added. "Well, you're a nice one, to be sure."

"I'm Ben Gunn, I am," replied the maroon, wriggling like an eel in his embarrassment. "And," he added, after a long pause, "how do, Mr. Silver? Pretty well, I thank ye, says you."

"Ben, Ben," murmured Silver, "to think as you've done me!"

The doctor sent back Gray for one of the pickaxes, deserted, in their flight, by the mutineers; and then as we proceeded leisurely downhill to where the boats were lying, related, in a few words, what had taken place. It was a story that profoundly interested Silver; and Ben Gunn, the half-idiot maroon, was the hero from beginning to end.

Ben, in his long, lonely wanderings about the island, had found the skeleton—it was he that had rifled it; he had found the treasure; he had dug it up (it was the haft of his pickax that lay broken in the excavation); he had carried it on his back, in many weary journeys, from the foot of the tall pine to a cave he had on the two-pointed hill at the northeast angle of the island, and there it had lain stored in safety since two months before the arrival of the *Hispaniola*.

When the doctor had wormed this secret from him, on the afternoon of the attack, and when next morning he saw the anchorage deserted, he had gone to Silver, given him the chart, which was now useless—

given him the stores, for Ben Gunn's cave was well supplied with goats' meat salted by himself—given anything and everything to get a chance of moving in safety from the stockade to the two-pointed hill, there to be clear of malaria and keep a guard upon the money.

"As for you, Jim," he said, "it went against my heart, but I did what I thought best for those who had stood by their duty. And if you were not one of these, whose fault was it?"

That morning, finding that I was to be involved in the horrid disappointment he had prepared for the mutineers, he had run all the way to the cave and, leaving the squire to guard the captain, had taken Gray and the maroon, and started, making the diagonal across the island, to be at hand beside the pine. Soon, however, he saw that our party had the start of him; and Ben Gunn, being fleet of foot, had been dispatched in front to do his best alone. Then it had occurred to him to work upon the superstitions of his former shipmates; and he was so far successful that Gray and the doctor had come up and were already ambushed before the arrival of the treasure hunters.

"Ah," said Silver, "it were fortunate for me that I had Hawkins here. You would have let old John be cut to bits, and never given it a thought, doctor."

"Not a thought," replied Dr. Livesey cheerily.

And by this time we had reached the gigs. The doctor, with the pickax, demolished one of them, and then we all got aboard the other, and set out to go round by sea for North Inlet.

This was a run of eight or nine miles. Silver, though he was almost killed already with fatigue, was set to an oar, like the rest of us, and we were soon

skimming swiftly over a smooth sea. Soon we passed
out of the straits and doubled the southeast corner of
the island, round which, four days ago, we had towed
the *Hispaniola*.

As we passed the two-pointed hill we could see the
black mouth of Ben Gunn's cave, and a figure standing
by it, leaning on a musket. It was the squire, and we
waved a handkerchief and gave him three cheers, in
which the voice of Silver joined as heartily as any.

Three miles farther, just inside the mouth of North
Inlet, what should we meet but the *Hispaniola*, cruis-
ing by herself. The last flood had lifted her, and had
there been much wind, or a strong tide current, as in
the southern anchorage, we should never have found
her more, or found her stranded beyond help. As it
was, there was little amiss beyond the wreck of the
mainsail. Another anchor was got ready, and dropped
in a fathom and a half of water. We all pulled round
again to Rum Cove, the nearest point for Ben Gunn's
treasure house; and then Gray, singlehanded, returned
with the gig to the *Hispaniola*, where he was to pass
the night on guard.

A gentle slope ran up from the beach to the entrance
of the cave. At the top the squire met us. To me he
was cordial and kind, saying nothing of my escapade,
either in the way of blame or praise. At Silver's
polite salute he somewhat flushed.

"John Silver," he said, "you're a prodigious villain
and impostor—a monstrous impostor, sir. I am told
I am not to prosecute you. Well, then, I will not. But
the dead men, sir, hang about your neck like mill-
stones."

"Thank you kindly, sir," replied Long John.

"I dare you to thank me!" cried the squire. "It

is a gross dereliction of my duty. Stand back."

And thereupon we all entered the cave. It was a large, airy place, with a little spring and a pool of clear water, overhung with ferns. The floor was sand. Before a big fire lay Captain Smollett, and in a far corner, only duskily flickered over by the blaze, I beheld great heaps of coin and quadrilaterals built of bars of gold. That was Flint's treasure that we had come so far to seek, and that had cost already the lives of seventeen men from the *Hispaniola*. How many it had cost in the amassing, what blood and sorrow, what good ships scuttled on the deep, what brave men walking the plank blindfold, what shot of cannon, what shame and lies and cruelty, perhaps no man alive could tell. Yet there were still three upon that island —Silver, and old Morgan, and Ben Gunn—who had each taken his share in these crimes, as each had hoped in vain to share in the reward.

"Come in, Jim," said the captain. "You're a good boy in your line, Jim, but I don't think you and me'll go to sea again. You're too much of the born favorite for me. Is that you, John Silver? What brings you here, man?"

"Come back to my dooty, sir," returned Silver.

"Ah!" said the captain; and that was all he said.

What a supper I had of it that night, with all my friends around me; and what a meal it was, with Ben Gunn's salted goat, and some delicacies and a bottle of old wine from the *Hispaniola*. Never, I am sure, were people gayer or happier. And there was Silver, sitting back almost out of the firelight, but eating heartily, prompt to spring forward when anything was wanted, even joining quietly in our laughter—the same bland, polite, obsequious seaman of the voyage out.

☆ XXXIV ☆

And Last

THE NEXT MORNING we fell early to work, for the transportation of this great mass of gold near a mile by land to the beach, and thence three miles by boat to the *Hispaniola*, was a considerable task for so small a number of workmen. The three fellows still abroad upon the island did not greatly trouble us; a single sentry on the shoulder of the hill was sufficient to insure us against any sudden onslaught, and we thought, besides, they had had more than enough of fighting.

Therefore the work was pushed on briskly. Gray and Ben Gunn came and went with the boat, while the rest, during their absences, piled treasure on the beach. Two of the bars, slung in a rope's end, made a good load for a grown man—one that he was glad to walk slowly with. For my part, as I was not much use at carrying, I was kept busy all day in the cave, packing the minted money into bread bags.

It was a strange collection, like Billy Bones' hoard

for the diversity of coinage, but so much larger and so much more varied that I think I never had more pleasure than in sorting them. English, French, Spanish, Portuguese, Georges, and Louises, doubloons and double guineas and moidores and sequins, the pictures of all the kings of Europe for the last hundred years, strange Oriental pieces stamped with what looked like wisps of string or bits of spider's web, round pieces and square pieces, and pieces bored through the middle, as if to wear them round your neck—nearly every variety of money in the world must, I think, have found a place in that collection; and for number, I am sure they were like autumn leaves, so that my back ached with stooping and my fingers with sorting them out.

Day after day this work went on; by every evening a fortune had been stowed aboard, but there was another fortune waiting for the morrow; and all this time we heard nothing of the three surviving mutineers.

At last—I think it was on the third night—the doctor and I were strolling on the shoulder of the hill where it overlooks the lowlands of the isle, when, from out the thick darkness below, the wind brought us a noise between shrieking and singing. It was only a snatch that reached our ears, followed by the former silence.

"Heaven forgive them," said the doctor, " 'tis the mutineers!"

"All drunk, sir," struck in the voice of Silver from behind us.

Silver, I should say, was allowed his entire liberty and, in spite of daily rebuffs, seemed to regard himself once more as quite a privileged and friendly de-

pendant. Indeed, it was remarkable how well he bore
these slights and with what unwearying politeness he
kept on trying to ingratiate himself with all. Yet,
I think, none treated him better than a dog; unless it
was Ben Gunn, who was still terribly afraid of his old
quartermaster, or myself, who had really something
to thank him for; although, for that matter, I suppose
I had reason to think even worse of him than anybody
else, for I had seen him meditating a fresh treachery
upon the plateau. Accordingly, it was pretty gruffly
that the doctor answered him.

"Drunk or raving," said he.

"Right you were, sir," replied Silver, "and precious
little odds which, to you and me."

"I suppose you would hardly ask me to call you a
humane man," returned the doctor, with a sneer, "and
so my feelings may surprise you, Master Silver. But
if I were sure they were raving—as I am morally certain one, at least, of them is down with fever—I
should leave this camp, and at whatever risk to my
own carcass, take them the assistance of my skill."

"Ask your pardon, sir, you would be very wrong,"
quoth Silver. "You would lose your precious life, and
you may lay to that. I'm on your side now, hand and
glove; and I shouldn't wish for to see the party weakened, let alone yourself, seeing as I know what I owes
you. But these men down there, they couldn't keep
their word—no, not supposing they wished to; and
what's more, they couldn't believe as you could."

"No," said the doctor. "You're the man to keep
your word, we know that."

Well, that was about the last news we had of the
three pirates. Only once we heard a gunshot a great
way off, and supposed them to be hunting. A council

was held, and it was decided that we must desert them on the island—to the huge glee, I must say, of Ben Gunn and with the strong approval of Gray. We left a good stock of powder and shot, the bulk of the salt goat, a few medicines, and some other necessaries, tools, clothing, a spare sail, a fathom or two of rope, and, by the particular desire of the doctor, a handsome present of tobacco.

That was about our last doing on the island. Before that, we had got the treasure stowed and had shipped enough water and the remainder of the goat meat, in case of any distress; and at last, one fine morning, we weighed anchor, which was about all that we could manage, and stood out of North Inlet, the same colors flying that the captain had flown and fought under at the palisade.

The three fellows must have been watching us closer than we thought for, as we soon had proved. For, coming through the narrows, we had to lie very near the southern point, and there we saw all three of them kneeling together on a spit of sand, with their arms raised in supplication. It went to all our hearts, I think, to leave them in that wretched state, but we could not risk another mutiny; and to take them home for the gibbet would have been a cruel sort of kindness. The doctor hailed them and told them of the stores we had left and where they were to find them. But they continued to call us by name, and appealed to us, for God's sake, to be merciful and not leave them to die in such a place.

At last, seeing the ship still bore on her course, and was now swiftly drawing out of earshot, one of them —I know not which it was—leaped to his feet with a hoarse cry, whipped his musket to his shoulder, and

sent a shot whistling over Silver's head and through the mainsail.

After that we kept under cover of the bulwarks, and when next I looked out they had disappeared from the spit and the spit itself had almost melted out of sight in the growing distance. That was, at least, the end of that; and before noon, to my inexpressible joy, the highest rock of Treasure Island had sunk into the blue round of sea.

We were so short of men that everyone on board had to bear a hand—only the captain lying on a mattress in the stern and giving his orders; for, though greatly recovered, he was still in want of quiet. We laid her head for the nearest port in Spanish America, for we could not risk the voyage home without fresh hands; and as it was, what with baffling winds and a couple of fresh gales, we were all worn out before we reached it.

It was just at sundown when we cast anchor in a most beautiful landlocked gulf and were immediately surrounded by shore boats full of Negroes, and Mexican Indians, and half-bloods, selling fruits and vegetables and offering to dive for bits of money. The sight of so many good-humored faces (especially the blacks), the taste of the tropical fruits, and above all the lights that began to shine in the town made a most charming contrast to our dark and bloody sojourn on the island; and the doctor and the squire, taking me along with them, went ashore to pass the early part of the night. Here they met the captain of an English man-of-war, fell in talk with him, went on board his ship, and, in short, had so agreeable a time that day was breaking when we came alongside the *Hispaniola*.

Ben Gunn was on deck alone, and as soon as we

came on board he began, with wonderful contortions, to make us a confession. Silver was gone. The maroon had connived at his escape in a shore boat some hours ago, and he now assured us he had only done so to preserve our lives, which would certainly have been forfeit if "that man with the one leg had stayed aboard." But this was not all. The sea cook had not gone empty-handed. He had cut through a bulkhead unobserved and had removed one of the sacks of coin, worth, perhaps, three or four hundred guineas, to help him on his further wanderings.

I think we were all pleased to be so cheaply quit of him.

Well, to make a long story short, we got a few hands on board, made a good cruise home, and the *Hispaniola* reached Bristol just as Mr. Blandly was beginning to think of fitting out her consort. Five men only of those who had sailed returned with her. "Drink and the devil had done for the rest" with a vengeance; although, to be sure, we were not quite in so bad a case as that other ship they sang about:

> *"With one man of her crew alive,*
> *What put to sea with seventy-five."*

All of us had an ample share of the treasure and used it wisely or foolishly, according to our natures. Captain Smollett is now retired from the sea. Gray not only saved his money but, being suddenly smit with the desire to rise, also studied his profession, and he is now mate and part owner of a fine full-rigged ship; married besides, and the father of a family. As for Ben Gunn, he got a thousand pounds, which he spent or lost in three weeks or, to be more exact, in nineteen days, for he was back begging on the twen-

tieth. Then he was given a lodge to keep, exactly as he had feared upon the island; and he still lives, a great favorite, though something of a butt, with the country boys and a notable singer in church on Sundays and saints' days.

Of Silver we have heard no more. That formidable seafaring man with one leg has at last gone clean out of my life, but I dare say he met his old Negress and perhaps still lives in comfort with her and Captain Flint. It is to be hoped so, I suppose, for his chances for comfort in another world are very small.

The bar silver and the arms still lie, for all that I know, where Flint buried them; and certainly they shall lie there for me. Oxen and wainropes would not bring me back again to that accursed island; and the worst dreams that ever I have are when I hear the surf booming about its coasts or start upright in bed with the sharp voice of Captain Flint still ringing in my ears: "Pieces of eight! pieces of eight!"